Praise for

DRAGONS DEAL

"Another enjoyable addition to the saga of the McCandles family." —*Night Owl Reviews*

"Enjoyable [and] . . . hard-boiled . . . a wild family-affair final twist setting up the next thriller, *Dragons Deal* is a fun fantasy frolic." —*Midwest Book Review*

DRAGONS LUCK

"Joyous fantasy with continuous action and a creative cast of characters." —*SFRevu*

"[The] paranormal support cast is three-dimensional . . . The whodunit is [a] fun sort of a paranormal version of Fritz Lang's *M*." —*Genre Go Round Reviews*

DRAGONS WILD

"*Dragons Wild* is a lot more straightforward urban fantasy, complete with the semi-standard trappings of a secret race of supernatural beings dwelling amongst, and influencing, normal people. But Asprin pulls it off with skill and style, delivering a thoroughly satisfying, energetic story that begs for continuation. In fact, it's actually one of the best things I've ever read from him in terms of entertainment and atmospheric value . . . Is it fun? Oh yes." —*The Green Man Review*

"Asprin tackles a new kind of comic fantasy, a little more serious and hard-boiled than previous books. Featuring a likable rake and plenty of action and quirky humor, this series opener belongs in most adult and YA fantasy collections."

—*Library Journal*

"Colorful." —*Publishers Weekly*

continued . . .

"This is the start of what looks like will be a great urban fantasy series that is funky, funny, and fun . . . Robert Asprin has begun another fine myth with his first entry in his wild dragon culture."
—*Midwest Book Review*

"Delightful."
—*Monsters and Critics*

Praise for Robert Asprin's MYTH series

"Stuffed with rowdy fun."
—*The Philadelphia Inquirer*

"Give yourself the pleasure of working through the series. But not all at once; you'll wear out your funny bone."
—*The Washington Times*

"Breezy, pun-filled fantasy in the vein of Piers Anthony's Xanth series . . . A hilarious bit of froth and frolic."
—*Library Journal*

"Asprin's major achievement as a writer—brisk pacing, wit, and a keen satirical eye."
—*Booklist*

"An excellent, lighthearted fantasy series."
—*Epic Illustrated*

"Tension getting to you? Take an Asprin! . . . His humor is broad and grows out of the fantasy world or dimensions in which his characters operate."
—*Fantasy Review*

DRAGONS DEAL

ROBERT ASPRIN
AND JODY LYNN NYE

ACE BOOKS, NEW YORK

THE BERKLEY PUBLISHING GROUP
Published by the Penguin Group
Penguin Group (USA) LLC
375 Hudson Street, New York, New York 10014

USA • Canada • UK • Ireland • Australia • New Zealand • India • South Africa • China

penguin.com

A Penguin Random House Company

DRAGONS DEAL

An Ace Book / published by arrangement with Bill Fawcett & Associates

Ace Books are published by The Berkley Publishing Group.
ACE and the "A" design are trademarks of Penguin Group (USA) LLC.

For information, address: The Berkley Publishing Group,
a division of Penguin Group (USA) LLC,
375 Hudson Street, New York, New York 10014.

ISBN: 978-0-425-27266-4

PUBLISHING HISTORY
Ace trade paperback edition / December 2010
Ace mass-market edition / July 2014

PRINTED IN THE UNITED STATES OF AMERICA

10 9 8 7 6 5 4 3 2 1

Cover art by Rob Johnson.

DRAGONS DEAL

One

"Hoooaggh! Huunngh!" Val's voice echoed inside the toilet bowl. She knelt on the floor in the small, dark bathroom, her eyes squeezed shut.

Mai held back Val's long blond hair and patted her soothingly on the back.

"This is good!" she kept saying. "This means your baby is healthy. This is good that you are sick."

"Is it?" Val asked, raising bloodshot eyes from inside the rim. The tiny Chinese woman looked as placid and chic as if she were sitting on a chaise longue in a cheongsam with a champagne glass in her hand, not sitting on an ancient tiled floor in tailored black slacks, black high-heeled slingbacks, and a teal-colored silk blouse, helping a barely-showing-as-yet pregnant woman deal with the horrors of morning sickness.

Mai rose gracefully to her feet and hauled Val up after her. Though Val was almost a foot taller, she knew that in a contest of strength with Mai, she would probably lose. Powerful things came in very small packages. She was learning not to judge things by appearance. A few recent, bitter lessons had hammered that old maxim into her. Luckily, Mai was her friend, but in this case it was no comfort. She gave Mai a sour look.

"You could at least look less happy that I'm heaving my guts up every morning."

"Why would I be unhappy?" Mai asked. "Do you know

how hard it is for dragons to become pregnant? You are a rare and wonderful person in the eyes of the clans today."

"Not everyone," Val said darkly. In her mind, she saw the handsome, debonair, smirking face of Nathaniel, who by now must know he was going to be a father but had the sense not to get anywhere near Val. Or her brother. Or any of their friends, dragon or not. At least, she mused, the child she was carrying would be good-looking.

"Not everyone will be happy, perhaps, but they will be envious as well. A child of your lineage means power. He . . ."

"Is it a boy?" Val asked. She clapped her hands to her ears. "No! I don't want to know!"

Mai grabbed her left wrist and pulled it down. "Or she. I could look, but I don't care. It doesn't matter, Valerie. This will be a dragon baby. You should be proud."

"I'm not ready!"

"It doesn't matter. That is why it takes eleven months to bring one into the world. It gives you time to prepare."

"Eleven! It only takes nine months to have a baby!"

Mai shrugged. "We are not humans, however we look. Our gestation period is different."

"Ohhh," Val moaned. She rubbed her forehead. "I was just about reconciled with nine months, and now you tell me it's going to be longer?"

"I did tell you before. You just didn't want to hear it. Some women blossom in pregnancy."

"Not me. I'm already starting to walk funny," Val said, tottering out into the bedroom and sinking onto the edge of her bed. "The extra weight's throwing off my pace when I run."

Mai followed. She lit gracefully on Val's desk chair like a butterfly touching onto a flower. "You will cope. All females have coped since the beginning of gender. You should be thinking of more important matters."

"Such as?"

"For a start, in what surroundings you will bring up this marvel." Mai looked around the small room, her mouth pursed with disapproval. Val was suddenly keenly aware of the laundry piled on the dresser and the smudgy windowpanes. "It is a shame you live this way."

Val was hurt. "On my salary, this is what I can afford."

"There are resources. You can avail yourself of them."

"I don't like the idea of throwing me or Griffen in debt to anyone."

Mai tossed her head. "Why look at it that way? Plenty of people would like to do you favors. It is an honor to serve you. Nearly pure-blooded dragons are powerful. Those who are their friends benefit by association."

Val thought of the carnage of the Halloween party after the convention and wondered if anyone really thought that way. She shook her head.

Mai tilted hers. "Even that," she said, guessing what was on the younger woman's mind, "is not enough to change the minds of people who will care for you, and who follow Griffen."

Val didn't shirk at responsibility, but she found it hard to reconcile the life she had left behind at college for the absolute disconnect from reality that was New Orleans. Or, perhaps she should call it a reconnect instead. To learn that she and her brother, alone in the world for years, were not human at all, but hereditary dragons of nearly pure blood. She had never believed in Santa Claus or the Easter Bunny, let alone mythical creatures. To discover that not only did she have to believe in dragons, but vampires, werewolves, fairies, ghosts, and a dozen other kinds of beings that not only existed, but had as many problems as she and her classmates—plus other matters that the unsuspecting human population would never associate with a magical existence. Eleven months of pregnancy was just the worst at the moment.

She and Griffen had more or less fled their homes several months before, and been urged to come to New Orleans by an old college buddy of Griffen's named Jerome. As it turned out, Jerome was also a dragon, though not as pure-blooded as they were. Like Mai, he wasn't as young as he looked, either. He had been sent to watch over Griffen by *another* dragon, an elder named Mose, who put them under his protection when they reached New Orleans. She liked Mose. He was the father figure they had not had since they were small children. Until recently, he had been there to advise them as well as urge them to solve their own problems when it was appropriate. It was strange that Mose had begun to defer more and more to the authority of her brother but only because Griffen outranked him in dragon circles. Griffen was virtually running Mose's gambling operation and collecting followers as if he were actually a king. For a long time, Val had felt left out of things, but she had since learned to make her own way, taking a job as a bartender in the Quarter and finding her own friends and social contacts.

That had been a mixed blessing. Some people she was glad to have found, like Gris-gris, her boyfriend, a quick, thin, dark-skinned black man who had run a minor gambling organization and had treated her, well, better than she deserved at least once. Some had been a disaster, like Nathaniel. He had glamour—not in the fashion sense, though he was handsome, dressed well, and walked like he owned the world—but the magical ability to cloud minds and bend them to his will. It had worked on her for a time; it never would again. He had left town before she and Mai could take revenge on him for seducing Val. If he was smart, he would never come back to New Orleans.

She couldn't blame anyone for her bad choices. She just had to learn to live with them. That meant, for the moment, putting up with morning sickness and possibly having to find a bigger place once the baby came. She and Griffen had been comfortable in the pair of cozy apartments in what had in the eighteenth and early-nineteenth century been slave quarters in the inner courtyard of one of the huge gated houses of the French Quarter, but they were never meant to be the siblings' permanent homes. Val knew it, but she hated to leave the protected confines. Still, it would be better to start looking for a new place while she could still get around easily. She promised herself to ask Jerome for leads. He had been the one who got them these apartments. He must know of something that was affordable and close by. The rents she had seen listed in the classified section of the *Times-Picayune* struck her as exorbitant, far beyond her means as a bartender; but the underground economy of the French Quarter usually meant that word of mouth was far better than using commercial services.

The telephone rang. In keeping with the vintage feel of the small apartment, it was a hefty black monstrosity attached by a thick wire to the wall. It sat on an antique table that had a small cabinet to hold a telephone book, as if anyone ever used those anymore. At least it was a push-button phone. Val swung her legs over the bed and picked up the receiver. It couldn't be Griffen or Gris-gris; both of them knew to call her cell phone.

"Hello?"

"Is this Valerie McCandles?"

The voice was a strong female alto. Valerie made a note of the clipped, forceful diction, as if the owner was used to command but was holding herself back.

"Yes. Who is this?"

"My name is Melinda. I believe you have heard it."

Valerie felt a chill hand take hold of her throat and squeeze. Nathaniel and Lizzy's mother. She drew herself up to her height of nearly six feet and held her back rigidly erect. "I have heard of you. May I ask why you're calling?"

"You don't ask what I want. That's interesting." Val stayed silent. "I am calling for two reasons: My daughter was badly injured, and she says that you are responsible."

"She attacked *me*!" Val blurted out. Mai's almond-shaped eyes went wide. *Who is that?* she mouthed. *Melinda,* Val mouthed back. The small Asian woman stood as still as a porcelain statue, her rose-tinted lips pressed together grimly. "She tried to run me over!"

"She admits that, not that she is the most reliable of my children," Melinda said. "I apologize for her behavior. She has . . . impulse-control problems."

"She ought to be locked up!"

"I understand why you might feel that way, but that is not the most important reason I called," Melinda said. "She tells me that you are carrying my grandchild. Is that true?"

"None of your business," Val snapped out.

"It is very much my business." The commanding tones came out in full. "You are young, and I understand that up until this year you have had little or no contact with the dragon community. Your uncle Malcolm has a lot to answer for. I can advise you, guide you. I have had three children."

And a rotten job you did with all of them, Val wanted to say. She limited herself to a somewhat terse, "So?"

The tone turned pleading. "You'll need help. I can give it. Have you got an obstetrician?"

"That is also none of your business," Val said.

"That means you don't," Melinda deduced, with devastating clarity. Val winced. "You need a dragon physician. A human won't know the signs of a healthy dragon fetus. Are you more comfortable with a male or female doctor? I know the names of the best in the clans. I can get any of them to take you as a patient. Valerie, I want to have contact with my grandchild. Let me meet you. We can discuss the future."

"My future is not your concern," Val said, wanting desperately to hang up. "I've got to go now."

"Valerie, this is not the end of our conversation," Melinda said. Now she sounded like a mother. "I am in town, taking care of my daughter. I will call you again to arrange a meeting."

"I'll think about it," Val said, feeling as if she had already lost the battle.

The voice continued on as though she had not spoken. "Have a place in mind by the time I call you again. You can have your brother present to protect you, or any number of people you wish, if you don't mind having your personal life discussed in front of them."

"I don't need anyone to protect me," Val said. Her cheeks were hot with anger. She felt something brush her head. She looked up and realized she had grown tall enough to touch the ceiling. For the last few months, since she had learned her heritage, she had grown in size when she was under stress, the way that Griffen broke out in scales on his skin. She had to get her feelings under control.

There was a wry smile in the voice. "My daughter's present condition tells me that you are probably right, but I want you to feel secure in my presence. We *will* meet. You may choose the time and place. Just don't wait too long."

The line went dead. Val found herself staring at the old-fashioned handset.

"Are you all right?" Mai demanded. Val looked down. Mai seemed even more tiny than usual. Val forced herself to breathe deeply. With each calming breath, the excess size receded. She shrank from ten feet down to six. "Your face is beet red. What did that nasty bitch want?"

"She wants to meet me," Val said. She sank onto the bed, feeling helpless.

"Don't go," Mai said, sitting beside her. "You could find yourself tied up in magical bonds and spirited away to a cave in South Africa until you have that baby."

Val was horrified. "She would do that?"

"To get a child of those two bloodlines, there isn't much she would stop at. It's the future of the clans you are talking about. But she can't get her hands on you if you don't let her. Stay away from her."

"I plan to," Val said, "but it sounds like she's leaving me no choice. She wants to see me. She's here in New Orleans, somewhere. With Lizzy."

"That is bad news," Mai said. "You need protection, no matter what you just told her. Tell Griffen, immediately. He can call in some favors, have people be on the lookout for her goons." She offered Val her cell phone.

Val gawked at the gesture. "You didn't want me to let him know last time!"

Mai shook her head. "I know I told you when you first learned you were pregnant not to burden him because he had so many other problems to deal with, but this is a peril he needs to see coming, from as far away as possible. No more surprises like the last time. Melinda is dangerous. If she wants to be involved in your pregnancy, she will find a way."

"I doubt she is coming to throw me a baby shower," Valerie said dryly.

"I wouldn't put it past her to put on the trappings of a grandmother, but there will be strings attached to any gift she makes you. There always are. If you do not feel fit to negotiate with her, refuse to see her until you are, or have someone with you whom you trust."

"I trust you."

"Melinda hates me. And I represent the Eastern dragons. She will see me as a rival who might assume influence over this baby."

Val was alarmed. She knew little about the politics going on among the other dragon clans, and didn't want to know. She was young. She wanted to enjoy her life! Could Mai, in whom she had confided so much, be interested in stealing her child for her own purposes?

Mai must have read Val's mind. She pursed her lips, producing minute indentations next to her perfect rosebud mouth. "I would never hurt you," she said. "I would remove myself from the scene if it came to a choice between your family and my clan."

Mai didn't mention the plans she had made, sowing seeds throughout the French Quarter, or what her clan wanted her to do with regard to the McCandles siblings. That would only frighten Val into doing something rash. That was not her intention. Not yet, anyhow. Val was too preoccupied to notice the hesitation.

"What about Griffen?" Val asked. "Is he the right one to keep Melinda away from me?"

"I think he is the right choice but also the most perilous one you can make. Melinda is the head of a powerful clan. He will be in danger if he tries to keep her from laying claim to a child of her blood. It is not only a possibility, but a probability. All dragons have heard the prophecy of a powerful dragon coming to unite the clans. Undoubtedly, Melinda believes *she* is the one, though if she is, why has she not united them already? I know that all of the dragons who live here believe it is Griffen himself. That is why they are aligning themselves to be close to him when he does. But you must inform Griffen of all that has passed today." Mai smiled, hoping to elevate the mood. "Except the vomiting part. Too much information. Few men want all the details about pregnancy, particularly brothers."

Val nodded. "I promise. I'll tell him as soon as he comes back."

"Where did he go?"

"I don't know. I hope it's not more trouble."

Mai laughed, a tinkling sound that Val might once have associated with Disney fairies. "Trouble comes in many guises in this city. Either it is the kind he must fight, the kind from which he must run, or the kind to which he must say no. He is prone to the third more often than the first two."

Two

Griffen looked up at the massive, colorful sculptures, astonished by their variety and artistry. These would have stood out like a sore thumb in Ann Arbor, Michigan, where he and his sister had been raised, but looked completely at home here in New Orleans. Around the walls of the huge warehouse, kings and queens, gods and goddesses, jesters, leering demons, angels, cats, tigers, wolves, and dragons all stared at him from eyes the size of his head. The faces were incredibly lifelike. Some of them grinned at him. Some smirked. Others looked threatening. They were Mardi Gras floats.

He had only seen floats before on television, in the inevitable annual footage taken by the national news services of the parades at Carnival time and run during the feature segment of the news, filled with people in colorful costumes throwing things to the cheering, laughing, dancing crowds that lined the streets, to the accompaniment of loud jazz music, heavy on the horns. Since he had moved to New Orleans, he knew now that the street down which the parades progressed was almost always St. Charles Avenue, not in the French Quarter that had become his home, that the costumed people were members of societies called "krewes," and that what they were flinging to their audiences were known, appropriately enough, as "throws." Beyond that, he knew nothing.

He had not been in town long enough to see the festival

yet. It was still months away. He was looking forward to Mardi Gras, but not with the enthusiasm of the people around him, who were working on building floats. Men and women in protective eye and ear gear, aprons, and gloves leaned over spinning, howling lathes, carving out the framework of the giant heads that would be attached to the fronts or rears of the theme floats. Others slid tools over pieces of timber, flicking curls of orange wood to the floor, where they became lost in the heaps of shavings already there. When those carvings were finished, they joined heaped pieces of frame at the side of the several unfinished floats, which looked like stripped-down flatbed trucks. Busy crews—or should Griffen say krewes?—hoisted the pieces into place to form the sterns of galleons, or regal, high-backed thrones, or demicastles. After them came men in dusty coveralls and breather masks, spraying fiberglass or papier-mâché to fill in the spaces in between and give shape to the design. Expert decorators worked at putting the huge faces into place, painting, varnishing, and gilding. The acrid fumes made his eyes water. The colors were every hue in the rainbow, but gold, green, and purple predominated. Griffen was fascinated.

"It woul' mean a lot to plenty of people if you woul' say yes," the scruffy-haired man at his side said, patting the nose of a roaring lion taller than he as if it were a friendly dog. Etienne de la Fee was a few inches shorter than Griffen and much thinner, with a dusky skin that an artist might have called olive, attesting to a heritage mixed from several different lines. His tightly curled hair, cut fairly short, spoke of African descent, but the color, dirty blond, attested to at least one European ancestor. His wide, light brown eyes had a wild look in them, but he spoke in the calm, loping cadence of a lifelong Louisianan. Though the morning weather was relatively cool, about the middle fifties, he wore olive khakis and a bronze-colored polo shirt. "Been decades since the Krewe of Fafnir was last active, but it was time to get it goin'. Seems as though you the man to help make it all happen again. Been nothin' to it, gettin' it all together again, like it never stopped. Mardi Gras is big business in N'awlins, Mr. McCandles. Everybody's excited to see it back up and going. Already started, a lot of it. You can see the lead float over dere, just about done." Etienne pointed to a corner. Griffen almost jumped out of his skin to see an enormous gold dragon with a curling purple tongue jutting out between lips lined with fire-engine red and rows of pointed white teeth longer than his hand. Smaller dragons jutted out around it as if they were its young riding on its shoulders. A young woman with a long black ponytail and clad in a paint-stained denim shirt outlined the dragons' scales with brilliant green. "Dat'd be the float you'd be ridin', right behind me and the committee. We'd be on horseback, of course."

"Wow!" Griffen said, admiring the dragon. "That looks real!"

"You know anybody like dat?" Etienne asked, curiously.

"No, I mean, it looks like it could get up and fly around," Griffen said hastily.

Etienne smiled with understandable pride. "These artists here are some o' de best o' de best workin', Mr. McCandles." His manner of speaking came from the deepest reaches of the Cajun backcountry, so that he tended to drop or soften consonants.

"Griffen, please," Griffen said.

"Thank you, Griffen," Etienne said, formally. "Y'know, everyone is excited to get Fafnir roarin' again. Been a hole in the festivities, you might say, since it stop rollin' wit' the others. A lot of people have put a lot of effor' into bringin' it back, countin' on you to agree to be dis year's king. Even arrange for the permits and everything. You have no idea how tough that was, pullin' off a permit wit' only half the details in place. But it went like . . . magic." Etienne grinned.

Griffen grimaced. To him, "magic" was more than just a metaphor. But his companion wasn't throwing the word around as part of a lame metaphor. In spite of Etienne de la

Fee's delicate-sounding name, he was a werewolf. He had a small amount of dragon blood, but the rest of him was lycanthrope. Griffen had recently run a conclave at a local hotel that had been attended by a number of shape-shifters, werewolves included. They were mostly decent people, even including the loup garou. The part of the conclave he had enjoyed the most was meeting beings that he had only read about in books of fiction. The reality was a lot different than the stories. Werewolves weren't the scary menaces that the movies loved to depict though they weren't tame or predictable creatures, either.

"Taking on the kingship sounds like a lot of work," Griffen said, considering the proposal that Etienne had made, talking it up all the way to a nondescript yellow stucco building on Napoleon Avenue. It was hard to keep perspective in mind when he was faced with the glorious concept of riding at the head of what was going to be a pretty spectacular parade, but he had promised Jerome that he was going to pay much closer attention to the business he was supposed to be running. "I'm pretty busy, you know."

"Bring in more business to ya," Etienne said, promptly. "Folks woul' take it well that you support Mardi Gras. They'd feel real generous. Gettin' de Fafnir parade back on track's been a special dream of mine. 'Course I couldn' do nothin' about it alone, not bein' a pure-blood dragon myself. But once word got around I was goin' after you for king, people from the best families jumped on in."

Griffen frowned. "I haven't said yes yet."

"Yes, sir," Etienne said, dreamily, spreading his hands out as if plastering a vision on the air. "I can just see it now: parade windin' along St. Charles Avenue, jazz bands, dance troupes, clowns, fire-eaters, stilt-walkers, pretty ladies, and handsome gentlemen in traditional scaled costumes tossin' out t'rows to the crowd, the gold gleamin' on the floats . . ." Griffen found himself caught up in Etienne's vivid description. He started to picture himself standing on the lead float behind that massive dragon with a gold crown on his head, waving and smiling as confetti peppered him from the sky. He shook himself fiercely, refusing to fall into a reverie.

"When did you get all this started?" Griffen asked. "It sounds like it's a lot of work.

"Well, you gotta build all the floats by hand," Etienne said, rocking back on his heels with his thumbs hooked into his belt. "Magic's allowed, of course, or money—you can pay to have 'em built, but Fafnir always made deir own. Matter of pride. A little magic helps 'em hold together better. They can take months. Den dere's they costumes. A fancy beaded one might take a year. People like to make deir own. The permits take a long time, even if Fafnir's a historical krewe. The city government want to make sure it's a legitimate society. We really started in on it full force about two years ago."

"Wow," Griffen said. He watched a young woman standing on a skid-loader platform raised to eight feet above the ground, threading small lights onto the framework of a float that looked finished, to his untrained eye. "This all looks pretty expensive. How does the krewe pay for all this?"

"Oh, well, the membership pays in its dues," Etienne said. "We also hold fund-raisers. Den dere's rider fees. I been part of other krewes and marchin' societies before, and sometimes on big parades the riders about pay for the whole thing. But the parade's not all dere is, Mr. Griffen. We hold a ball during Carnival season, plus a few other parties. Den there's selectin' the court. Dat'll help to cover the cost of the ball, which is food, invitations, clothes, favors, and doubloons. And don't forget t'rows. I know the best suppliers. You could count on me and my family to help you find anytin' you need. We got connections. And then there's the king's party. You have a tuxedo? If you want to hold it in a good place, you better get off the mark, son, 'cause most of the krewes have got deir reservations in for the last fifty years. Only a few hotels and restaurants got any space open. I got four of the best places holdin' rooms waiting to hear from you 'cause you Griffen McCandles. I have menus for you to take a look at. It'd help if you make the choice right away. Most of 'em is about sixty a plate, give or take ten."

Griffen was aghast. "Sixty a plate! Sixty *dollars*?"

Etienne shrugged. "If you don't like any of 'em, there's some other restaurants that'll give you a room they been holdin' for someone else."

"How many people will I be expected to invite to the party?"

The other man frowned and gazed up at the ceiling, calculating. "About two hundred," he said at last.

Griffen's head began to spin.

"*How* many?"

"Well, that's just the krewe and their spouses, 'cause sometimes only one of 'em wants to participate. Fafnir is open to men and women, though you got to be sixteen or older 'cause of the *in*surance. And then there's special guests, like the mayor and the governor. And if you have friends you'd like to have, dat's the party you can invite them to. It's a big honor. Unless people belong to a big krewe, they never see the inside of most of de parties or balls. They's all private. Have been since the beginnin'."

Griffen steeled himself and turned away from the gorgeous faces. "Sorry. Maybe next year. I'm still paying damages from the Halloween ball."

"Mr. Griffen, this is the year," Etienne said earnestly. "The committee know you'll say yes. They been countin' on you. You can't let 'em down."

"But there isn't time for me to organize a whole krewe and parade," Griffen said, feeling more and more desperate.

Etienne threw back his head and laughed. The hearty peals echoed off the high, beamed ceiling. People stopped working and turned to look at them. "Mr. Griffen, you are the most fun! You don't have to organize nothin'! You just the king. Dat's all. You got no special duties 'cept bein' on that float, where we need your power. And de king's party. That ought to be no big deal to you, considerin' what you already run."

Griffen gawked at the small man. "That's all?"

"'That's all?' Dose two are important, man! The first, 'specially."

"Oh. I thought I had to take over and chair this."

"No, Mr. Griffen," Etienne said, straightening himself up. From being a skinny, nerdy-looking male, he suddenly looked as if he could command a regiment. Griffen was abashed. "I'm the captain. Authority's all mine. So's the responsibility. You come along to the meetin's, you can see how it all works. In fact, I hope you will. What do you say?"

Griffen looked away from his eager face and scanned the warehouse. So many people, engaged upon the mysterious business of Mardi Gras.

"You did all this assuming I'd be in on it? Why?"

"Man," Etienne said, with a sharp-toothed grin. "I know you will. I been dreamin' 'bout you since I was ten."

Griffen was about to scoff out loud with disbelief, but stopped. He had heard stories of the gift of foresight but had never met anyone who had it. Oh, he'd had intuition strike in the past, saving his life once in a while, but it was a passing thing he put down to chance, or déjà vu. Since he had learned about his dragon heritage, he could not afford to deride anything about the supernatural. After all, someone who had been given beads by a long-dead voodoo queen and hung out with shape-shifters did not have a stone to throw at anyone else's glass house.

"But I could just walk away, say no."

"You won't," Etienne said confidently. "Everybody's countin' on you. I invested everything I had, called in every favor, to make sure Fafnir was revived for dis year. And I counted on you from the moment I seen you. I knew you was de one all dis has been set up for."

Griffen hated to be the object of a prophecy. It made him as uncomfortable as being the center of attention. He hadn't earned his college nickname of "Grifter" by attracting a lot of attention. He preferred to work outside the spotlight.

"So why approach me now, not when I arrived in the Quarter?"

Etienne wriggled his shoulders uncomfortably. "Because you didn' really know who you was den. And you had some workin' out to do. Still do, but you gettin' you feet under you. People respect you, but now you respect youself. No king should stand on a Mardi Gras float who don't respect himself."

"I did have self-respect!" Griffen protested.

"Not from what I seen," Etienne said, with a knowing shake of his head. "You put on a good show, but you didn't think you deserved what you got. Maybe now you see you do."

"I bet you got beaten up a lot at school," Griffen said, wryly.

"Never mentioned the gift but the once," Etienne said. "I had to test it out to show that I believe in myself, too. Foreknowledge ain't worth a damn if the user is dead. How about it? You can't say no, Mr. Griffen. Destiny's waiting for you."

"Not *my* destiny," Griffen protested. "Just because you dreamed something doesn't mean it's going to come true. I don't have to follow what you think you know. The future's malleable."

"Not so much as you tink it is," Etienne replied with an assurance that roused ire in Griffen.

"Why should I do it?" he demanded.

"To stop Fate," the werewolf said simply. "The bad things that will come if you don't. You a good man. You wouldn't let anyting happen to this city. You've made youself at home here. N'awlins has welcomed you, son. You bring people together in a good way. You gotta keep on doin' it, and the Krewe of Fafnir's part of it." He grasped Griffen's forearm and looked into his eyes as if searching for something. "C'mon along on Tuesday evenin'. Meet the department heads. Don't say no now. What do you think?"

Griffen gave one more good look at the roaring dragon's head in the corner. Its eyes seemed to glitter at him.

"I'll think about it," he said.

He had to get out of there before he agreed to the offer. It was too tempting. If there was anything he had learned in the last few months, it was to go over the details and ask questions, and more questions, before saying yes. He'd been guilty of rash behavior that had hurt him and the people who loved or trusted him—or both. He turned to leave.

In the wide doorway, a broad silhouette stood between him and the outside. Griffen recognized the shape of a man who might have been mistaken for a big-boned, muscular, and somewhat overweight biker. His heart sank as the figure swaggered toward him.

"You thinking of running a krewe, on top of everything?" Detective Harrison asked, his broad face skeptical.

Matters were still not perfect between Griffen and Harrison, not since the masquerade ball at the end of the conclave in October. The New Orleans detective had learned about Griffen's secret in the course of his investigation of a crime. They'd gotten along so well before that. Griffen had thought they had formed a cooperative bond that would do them both good, but he had left out one little detail—that he was a dragon. He had believed that he could keep the truth about his heritage hidden, but it had all come out in a completely disastrous way.

Most humans were going to be freaked out about learning that heretofore mythical creatures existed, let alone lived anonymously side by side with them. Especially when someone trusted you, and you didn't let the person in on the little secret, "Oh, by the way, I'm a hereditary dragon, and so is my sister. There's a bunch of us around town. We're generally not a problem, but you have to look out for the vampires, werewolves, fairies, shape-shifters, selkies, and others who are here, too." To the man who is trying to enforce law and order with no more than his wits, some martial-arts training, and standard police-issue weaponry, the world is going to seem like a much scarier place. Griffen had pulled the figurative rug out from under him and rendered him less effective at his job. Harrison was finding it hard to forgive the omission. Griffen did not blame him; he blamed himself. He had been avoiding Harrison until he could figure out a way to make it up to him. Simple explanations were out of the question. A full disclosure, over a really good meal and drinks, with time for as lengthy a Q&A session as Harrison chose, plus the acknowledgment that Griffen owed him a favor, a big one, might do the trick, but Griffen had not yet felt ready to do it.

"Uh," Griffen said, lamely. "I've been asked to be king."

"Good idea," Harrison said, with a nod. "Make you fit in better, especially if you are reviving a dormant krewe. Tradition means a lot around here. We've got more of it than you folks from up North."

"I'm considering it," Griffen said, determined to be honest with Harrison. "I'm not sure I have the manpower to cover the responsibilities I would have. I was spread too thin . . ." He had started to mention the convention. Harrison stiffened, but Griffen didn't have a choice except to continue in that painful vein, "over Halloween, and I don't want to screw up something as important as Mardi Gras."

"Good that you're taking the time to think something through," Harrison said grimly. "You got all the permits?"

"Yes, sir," Etienne said.

"You have a theme worked up yet?" Harrison scanned the room, taking in the half-finished floats with an experienced eye.

"It's a secret, Detective," the werewolf said, with a grin that was almost a leer. "But you invited to the tableau ball. C'mon around and see."

Harrison echoed the grin, which looked no less feral than Etienne's. "I'll do that, if only to look at this guy in his king costume."

Griffen was alarmed. "Uh, no. I'm not even sure I'm going to do it."

Harrison's face changed from grim to shrewd skepticism. "Oh, you'll do it, McCandles. I know you—or I thought I did."

He turned and marched out into the sun. Griffen couldn't help but gawk after him. *I deserved that*, he thought. *That's a bridge I have to rebuild, and soon.*

Three

A deck of red-backed Bicycle cards flicked neatly out into a double fan. Each half arched like stretching cats, then flew at one another until they formed a single neat rectangular cube. The white French cuffs surrounding the spare wrists of the man folding the cards in and out between one another were bedecked with warm gold cuff links, each containing a single green, cabochon-cut stone. To the casual onlooker, they looked like smooth pieces of glass or perhaps plastic, almost translucent. To anyone who knew their stones, they were flawless Imperial jade, worth more per carat than diamonds. The suit was equally expensive and understated: pure, fine wool in a cool gray just a shade under charcoal, a cut between Armani and Bond Street, but clearly bespoke tailoring. The man wearing it, Jordan Ma, had a narrow face, an inverted triangle with broad temples, a straight nose, sharply etched cheekbones, long brown eyes with epicanthic folds that helped conceal his expressions—if he wore any—and thin lips outlined at the corners with tiny, deep-cut parentheses. He dealt cards to the three people sitting at the table with him.

Rebecca Tan, the youngest of the three, picked up her cards as they came to her. Her face was small and round, with black eyes, a flattened bridge to her broad nose, and an exaggerated cupid's bow to her mouth. Her chin-length hair was brown and frizzy, an obvious affectation since she could easily have taken control of it. She favored scarlet silk dresses, tailored devastatingly tightly around her slender, small-breasted figure, but the style was a dare, not an invitation, and not a dare that invited casual onlookers. She did not look dangerous, but Jordan knew her to be an evilly dirty fighter both at and away from the poker table. She was not his protégée, but that of the man to her left. She looked to Winston Long occasionally for approval. If Long showed it, it was in some subtle fashion that Jordan missed.

Long was old, very old. He allowed fellow poker players to play around with his name during a game. He had been called Cigarette, Silly Millimeter, and the one that he rather liked, Pack. It never occurred to the Westerners with whom he played that his family name meant "dragon." His face was smooth except for the fine wrinkles around his mouth and eyes. His suit was smooth black with a patina of green and looked as if he had been wearing it for fifty years. Jordan was too young to know for certain, but Long used it often. He raised his cards, perused them briefly without rearranging them, and set them facedown on the tabletop.

The fourth Jordan knew the least. Peter Sing had been wished upon Jordan by those who were senior to him. He wore his long black hair gelled up on one side as if a sudden windstorm had come along and blown it upward. Jordan was not an obsessive person, but the impulse to hold Peter down and smooth out his cockscomb threatened to overwhelm him. Peter gave him a cheeky grin, as if he knew exactly what Jordan was thinking. Peter was ambitious. Not a bad trait to possess, but he was impulsive. He had, against the orders of the elders, entered the World Poker Roundup in Las Vegas seven times, only once with his own face, and had made the feature table six times and the final table once, though he had lost to a combination of bad luck and impetuousness to the reigning king of televised poker, who had eleven of the diamond-encrusted belt buckles to his credit. The elders were furious that he had risked revealing himself on national television, but Peter wanted one of those belt buckles so badly that Jordan was certain he would try again. He deplored having to deal with Peter on such an important assignment.

Jordan set the remaining cards down firmly and picked up his own hand. King high, queen, nine, three, two. An average to poor hand, but no one would ever know it from his face. He nodded to Rebecca, sitting immediately to his left, to begin the betting. She slid a coin into the center of the table to augment the ante. The other players followed her lead, called her minimum bet.

No food or drink was present to distract the players from their game. The light was good, neither too strong nor too faint, coming from shaded table lamps and brass standing lamps rearranged by Jordan so that no shadows would fall on the players' faces. Any small tells that they had would be in full view of the others. If a hotel employee had entered the room at that moment, he or she would have thought nothing special of the tableau: four people gathered for a casual game of poker. Perhaps they were in New Orleans for one of the countless conventions that enjoyed the Big Easy as a hospitable venue. Perhaps they were there to see the Saints play the Vikings during the next day's game at the Superdome. The difference was that instead of chips, the four strangers were playing cards for neat stacks of bright, blank-sided disks of pure gold.

The warm gleam of the metal aroused twin feelings of satisfaction and greed in Jordan Ma's soul. He wanted to possess all the coins on the table, as did each of his fellows. The game was "for keeps," as the quaint colloquialism had it. The participants came with their own stakes, and what they lost, they lost. That made play serious. At one time, he mused, they might have been at one another's throat for the treasure; but they had learned over time that though they were solitary creatures, they could cooperate for the common wealth. As now.

Rebecca dropped a card and signed for its replacement. She sorted her hand and pushed two more disks into the pot. Her face betrayed no emotion. *Good,* Jordan thought. *She controls herself well.* He could not tell what she was holding by her posture or expression. That was the mark of a good poker player. Long had taught her well.

"Have you made inquiries how to join a game?" Jordan asked.

"I did," Winston said. He discarded all but one card. Jordan dealt him four. Long glanced at them and put them down. Jordan let his eyes flick toward the older man's face. Long caught his glance. He spotted a hint of amusement in the old eyes in their nest of wrinkles as Winston dropped five disks into the pot, one at a time. Their musical clinking sent a pleasant frisson up Jordan's spine. "I asked the pleasant young man at the bell desk how one could find companionable colleagues for an evening of chance. It was necessary to guide him toward specifics. He found it difficult at first to get past the words 'companionable' and 'evening.' I had to assure him I did not want a bed partner."

Peter let out a short bark of laughter. "What do you expect? I am sure that it is by far the more common inquiry." He discarded one, accepted a card, and saw Winston's bet, five disks.

"And once that was straightened out?" Jordan asked, ignoring Peter. He discarded the three and two and dealt himself their replacements. Another king and a seven. One pair. Long had trusted to chance by taking four new cards. The odds were that he had little but an ace high. Rebecca probably had something of low value, since she had asked for a card and only bet two. She would almost certainly drop out. Peter stood the best chance of having a good hand because he had not hesitated to bet. Jordan felt that he might be able to bluff the other out of the round. He tossed five coins into the pot. As he had guessed, Rebecca threw her cards in. Jordan gathered them into the discarded pack. Her face still did not change expression.

"I was directed to a young black man who was, I may say, loitering with intent by the check-in desk," Winston continued. He added three coins to the growing pot. "Quality clothes, though of casual cut. Just the right note to strike, I believe. His name is DeShawn. He called me Mr. Long. He was happy to accommodate me. A few other travelers of the same inclination as mine will meet this evening. I am welcome to join them. The evening would be very informal, but pleasant. Refreshments will be provided. I had but to state my preferences as to drink, comestibles, music, even the type of chair I prefer. Smoking, DeShawn warned me, was permitted, and hoped it would not inconvenience me. I assured him that was not a concern. He did not take notes, but he seemed of quick wit. He suggested that if I find the company congenial, it would be available to me when I chose."

"Very well organized," Peter said, with a small nod. "Detail oriented. Makes for greater satisfaction of the clientele. I am impressed."

"Only if they follow through," Rebecca countered.

"He did not write down anything?" Jordan asked.

"No." Long pushed coins into the center of the table. Five. It was a modest bet, but it committed him to the hand. Jordan took that into account.

The tiny curves at the corners of Jordan's mouth indented. "Good. We can exploit that."

"How long do you think this will take?" Peter asked. He raised to eight.

"To bring down an entire gambling empire?" Winston asked, regarding him with amusement. "Not in a day, young one. Be patient. Our job is to cut away at all the legs that support this organization and make certain it cannot rise again. That will take time. You must be patient."

"I don't want to stay here forever," Peter protested. "It smells of mold. The people move too slowly."

"A river moves slowly, but it is powerful in its depths," Winston said. "Don't forget that. If you are arrogant, you will underestimate those who might have something to teach you."

Bored, Jordan found himself drawing a little circle on

the back of his cards with the tip of his forefinger. Winston was right, of course, and Peter was wrong, but if they were going to disagree every day, this assignment would become unbearable.

"At least let us agree we are united in our aim," he said.

"No problem," said Rebecca. "It is very simple. I have also made a connection to be admitted to a game. A man in a bar who wanted to pick me up also turned me over to a nicely dressed white male whom he claimed as a friend. Only," she added, letting her smile spread slowly over her face like melting butter on a hotcake, "this friend's name is Griffen."

"So you have met him," Jordan said, his eyes widening a fraction of a millimeter. "What is he like?"

"He does not move like a dragon when he is among others," Rebecca said, thoughtfully. "But when he forgets to think about being human, you can see it. Anyone could."

"He doesn't hide his heritage, then," Jordan said. "That is good. At least he is proud. That will make him a worthy adversary. The elders did not think it would be easy. But rewarding. Call." He regarded his twin kings once, then tossed eight disks into the pot.

Winston studied him for a time. Jordan knew there was nothing to see, but he concentrated on keeping his aura empty of clouds or beams of light. Clarity was all. He waited. Winston smiled for a moment, then placed his cards facedown on the table.

Peter put five disks more into the pot. Jordan matched him. He waited. Peter put three more in, but the growing shadow of doubt in his aura told Jordan he was flagging. Jordan added three. With a curl of his lip, Peter flicked his cards in. Jordan did not smile as he raked the pot toward him and stacked his winnings at his left hand. The tall pile of coins pleased him. Peter narrowed his eyes at him.

"You must watch your moods," Jordan told him. "If I can see it, even a human with a spot of intuition will see it, too, let alone a fellow dragon."

"And what about Mai?" Winston Long's dark eyes glowed.

"That bitch!" Rebecca snarled.

"She is unimportant," Jordan said, gathering up the cards. "We disregard her unless she interferes with us. She had her chance to bring down McCandles. The elders no longer trust her to try. That is left to us now." He separated the cards and shuffled them.

Four

Of all the places that Griffen had come to love over the last several months in New Orleans, nothing had come to feel like home as much as the Irish pub in the French Quarter two streets off Bourbon. Strangers usually passed it by most of the time. It wasn't fancy. It didn't offer strippers or live jazz bands. True, there were two pool tables, occupied most of the time in the evening. The walls were full of interesting junk. None of that looked like enough of a reason for travelers to spend their scanty vacation time hanging out with the locals when they could drink an overly sweet Hurricane from a plastic glass and wander down Bourbon Street dipping in and out of the music clubs or huddle in the dark watching women in sequin bras and G-strings making love to a brass pole. The music was out there when Griffen wanted to go listen, of course, a string of Christmas lights that hung from the wineglass rack over the bar substituted just fine for all the neon, and with two lovers, he had no need for the live nude shows. What made the Irish pub his favorite spot was the company. Anyone who came in for a drink and stayed became part of the conversation. The subject matter ranged from how the Saints were doing that season to monetary policy in Elizabethan England to what to do with a brother-in-law who had overstayed his welcome to the latest electronic gizmo and whether or not it would change the world. He and another regular named Bone were the reigning experts on all movie trivia. All of his friends knew that if they wanted to find him, chances were they could locate him there.

A couple of dogs, mismatched as to size, who more or less lived in the bar, came over to sniff his hand in hopes of pieces of sandwich or bar snacks. The small dog belonged to the bar owner, a big, burly man named Ed. The bigger dog, a rangy hound mix, used to run with a man named Slim, who had power over animals that he rarely used, or had to use. Animals, especially dogs, loved and trusted him. Griffen, too, had the power to control animals, but had been working hard not to use it unnecessarily, since Slim had taught him how easily it could be misused. Slim had been killed by a ruthless monster that had been trying to cause trouble for Griffen. Griffen still felt responsible for his death. He and the dogs missed Slim. The dogs would not lack for homes, since the denizens of the Quarter took care of their own, whether with two legs or four legs, but he gave them special attention when he saw them. As it was for Griffen, the bar had become their permanent hangout.

Griffen held up one end of the bar on the "family side," nursing an Irish whisky with a little water on the side, listening to Maestro, the fencing master who taught students on the upper floor of the Yo Mama's Bar and Grill, debating with a pale, thin woman with blond hair, round blue eyes behind thick glasses, and a blunt nose about which was the more authentic American music, blues or jazz. Griffen liked both types of music and had an extensive collection of CDs. He, like the rest of the patrons hanging out on the family side of the bar, listened with interest, throwing in a comment here and there to help fuel the fire. They had heard Maestro, a slim man in his middle years with a deep bronze complexion, silvering black beard and mustache, wavy hair held back in a ponytail, and wire-rimmed glasses on his nose, arguing both sides of the debate on different occasions. Like Griffen, Maestro was from Ann Arbor, Michigan, but had settled down in the French Quarter as if he had been born there. He, too, had a little dragon blood but didn't know it.

Maestro shouted over the jukebox and the crowd who were watching a hockey game broadcast live from Calgary.

"There's no doubt that the blues tradition came from the Southern slaves," he bellowed, "but their songs were based on the ones they brought with them from Africa. Jazz arose from that, on this continent."

"Blues is original American, too!" the blond woman argued. "Based on American rhythms, not songs direct from Africa."

"They can trace melodies to their native countries," said Maestro. "Not all of them, but many."

"What about the ones they can't trace?" the woman countered. "That proves my point!"

For one who had been raised in Ann Arbor, Michigan, coming to live in New Orleans had been an adjustment. Griffen loved almost everything about the city except for the never-changing climate. By now, the trees in his former home would be bare, the sky would be iron gray, with heavy, bulging clouds that looked like they were going to come down on you like a waffle iron closing, and there'd be tons of snow to shovel. He actually missed it a little. Instead, it was sweltering in the bar. The miasma of cigarette smoke was mixed lazily with the smells of beer, sweat, plaster, and mildew by the ceiling fans, which did little to cool the place down. Music blared as a counterpoint to human voices and the unmistakable pock of pool balls being knocked around the tables. Griffen had seldom been so happy.

He had spent the afternoon at the Presbytery, one of the majestic white buildings on Jackson Square, going through its permanent collection of Mardi Gras memorabilia. He had never dreamed that there was so much work involved in putting together a yearly spectacle. If you added up all the hours that it would take to build the floats, sew the costumes, organize the parties, create all the souvenirs and all the thousands of other details, it would come to more than there were in a year, no matter how many people were working on it. Still, it happened, and the parades ran on time, to the delight of the thousands who came to New Orleans to see them. Etienne was right: It was like magic.

Films ran on a continuous loop throughout the museum displays, showing parades in progress. The floats, even in the daytime, were lit up with strings of Christmas lights, neon and strobes. The costumes, with all their glitter and sequins, were dazzling. The Presbytery's docents, most of them middle-aged women who had lived in New Orleans all their lives, on hearing that he had been asked to be a king, were thrilled for him. They told him stories of Mardi Gras celebrations going back into the middle of the nineteenth century, heavy on the glamour and intrigue. They handed him leaflets and gave him Web site information about other krewes and directions to the famous maker of the best floats in New Orleans. Their enthusiasm excited his, so by the time Griffen left, he was ready to call Etienne and agree to anything just so he could accept that honor few people ever got, step up onto that float, and ride through the streets. But, a hundred steps out the door, back in the New Orleans that he knew, hard reality took hold.

The financial investment sounded like it would be substantial. He would have to sit down with Etienne and the rest of the committee to see what it would cost him to participate. The range for kingship seemed to run between ten thousand and a hundred thousand dollars. Even though his bank balance had been depleted severely over the last few months paying for the damage to the conclave hotel ballroom and some ill-considered bets on pool with another dragon named Flynn, he might be able to swing the lesser end of the scale. The greater end was beyond his means and out of the question, no matter how great an honor or how long Etienne had been dreaming about it. Still, he was intrigued with the idea of being part of Mardi Gras.

"Where y'at?" a feminine voice asked, interrupting his thoughts. Griffen jumped. He had been miles away. He put away the mental strings of beads and gathered up the small redheaded woman for a kiss. Fox Lisa kissed him back with interest, then leaned over to bestow a solid smooch on Maestro's cheek. Griffen thought of her as a protégée of the older man, but he never asked. If the relationship went deeper than that, it was none of Griffen's business. He wasn't seeing her exclusively, either. Maestro pecked Lisa back without losing the flow of his argument with his visitor and held up his empty glass to the bartender.

"You looked like you had something on your mind," Lisa said. A frame suspended rows of wineglasses upside down by their bases over their heads. Fox Lisa put an elbow against one of the wooden pillars that held it up. "Anything I can help with?"

He glanced around. "I have some news, but Val isn't here yet. I want to tell her, too."

"Sure," Fox Lisa said, making herself comfortable on the stool at his side. Griffen ordered her a drink. "Is it something bad?"

"No, I think it might be great . . . but can I wait?"

"Sure, no problem," Fox Lisa said. A native of New Orleans, she embodied the easygoing mood of the city. "Want to go to the clubs?" she asked. "I've been thinking all day about some live music." She gave him a wicked look from under long eyelashes. "Got me in a good enough mood to share."

Griffen grinned. "Sounds great," he said.

"What does?" Mai asked, at his elbow. Griffen watched cautiously to see how Fox Lisa would react to Mai. The two of them were Griffen's lovers, even joining him in the same bed at times, but both had let him know they liked their private time with him. He felt fortunate that they were on such good terms, but he did not like to push it. Even considering bloodlines, no man wanted to stand between two strong-willed women.

Fox Lisa tossed her head. "We're gonna go out and listen to some music in a while. You can come, too, if you like." So her good mood extended to others that evening. Griffen relaxed. No matter how it ended, it should be enjoyable.

"I am hanging out with Val this evening," Mai said, tilting her small head toward the tall blond girl. Val had not made it in past the doorway before she was greeted by friends who sat at a table near the door. Griffen glanced at his sister. She had been more tired than usual lately. He didn't like the shadows under her eyes. "I will ask what she wishes to do."

"What do you want to drink?" Griffen asked. It was a Saturday night. His week's pay was still in his pocket from the day before, and he felt generous. The gambling operation was doing well. Five games in various hotel rooms around the city were going on that evening, and so far Jerome had not called him with any problems. Val's drink was diet cola, as it had been since she found out she was pregnant. Mai asked for a Cointreau. She liked fine wines, but he knew she felt liqueurs were more reliable in bars. It wasn't really true in the Irish pub, where the bartenders were careful about corked or bad wines; but when Mai got an idea in her mind, he had never been able to persuade her to shake it.

Val looked up and waved to Griffen. She squeezed the hands of the friends in farewell and made her way around the bar to them. Unusually, she barged in between him and Fox Lisa. The redheaded girl made a face but said nothing.

"I've got something to tell you, Griffen," Val said, in a low voice. Mai sat poised on her bar stool. Fox Lisa's annoyance turned to concern.

"Me, too," Griffen said. "But you first."

Val glanced past Griffen to Mai. Mai nodded encouragement to her. She wished Fox Lisa hadn't been there. Val got along with her, but she didn't want anyone else involved in what might turn out to be nothing. Still, Lisa had been a friend to her, too, and she didn't want to upset the balance. Griffen was so oblivious to the byplay between his two lovers. They got along, but each was determined to be the last one standing on the ground. But they did like each other. It was a complicated relationship. Griffen was wise not to inquire into the specifics. He would not want to know them.

Hers were just as complicated, but she didn't have a choice. And she needed help.

"That . . . that woman!" Val sputtered out.

"What woman?" Griffen asked.

"Melinda," Mai said. "She is here. She wants to see Val."

"Where is she?" Griffen demanded, looking around.

"Not here, here," Val said, exasperated. "She is in New Orleans. I don't know where. But she knows about the baby. She wants to be involved with it."

Griffen looked furious. He clenched his fist on the edge of the bar. "She doesn't get to make that choice. You do. What do *you* want?"

Val had been scared to pieces at the Halloween ball, facing Lizzy. Though Melinda's daughter had been tiny, she had the strength of the completely insane. Their fight was as fearsome as a nightmare. Lizzy was strong and faster than a normal person—all right, dragon—but Val had won out in the end. On the phone, Melinda sounded as sane as the US Constitution and just as firm on her rights. But did she really have any? Val hardly knew what normal human family life was like, let alone dragon. Val and Griffen had been orphaned while still young. Their uncle Malcolm had stepped in to raise them, but he had been a distant guardian, leaving them in the care of nannies and housekeepers as he took care of his extensive business interests. As a result, they had developed little family feeling or loyalty for anyone but one another. To have a mother come in to fight for her child . . . Val frowned. She had probably better think about that a good deal herself. Would she kill or die for this unknown lump she was carrying?

The answer surprised her: an unequivocal yes. It wasn't just biology. This child hadn't chosen to be conceived; she had been tricked, but it was helpless, and it was *hers*. One day it would be out in the world and able to make its own choices. Val had to give it that time to be born and live and learn. To her surprise, she felt deeply about nurturing it and loving it. She had never had a little brother or sister, but she looked forward to experiencing all the baby things, the sounds, the feel of silken infant skin, the tiny hands that reached out for her. She found herself smiling stupidly at the bar mirror and took a hasty drink of her soda. The bubbles went up her nose and made her sneeze. She could not wait to be able to go back to whisky and soda. The fizz did not take the edge off her feelings. Those experiences were hers, and not to be taken away by the mother of her unscrupulous seducer. She resolved to withstand Melinda and her demands. She was a dragon, too! She was powerful . . . if untrained. Lizzy had been the one who attacked *her*. Didn't she get any points for that?

"Absolutely not," Val said. "I don't want anything to do with her."

"Then she had better leave you alone," Griffen said. "I'm behind you."

"And I," Mai promised.

"Who's Melinda?" Fox Lisa asked.

"The mother of the crazy girl who attacked Val on Halloween," Mai said.

Fox Lisa's eyes flashed. "You can count on me, too, Val." She had a little dragon blood as well, though as yet Griffen hadn't found the appropriate time to explain it to her.

"Thanks," Val said, her throat tightening. She didn't know what any of them could do, when Lizzy had had no trouble finding her. Melinda undoubtedly had resources her crazy daughter didn't. "All right, I'm ready to talk about something else," she said, turning to Griffen. "You said you had some news. Good news, I hope?"

Griffen grinned sheepishly. "Well, I think so. But I'm not sure if it's something I'm going along with."

"Enough with the prologue," Mai said, pushing his shoulder impatiently. "What is it?"

"Well . . ." Griffen found that he was enjoying the suspense. He glanced at each one in turn. "You know Mardi Gras is coming up in March."

"Ye-es," the three of them said in unison. Fox Lisa caught the others' eyes and giggled.

"Well, a man named Etienne de la Fee asked me to be in his krewe's parade."

"Big deal," Fox Lisa said. "Thousands of people ride on floats. It's fun, but it's their way of raising money. Cost you between two hundred and five hundred for a year's membership. Maybe more if it's a big krewe. You'll have to supply your own throws. Maybe another three hundred on up for those."

"But that sounds like fun!" Val exclaimed. "You get to ride on a float! That'll be awesome. I'll have to tape it."

"Oh, he'll have to wear a mask," Fox Lisa corrected her. "Riders are anonymous in most parades."

"Well, what fun is that?" Mai asked, waving her hand. "I would not pay sums of money for the privilege of anonymously flinging cheap plastic toys to screaming hordes."

"A lot," Fox Lisa said, her nose turning red in annoyance. "People enjoy being generous at Carnival."

"Useless," Mai said. "If you want to give charity, pick something worthy. Junk means nothing. Don't waste your time, Griffen."

"Are you dissing our festival?" Fox Lisa asked, dangerously. "Being a krewe member is fun, and it makes you feel good, no matter that no one knows who you are!"

"No." Griffen felt that he had lost the momentum he had been building up, and he had to get between his two lovers before they raised the argument further. He raised his voice over theirs. "I'm not going to be a plain krewe member. Etienne asked me to be their king!"

"The king? Really?" Val asked, her eyes bright. "Why you?"

"He said everyone in the krewe had some dragon heritage," Griffen said, dropping his voice down. "They want me because of my bloodline."

"That sounds much more reasonable," Mai said, nodding.

"Wowee!" Fox Lisa exclaimed, throwing her arms around his neck and kissing him. "That is fantastic news! What an honor! You have to do it! You can't turn it down."

"How difficult is it to get to be royalty on a float?" Mai asked, speculatively.

"Just about impossible," Fox Lisa said. "Unless you have been a member of the krewe for years and years, and it's come around to your turn, then *maybe* if everyone is willing to vote for you. Or you drew the lucky ticket in a random drawing. It varies a lot how krewes pick the king. The only outsiders who are ever asked to be king are usually celebrities." She beamed at Griffen. "That means you've been accepted as a local, Griffen. Congratulations!"

"What's the congratulations about?" Maestro asked, coming up for air from his discussion.

"Griffen's going to be a Mardi Gras king!" Fox Lisa exclaimed. "Oh, I am so happy for you!"

"What krewe?" Maestro asked.

"Fafnir," Griffen said.

"That one's been defunct for years," Maestro said, with a lift of his eyebrow. "Did they say why they're reviving it instead of starting a new krewe?"

Griffen shook his head. "I guess I can ask all that at their meeting on Tuesday," he said. "I don't know much yet, only that it's going to cost me a bundle."

"Do it anyhow," Maestro advised. "It's a once-in-a-lifetime opportunity. I can't believe you're even hesitating."

"Neither can I," said Val. "It's not like you."

"It's a pretty expensive proposition," Griffen said.

"So what is money for?" Mai asked. "If it is something you will enjoy, spend it. I would."

Griffen looked at the eager faces around him. "Well, okay," he said, with a huge show of reluctance.

"You phony!" Val said, laughing. Griffen grinned back.

"That's better," Mai said, studying him critically. "If it does you good in the community, it sounds like a worthwhile opportunity."

"Well, it's got responsibilities, too," Griffen said.

"Purely ceremonial," Maestro said, sitting back with his drink in his hand. The second and subsequent drinks of the night were always Diet Coke. He raised the glass. "Cheers, King of Fafnir. Just one question: Who's your queen?"

Griffen felt his eyebrows lift. "Queen?"

"Yes. Not all krewes have 'em, but if I recall correctly, Fafnir had both a king and queen."

Griffen frowned. "I don't know anything about that. Won't they ask someone, just like they asked me?"

"Not necessarily," Fox Lisa said, her eyes shining. "Sometimes the king gets free choice. Did Etienne tell you?"

"No," Griffen said, though he wasn't a hundred percent certain. The conversation he had had was a faint noise in his memory underneath the sounds of saws, planes, hammering, and shouting. He had been far more interested in the intricate floats.

"Maybe he just didn't mention it," Val said. "He probably thought you were going to go away and think about it."

"Wow," Griffen said, sipping his whisky. "Maybe."

"Who would you choose?" Mai asked. Griffen almost choked on the mouthful. That had not been a casual question. He looked up. The eyes of all three women drilled into him. Griffen, a practiced poker player, concentrated on looking noncommittal.

"Me?" he asked.

"Well, they usually choose a local," Fox Lisa said eagerly. "I've lived in New Orleans all my life. I'd do it if you wanted. I'd love it."

"But they want a highborn dragon for king," Mai said. "That means they would want the same for their queen. I would be an excellent choice."

"But I'm your sister," Val said. "My bloodline is the same as yours, Griffen. You should tell them I'm interested."

"The king and queen as brother and sister? That sounds like incest," Mai said, her eyes aglow. "It would be far more logical to ask me."

"It might not have anything to do with that!" Griffen said. He realized what kind of a minefield that Maestro had led him into, and from the amused glint in the older man's eyes, he had done it on purpose. "Look, it's premature to get into a discussion about it. I hardly know a thing. Why don't we just forget about it for now and talk about it after I've had a chance to ask Etienne."

"That's right," Fox Lisa said. She ducked under Val's arm and cuddled up against Griffen's shoulder. Her fingers played with the top buttons of Griffen's shirt. She looked up at him coyly. "We were gonna go listen to music, then go home. Why don't we get going?"

"That's a good idea," Mai said, taking Griffen's other arm. "We'll go and have some fun."

Val looked disgruntled. Griffen remembered that Mai had come in with her and had been planning to spend the evening with her.

"We could all go," he offered. "I hear Beth Patterson's on tonight. She said her new CD might be ready by this week."

"No," Val said, her eyes sparking. "I'm going home. If I can't count on support from my own brother, then I just want to be by myself for a while." The air trembled with tension.

Griffen had had his fair share of Val's melodrama when they were teenagers, but with the advent of her dragon powers and her pregnancy, the pout took on a more frightening attitude. She had enough control not to grow to giant size right there in the bar, but the resident dogs rose from under Griffen's bar stool and retreated to the corner, whimpering. He had better intercede before the human denizens joined them.

"Come on," Griffen said, with his most persuasive smile. "I don't have a clue whether I have any say in the decision. I bet they have some society woman with a pedigree dating back to the real Fafnir. Etienne knows all about me. I bet he has something special in mind for you. For all of you," he added, knowing how lame the evasion sounded.

"Griffen, I have known you for many years, since we were freshmen, and you know me," Mai said, not taking his hint at all. Her small face was as expressionless as a mask, which had always boded trouble for him. "The least you can do is say that you know I would be a wonderful queen."

"I . . ."

"What about me?" demanded Fox Lisa. "This is my city! If anyone, you ought to consider me."

"I'm going home," Val said, standing up suddenly. Her eyes were very bright. The glasses hanging from the frame above the bar began to crack one by one.

"Val, no . . . !" Griffen said, alarmed. "Come on, calm down. We'll talk about this."

"What's to talk about? If what's important is being a dragon, I can't believe you wouldn't ask me, your *only sister*." The glass in front of him let out a *snap!* A thin crack appeared in its side. A thin drop of whisky and water seeped down the side and onto the bar.

"But it doesn't have anything to do with that," Griffen protested, mopping up the liquor with a paper napkin. "At least, I don't think so."

"But you didn't even say you'd nominate me if it was pertinent," Val said. Now a tear had started in each eye. Griffen knew that Val only cried when she was really angry.

"Or me!" Mai said.

"How do you think you figure into this?" Fox Lisa demanded, standing up to Mai. She was a couple of inches taller than the Asian woman, but her anger made her seem much bigger. One would think she would be frightened considering what she knew about Mai and the others, but as she had accepted Griffen's dragonhood with little more than a "hey, cool!" she had much the same reaction to Mai's trying to prove she was superior. Griffen admired her easy attitude and her courage. "You barge into this town, like you're some kind of big deal. Who the hell do you think you are?"

"Uh, guys? Do you think you could keep it down a little?"

The bartender leaned over the counter toward them. Griffen ducked his head apologetically.

"Sorry, Fred," Griffen said. "The discussion's just getting a little, uh, emphatic."

"Look, Griffen, I sympathize, but your ladies are scaring the customers," the bartender said, tilting his head in the direction of the door. The groups that had been seated at those tables were pushing out of the chairs and scrambling in their pockets for money. "I'm real sorry, but I think you ought to take it somewhere else for a while. No offense."

"None taken," Griffen said, embarrassed. He was suddenly aware how many people were looking at him. A few were strangers in the French Quarter, but most of them were people he knew. Many looked sorry for him. "Mai . . . ?"

"What?" Mai exploded, turning to him. Her eyes were all but glowing green. Val had grown five inches taller in the last few minutes. Fox Lisa's complexion just about matched her hair.

"We've got to go," Griffen said, firmly. "Come on."

Fox Lisa looked annoyed but triumphant.

"They're kicking her out?" she asked.

"You, too," Griffen said, taking no prisoners. "And us, Val," he added.

At once, Val subsided. She looked shocked.

"I've never been kicked out of a bar in my entire life!" she said. "This is your fault, Griffen!"

"Yeah, it is," Griffen said. He shot a grim glance at Maestro, who had the grace to look abashed at the results of his mischief-making. Griffen plucked bills out of his wallet and put them on the counter. "Come on." He took Val's arm. She started to yank it away, then let him hold on to her as he marched her firmly out onto Burgundy Street at the corner of Toulouse. The two other women, still arguing, followed in their wake.

As soon as they were outside, Fox Lisa poked him in the chest with her forefinger.

"This isn't over," she said. "You're gonna have to figure out what your priorities are, Griffen McCandles." She marched away up Toulouse. Griffen watched her disappear into the evening crowd, feeling dismayed.

"She's right," Mai said. "And *who* is really important to you." She sashayed off in the opposite direction. Griffen and Val found themselves standing alone in front of the Irish pub's door.

"Can I walk you home?" Griffen asked Val.

"No, thanks," Val said tersely. Her eyes were still shining. "Gris-gris said he and his cousins would be hanging out in the bar at the restaurant. I think I'll join them. No offense, but I don't want to be with you at the moment."

Griffen slunk toward home by himself, wishing his dragon skills ran toward letting him turn invisible. His big opportunity didn't seem so wonderful anymore, and he hadn't even agreed to it yet. He'd been all set to spend the evening barhopping with one or more of the ladies. Now the best prospect seemed to be microwave popcorn and a couple of DVDs. He had just rented the classic *Frankenstein* and the original *The Mummy*. Taking himself out of the here and now felt like a good idea. At least the people in the movies *knew* they were creating monsters.

As he turned into Royal Street, a couple of shadows detached themselves from a group near the door of a bar and followed him at a distance of approximately thirty feet. Griffen didn't even notice them.

Five

Late Saturday night, two o'clock Sunday morning, really, was an excellent time for a young man to be out and about in the French Quarter. He had a pocketful of money. The hours he had just spent at the poker table in the Marriott on Canal Street had been more than profitable. The bars were still open, and playing live music good enough to shake one's soul and loud enough to be heard all the way over on Royal. And his girlfriend had left a message on his cell phone to tell him she forgave him being a jerk, and to come over as soon as he was free—whenever that was. She didn't care how late. He grinned at the vagaries of good fortune. *What a great word that was,* he thought, taking a deep breath of the warm, moist air. Louis Armstrong was right. What a wonderful world it was, too.

He heard a faint *click* of footsteps on the brick street, maybe ten or twelve yards behind him. He could hardly believe it. There were a couple of guys following him, probably hoping to get ahold of the money he was carrying. Obviously they didn't know who he was. He glanced back, and they sidestepped into a doorway. He shook his head and grinned. Amateurs. They were going to get a surprise, one they did not and could not possibly expect. He flexed his fingers, letting the tips of claws emerge just a tiny bit. He kept walking, heading for a corner he knew was dark at this hour. He undid his black bow tie and stuffed it into the pocket of his black, light wool pants. No sense in letting it get messed up. His white shirt was probably going to suffer, though.

Jesse Lee had been downright trepidatious at first to work for Griffen McCandles, though all his instincts told him that he was taking advantage of a great opportunity. He had started dealing poker and blackjack at the big casino when he was eighteen but was approached by the elders of the Eastern dragons to shoot cards at private card games around New Orleans almost three years ago. He prided himself on being the fastest and most nimble card handler in the city, probably the whole state of Louisiana. He had tried to get them to start calling him "Jet" Lee, in tribute to the movie star, but it just had not caught on.

He did tricks before and after games to amuse the paying players, which earned him sizable tips, like the wad that made his wallet bulge, but during the game he was irreproachably precise and neat. The elders as well as his clientele had told him that his skills were appreciated. Still, when Griffen McCandles came to the city a few months before, he had felt irresistibly drawn to the younger man. In spite of warnings from his then-current employers, he had quit working for them and gone to deal for McCandles. He'd shown respect to the elders but had been firm that that was his choice. The Eastern dragons had let him go, but with a warning. Griffen and Jerome knew his situation and never put him into a venue where one of the Eastern dragons' games was going on at the same time as his. Griffen cared about what happened to his people. That pleased Jesse. It was so uncharacteristic of a senior dragon of his rank. Jesse wanted to enjoy the novelty before Griffen came into his full powers and started acting just like the rest of them.

He cut through Pirate's Alley and went into Jackson Square. The high building around him felt protective, though the wide public area was deserted except for a man in ragged blue jeans and a woven poncho singing to himself on the grass square bordered by the flagstone sidewalks that ran along the four sides. Jesse angled around the central garden, past the iron fence where in daytime artists hung their paintings and drawings for sale. He flattened himself against the far side and glanced back around the bushes at the thugs. Their faces were in shadow. Their bodies were both thick— not fat, but strong. Their legs looked short, but only until he realized that bulk made them look broad in proportion to their length. They looked like hired musclemen, not muggers. Jesse's heart pounded. Who had he pissed off? He didn't owe anyone money. He hadn't insulted anyone that he could remember. It couldn't possibly be one of the players wanting to recoup on the evening's losses; the other players would be the ones to go after, not him!

Jesse stopped briefly, pretending to look into a window of the one of the closed shops. The two behind him moved toward him purposefully, not minding now that he was watching them. He grinned to himself. Weren't they going to get a surprise?

He had taken martial-arts training since he was young. The discipline had no name; humans had fragmented the original into several traditions. They weren't capable of understanding the whole. He had other advantages owing to his heritage, including impenetrable skin. It might hurt to get stabbed, but knives and bullets could not kill him. Discovering that would disorient his would-be attackers long enough for him to use disabling moves on them. He hoped he would not have to kill.

He eased in the direction of Chartres, the northwest exit of the square, keeping close to the wrought-iron fence. The others sped up their pursuit. They were coming for him openly now. Jesse was alarmed by how confident they seemed. One of them wound something around his right hand. That meant they were there to teach him some kind of lesson. But who sent them? As far as he could remember, he had been open and aboveboard with everyone. He had informed the elders to their faces that he was changing jobs. His girlfriend had not been attached to anyone else when he started seeing her. Even his taxes were up-to-date, though the details of his profession were a little in the gray scale as far as the government went. His conscience was clear. His breathing sped up. The moist air was an impediment to getting enough oxygen. Why should he be afraid of two human muggers?

That was it: He sensed an otherness about them. They weren't a hundred percent human. The way the bigger one moved was too sinuous to be ape-descended. And they just didn't seem in enough of a hurry to hunt him down and deliver their message. Almost as if they were waiting for something.

Or someone.

As Jesse reached the corner of Chartres and St. Ann, a figure turned out of the shadows and grabbed for his neck. Jesse gasped. His reactions, which he always prided himself were as fast as lightning, kicked in. He jumped back and dropped into the primary defense stance. Knees bent, he arched his fingers and let his claws grow.

His assailant slashed at him with an open hand. His fingers were claws, too. Jesse grabbed the passing wrist, stepped backward into the man's path, and dragged the arm all the way down. The man's body fell across Jesse's back. His feet went up, and he landed heavily on his back in the street. Jesse ran.

Footsteps rang out behind him. The other two men were coming for him. Jesse had been making for his girlfriend's apartment, but he didn't dare lead these thugs to her. He ducked left along St. Ann, making for Bourbon Street. They couldn't follow him into a bar full of people. Maybe they'd back off and go away. He'd deal with the future later.

His pulse thundered in his ears. The street was dim at this hour. He ran in between the reproduction gaslight lampposts, fearing the shadows. Ahead was a bar with its doors wide open. They wouldn't close until at least four. Zydeco music poured out into the night. Jesse had one pool of darkness to cross to reach it. It was twice as wide as the other voids. A small alley opened to the right between a closed drink stand and a gated apartment complex.

A dark form whooshed over his head. The third man landed in the shadow, his eyes gleaming green. Jesse turned ninety degrees and zipped across the street. A lone taxi missed him by inches. It honked at him. A gate stood ajar. Jesse ducked inside it and found himself in a passage leading to a courtyard. A dozen men and women sat around a fountain in the center. Two of them played guitars. The others were singing along with the music.

"Hey!" he cried. None of them looked up. "He—"

His second cry was cut off. Something had dropped around his throat and squeezed. Jesse gasped for air. He hooked his claws under the narrow ligature and tried to snap it. The person holding on to the ends was strong. He felt himself being dragged backward. He kicked behind him. His heel connected with a shin. Its owner flinched, but the movement only served to tighten the cincture around his neck. Jesse let go of the wire and flailed with all claws out. He connected with an arm, a leg, a rib cage, but his blows had less and less force. A red ring flared around his vision. It grew smaller and smaller. He was running out of oxygen. He felt his body sagging even as he fought for life. The sound of the music thudded against his eardrums. He reached out a hand to the singers in the courtyard. Why didn't they see him?

A knee in the back shoved his neck harder against the ligature. Jesse dropped to his knees. All three figures were around him then. He tried to tilt his head back to see them. One bent over and grinned at him. He thought he knew the face, an oval topped by a cockscomb of shining black hair. The man gave a vicious tug to the garotte. Jesse's vision darkened. He felt himself drowning in a sea of red pain. It swallowed him up and closed over his head.

The guitars finished with a flourish, to the applause of the singers. None of them looked up as the three men slipped out of the darkened passageway and out onto St. Ann Street.

Six

Griffen arrived at the New Orleans Forensic Center, a grim concrete structure between a wig warehouse and an old gray house on Martin Luther King, Jr. Boulevard. The street was a boulevard in the classic sense, in that it was wide and gracious enough to promenade down, with what must once have been handsome gardens dotted with trees running up the center, but the paint on the houses on the opposite side had peeled into a mosaic impression, and the row of garbage cans on the curb in front of the corner restaurant had not been emptied yet.

Jerome was waiting at the door. Griffen, barely awake, blinked up at him. It looked as if the other man hadn't had much sleep, either. His usually well-styled clothes were rumpled, and his hair was flattened on one side.

"We got troubles," Jerome murmured, as soon as Griffen was close enough to hear.

"Who is it?"

"Jesse Lee."

Griffen winced. "He was a good guy."

"One of our best. I had a lot of hopes for him."

"What happened?"

Jerome tilted his head toward the door. "You'd better come and see."

Griffen had never been inside a morgue. All the television shows had one thing right, though: The smell hit him before anything else. It wasn't decay that made his eyes water, it was antiseptic cleaning fluid. They must have used it by the gallon, undiluted. The industrial beige of the walls went well with the stink. He never believed in restless spirits before he had come to New Orleans and met a deceased voodoo priestess, but no self-respecting ghost would hang out here. All kinds of people, well dressed in suits and dresses or jeans and hoodies, huddling together for support, wept loudly into tissues. The staff behind the desk paid little attention to them. They had to deal with the details of death every day. Griffen didn't think he could ever get used to it. He didn't want to sit down. He had a feeling of déjà vu from watching movies all night about animated corpses. If Jesse was really dead, Griffen hoped he wouldn't manifest on him unless he had information on what caused his death.

A familiar face leaned out the door next to the counter. Detective Harrison glared at Griffen.

"What took you so long?" he demanded. "Come on back."

The heavyset detective strode ahead of them on slightly bowed legs that always reminded Griffen of the gait of a longtime biker. His dark hair was thin on the crown of his head, and sweat beaded the thick flesh between his hair and the collar of his shirt. The usual leather jacket must be hanging up somewhere. It was much cooler in this office building than in most of New Orleans, but Griffen put that down to necessity. Harrison indicated a door on the left side and ushered them in.

The gray-painted room was not the kind of viewing chamber set aside for sensitive relatives to identify a loved one under genteel circumstances, with a curtain and a window. This laboratory had steel tables with hanging sprayers and scales, plus plenty of other devices and machines that Griffen did not want to know about.

Harrison brought them to a wall full of square steel doors. He nodded to a young black male technician wearing green scrubs and cloth baggies over his shoes and hair. The technician, whose name was Shore, according to the name badge attached to his tunic, nodded and pulled open a door. From inside the cubicle, he slid out a gurney. A narrow form covered by a white sheet lay upon it. He threw back the white sheet and withdrew to the side of the room out of earshot, but Griffen saw his keen gaze still on them. He looked down. The corpse's face was dark purple, and the eyes seemed to bulge unnaturally under the lids, which were closed, Griffen was grateful to observe. It was almost redundant to note the deep red line on the neck that indicated that Jesse had been strangled.

"Name?" Harrison asked. Griffen took a deep breath, as if to reassure himself that he could still take one.

"Jesse Lee. He was one of my poker dealers. Nice guy. Single. Decent and honest."

"I knew this guy was one of yours," Harrison said. "You are sure some lucky that I was on duty this morning when the call came in from a house on St. Ann's."

"You met him before?" Griffen asked.

"No," Harrison said. "But I could guess." He lifted the corpse's left hand. It looked completely normal except for the forefinger. It was covered in pale gold scales that almost blended with the rest of the skin, but the nail curved up in an arc and came to a fearsome point. "I could try and convince the medical examiner that he had some kind of exotic skin condition, but the claw's past my ability to lie with a straight face. Also, the corpse is resisting being autopsied. They can't get a knife into him. That's what made me figure he was one of yours. The ME is trying to call it scleroderma or some other natural thing, but I don't have to have it written on the wall by a fiery hand to figure out the real reason."

Jerome tilted his head. "That why Mr. Shore over there is so interested?"

"Well, you don't have to be a genius to figure it out," Harrison said, with a scowl. "You could say it attracted attention. But the claw is the real standout. Anyone can see it."

Griffen stared at the hand. What made it possible for ordinary humans to exist side by side with his people was the fact that, as Tommy Lee Jones said in *Men in Black*, they do not know it. Part of his mind raced, trying to find a good reason for an ordinary card dealer to have a finger like a reptile's. The other part was yelling inside his head that someone had managed to kill a dragon, and if he was unsafe, what could happen to the rest of them?

"What can I do to keep mention of this from getting out?" Griffen said.

Harrison snorted. "You can't stop the rumors. The ME's photographers took about a hundred snapshots. Not to mention someone will undoubtedly have taken a cell phone picture of that finger and put it on the Internet already. But we can keep it low-key if you don't make a fuss about the guy's wallet."

"What?"

"When we put this guy on the stretcher, he had about eight hundred dollars among his personal effects, plus some fancy jewelry: a big gold ankh, a jade ring, solid gold cuff links. So, robbery wasn't the motive. The cash is missing. Not a big surprise, considering the wages we public servants get paid, but it would cause embarrassment if it came out, and the powers that be would be more than happy to return the embarrassment to you. If you threaten to kick up a fuss, everything will slow to a molasses crawl, more chance for the facts to come out. Just act normal."

"We can say it's a fad, plastic surgery or something," Jerome suggested. "This isn't the first time someone . . . has died in New Orleans."

Harrison raised an eyebrow. "You, too?"

Jerome's dark skin glowed with a red undertone. "Yes, Detective. Griffen here trusts you, so I'm trusting you."

Griffen held himself steady as Harrison studied him up and down. "You folks talk to ordinary people like me?"

Griffen was abashed. "I've been remiss in not finding the time to sit down with you. That place in Jackson Square on

St. Ann. I owe you a dinner. Wednesday night, okay? I've got to be somewhere Tuesday."

Harrison's expression didn't change, but his stance softened a degree. "I don't mind. That won't alter the facts, however. This is still a murder investigation, and it happened in the Quarter, so I am the primary on it. I will solve this crime. I want to know why this man died. If it's because he worked for you, I want to know that."

"We'll cooperate in every way," Griffen promised. Jerome nodded.

"No holding back facts. You think I like keeping your crazy-ass secrets? But murder is my territory. You'll help me this time."

"Yes, Detective." Griffen sighed. "No more evasions. If you can take it, I'll tell you anything you need to know.

Harrison stuck a finger in his chest and thumped. "No. You tell me anything I ask you. I'll decide if it's something I need to know or not."

Dragon skin or not, the poke hurt. Griffen rubbed the spot. "I understand."

Harrison glared at him, then raised his chin. "Plastic surgery, huh?" he asked loudly. "People will do any stupid damned thing to themselves these days." Shore, the technician, looked crestfallen. "Do you know who's next of kin?"

"Can find out, Detective," Griffen said. "Jesse had a girlfriend. It'll be in our records. She might know family."

"Call me, not her," Harrison said. "Got that?"

"We got it, Detective," Jerome said.

"Get out of here," Harrison said. "I'll call you when I need something." Griffen nodded to Jerome, and they headed toward the door. "That Wednesday's fine, by the way."

Griffen felt his mood lift just a little, but he didn't let it show. The technician was still in the room. "Whatever you say, Detective."

Seven

The suite in the Royal Sonesta had an excellent view of the courtyard, a gracious haven when the hustle and noise of Bourbon Street was so close by. Jordan Ma sat with the other players for the day.

"So, what's your business, Jordan?" asked Luis Serafina, who "dabbled in a little of this and that" in Miami. He was middle-aged, sallow-skinned, small-boned, balding, with sharp-cut nostrils and lips that made him look bad-tempered, when he was anything but. He was expansive, avuncular, and, Jordan could tell, liked it when people got along.

"Textile imports," Jordan said. "Silks for the high-end fashion industry."

"Very nice," Luis said. He poured himself a vodka on the rocks from the selection of bottles on the open bar. A young, light-skinned black man in a tuxedo shirt and bow tie stood behind the bar. Once the game began, the players had been told, Marcel would serve them at the table. Rectangular chafing dishes hung in rows over canned heat contained savory snacks. Jordan scented ginger and scallions. He smiled. Care was given even to the catering of these private games. Luis twisted a strip of lime peel and dropped it into his drink. "How about you, Carroll?"

The thickset bald man in the blue silk suit looked as if he were just about to fall asleep. His heavy eyelids drooped low over very light blue eyes. Jordan wondered if he was as shrewd as he looked. "Entertainment lawyer," he said. "I'm stealing a day or two away from my clients. Technically, I'm on call, but no one's suing each other over the weekend so close to Christmas."

The others chuckled. The remaining players were a married couple from Toronto. Marion was tall, bony, and outgoing. Len was stocky, dark, and observant. None of the five had met before. Luis was the old hand, a veteran of many visits to the French Quarter for pleasure and poker. He played at the casino when he was in town, but spent a few evenings per trip at one of the games organized by Griffen McCandles. Jordan listened to the chatter, interjecting a friendly comment now and again while the dealer, a young, dark-skinned woman in her early twenties, also wearing a white tuxedo shirt, set up the table. Jordan had brought with him forty thousand dollars in cash, in neat bundles of fifty hundreds, tucked into a long billfold in his inside breast pocket. The chips being set out were in minimum denominations of fifty dollars, going up to a value of a thousand dollars, as agreed by the players as they had arrived. When all was ready, the dealer signaled them over.

Jordan sat at the end of the table between Luis and Carroll, feeling like the Jabberwock, readying himself to strike. The dealer was at the center of the table on the long side. Her back was to the window, a seat that none of the players would have desired. Jordan sat opposite the married couple from Toronto. As soon as they sat down, they ignored each other and chatted with the players to either side instead. Jordan smiled. They had almost certainly met over a poker table. They would be his designated victims for the night.

One at a time, the dealer traded chips for the stakes pushed toward her by the players. Jordan handed over his money and pulled the stacks of chips toward him to arrange as he liked. The dealer opened a new pack of cards, Bicycle blue diamond backs, removed the jokers, and shuffled it.

"What game, madam and gentlemen?" the dealer asked, flashing a brilliant smile at them.

"Texas hold 'em," Jordan said at once.

"Oh, yeah," Luis said, eagerly. "How about it, folks?"

"Sure," said Len, his face giving away nothing. "We play a little of that up North."

"Very well," the dealer said. She placed the button in front of Len, and play began.

Jordan examined his cards long enough to see that he held queen-seven, suited. Not an easy winning hand, but buildable, depending upon what the flop showed. He used the time, instead, to observe his fellow guests.

Luis was expansive during play, talking about his business, his three children and seven grandchildren, and how much Florida was changing.

"There are shopping malls everywhere," he said. "And the snowbirds, they don't go to the beaches when they come down—they go shopping! It's good for the economy, but why bother to come to Florida and spend your whole day in the air-conditioning? The sun and the sea, baby! That's what's great about Florida."

The chatter, Jordan quickly discovered, was to cover up the number of nervous tells that Luis displayed. If his hand was bad, he darted his eyes back and forth. If it was good, he kept drumming his fingers on the back of his cards. If it was marginal, he played with the edges of the cards. It was a marvel no one had cleaned him out based on reading him alone. But unconscious tics aside, Luis was a careful player. He did not overbet. In fact, he underbet so badly on good hands that Jordan wanted to take his money just to teach him a lesson. But he was not there to teach them to play cards; on the contrary, the better they thought they were, the fewer defenses they had against him.

Carroll had the fewest tells. He kept himself very still except when drinking a sip of white wine or eating a canapé. Jordan would not have been able to tell what he held simply by reading his body language. He could glimpse reflections of the hand in the man's corneas, but only occasionally. Carroll kept his eyes slitted. It would take a psychic, not a dragon, to get more information from him.

But the Canadian couple was easy. Len led with his left hand when his hole cards were good.

As he had predicted, Jordan had to fold the queen-seven. His next two hands were also unremarkable. He tossed in a three-two unsuited as soon as it appeared. The pair of sevens he kept until he knew by the avid look on Marion's face that she was holding something solid. She and Luis ended up in a modest series of raises until Luis finally dropped out. Jordan saw that he had been holding a trio of tens against Marion's three twos. He closed his eyes to shut out the pathetic sight. All the more reason, therefore, to continue with his plan.

The dealer expertly shot him two new cards. He knew by the residual energy on the first that it was the queen of hearts he had held before. Once he had touched the thin pasteboards, he could identify them anywhere in the room. The other card, at which he had to look, was the ace of hearts. Good enough. When it was his turn to bet, he pushed fifteen hundred into the pot. Luis's eyebrows went up. The Miami native launched into another story.

"Did I tell you about my daughter-in-law?" Luis asked. "She bought one of those laptops, but she didn't understand about the CD drive that pops out of the side?"

"Don't tell me she used it for a drinks holder," Marion shouted jovially.

"No, no, not that bad," Luis said. "She put a program CD in it and wondered what happened to the music!"

Jordan chuckled. Luis was going to be nothing for him to worry about. He won the hand.

The group settled down to watch one another and make the most of advantages as they arose. They were all fairly experienced, so no one had to learn as it went along. Texas hold 'em was not Jordan's game of choice, but it had become so popular that it was almost certain that any group would have a majority of aficionados or at least players who had watched one of the televised series. As it was so much newer than five-card or seven-card draw or stud, many of the older players had not completely adjusted their playing style to conceal their feelings about the hands they held. That was changing rapidly. Jordan's usual task for the elders was to monitor human behavior and report its progress according to region.

After ten or twelve hands, the young dealer gathered up the deck of cards and dropped it into a plastic bucket at her side.

"New cards," she said, brightly. She reached into a basket lined with a chintz cloth that contained rows of boxed decks of cards still in their cellophane. She stripped the wrapper off with expert fingers, opened the deck, fanned it, removed the jokers, and shuffled. The crisp sound was satisfying to the ear. "The old ones were getting a little tired, madam and gentlemen."

"I'm the one who's tired," Luis joked. "Can you get a new one of me out, too?"

Len laughed. "Me, too, miss," he said. The dealer smiled at them and sent cards flying around the table.

Jordan understood the necessity of changing decks. An expert card mechanic could mark a deck after a short time, by notching the sides or backs of the cards with a fingernail, or bending the corners slightly. When a cheat could cause thousands of dollars to be lost in a single hand, it was simpler and cheaper to open another deck and make the cheat start over. He deplored the fact that he was the one who must begin again, but the stakes were high.

With nothing to give away what he held or what he was thinking, Carroll took an early lead. He smiled at the jokes, nodded acknowledgment of Luis's stories, and exchanged brief pleasantries with everyone else, but he was there to play poker. Jordan appreciated his application. In fact, he would have enjoyed the game very much if he had not been there to lose spectacularly.

The second time the young woman collected the cards, Marion let out a noise of protest.

"But that looks so wasteful just to toss them out!" she exclaimed.

"Oh, don't worry, ma'am," the dealer explained. "We used to just throw them out, but now we take the bucket down to the men's shelter about once a week. They separate out the decks again."

"For sale?"

"No, ma'am, they play with them. Gives them something to do. They donate some to the VA hospital and the long-term wards at the hospitals."

"I've never heard of that being done before," Marion said. "That is very generous of you."

"I am impressed," Carroll said, letting a rare expression of pleasure show on his broad face. Jordan's first thought was that going to such an effort was needless, then realized it was a stroke of genius. Why shouldn't someone else benefit from the castoffs of the well-to-do? Also, in the depths of his manipulative soul, he knew it was good for publicity. Griffen McCandles could not help but see his halo polished for a gesture of generosity that really cost him nothing.

"So am I," Jordan agreed.

The third time the cards thumped into the bucket, Luis kicked his chair back. The sun had gone down sometime before, and the lights around the swimming pool in the courtyard had come on.

"I need a break," he said, stretching his arms high over his head. "Anyone else?" He went over to the bar and fished a beer out of the tub of ice beside it.

"Absolutely," Marion said. She made for the room's only lavatory. When she came out, the dealer excused herself and went in. Jordan took that opportunity to examine the wrapped decks of cards in the basket. He sent his consciousness deep inside the first one, a deck with two red-spoked wheels on the back, letting each individual card impress upon his psyche until he could see the spades, hearts, clubs, and diamonds pressed up against one another. He would be now able to read them as they were used. He put it down and concentrated upon the next, a blue deck with the image of a leering joker riding a bicycle.

The sounds of water rushing and a door opening caused him to glance up as he was reading the third deck. The young black woman came toward him, alarm on her face.

"Sir, don't touch that!" she insisted. She hurried to take the basket away and set it down.

"I'm sorry," Jordan said, evincing contrition. He handed back the third deck. She replaced it at the left side. "I didn't realize they were off-limits."

"Yes, sir, I'm afraid so," she said, allowing herself to be slightly mollified. "It's . . . I must be the only one to handle these cards."

"I apologize. I only wanted to see the backs. There is a large variety, isn't there?"

"Well, there is," she said. "There are more than fifty designs. I don't have to repeat a design during the entire evening, so there's no question . . ." She let the sentence tail off.

"I understand," Jordan said. "You have to be careful to prevent cheating. I was just curious."

She looked reluctant but did not want to seem inhospitable to a guest. "If I handle them, you may see them all, sir. Just please, don't touch."

"I won't," Jordan said. She showed him deck after deck. He hoped she would not change the order, but she put them back in the basket the same way they had been before. Now he had to finish the situation before she used up the three he had touched and went on to one he could not read.

He glanced up. The others were finished with their breaktime activities. Luis whispered to them until Jordan met his eyes. He broke off, looking uncomfortable. They had been talking about him. It did not matter. Jordan was not there to make friends.

It was easy going from then on. The others clearly suspected him a little of wanting to cheat, so they kept an eye on him. Jordan moved his hands in an open and ostentatious manner so there was no question that he was handling only his own cards and for as brief a time as possible. He let three promising hands go, to the benefit of Len and Marion, especially Len, so that their piles of chips grew. Seeing him lose made the others relax a little. Luis told stories. Marion laughed at them in her loud, easygoing way. Len and Carroll peered noncommittally at their cards and pushed chips in.

Carroll let out a soft exhalation of breath as the dealer passed him cards. Jordan did not look up. It was the first such noise he had heard the bald player make. Was this a tell, at last? Then Carroll burped and grunted. He left his cards where they lay on the table. Jordan was frustrated. He must get that man out of the game so he could concentrate on players he *could* read. Jordan checked his own cards. A pair of kings. A good start. He began to concentrate energies upon Carroll, urging him to take action.

"Two thousand," the bald man said.

"Raise," Jordan said, adding another five thousand to the pot. Carroll's eyebrows rose a fraction.

"Too rich for me," Luis said, with a laugh. He passed his cards to the dealer. Len and Marion followed suit. The flop was revealed; none of them were face cards. Carroll checked. Jordan raised a thousand. Carroll threw his cards in. Jordan felt a twinge of annoyance, but at least he had created some movement in the silent man's psyche.

It took four hands to lure Carroll in so that he was betting on each hand. By then, the dinner hour had passed. The server behind the bar brought selections of one-bite hot snacks to each of the players. The food was delicious but not meant to interrupt concentration. Jordan needed every erg of it he had. He held the first pair of aces in the entire game in his hand, spades and diamonds. He kept as still as a snake prepared to strike. No matter. Even if Carroll had an ace, it was not in suit. Marion was on the button, so Jordan bet first.

"Five thousand," he said.

"Raise one," Luis said. Jordan was unconcerned about the Miamian. He had seven-eight suited.

Marion folded, and Len added his chips to the pot.

"See you," Carroll said.

Jordan saw Luis's raise.

They all watched the dealer avidly as she peeled three cards off the top, then turned up the next three cards. Two nines and a queen. Jordan added another six thousand. Luis and Len held on. Carroll's broad face broke out in pinpoints of perspiration.

"Hey, you hear of that sting that the Feds played at the Miami Port Authority?" Luis asked.

"I saw it on the news," Jordan said. Luis beamed at him. He loved it when people got involved in his stories. Jordan kept up the conversation, but his attention was on Carroll. The bald man pushed three stacks of chips into the center. Everyone, including Luis, stopped talking.

"All in," Carroll said.

"Call," Jordan said immediately.

They turned up their hands.

"Very nice," Marion said, as they saw the three nines. Carroll smiled at her. Luis had a queen and a seven. Len had another queen and a six. They glanced at one another, each sizing the others up. Jordan hoped his count was accurate. Three cards below the deck remaining in the dealer's hand was a queen. Three cards below that was an ace. He turned his attention from Carroll, taking a great risk, and put it on the young woman. She winced as she felt his subconscious push, but said nothing.

The players leaned toward the center of the table. Jordan felt her will bend to his. One, two, three. The queen was revealed on the turn.

"Oh, ho!" Luis chortled. "Is there another pretty lady in there?" Len pushed his cards in. Even if the last queen did appear, his hand would fall on the six. Carroll looked smug. The chances of two in the bush was low compared with the one in the hand.

One, two, three. Everyone held their breath. The dealer must have sensed the tension. She paused a moment before turning up the river card. Jordan, even though he knew it, felt his heart pounding with anticipation.

Ace.

"Ooooh!" Luis moaned. "Rocket ship!" He flicked his cards in.

Carroll's eyes went from the cards to Jordan's face and back again. There was no way that Jordan could have engineered a cheat. Carroll had simply lost.

"Bad luck," he said. He extended a neat, hairless hand to Jordan, who shook it politely.

"Bad luck," Jordan agreed. He almost wiped his forehead in relief. Carroll pulled his chair back from the table and went to the bar. The server poured him a stiff drink. Carroll returned and sat with his back to the window to watch the others play.

Jordan steeled himself. One last deck that he had touched lay in the basket. He must not go beyond that. He needed a big finish.

He won moderately, allowed himself to be bid up, then dropped out of a hand Luis won. Luis had just enough chips remaining to stay at the table. Carroll was in a good position to see everything except the dealer's hands and Marion's. Now was the time for Jordan to strike.

He used a tiny trickle of power to cause the ace of hearts to be ignored, then to stick to the underside of Marion's arm as she leaned over the table to watch. She never noticed. It was prepared.

Jordan went up against Len, knew this was the hand he wanted. Perfect. He went all in against Len, who had no choice but to match him though he still had a stack of chips in reserve. Straight. Straight flush. When Len won the next hand, Jordan showed that his hand would have won but for the missing ace, which Marion was holding.

"There's no way to assume you would have been dealt the ace of hearts," she protested.

"There certainly is no way for me to have been dealt the ace of hearts if you were concealing it, madam," Jordan said.

"You think I did that on purpose?" she asked, with horrified realization. "I would never cheat."

"Sure looks like it to me, lady," Luis said.

Jordan turned to the dealer. "This game is a farce. I believe that I would like my money back. Who knows how long this has been going on this evening?

"How long what has?" Len demanded. He was not the openly emotional person his wife was, but he flared like an ember that had been poked. "Are you calling my wife a cheater?"

"Since you won on a hand that depended on the missing card your wife was holding, I would call it collusion," Jordan said, his eyes burning. "I want my stake returned to me."

Len lifted his chin pugnaciously. "You can't have it. I won that money! You lost it. That's poker!"

"Gentlemen!" the dealer said, looking terrified. She held up her hands. "Please, give me a moment."

The young woman retreated to the end of the room with her cell phone. She spoke in low tones at length to the person on the other end of the line. Her eyes filled with tears. Jordan heard her voice break. She wiped her face before she returned and managed, with some effort, to regain her composure.

She sat down at the table and smiled at them.

"Would you like to take a break, madam and gentlemen?" she asked.

"I think that would be a good idea," Marion huffed. Her pale cheeks sported red spots over the cheekbones. She sprang up and marched as far away from the others as she could and stood glaring at them. Len joined her. He could not look at anyone. Jordan stood with Carroll and Luis by the window. The dealer remained at the table, guarding the cards.

Within minutes, a well-dressed black man named Jerome arrived. He went to the dealer's side. The girl blurted out her story in a whisper. Jordan, the only one who could hear, was impressed by her accuracy and powers of recall.

Jerome was of interest. Jordan felt dragon blood in him. He hoped that his own dragon blood was concealed enough by strong magic not to be detected outright. Jerome left the table and came toward the men with his hand out.

"I am sorry you folks didn't have a good a time as you should have," he said. "It seems clear that the, er, friendly nature of the game was ruined. I've thought about it hard, and I think that the only fair thing to do, folks, is to return your original stakes to you. With a 10 percent premium, on the house. What do you say?"

"But I won that money fair and square!" Len said. "I should keep it."

"I beg to differ," Jordan said, coldly. Inwardly, he was shouting for joy. "I want satisfaction. I did not know I would be sitting down with practiced con artists."

"I been playing with these people a long time," Luis said, sneering at Len. "I don't like cheaters. I don't care what you think you can get away with. I'm in for your deal, Jerome."

"Thank you, Mr. Serafina," Jerome said. Carroll murmured that he agreed, too. Jordan, with a great show of reluctance, nodded his consent. Jerome took the money out of the bank under the table. The dealer handed him her notebook of the original stakes. Jerome counted it out to them, then added extra money from his own wallet.

Jordan accepted forty-four thousand dollars, then peeled off a pair of hundreds and put them down in front of the dealer.

"No reason for you to take a loss because of *them*," he said, tilting his head toward the unhappy Canadians.

"Yeah, good idea, Jordan," Luis said. He added a couple hundred of his own. "Buck up, sweetie. You didn't do anything wrong. C'mon and have a drink with me, Jordan. You, too, Carroll. I know a place with the best cocktails."

"Thank you," Carroll said. His smooth forehead displayed one horizontal fold of pleasure at having the money he had lost returned. "You're on."

It was the fairest outcome. No one was happy with the arrangement but Jordan, and that glee was entirely inward. No one was at a loss except for the house, but they all felt as if advantage had been taken of them. The three men gathered up their belongings and went to stand in the elevator bay.

The suite door stood open only yards from them. Luis shook his head with disapproval as he punched the DOWN button.

As they waited, with his heightened senses, Jordan listened to Jerome. The black man had held back the Canadian couple for a private chat.

". . . I am sorry to tell you that under the circumstances, you won't be admitted to another game in our operation."

"But we came here to play poker," Marion insisted.

Jerome was patient and polite, but obdurate. "I suggest you try the casino, ma'am. I have no way of knowing for sure what happened here, but it just can't happen again. I appreciate that you came to visit us today. I'm very sorry."

"I'll report you! What you're doing is illegal!"

"Hypocrite," Luis muttered. "She was okay for it to be illegal when she was winning."

Jerome knew it, too, but he didn't throw it in her face. "The cops know about us, ma'am. But go ahead if you want. We can file countercharges. I have witnesses. What would you like to do?"

Marion didn't say another word. She stormed out of the suite with Len in her wake like an unhappy water-skier. She paced back and forth at the edge of the elevator bay. Jordan felt the tension in the air as thick as honey. The Canadians found it too uncomfortable to wait with the others who had accused them. Marion threw open the stairway door and stomped down. Len, with a glare at Jordan, followed her out.

Jordan assumed that McCandles would ensure that none of the five players would ever meet again over a table, but how many of them would return to play again in a McCandles-sanctioned game? Few, he was sure, if the conversation over cocktails with Carroll and Luis was anything to go by.

After an hour in a quiet club on Royal, he left the two men still commiserating, and returned to the Royal Sonesta.

His colleagues glanced up as he appeared in the doorway of the Mystic Bar. He spotted their energy signatures at once and made his way to them.

"How did it go?" Rebecca asked.

"Perfectly," Jordan said, with a smile. He raised a long finger. The cocktail waitress bustled toward him, the tiny tray balanced on her hand. "It was almost too easy."

Once he had given his order, he gave them details of the game. "I had hoped for a better opponent, but it didn't matter. The outcome was all that counted. Too bad that Griffen himself did not come."

"We have not caused enough trouble to bring out the man himself," Peter said.

"Soon enough," Winston Long said. "But we want to bankrupt him first, then disgrace him. If players believe that they are coming to games where they will deliberately be fleeced, he will lose all his business. Then we can retake this city."

The waitress placed a brandy glass in front of Jordan and withdrew discreetly. Jordan raised it to each of his colleagues.

"Hear, hear," he said, and drank.

Eight

Griffen got out of the taxi in front of the grand, white-painted house on a boulevard in the Garden District, and eyed the house uncertainly. He had grown up in a modest little house in Ann Arbor, three bedrooms, two bathrooms, and an eat-in kitchen on a quarter acre in a neighborhood full of similar if not identical homes. This gracious, white-painted mansion with robin's-egg blue storm shutters was easily three times the size of that house, and it stood in its own landscaped gardens. In fact, the gardener, a scrawny man in coveralls who could have been anywhere between thirty and ninety, was on his knees pulling weeds on the left side of the house in the last light before sunset. The Spanish moss hanging from the branches of the enormous catalpa trees just inside the wrought-iron fence drew sinister shadows on the close-trimmed lawn.

"Y'all need to arrange for a pickup?" Doreen asked. An African-American woman in her forties, she ran a cab service based in the French Quarter. Her clientele tended not to own cars, since parking was difficult to find in the narrow old streets. Important clients like Griffen she drove personally.

"I'll phone you," he said absently. He leaned in the window and handed her a five. "Not sure how long I'll be."

"You got it, baby," she said. She glanced at the big house and patted him on the cheek. "Don't believe the half of what you hear in there. You can keep your head on your shoulders, I know it."

"I try to," Griffen said. "Sounds like you already know what's going on."

Doreen grinned at him. "'Course we do, baby. We're all proud of you. I'm gonna be out to see your parade with my grandbabies on a ladder. Make sure you throw us something, you hear?"

"I promise," Griffen said. All the new customs he had to absorb in a short time made him feel a little overwhelmed. Doreen seemed to pick up on his mood. She poked him in the arm.

"Don't you think a thing about these people. They all came into the world the same way as you and me."

That was true, he mused, as he straightened his shoulders and marched toward the Greek-Revival portico held up by four pillars painted green. At least for him. Doreen wasn't a dragon, though he doubted few people of any descent could stare her down. She was noted for getting fares—and tips— out of drunk tourists when other cabbies were just grateful to get them out of their cars without having them vomit all over the upholstery. Still, it was good advice not to let dragons who were better established than he was lord it over him. *Always walk in as if you own the place* had been his longtime motto.

Easier said than done, he realized, as he entered the grand house. A tall, thin woman with large eyes and an ascetic nose in a nice blue dress admitted him with all the airs of a duchess. She leaned back slightly to regard him. Though he was several inches taller, he felt as if she were looking down on him instead of the other way around.

"May I help you?" she asked.

"Mrs. Fenway?" Griffen asked.

"No, I'm the housekeeper, Edith," she said, the austere look changing to a kindly smile. "And you must be Mr. McCandles. The Fenways are in the den with Mr. de la Fee and the others. This way, please."

The intimidation quotient ratcheted right into overdrive as he sauntered behind her through the high-ceilinged corridor. The interior walls were painted white over stuccoed plaster. The doorways were outlined by wooden edging stained dark brown and as wide as his outspread hand. Each piece had been routed with five parallel lines that converged in a roundel every three feet and at the corners of the frames. He realized every one of them had to have been made by hand. All the knickknacks gleamed with the warm flicker of money. Griffen had seldom been in a home like that which wasn't a museum with little labels on it indicating the name of the piece, the designer it had been made by, and in what year. No one he knew lived like this. He thought he might like to have something like it himself one day.

At last, Edith opened a door into a glass-walled observatory. It alone was as large as the house he had grown up in. Exotic plants hung from wrought-iron or knotwork hooks. He recognized orchids and miniature roses, but he had no idea what the rest were. The room was divided unofficially in half by a slate-bed pool table that made him more envious than the rest of the display of wealth had. On the far side, a couple of dozen comfortable-looking armchairs were arranged in a rough circle. Small, circular tables about the size of a dinner plate stood at the elbow of each one, no doubt to hold drinks. Griffen approved.

The twenty or so people already present in the other half of the room turned to look at him. All of them, of white, African-American, and mixed heritage, were men except for one woman in a deep green two-piece dress suit. Griffen had learned a little about clothes in the last few months. Everything they wore was so understated and well fitted that he knew they had top-tier designer labels hidden inside. He was glad he was wearing his best black wool pants and a handsome, long-sleeved Fuji silk shirt in pale blue, but he still felt as if he had been hired for the afternoon instead of invited as a guest.

Etienne was the only one who was dressed as casually as he was. He spotted Griffen and wormed his way out of the crowd he was talking to. He came up with his hand extended.

"You here!" he said. His grip was powerful enough to make Griffen wince. "Good! I was just tellin' Mr. Fenway how much you liked the floats. He is in charge of the floats committee. Let me introduce you to everyone, all right?"

By the time he had dragged Griffen over to the largest group, the most elegant of the men had his own hand out to take Griffen's. His long, almost spidery fingers wrapped around Griffen's hand and shook it firmly.

"Callum Fenway, Mr. McCandles," he said. "Nice to meet you."

Callum Fenway's narrow face threw his large, dark brown eyes into relief against his café au lait skin. His hair had been straightened into shiny, floppy waves that made him look like a romantic hero or a cocker spaniel.

"Call me Griffen, Mr. Fenway," Griffen said.

"Well, thank you, Griffen," Callum said, with the air of a schoolteacher speaking to a first-grader. The attitude made Griffen nervous and annoyed at the same time. "We do hope that you will be joining our exclusive little number." He turned to speak to a woman at his side. "My dear, Griffen McCandles. Griffen, my wife, Lucinda."

Lucinda Fenway was a surprisingly lovely woman whose face was almost a perfect heart shape. Her long, nearly black eyes boasted sweeping eyelashes like delicate lace fans. Her figure was tiny at the waist but lush above and below. If she hadn't been a dragon, he would have put her at fifty, but he did not dare guess her real age. "How nice of you to come. Will you have a drink?"

"Irish whisky, if you have it," Griffen said, making it sound as suave as though he were James Bond requesting a vodka martini. "Thank you."

Lucinda turned her head and raised her eyebrows just a trifle.

One of the infinite number of young, twentyish women who worked temporary jobs serving at private parties on their days off from the elegant restaurants downtown slipped through the crowd and pressed a cold tumbler into his left hand. Griffen took a grateful swig as Lucinda recited name after name to him. He did his best to retain them, but he had a dozen tricks for getting people to reintroduce themselves to him. He just smiled and shook hands.

". . . And Terence Killen, who is in charge of our membership committee. I hope you two will be having a nice little conversation later on," Lucinda concluded, coming to the last person, a plump, ruddy-faced man with a head of executive-class silver hair.

"Griffen."

"Mr. Killen," Griffen said formally. He held his temper in check. The krewe should have invited him by the third or fourth introduction to use their first names, too. The longer it went on, the madder he got. It was a power move to deny him the familiarity, but he determined he would not show that it bothered him. Better to make it sound as if using the honorific was what he did to keep his distance. He smiled superciliously at the membership chairman, who squirmed a little, then caught himself. Yes, they knew what they were doing. So did he.

"Well, let's get started," Callum said. With his glass, he gestured toward the circle of chairs beyond the pool table. Griffen waited for the others to lead the way. To his surprise, they all deferred to Etienne.

The werewolf-dragon hybrid loped toward a seat set with its back to the center of the white-painted fireplace. The set of brass irons that stood beside it made it look as if Etienne had his choice of scepters to wield. He settled down and put his right ankle on his left knee. The rest of the men followed and took seats in the circle. If there was a system governing who sat where, Griffen had no idea. Callum went to take his place at Etienne's right hand. The chair at his left remained empty. Etienne waved Griffen over.

"C'mon, man! This is where you belong," he said. Griffen, feeling the eyes of the rest rake him as he went by, sat down where he was directed. Etienne took a battered three-by-five spiral-bound notebook out of his back pocket and flipped to a page. "This is the ninth meeting of the Krewe of Fafnir since its refounding late last year. As you captain, I call for news from my lieutenants on the progress of each of you departments." He grinned sideways at Griffen. "This isn't the whole krewe, of course. We're just the heads of all the committees. We meet from time to time to catch up on what's done and what still needs to be done. There's an encyclopedia of work to get through. Just get up and walk around if you get bored."

"I won't," Griffen said. He glanced at the circle of men. "Uh, aren't there any women lieutenants?"

One of the eldest men present, sallow-faced and with pouches under his eyes that made Griffen think of a deflated frog, cleared his throat. "You're out of order, Griffen," he said, in a squeaky voice that would have sounded natural in a pond.

"Wait," said a young man with shiny dark hair and dark eyes and a pale complexion. "That's going to be a matter for discussion in future years, but it was like this when this krewe last organized a parade. If you join us, you can have a vote. The discrepancy with modern society, uh, has been noted. But that's not what we're here to talk about today if you don't mind."

Griffen felt he'd been slapped down, but it *was* none of his business unless he put his money where his mouth was. Mardi Gras krewes didn't get any support from the government, so fairness laws didn't apply. If he wanted to make a change in their structure, he would have to change it from the inside.

"Okay, then," Etienne said. "Let's go down the list. Treasurer?"

No surprise that Callum Fenway was in charge of money. He stood up and produced a BlackBerry from his jacket pocket.

"At present the checking account has eighty-four thousand sixty dollars and twelve cents in it. Got some big upcoming payments, to Nautilus and Blaine Kern, for float rental and construction, to Bourne Range for the den rental, Howson's for fabric and notions for costumes, and Mimi's Masks on a down payment for our parade masks. We won't know exact numbers until about a week before the parade date, so final payment has yet to be determined. This week, I have processed nineteen requests for riders. All their checks have cleared."

"Okay," Etienne said. "That'll leave it to Terence to make sure there's no problem with other krewes before we accept 'em." Terence Killen nodded and accepted a document from Callum. "Sounds good. How many riders we got so far?"

"Three forty-five," Terence said. "Counting krewe members who've paid."

"Oscar?" Etienne asked. "What about the riders?"

Oscar hitched his big belly over his belt buckle. "I'll get on the float captains. We've got a meeting on Thursday. They are recruiting, but they've got to close the deal and get them to pay up. They're into the concept, though. Real excitement. Could be over eight hundred by parade date."

"Nice. Well, then, Doug, where y'at on liaison?"

The dark-haired man stood up. "I was on the phone with our friends in the Krewe of Antaeus, the Krewe of Nautilus, and the Krewe of Aeolus. It is agreed: We are going to be the fourth to step off on the twenty-fourth of February, at seven o'clock in the evening. They're looking forward to the group meeting on Twelfth Night. Aeolus is hosting it at Antoine's. Should be a mighty fine party."

"Sounds fine," Etienne said, checking off an entry on a page and flipping to another. One by one, the men got up to report, reading from extensive notes. Every lieutenant had a checklist, a clipboard, a handheld electronic device, or something equivalent on which he could jot down details.

"Mitchell, how's the tractor situation?"

"We're gonna have enough," said a chocolate-dark African-American in a charcoal gray sports coat and yellow polo shirt. "Got nine big ones to pull the double-decker floats . . ."

"Nine?" Griffen echoed, impressed.

"Really, that's nothin', young man," Mitchell said, with a humorous glance toward him. "Proteus, Rex, Zulu, Bacchus, they'll have dozens of the big floats in between all the smaller ones, and the bands and the other units. We're just getting started. You wait ten years, and we'll be ready to rival them for a really long parade!"

"Hear, hear!" laughed Terence.

Mitchell went on. "Sounds like we'll have twenty-four small floats, and I have got enough tractors and drivers to manage them, plus some spares. Fifteen of the smaller floats are still under construction, and not all in the den yet. I've got one in the barn out back of my mother's house. The rest of each committee's got them in various places, in pretty nearly every stage of disarray. It's just too soon to start moving even the finished ones, and we don't want to tip our hand too soon on the theme. They'll start to migrate to the den after Twelfth Night."

"Our formal ball will introduce you and the parade theme on January 18," Etienne told Griffen.

"What is the theme?" Griffen asked.

"Well, that kind of information is not open to the public," Mitchell said flatly. "Until you join Fafnir, you are still the public. We can't count on outsiders keeping our secrets."

Griffen tried not to scoff. "You make it sound like a big deal."

Mitchell lowered his brows. "It is a big deal, young man. We have rituals drawn from history, going back centuries. Fafnir has been the guardian of fire in this place, well, since its founding."

"But what about the people at the ball?"

"Ah, well, they won't be present for the underlying rituals of our krewe, just the announcement and the party. Your guests will be welcome to come to the ball, too. There are plenty of family members invited who are not part of the krewe, and they don't have to keep secrets."

Griffen immediately saw a way to keep peace among the three ladies in his life. "And how much are tickets?"

"We're projecting about three-fifty apiece," Callum said. "That right, Ralph?" A white man with a short brown beard nodded. Griffen swallowed hard. Three for the girls, one for himself, and at least two others added up to over two thousand dollars right off the bat. Callum had undoubtedly seen the apprehension on Griffen's face. "But all that's by the way, unless . . ."

"Unless what?"

"Unless you say no." Callum nodded toward Etienne.

Nine

The captain nodded around the circle and flipped to the next page in his notebook.

"Well, now, all old business bein' taken care of, is there any new business?" Etienne asked.

Terence raised a hand. "I want to know, do we have us a king? Griffen? You've been listening to us beat our jaws for hours. What do you think? Are you in or out?"

"I'm in," Griffen said, trying not to look as eager as he felt. "I want to do it."

The others burst into applause. "See, I told you," Etienne said, his thin face alight. "Welcome, Griffen. Well, then, let's get the membership festivities going."

Griffen felt every eye fix on him again. They looked like lions at feeding time. "What festivities?" he asked.

"Well, to start with, you need to enter your membership and pay for it, here if possible," Terence Killen said, flipping up papers on his clipboard and detaching one. "I've got the form to fill out right here. It's not too long. I'll take a check or cash. We're not set up with the credit cards yet, just PayPal online."

"How much?" Griffen asked.

"The basic membership is four hundred dollars for the first year," Terence said.

"No problem," Griffen said, reaching for his wallet.

Terence went on. "But there are higher fees for the officers and honorees of the krewe. We pay a premium for our ranks.

As you are the king, and we are a smaller krewe, we ask only twelve thousand dollars."

Griffen blanched. "Twelve *thousand*?"

Terence nodded. "Yes, sir. That covers your costume for the parade, and an allowance for throws, ball ticket, and some of the cost of striking you into doubloons."

"What?"

"Well, one of the throws that we distribute is a doubloon. An aluminum coin. Sometimes plastic, but we prefer the feel of metal. Used to be wood, or bakelite, back in the old days."

"I know," Griffen said. "I saw some on display at the Presbytery."

Terence seemed pleased that Griffen knew. "That's right. Rex started it. The parade theme is depicted on one side, and the face of the king is on the other. That's you. It's a great honor. You've got a good profile, and it'll look pretty handsome. We'll make sure to give you a presentation case with at least one of each color for your wall. I know it's a bunch of money all at once. I can take a deposit against the rest. We know you are good for it. At least, that is what Etienne tells us." Killen chuckled, and the others shared the laugh.

Until he said that, Griffen was going to give them a few hundred, but then he felt stung by pride to show he was a person of consequence. How much could he spare? He did a quick calculation to make sure he would have enough left to cover his taxi fare home and dinner. Dinner! He would have to go to an ATM to withdraw enough to pay for dinner with Harrison the next day and live on savings the rest of the week. But he was able to hand Terence Killen two thousand dollars, a sum that pleased the others.

"Thank you, sir," Terence said, removing a handsome deerskin billfold from his inner pocket and tucking the money away. He took the application that Griffen had hastily filled out and signed at the bottom and put it back on the clipboard. "Well, now that you have agreed to join us, there is an ordeal to seal the commission."

"An ordeal?" Griffen scanned the room for a means of quick exit. "I don't like the sound of that," he said.

"It's not a true ordeal," Callum said. "We've got rituals. Pete? He's Keeper of the Mysteries of Fafnir." He signed to a wiry man with tightly curled brown hair and pale blue eyes, who took a metal box off the floor. From it, he removed a scroll, an actual scroll of yellowing material that crackled when it was unrolled. Griffen hadn't seen anything like it since the last time he had visited a Renaissance fair. Matt stood up. Griffen got to his feet. The man began to read.

"You wish to join us as a member and king of the Noble Krewe of Fafnir, Griffen McCandles. Do you declare that you are of pure dragon blood?"

"As far as I know," Griffen said. He suddenly felt that every eye in the room was on him, peering at him as if they were looking into his bones. Even Lucinda Fenway, not included in the circle of lieutenants, was staring at him avidly.

"Will you manifest your power here and now, to prove without a doubt the truth of your bloodline?"

"What do you want me to do?"

"Anything you can, son," Callum said, his eyes fixed on Griffen. "You've surely been exercising your abilities by now. Give us a small demonstration. Anything you can."

"I . . ." Griffen hesitated. The tension that the others displayed drained out of them like the air from inflatable beach toys. Doug groaned.

Mitchell scoffed. "Etienne, you are full of it," he said, flicking a hand at the captain. "You bring a kid here that you swear you dreamed about as the big, all-powerful one true dragon, and he don't have no more power than a burnt-out lightbulb. Shouldn't have expected no better of a moon-howler who's got about as much dragon in him as a lizard."

That lit Griffen's temper.

"Are you calling me a phony?" Griffen asked, dropping his voice to just above a whisper.

Mitchell looked taken aback at Griffen's tone, but he held

his ground. "I am saying that maybe Etienne is mistaken. I have known him since we were together in school, and sometimes he lets his visions get the best of him."

"That's not what it sounds like to *me*," Griffen said, meeting the other man's eyes. Mitchell leaned back and folded his arms.

"You take offense at what I say? Well, then, prove I'm wrong!" he said.

"Now, don't rush him," Etienne said. "Don't you worry about a thing, Mr. Griffen. Go ahead. Just relax."

The lieutenants looked skeptical and amused, not unlike a tableful of poker players meeting a rookie at his first game. Sometimes, Griffen would play the innocent until he had figured out just how good his new opponents were, but this time he wanted to prove he knew what he was doing, for his own reputation's sake and that of Etienne, who had brought him there. He decided to give that bunch a taste of a skill that he had learned but seldom used: that of animal control. He didn't have to close his eyes to concentrate. He reached out into the walls and under the floor of the mansion, and sent out an irresistible summons: "Come to me."

Most people in the South called them palmetto bugs. Griffen didn't doubt that there was a fancy Latin name giving genus and species, but as far as he was concerned, they were hypertrophied cockroaches that lived everywhere in New Orleans unless one sprayed the living hell out of one's apartment to keep them at bay. The Fenways probably had an exterminator come in monthly or even weekly to hold off the arthropodia, but no insect could withstand the call of a dragon's control. Griffen waited. He heard a slithery noise begin at a distance. Some of the other men glanced up. The sound got louder and more complex as more palmetto bugs joined the throng. By the time the first of the three-inch-long cockroaches stuck its antennae under the door of the conservatory, thousands were at its back. They swarmed into the room, filling the floor with a roiling carpet of brown. All of the krewe's lieutenants jumped to their feet. In spite of her tight pencil skirt, Lucinda leaped onto a chair. Griffen stood in an empty ring of floor as his inquisitors stomped, kicked, and brushed at the army of insects. Etienne didn't seem particularly bothered as the giant bugs raced over his shoes, but Mitchell beat at them with his hands and feet. His eyes showed the white all around the irises.

"Get them off me! Get them off me!" he bellowed.

"Griffen, get those things out of my house!" Lucinda shrilled from her post.

"Yes, ma'am!" Griffen said. He let the summoning energy die down and replaced it with an order to retreat. As smoothly as a wave receding, the brown insects turned around and fled the room. Some of them seemed to melt into the crack between wall and floor, but the majority slipped underneath the doors under which they had entered. In seconds, there were no palmetto bugs left except for the few that the flailing feet of Etienne's lieutenants had crushed.

"Thank you!" Lucinda said. Callum, recovering his dignity, hurried over to offer his wife a hand to climb down from her perch. She brushed invisible dust from the seat and sank into it.

"That was fun!" Etienne said, laughing heartily at his companions. "No one has ever done that before! You gotta admit, it was original!"

"No one will ever do that in my house again!" Lucinda insisted.

"No, ma'am," Etienne said, dampening down his enthusiasm. He winked hard at Griffen, who tried not to grin back. "We'll exclude that from future demonstrations, ma'am."

"Impressive," Mitchell said at last. His composure had returned. He regarded Griffen with respect. "Pretty comprehensive animal control you've got there. Been workin' on it long?"

"Not that long," Griffen said, as casually as he could. Mitchell gave him a wry half grin.

"Top of your class, young man," he said.

"Animal control! Anyone with a little talent can do that!" Callum said, scornfully. "That's a street-corner trick. That's not a manifestation of real dragonhood!"

The satisfaction of performing a genuine exercise of power well faded into red-hot anger. "Street-corner trick?" Griffen asked, coldly. "I learned that from a man with more talent and integrity than almost anyone else I know." The fact that Slim *had* worked on street corners had nothing to do with his skills. He had been a mime statue, surprising tourists for tips.

"Belongs in a carnival," Callum said, with a dismissive wave. He sat down and folded his arms. "I declare it to be a nonstarter."

"I disagree," Mitchell said. "That was more than worthy, Callum."

"Me, too," Etienne said. "It was damned good. Go on to the next part, Pete."

Griffen raised an eyebrow. The next part? The curly-haired man raised the scroll again as if to ward off Griffen's gaze, and read.

"Will you manifest your true self here, to prove without a doubt the truth of your bloodline?"

"This is my true self," Griffen said.

"Not what you show the outside world," Terence said. "Your dragon soul."

My dragon soul? Griffen thought. Up until a few months before, he had no idea that he had dragon *blood*, let alone a soul with scales on. What did that phrase mean to him?

Did they want him to transform for them? He had hardly ever managed to do it except to defend himself from an attack by the George, a chimeric hunter. Could he bring about the change even though he was not really under threat?

"Go on, young man," Mitchell encouraged him. "*Be* the dragon."

"If he can," Terence said.

"Yeah, we're gonna find out that he's a weredog or something low down like that," Callum cackled, sitting back in his chair. "No offense, Etienne, but your boy is faking it."

Faking it! Griffen's temper reached a boiling point. He felt steam curling in his nostrils. This whole ordeal was an attempt by these self-satisfied jerks to make him display himself for their amusement! Not one of them felt as strong as he did! How dare they demand anything from him? He didn't have to put up with abuse, not for the sake of leading a *parade*!

The sensation he had felt only a half dozen times in his life surged through him. He felt his tail grow from his lower spine and whip back and forth against the backs of his legs. The claws that were often just barely under the surface of his skin burst out and curved into miniature scythes. His skin took on a green hue as it covered itself with scales. His whole musculature shifted, increasing the strength in his back and shoulder joints and making his entire body more flexible. Griffen's perspective changed as his eyes transformed from ordinary hazel irises into multicolored orbs that could see on wavelengths no human could imagine.

In his enhanced vision, he saw the cool image of Fenway sitting in his chair, laughing. They had goaded him on purpose! Furious, Griffen leaped for him.

Fenway's eyes went wide. Griffen was on top of him in a split second, the pointed teeth in his elongated jaw clamping the man's neck. In the next split second, Fenway had transformed, too—but only partway. His skin covered with scales, but his face remained largely human. His claws were only half as long and not as well developed as Griffen's. How dare these thin-blooded dragons insult him like that?

His jaws tightened. He knew he couldn't easily penetrate another dragon's skin, but the pressure was making Fenway's eyes bulge out. Griffen felt hands pounding on his back and shoulders, pulling on his wings. A fanged face intruded into his line of vision, a weird combination of fur and scales.

"Mr. Griffen, let him up!" the creature shouted in Etienne's voice. "I think he's convinced now!"

Griffen let himself be pulled up. As swiftly as it had come upon him, the transformation faded. He found himself standing in his shorts on the ruins of his best trousers. His silk shirt was split at the shoulders where his wings had popped through. Luckily, his underwear was made of stretchable cotton. Fenway, much more experienced at transforming, rose to his feet with all of his clothes intact. He clutched his throat. In human form, two lines of bruises showed on either side of his neck.

"Well done, there, Griffen," Callum said. He stopped to swallow hard. Griffen was grimly pleased that his neck hurt. "We wanted to see if you were a true dragon. I must say we are . . . impressed by your abilities."

"He is twice the dragon of anyone else here, Callum," Mitchell said, slapping his hands together. "Damn! A pure manifestation. I never thought that I would live to see one that ideal. I can't do that. None of the rest of us can, not that good—or that fast. Wish I'd taken a picture."

"Do you want to explain to the people at the drugstore counter when you pick up your prints?" Matt asked, scornfully. "Give me a break, Mitch."

Griffen shook his head. "I know half a dozen shape-shifters who could do the same thing, faster and maybe better."

"No way, son," Terence said. "We can feel the difference, like a jeweler can tell a cubic zirconia from a diamond. The real thing shines through in a way no fake can copy."

Griffen nodded. That made sense.

"Why did you jump on me?" Callum asked.

"I wanted to see if you're the real thing, too," Griffen said, offhandedly. "Fair's fair."

"You can sense us, son," Callum said. He felt his neck one more time and let his hand drop. "I take your point. We did goad you into that, I admit, but we often find that a temper storm is the best way to help someone lose his inhibitions.

You can see that it worked. You're not a puppet to dance for the masses. But we take our mission very seriously, and we don't want to put our trust into the hands of someone who can't handle it."

"So, I passed your little ordeal?" Griffen asked, letting himself be mollified.

Callum smiled. "You bet you did. You shall be king. Lord above, you could be king in truth if you really wanted to."

"You are even more than Etienne said you were," Terence Killen said, slapping him on the back and guffawing. "My lord, how long has it been since we saw someone like you? Well, you have got good blood. I have heard of the McCandles line, up North, but what is your mother's family?

"Her maiden name was Flambeau," Griffen said.

"Another good line, hardly diluted over the centuries. You have a sister, I believe?" asked Terence. "She must be something."

"She is," Griffen assured them. "About that, I . . ."

Lucinda appeared at his side and handed him a tumbler. The scent of good Irish whisky rose. He took a deep and appreciative drink.

"Thanks, Mrs. Fenway," he said.

She patted him on the shoulder. "Call me Lucinda. Call them by their names, too, Griffen. These old fools stand too much on their dignity. I'll bring you a pair of our son's pants. I think you're about the same size. Dinner's in about five minutes. Be right back."

"Thanks, Lucinda," Griffen said.

". . . Think it's the prophecy?" Doug asked, as he turned back to the conversation.

"Oh, not that again!" Matt moaned. Griffen pretended not to hear. But the speculative gazes turned back to study him.

"Well, that's it," Callum said, standing up to offer him a hand. "Welcome, King of Fafnir. This is going to be a fine Mardi Gras."

Griffen gripped it firmly. The gesture was no longer a challenge, so he kept his shake friendly. "It sure will," he said.

"Come on, folks," Callum said, leading them toward the door. "We'll talk more later. Lucinda will have my head on a white china platter if the food gets cold."

Ten

Griffen left the Fenway mansion after midnight. He wore a pair of black sweatpants and T-shirt borrowed from the wardrobe of their elder son, who was away at college in Texas. He refused the offer of a ride home from a number of the members who had offered to drive him. It wasn't that far from the Garden District to the French Quarter. He wanted some time alone to clear his head. What an evening!

Lucinda had been a wonderful hostess. She had served them an epic gumbo, bursting with shrimp, sausage, and, for a wonder, crisp okra. He had never tasted it before he had come to New Orleans, but he could never imagine becoming tired of andouille sausage. The fire of the spices still played upon his tongue. Dessert had been a play on the famous Brennan's bananas Foster: a blond layer cake with frosting flavored by banana and orange, served with a brandy caramel sauce that was still on fire when the regal Edith brought it to the table.

The excellent dinner made up a little for the fact that he had almost turned his pockets inside out for the membership fees, and he still owed the krewe ten thousand dollars for his kingship. He ached for his bank account. It had further suffering ahead of it; the lieutenants wanted to know (1) if he was going to host a king's party, (2) if he had given any thought to where, and (3) how many people he was thinking of inviting. An address list for the entire krewe was available to him as a printout or a computer file.

He had called all four places holding rooms on Etienne's

say-so, and the damages would be a king's ransom, around ten thousand for a large-scale blowout in the most expensive of them for the entire krewe plus spouses or "plus-ones." There would also be the cost of invitations and favors, plus entertainment, and so on. And tuxedo rental. Griffen had a slip of paper from Etienne's little notebook with all the things he was expected to do in the coming season, and what would be supplied to him by the krewe.

Once he had passed the dragon test, as he was calling it in his mind, the other members had changed from casual smugness to polarization at two different extremes. They were starting to align themselves with or against him. He knew they had heard of the prophecy, but certainly weren't going to say whether or not they believed or even could consider Griffen the "young dragon." Still, he noticed Mitchell and Doug, for example, had begun to look directly at him when they were discussing krewe business, as if looking for his approval. On the other side, Matt kept his distance. He was not hostile, but Griffen felt he was not on his side. Others had yet to make their choice evident. Griffen was aware of a lot of speculation and jealousy, and not a lot of admiration. They had all accepted, as Etienne claimed he had known for years, that he was going to be their king.

Griffen didn't feel like a king. He felt like a little boy in the middle of a board meeting and didn't like feeling that way. The others showed him the deepest of respect. He didn't deserve any respect. He could not get past the fact that he had attacked another living being out of pique. His life hadn't been at stake. He had not been threatened; nor had his sister. Griffen had been tricked into transforming. That was not enough reason to let himself, well, go dragon. He was ashamed of how good it had felt, how natural. This must be what Terence Killen meant by his dragon soul.

The others had thought nothing of his outburst; all had accepted it. In fact, most of them had enjoyed it. But they had been raised as dragons. Was that kind of behavior acceptable in dragon society? Mose and Jerome had both warned him that dragons usually couldn't be bothered with "lesser beings," like humans. Griffen did not like the arrogance that seemed to be the hallmark of most of the dragons he had met so far. If superiority meant manipulation, humiliation, greed, casual violence, and scorn, he rejected it. He didn't like the way the other dragons looked down on Etienne. For all the captain's good nature and organizational abilities, he was only a fraction of a dragon, and the added werewolf blood made them consider him even lower than humans. They had made it clear, however, that they would like to socialize with Griffen. He had received invitations to dinners, country clubs, and golf outings, delivered right in front of the captain without including him. The lieutenants were snobs.

On the other hand, he mused, human beings acted like that, too. He didn't like the behavior any more when it came from them.

Griffen stopped in his tracks in the bougainvillea-scented dark. Funny, he had not separated himself from the "them" of humanity before. Perhaps he really was beginning to understand that he was different. But was it nature or nurture that governed one's real self?

It almost made him dizzy to know that he belonged to two different worlds, the one in which he had been raised and the one into which he had been born. He couldn't deny he was a dragon, but he refused to let go of those traits that were human, at least as he saw things. He needed to give himself time to think about that.

But there were good things going on in the krewe, too. Charity, for example. Phil Grover, one of the lieutenants, had bent his ear during dinner over a charity that Fafnir supported. Ladybug, Ladybug had been established to support families, especially children, who had been made homeless by fire. New Orleans's old houses were made of wood and asphalt shingles, both of which went up like torches in a fire. Even though the resurrected krewe had been in existence again less than two years and had yet to march, it had raised tens of thousands of dollars for good works. Phil had hit him up shamelessly for a donation, or, if he wished, to donate a portion of his business's proceeds to it, they would consider it a favor. A mandatory favor, Griffen understood, but he didn't really object. He knew he had been fortunate in his life. Now that he was making decent money, some of it ought to go to those who had worse luck than he. He had a stack of flyers for Ladybug, Ladybug that he intended to put on the table in every suite where his people organized a game.

But that wasn't Fafnir's primary mission. Callum had alluded to one, but when Griffen asked the others about it, they were vague. They said that their job was to protect the city. But wasn't everyone's?

He now had a list of the dates involved. January 6, the Feast of the Epiphany, the day after Twelfth Night, kicked off the Mardi Gras season. Fafnir's parade was scheduled for February 24 at seven in the evening. The parades ran for two weeks before Mardi Gras itself, the Tuesday that preceded Ash Wednesday, the beginning of Lent. On weekends, there were parades all day, but on weekdays they started after six o'clock. Fafnir would be the last of four to march that day. He had a map of the assigned route. Etienne emphasized more than once that they must kick off on time. The parade would last anywhere from three to five hours, depending on the pace and how many units would be marching. That still hadn't been determined, as more people got in touch with the krewe to be included.

The parade had a set order. As captain, Etienne would go first, followed by the lieutenants, all on white horses, followed by Griffen. His float was going to be pulled by a tractor. Griffen was a little disappointed. When Etienne had mentioned horses, he had visions of a team of a dozen white horses, but a tractor was more reliable and less prone to injury. The rest of the floats followed, first with the other honorees, then lesser floats populated by riders from the krewe itself and others who paid to ride. All of them were interspersed with other entertainers and affinity groups. So far the krewe had hired seventeen bands, including five from area high schools and colleges, troops of jugglers, groups of dancers, marching clubs including one from their designated charity and three from the fire departments. They were looking at some 150 units, which sounded to Griffen like an enormous number, but the others insisted it wasn't.

The ball was scheduled for Saturday, January 18, when he was to be introduced to the krewe and their guests. The king's party, and he was still not sure if he was having one, ought to be in between. Whether it was big or small was up to him, but it had to be elegant. Griffen had that feeling again of being a small boy at a board meeting.

The next krewe meeting was Monday, a day early because the next day was Christmas.

And he was now in possession of a true secret: the theme of the year's parade. It was "Dragons Rule." Mitchell and Langford, who was in charge of liaising with the costume manufacturers, produced photographs and a stack of color sketches for him to see. The floats would all express themes of dragons throughout history, literature, legend, and media of dragons who win. Griffen marveled over whimsical sketches of St. George losing to the dragon, giant snapdragons with eyes and darting tongues, a dozen different puns about dragonflies, the Welsh red dragon facing off against the white dragon of England, all five colors of Pernese dragon with one tiny white dragon on the end of the float, the nine sons of the dragon on a Chinese-themed float.

That last was the float on which the dukes would ride. Those were men who had been selected to be honored by the krewe. There were nine of them, as there would be nine maids, on a Dragon Lady float. Griffen admired the cut of the women's costumes, sexy but not revealing. Allure wasn't the purpose of Mardi Gras parade costumes since they were masques to conceal themselves against the devil. He found the whole concept exciting. Put end to end as if the parade stretched out before him, Griffen was more delighted than ever to be a part of it. Mitchell put down one more picture, of a float that resembled a huge gold dragon with green eyes. "That's the queen's float," he had explained.

Griffen had finally worked up the courage to ask the question. "Who's queen?" he asked, feeling as if he were echoing a line of dialogue. "I have, uh, a sister and two girlfriends who are interested, if you haven't chosen anyone yet. They, uh, asked me to ask."

The lieutenants had burst into laughter. Griffen had felt abashed.

"Not your problem," Etienne had assured him, his eyes twinkling. Griffen had forgotten his gift of foreknowledge. "You can tell those three fine ladies that they going to be maids. It's a big honor. They will ride on their own float and sit with the dukes of the court at all the parties."

"They aren't called duchesses?" Griffen had asked.

"Nope. That's not proper Mardi Gras terminology. They are maids, and they will have as fine a time as you will. I've seen it."

As a final treat, Etienne had shown him a photo album of the last Fafnir parade. The white leather-bound book bore the krewe name and the year, which Griffen noted was before the Second World War, when Mardi Gras had been suspended.

"I think you'll find the king's float the most interesting," Etienne had said, opening it to a page and pushing the yellow-edged book toward him. Griffen had studied the old black-and-white photograph closely, concentrating on the fine, shining surface at the man in white satin and a jeweled crown who sat majestically waving a multipointed scepter on a throne with dragon's-head finials on the uprights and the arms.

It was Mose.

Griffen stared. The man in the picture was wearing a crown that concealed his forehead, and he had a full beard, but Griffen was absolutely certain of his identity. Mose looked exactly the same as he had the last time Griffen had seen him. He looked up at Etienne, who grinned at him.

"Just wanted you to know that there's a tradition that it's right for you to uphold, Mr. Griffen," he had said.

Griffen was stunned. Automatically, he had reached for his cell phone and pushed Mose's number. His old mentor had gone to visit his daughter out of state, or at least that was what he insisted Griffen tell the others in the operation, but Griffen had to ask. The phone rang and rang before going over to voice mail. Griffen had hung up without leaving a message. Mose!

As he walked, Griffen's head spun at the thought of all that was going on and all that he had to do. He wished he *could* ask Mose about the krewe and get his advice. He worried that he was far out of his league. These people were all very experienced, knew the ropes, had been part of and helped dozens of other krewes over the years. They were proud to be restarting something that their parents and grandparents were part of decades ago.

He tried Mose again. The cell phone rang four times, then went straight to voice mail. Frustrated, Griffen punched the red button.

"He's not answering this late, especially since he knows it's you."

The quiet voice made Griffen jump.

He had not heard her fall into step beside him, but then he wouldn't have. Rose, a beautiful black woman in her thirties and a well-regarded voodoo priestess, had been dead for eight years. Her footsteps were silent.

"Why not?" Griffen asked.

"Because this is something he wants you to work through all on your own," she said. "It's too important. He wants you to make your own decisions."

Griffen nodded. "You never appear without a reason," he said. "Is my getting involved in the krewe important to you, too?"

"Very," she said. She gave him a wry smile. "I made a mistake not giving you more time before to decide whether or not to chair that conclave. This time, I wanted you to make up your own mind. If you hadn't said yes, I would have asked you. It's not true," she said, with a faint hint of mischief, "that ghosts can't learn anything new."

"Well, you don't strike me as an ordinary ghost," Griffen said. "Not that my experience has been very broad. What's so important about it?"

"Balance," Rose said. "This city requires it. Mardi Gras is part of the balancing act that New Orleans goes through year after year. All that indulgence before the deprivations of Lent is a balance, the feast before the willing sacrifice. It is most sincerely meant, by the locals. The visitors all think it is a big party. They do not see that the pendulum must swing from the opulent to the austere and back again. So, too, must the elements be balanced. It has been growing out of whack for a long while. I am glad to see that it will at last be redressed. You are doing the right thing. Do your part at the parties and most especially in the parade. Etienne needs you and your special skills."

"All I'm going to do is sit on a throne and throw doubloons," Griffen said, doubtfully.

"Not at all," Rose said, her serene face serious. "You are the focus, the channel. Keep your humility, but you are entitled to pride as well. Use the office well. Keep in mind your most important task."

"The balance," Griffen repeated.

"All power must be kept in balance, or destruction follows. It is part of history." Rose turned toward a streetlamp shaped like an antique gaslight. Griffen lost sight of her in the momentary glare before his eyes readjusted.

When they got used to the light, she was gone.

Eleven

Griffen threw a couple of hundred-dollar chips into the pot and restacked his five cards. Sun blazed in the window behind him. He wouldn't usually sit with his back to either a door or a window, but the least glare hit him in the eyes that way.

When he had returned to the French Quarter the night before, it was still too early to go to bed. He had walked over to the Irish bar to see who was around. Fox Lisa had been there with Maestro. She had wanted to hear every detail of the meeting. He told her what he could without breaking the krewe's confidence. She tried hard to worm the parade theme out of him. It had been hard to resist her, especially when she suggested they leave the bar and go back to his place.

She had fallen asleep afterward. Griffen had been too excited to drop off. Instead, he went out to his living room. He was starting to formulate ideas for his king's party. He found a notebook, made a batch of microwave popcorn, and put on *Masque of the Red Death*, starring Vincent Price, with the volume down very low. It was the only movie in his collection that had anything to do with Carnival. He would have to check out Tower Records or the DVD rental shop to find if there were any movies about Mardi Gras in New Orleans. Since Rose had given her approval, he wanted to do his best for the Krewe of Fafnir. Whatever he could do to help maintain balance, whatever that was, he would do. He needed to research more into the history to see if there was a reason for Carnival beyond the religious festival.

About four, Fox Lisa had discovered he was awake and joined him on the couch. Neither of them got much more sleep. She had to leave early to go to her job. Griffen went back to bed, but his mind kept racing, interspersing the sketches of the parade floats, Vincent Price, and Rose.

The phone rang just about eleven. Griffen groped for it with a hand and muttered a hello into it. At the sound of Jerome's voice, he opened his eyes to a headache and quickly shut them again. His head throbbed whenever he moved his head too quickly. But he had promised Jerome faithfully after the conclave that he would pay more attention to the business. He had kept his word. This was just one of the myriad small problems that he needed to help solve. He had been dressed, shaved, and on his way in fifteen minutes flat.

"Raise you," said Jerome, putting in three chips. He grinned at Griffen. Griffen refused to admit that he was bluffing. Let Jerome try to figure it out. Hopefully, it would cost him a bundle. Griffen held two pairs, twos and threes. It was pretty small, but it would beat even a pair of aces. He might even be able to make a full house. Even if he didn't, he might be able to convince the others to fold. Sadly, he was not there to play for blood.

Ellis and Mike, two white businessmen from Detroit, sat between them. They were executives from the auto industry. The game had been set up to run during the two-hour break the visitors got for lunch. The convention was being held in the function rooms and grand ballroom of the Astor Crowne Plaza, sixteen floors below them. If they were happy, they knew other executives who would like to join a hosted poker game. Jerome was determined to make sure they were happy. Griffen agreed that what they wanted mattered more than another hour's sleep for him. The suite was already rented. Lunch had been ordered in, and a full bar of drinks awaited them.

"I think you have a handful of nothing," Ellis said, with a laugh. He pushed in three chips.

"Pay and see," Jerome said, smiling broadly.

"Well, I have got nothing," Mike said, turning his cards back to Noah, the dealer, a light-skinned African-American in his forties with graying hair and light freckles. Peter put in the three and raised two more. The rest of them concentrated on the hand. It was a hard battle, but Griffen's two pair took the pot. The others emitted the obligatory moan. Noah shuffled and dealt again.

There should have been five players in the game. Two of the three locals they had expected to fill out the table had canceled, citing an important lunch date. The third simply didn't show up. Jerome had phoned Griffen and asked him to sit in. That made four. They were ready to settle for being one short, when a businessman in an Armani suit had happened to catch the eye of one of their spotters at the Marriott and asked if he knew where he could find some action. Marcel had put the man in a cab at his own expense. Peter, a dapper Chinese-American with slicked-up hair that stood six inches high, arrived just before the first hand was dealt. He sat to the right of the dealer, his fingers resting lightly on his downturned cards. Griffen had made a note to pay Marcel back with a bonus for quick thinking and sit down with him for a drink.

Marcel wasn't the only man in his employ who had shown initiative like that. Griffen realized he needed to get to know more of the people who worked for Mose's operation—now his. The wake-up call he'd received after the conclave had brought him around to understand being a responsible boss and member of the community meant more than just making sure payroll went out on time. It also meant recognizing those employees who wanted the business to run better and instituting improvements they suggested. They wanted to be part of a first-class, well-run establishment. He wanted that for them as well as for himself.

The first on his list to appreciate was Jerome. Griffen had sensed some disquiet from Jerome when Mose had installed him as heir apparent over the head of the dragon who had been in the team longer. He certainly knew the job better than Griffen did. There was no reason not to have given Jerome the position except for Griffen's bloodline. He was glad that Jerome seemed like he was starting to relax around the "Young Dragon." He was finally losing the chip off his shoulder he had after Griffen was promoted over him.

"Hey, Grifter, since you were off playing with your parade friends, I interviewed a new caterer," Jerome said. "What do you think of the canapés?"

Griffen ate a meatball from the plate by his elbow. The burst of beef flavor was accented with savory spices he couldn't identify, but enjoyed. "Very good," he said, reaching for another tidbit, a chunk of steamed fish with a green sauce on a rice cracker. It was as tasty as the first. "You should hire them."

"Already did. They're our go-to guys now when the hotels don't supply room service," Jerome said. "I checked out about twenty places. These were the best."

"Nice pick," Griffen said, pretending to doff a hat. "You have my respect."

"Hear, hear," said Mike. "Great eats."

"Stop passing the shit, man," Jerome said, though he looked pleased.

"Not shit," Griffen said, his expression severe. "Only one problem."

Jerome looked concerned. "What?"

"There might not be enough food. I'm going to eat about five pounds of this stuff!"

"So will I," said Peter, munching on another bite-sized morsel. "What do you call these things with the cheese and shrimp?"

"I don't name 'em, man. I just eat 'em." Jerome called for the caterer's assistant to refill everyone's plate.

It was funny. Griffen had come to understand he didn't really know Jerome at all. How Mose did without him those long months when Jerome was up at college with him in

Ann Arbor, he didn't know. He seemed to be able to juggle dozens of knives in the air all at once. Reserving suites, arranging players who would find one another's company pleasurable, hiring caterers as well as all the other people they used were only a few of the jobs he handled. He once asked if Mose knew all that Jerome did for them.

"'Course he did!" Jerome had said, scornfully. "It's his operation!"

Touché, Griffen thought. He had to lose his own ignorance, to be worth the people who worked for him.

"Play cards!" Ellis said. "We've only got an hour."

Griffen sat back at his ease to survey the others. He prepared to look for weaknesses in play and tells. He was amused to see they were all doing the same. Griffen couldn't take total advantage in this game. It was to benefit them, not him. He already took a piece of the gate, the percentage that came from the buy-in. He had to remember that and not play for blood. A little extra to cover his Mardi Gras expenses would be nice.

"Hey, I know you," Mike said to Peter. "I saw you on the World Poker Roundup! You made it to the final table four years ago."

Now Griffen turned to stare. The Asian man smiled modestly.

"Yes, I did," he said. "I did not win, though."

"You still took home a big purse. Over 350k, if I recall."

"That's right."

Jerome clapped his hands. "Well, we've got us a celebrity."

"Welcome," Griffen said. "It's an honor to have you at one of my games."

"Your games?" the man echoed.

"I'm Griffen McCandles. This is my operation. Thought I'd deal myself in today."

"Oh!" Peter seemed taken aback. "Well, it's a pleasure for me, then, too. This is a very nice arrangement you have. Five hundred."

He threw in his chips, and the game went on.

Griffen was curious to watch a professional at work. Peter had very neat movements, no wasted energy. His expression, when he was not chatting with the others, became a friendly grin. It was disarming, but Griffen knew better than to believe the surface appearance. He could sense dragon blood in Peter and wondered if he knew he had it.

At the hour, Noah dumped the current deck and smiled at the players. "Five minutes' break, please, gentlemen," he said.

"Hey, so what's it like playing cards for a living?" Mike asked Peter, as they got up to stretch.

Griffen went to load up on snacks from the chafing dishes on the caterer's table. He liked the suites in the Omni. Unlike some of the chains, the paintings weren't bolted to the wall, or the lamps to the desk. Hospitality meant not treating your guests like potential thieves, even though it meant that the ones who were took your towels home with them.

"Hey, man," Jerome said, appearing at his elbow. "Thanks for helpin' out."

"Happy to do it," Griffen said. "You handle so much. It's the least I can do. Any more flak from that game?"

They both knew what he meant. The cheating scandal. It still rankled with both of them. Jerome shook his head.

"No one's called it in to the police. Luis started talkin' about it at another game. The dealer had to ask him privately to knock it off, but you know how that guy loves to tell stories. No peep out of Len and Marion, but maybe they want to lie low."

"I can hardly believe that they would cheat," Griffen said, feeling at a loss. "Those two have been coming down here for years. *I've* played with him. He's cagey, but he's straight as they come. Almost pathologically honest. Mose said last time they were here they forgot to give one dealer a tip. They sent a money order from Toronto."

Jerome pressed his lips together. "I know, man. It's got

to be the other one, the one who kicked up the fuss. Jordan Ma, I think his name was. I don't know how it happened. He must have noticed the missing card stuck under Marion's arm and made capital out of it. Kitty, the dealer, is too new. She's freaked out being in the middle of that. I'm gonna ride herd on her for the next few times. She won't have to deal for that man again. We have a couple of experienced dealers who can handle accusations of cheating or horseplay."

"Maybe I'll bring everyone together for a seminar," Griffen said. "We have to keep our reputation straight. It's all that we've got." A painful memory struck him. "Speaking of that, I had to let Jimmy McGill go."

"I thought that boy looked too furtive," Jerome said. "What was with him?"

"He was dealing cocaine for Tee-Bo on the side. I told him when he started that I don't allow a sideline in drugs anywhere in our operation. I gave Tee-Bo a call. He didn't know that Jimmy was working for us, either. I called Jimmy in and told him to choose which employer he wanted to stick with."

Jerome shook his head. "He gave you a sob story, didn't he? Grifter, you can't be soft on them, or they'll just walk on you!"

"I wasn't," Griffen said, feeling terrible about it all over again. "He claimed it was all a lie. I knew it wasn't. It was the second time I had caught him. I gave him another chance after he begged me to keep him. This time I fired him. I don't think Jimmy's going to be working for either of us again."

"You didn't have a choice, head dragon," Jerome said, gently punching him in the arm. "You got to do what's right and keep things straight."

Reputation was everything in the Quarter, where so many deals were sealed with a handshake. Griffen had vowed to be honest with everyone. He didn't want illegal drugs associated with his games. He had made it clear to all the employees in the operation from day one, and to everyone he had hired since he started. He knew what it had been like not all that long ago. Mose had turned a blind eye to the junk. Maybe there were other land mines that Griffen hadn't found yet. This would be strictly a gambling operation. There was plenty of money for everyone in that alone. If they wanted to do something even more illegal, Griffen wanted no part of it.

"Hey, if you have a few more games for me to sit in on, I'll play," Griffen said, as Noah called them back. "Mardi Gras is going to run me dry on capital."

"You're not supposed to be takin' profit directly from our clients," Jerome said dryly. "But I think a lot of them would be thrilled to have the big man sit in on a game. Just don't take 'em for too much."

"Me?" Griffen asked, planting a hand on his chest. Trying to keep the innocent expression on his face made them both laugh.

They returned to the table. The dealer, Noah, did a fancy shuffle on the new deck of cards. "What's your pleasure, gentlemen?"

"Texas hold 'em," said Peter. Griffen didn't groan, though he felt like it. The man seemed to pick up on his displeasure anyhow. He peered at Griffen apologetically. "You don't like hold 'em?"

"I'm old-fashioned about poker," Griffen said, startled. No wonder the guy was a professional. He could read minds. "I like the old games, even five-card stud."

"More possibilities of a working hand with hold 'em," Peter Sing said.

"Statistically, you are right," Griffen agreed. "I didn't mean to denigrate your choice. You are the guest. And you've had a lot more experience than I have. I only played in college before I came here."

"No offense taken. It's natural you have a preference. But," he said, appealing to the businessmen from Detroit, "it's my game. Shall we play?"

"Oh, yeah!" said Ellis, grinning.

Noah produced a white plastic button two inches across and put it in front of Peter. "Ten-dollar bets, blinds one hundred and two hundred."

The table anted up, and Noah dealt.

It seemed seconds later when Ellis looked at his watch and nudged his colleague. "Got to go back. Damm it. Wish we could stay."

"Me, too," Mike said. "I'd like to have had a chance to get back some of my stake." He grinned at Peter. "But it was worth it to have had a chance to play with a real pro. Too cool. Listening to tabulations of sales figures and projections for next year is just not going to cut it. Probably fall asleep during the presentations."

The man with the cockscomb hair was the big winner, having taken about a quarter of the money on the table. Griffen was next, having made a little less than 20 percent on his investment. He was fairly happy. You couldn't get that from the stock market. The businessmen had both lost money.

"Sorry you didn't do as well as you hoped," Griffen said.

Ellis was gracious. "Not to a couple of players like you. It was an education."

"We'll definitely get our buddies in," Mike promised. "Perhaps a room like this, with double tables? Mr. Sing, will you come?"

"Sure," Peter said. "I'm in town for a few more days."

"That's fantastic!" The men were enchanted. "Thanks again, guys. It was great."

"Thank you, gentlemen," Griffen said. "Looking forward to seeing you back again."

"Count on it!" Mike exclaimed.

After giving a generous tip to the dealer and the server, they headed for the elevator.

"Got two games going this evening," Jerome said, as they got up. "Put your phone on vibrate in case I need you."

"Not after eight, Jer. Having dinner with Harrison. I'd prefer not to be interrupted. I know you'll be able to handle anything that comes along."

Jerome nodded. "No problem. A little PR?"

"Fence-mending," Griffen said. "Good job, Noah." He gave the man a tip, too.

"Thanks, Mr. Griffen. It was a good game. Fun to watch you play."

Jerome turned to offer Peter a hand. "Thanks for sitting in, Peter. Hope you had a good time."

"Thank you," Peter said, slapping them both on the back. "It was too short. I would have walked away with all your money if I had the time."

"Yeah," said Griffen. "You are welcome anytime. We'd love to have you sit in."

"Hey, Grifter . . . ?" Jerome began, a pinched look on his face.

"Just a moment. Here's my cell phone," Griffen said, jotting it down on a piece of paper. "Call me when you're free."

Peter produced a card from his pocket. "This is my number. Please call me when you have arranged more games."

The Eastern dragon grinned at them as he left the suite. He waited until he was alone in the elevator before he brought out his cell phone and pushed a speed-dial number.

"Yes, it's me. Better than you would ever dream." He grinned at the phone. "And you told me it was a liability that I played in that televised tournament."

Twelve

Griffen was nervous as he checked himself out in the mirror. He wore a dark blue matte silk shirt and a new pair of black wool trousers. He wanted to make a good impression, but not show off. Humble but honest was the name of the game. As a sly old sage had once said, sincerity was the key. If you can fake that, you've got it made. Griffen had been overcautious in telling Harrison what he needed to know to do his job, and the vice detective had let him have both barrels when he discovered how much Griffen was holding back. Griffen was concerned, and rightly so, that the human detective would freak out if he knew the whole truth, but it turned out for the wrong reasons. Harrison really wanted to know what he was dealing with. A homicidal fairy was not all that different in the damage he could do from a meth-head on a toot. As a result, Harrison had been on his case. There were no breaks in Jesse Lee's murder. Harrison blamed him for that. Knowing that the victim was a dragon made it Griffen's fault. Griffen understood the logic. He felt the same way. If Griffen hadn't been a dragon, Jesse Lee might not have been killed even if he had come to work for him. The Eastern dragons saw it as the first chip off their power base.

What Griffen didn't like was that Harrison was letting his guys in vice hassle the dealers and spotters just a little, just to remind him how he had erred. Griffen thought they were both being punished enough because an innocent man had been killed. He had to make peace with Harrison. They really could help one another.

Griffen took the long way to the restaurant, stopping off at Tower Records. He browsed through the "Musicals" section of the DVDs. He had had a yen lately to watch *Guys and Dolls*. He was developing a keen sympathy for Nathan Detroit's problem of keeping one step ahead of the cops but still maintaining the Oldest Established Permanent Floating Crap Game in New York. His players were counting on him. His employees were counting on him. And now, so were the people in the Krewe of Fafnir. Griffen felt he ought to own his own copy of the movie so he could refer to it from time to time. It'd be nice to think he could handle himself with the same style and aplomb as Frank Sinatra.

With the little bag under his arm, he turned back into the heart of the Quarter. The restaurant was on a corner facing Jackson Square. Griffen strode the four blocks north on Decatur Street, dodging tourists and traffic.

The heart of the square was full of artists, fortune-tellers, and street performers. Close to the eastern edge of the park, a couple of the teenage boys were dancing to a boom box for a small knot of tourists. By their posture, Griffen didn't think they were inclined to leave tips in the upturned hat on the ground. He diverted into the stone-flagged confines and removed a five from his wallet. Ostentatiously, he dropped it into the hat. The boys did sunfish rolls on their sheet of cardboard in thanks. A couple of the visitors reached for their wallets. He grinned and angled for the diagonal path that would take him to the restaurant on the corner.

He suddenly felt uneasy. Someone was watching him, but where? He glanced around. A man in a lightweight gray suit was not-looking near the wrought-iron fence. Griffen eyed the broad shoulders. That was no tourist. He was a cop or some other kind of law enforcement. He wasn't the only one. Another man, in a tan jacket and dark blue pants, was reading a newspaper with his shoulder propped against one of the replica gaslight streetlamps. All he was missing was the rectangle cut out of the paper to peer through. Why the obvious surveillance? Was Harrison trying to hassle him just before they had dinner together? Why?

Then he was there at Griffen's side.

"Nondescript" was the perfect word to describe Jason Stoner. He had absolutely no distinctive features, nothing to set him apart from any other ex-serviceman who had gone into civilian service. His hair was buzz-cut short. It could have been graying at the temples, but Griffen couldn't tell. What set Stoner apart was his uncanny stillness. He could have been a statue. He stood at ease on the balls of his feet. Griffen, who knew a little about martial arts, understood that the stance made him prepared to respond to an attack from any direction, even one coming from above or below.

"Mr. Stoner," he said.

"Griffen."

"To what do I owe the honor? I don't have time to spare. I have a dinner engagement."

"Yes," Stoner said, his eyes registering no emotion. "Detective Harrison. This won't take long. I told you that if you became involved in my interests, I would warn you."

"What interests are those?" Griffen asked. "Homeland Security?"

"That is my only concern with regard to you, or anyone else in this city," Stoner said.

"I have nothing to do with your business," Griffen said, alarmed. "I'm just trying to keep mine going."

"What about the Mardi Gras situation?"

"That's nothing," Griffen said. "The only thing that makes the krewe different from every other krewe in New Orleans is that all the members are dragons. I have no authority. I'm just the king. They're all hyperorganized, but it's nothing that should interest the government."

"Don't try to pretend you don't know what's going on," Stoner said.

"There's nothing going on," Griffen said, feeling desperate. If Stoner picked him as dangerous, he could end up in a federal penitentiary awaiting a trial that never came, or shipped off somewhere they didn't speak English and had no phones, or just plain killed. "I swear. It's accountants and bartenders playing dress-up for a day."

"Then you will cooperate with me. I represent your nation's government."

"What do you want?"

Stoner turned to face him. His eyes bored into Griffen's like awls. "These accountants and bartenders do want to interfere with my job. My job is to protect the United States from all attacks. These people are a threat to this country." Griffen hesitated. Callum and the others *had* implied that they had a mission of some kind, but never said what it was. Had Griffen fallen into the hands of terrorists? All of the altruistic talk about charities and generosity to the Mardi Gras crowd suddenly sounded too good to be true. All the enthusiasm he had felt soured in his stomach.

"Of course I will do anything I can to keep the country safe. I won't cooperate with anything that endangers it."

"And you'll report to me if you observe anything?"

"Observe what?" Griffen asked.

Stoner's eyelids lowered a fraction of a millimeter. "That is classified information."

Griffen felt his temper rise. "I don't work for you. I'm not going to spy on these people. It sounds like you have the place wired already."

"Not yet. No," Stoner said. "I don't want you to put a bug in for me." The way he emphasized "bug" suggested he had seen Griffen's little stunt, or knew about it. "This krewe has plans that will interfere with the country's safety. If you get involved in their scheme, I will have to take you down with them."

"I told you, I won't help with anything dangerous or subversive, but that is as far as I will go. I don't want to get on your bad side, Stoner, but I'm not going to do your job."

Stoner just looked at him. "I don't need you to do my job.

All I need from you is information if you get it, and for you to stay out of the way if I need to take these people down. Remember what I said."

Then he was walking away. Griffen jumped back. It was like watching a statue come to life. The defiant part of his mind said that Stoner would have made a terrific street performer.

He felt upset and confused. Was there really a plot to overthrow the government hidden among all those blueprints and artists' renderings? Rose wanted him involved in the Krewe of Fafnir. She couldn't be wrong about them. Or was there something else she hadn't told him?

His head spinning, Griffen jogged the half block to the restaurant.

Thirteen

Griffen checked his watch with annoyance. He was a few minutes late. He scanned the room for Harrison.

The burly figure holding up part of the wall opposite the maître d's desk detached himself and came to meet him. Harrison still wore his weather-beaten leather coat, but underneath it was a nice blue-and-white-striped Oxford-collar shirt—ironed—and a blue tie striped on the diagonal with red—neatly knotted. Griffen tried not to stare outright. Harrison gave him a squint-eyed glare of challenge.

"Thought you were gonna blow me off."

"Not a chance." Griffen grinned. "This is some of the best food in the city. I was going to eat here whether you made it or not." Harrison grunted. The challenge retreated but didn't disappear completely. Griffen smiled at the hostess, a statuesque woman named Nami. She knew him and his sister well. She held up a finger for patience.

"I have your usual table, Mr. Griffen. Just a moment, please."

"Your usual table, huh?" Harrison said.

"We come in here for special occasions," Griffen said. "The turtle soup is the best thing I have ever eaten. You'll have to try it."

"Can't be as good as my aunt Emily's," Harrison said doubtfully, as Nami picked up two tall, leather-backed menus and led them into the dining room. About thirty tables covered in white tablecloths stood well spaced for privacy but close enough to suggest intimacy. The lighting was mellow, adding to the cosy atmosphere. Somewhere, light jazz music played. It didn't interfere with the quiet hum of conversation. Nami brought them to a table for two by the wall underneath an Art Deco sconce. It was original to the restaurant's décor, as were other pieces of bronze and stained glass.

The restaurant had the potential to intimidate, but the staff, as in so many top New Orleans restaurants, defused the situation and made their guests welcome. The waiter, a middle-aged man with a shaved head and very dark skin, came out to greet them immediately. Edwin was Gris-gris's uncle. He wore the fine-dining server's uniform of a white shirt, a black bow tie, black trousers, and a long, plain, white apron tied at the waist.

"Mr. Griffen! And Detective Harrison. Welcome."

"You know each other?" Griffen asked.

"We've met," Edwin said. It didn't sound as if it had been a happy event, but the waiter was willing to forgive and forget, at least within the confines of the restaurant. "Let me give you a chance to look at the menu, and I'll get you some water and rolls."

Edwin bustled away. Griffen felt nervous again. He didn't know whether to mention Stoner. Harrison hated that the Homeland Security man might be interfering in *his city*. There was no good reason to raise his blood pressure unless Griffen needed his help. He had yet to figure out what Stoner had been talking about. Still, he had gotten in trouble for holding out on knowing about supernatural elements. He was torn as to what to do. Harrison gave him a curious glance.

"What're you staring at?" he asked.

"Nothing," Griffen said. "Nice tie."

"Sound surprised. You think I don't know how to dress?"

"You look fine, sir," the waiter said, returning. He filled their glasses from a silver pitcher and put a basket covered with a snow-white napkin on the table between them.

Fragrant steam rose from it. "Now, what may I get you to drink? We have some good wines, beer on tap, or something from the bar?"

"Coke," Harrison said, grimacing. "I hate insulting the food, but I'm still on duty today. This is my dinner break. Those slugs in IA would be happy to Breathalyze me to find out I'm drinking. Hope I get something to eat before I have to pull another body off the street."

"Diet Coke," Griffen said. It was a sacrifice on his part, too. The wine cellar was as excellent as the food. Even the modestly priced bottles were good. They also kept his favorite Irish whisky, Tullamore Dew, at the bar.

The waiter disappeared. Griffen leaned in a few inches and dropped his voice to an undertone.

"How's the investigation going?"

Harrison shook his head. He took a roll out of the basket and pulled a piece from it. He buttered the piece and ate it. "No progress. The girlfriend was flattened. They were gonna get married. Can you do something for her, Griffen?"

"Sure, we can. We already are. Were there any witnesses?"

"You know I can't talk about an ongoing investigation. But there were people within twenty feet, didn't see a thing. So," he said loudly, with a glance at the diners at the surrounding tables, "I can't answer your question about witnesses." He opened his menu.

Griffen got it and opened his own. A pristine white card announced the evening's specials, a fresh-caught Gulf lobster, prime rib, and a chicken breast with oyster stuffing. They all sounded good. "Remember, this is on me," he said. "Order what you want."

"Um-hmm." Harrison didn't look up. Griffen decided not to press the matter. He had already told Edwin ahead of time to make sure he got the check, no matter what argument Harrison put up.

"Well, do you have any more questions for me?" he asked.

"Not about that. I'll need to talk to any of your other employees who interacted with him in any way."

"Sure. I'll make sure they are around when you want them."

"Good. Enough shop. What's good?" he asked Edwin, who returned with a white paper pad in his hand.

A nod from Griffen urged him to go all out. Edwin applied the full force of his personality on the detective. "Our strength is our seafood, Detective. We've got fine black bass this evening. I can also recommend the seafood platter. Steamed mussels, roasted scallops, and a lobster tail. Everything's fresh and delicious, guaranteed."

Harrison frowned. He looked longingly at the seafood side of the menu, but his finger moved toward the specials card. "What about that chicken breast?" he asked.

Edwin snatched the menu out of his hands. "Hey! You insult my restaurant, Detective? *I'll* choose. That way you don't have to think about it. You'll enjoy it, I promise." Harrison looked annoyed but didn't protest or try to take it back. Griffen handed over his menu placidly.

"Sounds good to me," he said. "I trust you."

"All right," Harrison said. "But none of that nouveau cuisine. Ain't enough calories in that to keep a canary alive."

"Are you kidding me?" the waiter asked. "In this establishment?"

He disappeared into the dimness and reappeared in moments with two tiny china plates in his hands. He set them down with a flourish.

In the center of each plate was a golden brown round of bread topped by a dark green, ridged leaf Griffen thought was spinach. It was the setting for one plump oyster, still glistening with its liquor, sprinkled with white shavings and a single red dot that was unmistakably hot sauce. Griffen lifted the plate to smell the white shavings and recoiled slightly. Horseradish.

"Here's a little amuse-bouche to start you gentlemen off," Edwin said.

"That means a little appetizer . . ." Griffen began.

"You think I don't know my Franglish?" Harrison asked.

"This is my city. You just got here." He disposed of the oyster in a gulp. Griffen swallowed his own oyster. His eyes watered, and his whole body shuddered. He followed it with the brown bread and basil leaf. It filled his sinuses with a heady licorice scent that went perfectly with the horseradish and hot sauce. *That* was the way to enjoy a bivalve.

No sooner had Griffen recovered from the oyster than Edwin swooped in to remove the plates and replace them with two flat basins of warm, fragrant green liquid. Griffen inhaled appreciatively. The turtle soup was what brought him back time after time to this restaurant. He hoped it would mollify the gruff officer, and it did. The aroma made Harrison smile.

"It's made with sherry," the waiter explained, "but I had the chef flame it to take down the alcohol before he added it. Enjoy it."

"We will," Griffen promised. The rich liquid rolled on his tongue like cream, and the savory, meaty flavor made him feel all was well with the world. Neither of them spoke until the soup plates were empty. Harrison sat back in his chair.

"I'm gonna have to arrest the chef," he said.

"Why?" Griffen asked.

"He stole my aunt Emily's recipe."

Griffen laughed. "Are you sure? Should we check the kitchen to see if she's back there?"

"Now that you mention it," Harrison said, "I haven't heard from her in a while. Maybe she's moonlighting. Damned economy."

"I hear that a lot," Griffen said.

"Your business doing okay?" Harrison asked.

"Glad you asked," Griffen said, keeping it casual. "Your fellow guardians of the law came and tossed one of our games the other night."

"Keeping you honest. You guys don't pay taxes."

"Actually, we do pay taxes," Griffen said. "I have all my employees filing W-9s before the end of the year."

"Anyhow, we got a complaint from the hotel. Got to follow up on complaints. You're still unlicensed, unless you've swung *that* in the last few weeks."

"You have me there, Detective," Griffen said. "I prefer to think of it as operating in a gray area."

"You know I don't give a damn unless someone gets hurt." He glared at Griffen. Griffen spread his hands.

"Look, Harrison, we both want the same thing, for everyone to live in peace and make a living. You don't have to have a stick up your ass."

Harrison grimaced. "I don't like to relax around people like you. I might have to run you in one day for vice."

Griffen shifted uncomfortably, then noticed the mischievous gleam in Harrison's eye. The detective was ribbing him. He didn't know whether to counter with a retort or just accept it. Edwin rescued him from the awkward moment.

"Salad, gentlemen," he said.

"I hate frisée," Harrison said, as Edwin put the plate down in front of him and carefully drizzled dressing on it from a sauceboat. But he finished it. "Great dressing. Too bad they put it on weeds and grass clippings."

A busboy removed the empty dishes. Edwin and another waiter brought the main course out to them, big silver covers on the plates. At a silent count of three, the waiters whisked the domes away.

"The best of New Orleans. Enjoy."

A rush of hot steam washed Griffen's face. Contentedly, he contemplated a surf and turf at a far remove from ordinary family restaurant fare of fried shrimp and tough steak. The parsley-sprinkled bread-crumb crust on the filet of flounder was so delicate it broke like the snap of crisp snow on a winter morning. The tenderloin was sliced and fanned to show the red center in the rectangle of brown. Griffen applauded the chef's using a fish that was firm and hearty enough to stand up to the meat. Fingerling potatoes and baby vegetables filled in the empty places on the plate, and the entrée was surrounded by a savory sauce. Griffen had been schooled by Edwin and other servers at the finer restaurants that good meat shouldn't be covered by the sauce. That trick was for keeping Salisbury steak and turkey breast from drying out. Everything smelled so good it was hard to decide what to try first.

He had his eyes closed, enjoying a perfect bite of flounder, when Harrison's gruff voice interrupted his reverie.

"I have to keep learning all the time, or I'm gonna get killed out there," he said.

Griffen's eyes flew open. It was an awkward beginning, but at last the elephant-in-the-room subject was coming up. The tough street cop was appealing to the college kid from Michigan, and he did not like the uneven quality of the playing field. It took a brave man to admit he had a weakness. Griffen dipped his head to acknowledge it.

"Whatever I can do to help out the NOPD," he said.

"Forget the NOPD," Harrison said, chewing a miniature squash. "They'd lock me up in a mental institution if they could hear us now. How many of . . . you are there?"

"I have no idea," Griffen said, honestly. "I knew as little as you did until recently, and I still don't know everything that's out there."

"What about people like you?"

"Dragons." Griffen let out a low whistle. "There are a lot more dragons in New Orleans than I thought, and I know I haven't met all of them yet. And there are all the other ones."

Griffen paused while Edwin came and topped up their glasses.

"What other ones?" Harrison pressed.

"Uh, changelings, uh, werewolves. Shape-changers. Vampires. Ghosts. Wiccans. You know . . ." Griffen let his words trail off uncomfortably. Harrison's expression didn't change, but Griffen could almost hear the gears turning. The detective was handling the revelations better than he would have thought.

"I already knew about the wiccans," Harrison growled. "I feel like I'm living in Disneyland. Why's this city got more weirdos than anywhere else in the world?"

"I don't know if that's true," Griffen said. "I'd bet there's a higher percentage here, but I don't know. I haven't had that much experience living in many other places, and none before I knew about . . . you know. I know I would rather live here than anywhere else, and I'm a dragon."

"This is the best place to be," Harrison said. "It's worth protecting. Even with all of you in it."

Griffen held up a finger. "Wait a minute, Detective. It's not *in spite of* people like me. We're part of this city and this country, too. I may be new down here, but lots of others have been here as long as any human beings. They love this city. I love it. We're not interfering. We're part of the landscape."

Harrison chewed over the notion. Griffen could tell he found this tough to accept, but he swallowed it as he did the fish. "My granny had one of those scrolls that hung from a nail in her parlor that was called 'Desiderata.' She always told me it was a waste of energy to rail against what can't be helped. But is there some kind of secret password so I can tell what I'm dealing with?"

"No more than if you ran into a smuggler, an illegal alien, or a millionaire," Griffen said. "I can feel them, but that's a new skill I'm just picking up. Some humans have it, too. I used to call it the sixth sense, but it's more than that. And there are a lot of people with just a little blood from one of the groups. Plenty of them don't know they have it, like me and Val."

"You mean there's half vampires out there? Half swamp creatures?"

Griffen grinned at the mental picture of a half-flora, half-fauna baby in diapers in a crib shaking a catalpa-pod rattle. "Maybe. Some types can't interbreed. Some of them can have sex with other beings but can't have children with them. We don't all know about each other. I got thrown into this only a few months ago. I'm learning it just ahead of you."

Harrison had plenty of other questions. Griffen was impressed, as always, by the detective's shrewd intelligence.

Griffen found himself telling him about the conclave, who had what kind of powers, who got along with whom, and whether they lived in New Orleans or not.

"Now here's a special just for you from the dessert chef," Edwin announced. Griffen got off his elbows and made room for the dessert, a tower of pastry with caramel sauce and a chocolate cutout for each of them.

Both men dove into the confection with spoons. It tasted of vanilla, with a hint of coffee and chili. Harrison deconstructed it as he might a case and cut into each piece, dipping it in the crème anglaise in the center. Griffen felt his waistband tightening with every bite. He was going to have a stomachache later, but he couldn't stop eating. The chef had his own magic.

"That one who died, Slim? What was he? A shape-changer?"

"No. He had power over animals. They loved him."

"Then why was he posing as a statue for tips in Jackson Square? Seems like a waste. Could have been world-famous with an animal act. A real Doctor Dolittle."

Griffen shook his head. "Because he respected the animals as you would respect other people," Griffen said. "He wouldn't exploit them any more than you'd line up a bunch of humans and make them dance to earn a profit for you. He was very responsible with his power. I didn't understand that at first. The animal-control talents are very touchy, and they have reason to be. I want to save you the trouble of making the same mistake I did."

"Point taken," Harrison said. "Just seems like a lot of people would use a talent like that to make money."

"They would. Slim didn't like it. He did his best to protect animals from others. Like me." Admitting that reopened an old wound. "I made a lot of the same assumptions you did. He taught me better. I wish . . . I wish it had gone differently."

"You and me both," Harrison said, polishing off the last bite of pastry. "Well, if you are all such good citizens, then I need help. Did any of them see what happened to Jésse Lee? Anyone who has leads on open cases can let me know. I don't care where the information comes from."

"You don't know what you're asking."

"That's damned right, I don't," Harrison said. "But I have confidential informants you wouldn't meet in broad daylight with an army at your back. How much worse could your kind be?"

Griffen winced. "Don't even ask. But I'll put it out there. I got to know some people during the conclave who consider themselves good citizens."

"And some who don't?"

"Not as much as they don't consider themselves to be part of civilization if they can help it. We're all ruining their environment for them."

"Everybody's a rampant greenie these days," Harrison growled.

"Some literally," Griffen said. "At the conclave . . ."

"How was the food?" the waiter asked.

"Five stars," Harrison said. "Mr. McCandles here wasn't giving me BS when he said this was the best place. The tournedos de boeuf were perfect, red inside but done exactly to temperature. The panko crust suited the flounder. Don't need more seasoning than a little thyme and a sprinkle of salt. Your chef got that on the nose. Dill would have overpowered that and the beef."

"Yes, sir. He knows his fish. I saw that you appreciated our turtle soup."

"Flaming the sherry was an inspiration. Added a little smoky, aged flavor that just gave it another dimension. I have got to try that myself. Don't get a chance to really do any fancy cooking on my schedule, but I get a vacation once a year. Does he sauté the meat before he simmers it, or does he start with raw?"

"You better not overcook turtle, Detective," Edwin said, warningly. The two of them dropped into incomprehensible jargon including such terms as "the Maillard effect" and "*sous vide.*" Griffen was slack-jawed.

"I get the Food Network," Harrison said, defensively. "You can't live in this city and not become a food fan."

"Damm it, take the card!" A too-loud voice interrupted the restaurant review. All of them turned. A red-faced man in a light brown suit glared up at a waiter. Griffen could see from where he sat that the man's eyes were red, too. In fact, he looked a lot like the steak Griffen had just eaten. "It's fine! Run it again!"

"Sir," the waiter said, dropping his voice and leaning close, "I am very sorry, but it was declined."

"Declined, hell! You're just running it wrong! Do it again!"

"We did, sir. Would you happen to have some other means of settling your bill?"

The belligerent expression on the man's face told Griffen he was between tipsy and drunk. "That's the way I'm paying. Now, run the slip, because I am walking out of here in exactly sixty seconds whether you do or not."

"Sir, that won't do. They won't pay."

"Tough shit. What are you gonna do? You gonna call the cops?"

"No, I'm already here," Harrison said, striding to the man's side. The diner jumped. Harrison put a hand on his shoulder and pushed him back into his chair. Griffen followed along just to see the show. "I was just having a nice dinner, and I heard the commotion. I'm not gonna bust you up in here. Place is too nice for that, and it would just embarrass the hosts you were trying to stiff."

"The card's good!" the man protested.

"Instead of blaming the staff, you tried calling the credit-card company? Gimme your cell phone," he said to Griffen. Griffen immediately surrendered it. Harrison dialed the number on the back of the card and thrust it at the man. "Ask 'em."

The man recited his number into the receiver and waited. "What do you mean I'm over my limit? I had three thousand dollars credit before we left . . ."

Harrison took the phone. "Who'm I talking to? Well, ma'am, I'm Detective Harrison of the New Orleans Police Department. Yes, ma'am, good evening. No, I know you can't tell me anything about his account. But how about you tell Mr."—he glanced at the card—"Tadeuz if there was any big purchase recently? Uh-huh. You have a nice night." He handed the phone to the embarrassed tourist, who listened closely.

"The car rental," he told his scarlet-faced wife. "We declined the insurance, so they took a deposit on our credit card. But that's not fair!"

"You signed the agreement," Harrison said, his voice low and just on the soft side of threatening. "So maybe you remember that you have enough money in your wallet to pay cash. Otherwise, there're crimes known as theft of service, theft by deception, and a bunch of other charges that I could read out. I am sure you would rather pay your money for this excellent food and wine than for bail money." The guy was slightly drunk but not insensible. He got the point. His face was scarlet as he opened his wallet and counted cash out into the small black tray on the table.

"And the tip," Harrison said. "These people treated you really nice. Don't take it out on them."

Very grudgingly, the man put another bill on top of the others.

The man's wife, a nice-looking woman with gray, curly hair, lifted beseeching eyes to him. She was genuinely upset. "Really, Officer . . ."

"Detective," Harrison said.

". . . Detective, we'll see what happened. It wasn't deliberate. We have a high credit limit. Really!"

"It's okay, ma'am," Harrison said. "You enjoy the rest of your night, now." The couple gathered their belongings and rushed out of the restaurant. Behind Harrison, the family at the next table mimed applause. Griffen grinned. They went back to their table.

Edwin followed them and helped them be seated. "Well, Detective, we are very grateful for your help. We'd like to—"

"Now, don't you say another damned word!" Harrison snarled. Edwin halted, eyes wary. "I do not want to hear another word about it. I am just doing my job. No freebies." Griffen pushed down on the air with his flattened hand just behind the detective's back.

The waiter subsided. "Well, I will just go and make sure the coffee is as good as it can be." He bustled away.

Harrison's pager buzzed. He looked down just as Edwin brought a *café presse* to the table.

"Shit. I almost made it to the coffee," he said.

"We'll put it in a go-cup for you, Detective. I hope you enjoyed your meal."

"Sure did," Harrison said. He pointed a finger at Griffen's chest. "Don't think this takes you off the hook, McCandles."

"No, Detective, sir," Griffen said. Harrison hung around long enough for Edwin to pour his coffee into an insulated container. "And I want to make sure you're gonna pay for this meal."

"I know," Griffen said, reaching for his wallet. "Theft of service, theft by deception, and whatever else you can think of."

"Damned straight," Harrison said. "I'll use whatever tools are in my toolbox on you if I have to. Whatever makes it work down here so that life goes as peacefully as it is going to go."

He took his coffee and went out into the night. Griffen felt his shoulders relax as soon as the detective was out of sight. That hadn't gone as badly as it could have. They weren't exactly friends again yet, but they were allies. Harrison felt more in control than he had before. Griffen didn't mind letting him think he was on top of that hierarchy. It worked better for both of them.

Fourteen

Valerie looked back over her shoulder onto the street. Two men had stopped, one lighting the other's cigarette, just out of the light of the vintage streetlight. "They're still there."

"If you want, I will take them out," Gris-gris said, guiding her by the elbow to one of the naugahyde-covered booths. "It would be my pleasure. I just want you to relax and have a good time. You took a weekend night off just for me. I want you to be happy."

Val almost said yes. She kind of liked having a boyfriend who was willing to kill two people just because they were bothering her.

She hadn't really thought she liked the bad boys, but the mild men she picked up she often forgot a week later. The dangerous aspects of Gris-gris really turned her on. Griffen carried a knife in his pocket, but Gris-gris had actually used his. The boys she had dated at college would probably pass out if you showed them one. That was one reason why she continued to see him when there was so much variety in the Quarter.

"No," she said. "Unless they come in here. As long as they keep their distance, I'll be okay."

"Whatever you say. Hey, Clarissa!" he shouted. "You got some service coming out here?"

"You shut up, Gris-gris!" Clarissa shouted back. She was pouring coffee for a man at the counter.

"You want me to come and mess you up over there? My lady wants some service!"

"Hey, Val, honey," Clarissa called over. "That man bothering you?"

"No," Val said, grinning at him. "Not yet. Unless I get lucky."

She glanced out the window. The men had stopped on the other side of the street. They stood smoking and talking, but she *knew*, she could *feel*, that they were watching her out of the corner of their eyes. Her temper flared. The room suddenly seemed too small, as if her world was constricting.

A light touch brushed her hand. "Hey, sweet thing, keep it down. They only used to seeing one size of you in here, okay?"

Val looked at him in shock. She glanced at their hands. Hers were bigger than his. She had grown without thinking about it. She shot a hasty glance at the other people in the diner. "Did anyone see?"

"Maybe the two guys outside, but I think they already know. Right?"

Val concentrated hard on returning to her normal size. *Damm it.* She thought that she had gotten that reaction under control! It was the tension from worrying about Melinda jumping out and surprising her that was throwing her off. She had to get herself together.

The men outside had not been sent by Melinda but by Griffen. She was perturbed by his overprotectiveness even though she understood it. It was sweet. She knew it meant he cared; but they went everywhere she did, even when she went out running in the mornings. She hated the idea of being under surveillance. Even more, she hated the reason she had to be under surveillance. Mai insisted that Melinda was a fearsome opponent and would stop at nothing to get what she wanted. Well, if she wanted Val's baby, she was going to be disappointed.

She found herself getting angry all over again, but she

controlled herself before she started Hulk-ing out all over again.

"Sorry, I'm not being fair to you,". Val said to Gris-gris. "Thanks for asking me out this evening."

"We haven't really had any time alone lately," he said.

Val glanced out at the loitering men. "And we don't exactly now."

"Well, I hope they ain't gonna be following us *everywhere*." He looked her up and down with interest. Val felt her own response growing. Her body was changing, but not enough to interfere with lovemaking.

"They'd better not," she said, huskily. "I owe you my undivided attention for a while."

"And why is that?" he asked, studying her. She liked the incredible dark brown of his eyes. When he looked at her, they seemed to absorb her gaze so she couldn't break away.

"Well, all the nice things that you say and do for me."

He looked pleased. "You're a special lady. I'd do it just because you're you. But your family has treated me right, also. That means something to me."

Val looked into those deep eyes. She didn't want to fall in love with him. She was too young. They really didn't know each other well. She liked spending time with him. He let her take the lead on their lovemaking. That meant something to her. So little of her life before New Orleans had been in her control. Her uncle had chosen where they went to school, enrolled her in the college of his choice, even given her a clothing allowance in store credits so she had to shop where he chose. Gris-gris gave her freedom to act. Whether or not they had any kind of future together was something she didn't want to overanticipate. What happened, happened. She tore herself away from his gaze and gave him a sardonic smile.

"Did I tell you about Griffen's meeting with his krewe?"

"Yeah. Are you going to be a queen?"

"No," Val said, peeved at the memory. "And I am not buying Griffen's explanation that the krewe has chosen a queen and wouldn't tell him her name. I think he's just putting off having to choose one of us because he knows the other two are going to be mad at him. Still, being a maid sounds like fun. You'll come to the parties with me, too, won't you?"

"That's all out of my league, mostly," Gris-gris said, honestly. "Society people, rich people, educated people."

"But do any of those matter? I want you there."

He nodded. "Then I will be there, pretty lady."

Val hesitated. The subject of finance was a delicate one. She had no idea what Griffen was paying him as a runner and spotter. "We'll have to buy tickets. I think they'll actually cost a few hundred dollars. If it's too outrageous, I'll understand."

Gris-gris waved away the trouble. "I can afford that. It's my once-in-a-lifetime chance to escort a maid of Mardi Gras to the ball. I have to find me a suit, too. Can't go there in what I own."

"Oh! I have to find a dress," Val realized with a shock. "I'm so used to wearing casual clothes wherever I go around here. I don't think I have anything even remotely suitable."

"Plenty of places to find a gown," Gris-gris assured her. "You could even have one made. I've got an aunt who would love to dress you up."

"A tailor?" Val was delighted and momentarily distracted at the thought of having a dress made to order. "I've never had anything made for me."

"Yeah, but we do all the time," Gris-gris pointed out. "It's a lot cheaper than buying fancy clothes. There's probably as many tailors and dressmakers down here as there are in New York because of Mardi Gras and Halloween."

"I never thought of that, but yeah. I can see that. Michael Kors probably doesn't do a lot of parade costumes."

Gris-gris laughed. "Designer-line masquerade? That'd be something else."

Val was suddenly ravenous. "I need something to eat right now," she said. "Sorry. I could blame it on you-know-who"—she glanced down—"but it's just me. I forgot to eat lunch."

"Clarissa!" Gris-gris cried, without breaking eye contact with her. "You'd better feed my honey soon, or we'll go someplace that knows how to cook real food!"

"You think you know what it tastes like?" Clarissa asked skeptically. "Ain't been that long since you actually started paying for your meals."

"Look, mama, I am going to get beat up here if you don't deliver!"

A loud snicker came from the booth behind them. Val turned around to glare. "You poor hunk of scum," said a large man with tattoos all the way around his thick neck. "I'm watching you jump whenever that girl tells you to. You are so whipped, man!" He made a gesture with one finger like a flower stem wilting. His friend, who had a long scar from his ear to his throat, sneered.

"Yeah. She too much woman for someone like you. You ain't got enough manhood to please her, so you actin' like her personal servant."

Val was shocked and furious. She started to open her mouth. Gris-gris reached over and put his hand on her arm. She spun to look at him. He wasn't angry. He was smiling.

"Man," he said, "you only *wish* you were whipped like me." He sighed and grinned widely, the look of a satisfied man. "You would be luckier than a four-leaf clover to be whipped like me."

The others looked shocked. Their expressions shifted to something like admiration.

"That good, huh?" asked the large man.

"Oh, yeah," Gris-gris said. "There are ladies that are worth bowing down for, and this lady here is one of them. I have no shame for showin' my gratitude in public. You ought to think about that sometime." Val felt her cheeks burn. She was so flattered it made her breathless.

"Thank you," she whispered. Gris-gris gazed at her and dragged her into those deep eyes again.

"Honey miss, you are somethin' special. I don't mind what you do, as long as you take some time to do it with me."

"Forget about the food," Val said, taking his hands in hers. She squeezed them, as if trying to communicate her growing need to him. She did not need to. He looked as eager as she felt.

"Too late, Clarissa!" Gris-gris bellowed, a broad grin on his face. "Maybe some other time. Got somethin' better in mind!"

Arm in arm, they slipped out the door. For a while, Val managed to forget—or care—about being followed.

Fifteen

The young waitress at the Café du Monde set down a heavy white mug of coffee and a plate of fresh, hot, white-coated beignets in front of Griffen.

"Now, y'all watch it. They're hot!"

"They taste the best that way," Griffen assured her. She smiled, slapped a bill down, and went on to the next customer.

Griffen took a huge bite of beignet. The searing heat of dough just moments out of the hot oil parboiled his teeth, but it would take molten lava to hurt a dragon's mouth. He loved the sensation and the flavor of the fresh doughnuts. The chicory-infused coffee was just as hot. Its slightly spicy smell made the perfect counterpoint to the sweet, puffy, square doughnuts. No wonder this place was always full, at every hour of the day or night. It was a national treasure. The day they put him in charge of everything, he was going to grant Café du Monde landmark status.

As he took the next bite, the ringing of his cell phone surprised him. He inhaled at the wrong time and got a lungful of powdered sugar. He reached for the handset while trying to cough the white powder out.

"He-hello?" he hacked. "Yes, this is Griffen McCandles."

"Peter Sing. I sat in on your game the other day?"

"Yes!" Griffen said. Hastily, he drank a swig of coffee to clear his throat. "Hey, good to hear from you. What can I do for you?"

"I am in the mood to play poker," Peter said. "You said

you would be happy to have me in on any of your games. Do you have one going on tonight?"

Griffen hesitated for a moment. "Let me check my list," he said. He stared out of the restaurant across Decatur Street at Jackson Square. He was torn as to what to do.

Following the game at the Omni, Jerome had taken him aside and said he didn't trust the man. Coming from anyone else, Griffen could have ascribed any number of motives for disliking another person, but Jerome was different.

Jerome was smart, experienced, tough, and streetwise, but the main talent in which he excelled overall was as a judge of character. Mose had noticed it when Jerome was very young and relied on it from then on. Griffen would have been a fool to ignore his warning.

"I'm sorry, Peter," he said. "The only thing running tonight is a closed game for a few regulars. They're not very good. You'd outshine them, and they'd get pissed at me."

"I could hold back," Peter offered. "I really want to play."

"Sorry." Griffen was pleasant but firm. "Hey, how about this? I have a late-night game set up day after tomorrow, some really experienced players who want to come around after a show at Preservation Hall. They're high rollers. Much more your speed. You'd enjoy that a lot more. The action won't get started until after ten."

"That is not very good customer service." Peter sounded annoyed, so Griffen kept his tone apologetic.

"We really do try to give our clients what they want," Griffen said. "Do you want me to arrange a game for you tonight? I can try and set something up and get back to you with the details."

"That will not be necessary," Peter said tersely. "I will attend the game in two days. Give me the location."

"When I have it, I will let you know," Griffen promised. Sing signed off without saying another word. Griffen punched in Jerome's speed-dial number and told him what happened. "See if you can put something together with a few clients who won't mind losing money. I'm going to sit in myself and keep an eye on him."

Jerome sounded incredulous. "You listened to me? You actually listened to somethin' I said?"

"I've learned my lesson," Griffen said, humbly. "I hated turning down money, but if you don't trust him, I don't want him near the operation unless I can be there myself."

Jerome sounded relieved. "I just get the feelin' that he's the first snowball in some kind of avalanche. I'll set something up for Friday night."

"Thanks," Griffen said. When he hung up, he already felt better.

Sixteen

Griffen stalked toward the Fafnir den. Etienne's message had sounded urgent. Anything that got him out of bed before noon for the second time in a week had better *be* urgent.

He strode among the Mid-City warehouses. No part of the old city was much more seedy or run-down than any other part, but there was just something about industrial buildings that tended to look abandoned and derelict even if they were being used by a thriving business. The den, the bright yellow paint on its huge sliding doors slivering in the baking heat and humidity, seemed like it hadn't been used for years. According to Terence Killen, it was rented from a garden-furniture importer who had two other warehouses and wouldn't need that one until April, plenty of time for Mardi Gras staging and takedown.

Griffen reached the apron and felt as if he had been hit in the head by a hot, wet fish. The power that the old building exuded made him believe in science-fiction force fields. Passersby, mostly locals, walked around him on the sidewalk, meeting his eyes with a friendly expression of puzzlement but never looking at the nondescript warehouse itself. If they didn't feel it, why did he? What was it?

He managed to push his way through the sensation and enter the den by way of the small door next to the main entrance.

The contents of the bustling facility had changed since he was there before. It was not just that the floats there were much closer to completion, nor that dozens more people were working on them, or spreading plans out on tables, or conferring in corners. Something unseen was building in the very air. The feeling was much stronger inside than it had been outside. It was intense. Griffen wanted to fight back against it. Not that it was sinister, but it was powerful. Yes, that was it: power. It was concentrated here as he had never felt it, not even at the conclave. It must be true that dragons possessed far more power than the average being of supernatural heritage.

He let himself absorb the sensation for a moment. Like a perfume, it entered his body by every pore and orifice. His natural mojo fought off the intruding energy until he could accept it as nonthreatening. He even liked it.

With a proprietary air, Griffen surveyed the dozens of people working on floats. They were making the float that would carry him through the streets of New Orleans. He tried to pretend that he was a real king, and these were his lackeys. They were going to go out and do battle with the rush-hour traffic and the minions of the tourism industry. He would wave to his thousands of loyal subjects, many of whom would be young ladies who would show their loyalty to him by raising their shirts with nothing on underneath. Then the whole idea overwhelmed him with the absurdity of it. He laughed out loud. The big dragon in the corner seemed to wink at him. He had to stop getting his information from the evening news.

Somehow, the sound of his voice echoed above the noise of drills, lathes, and saws. Etienne and Terence looked up from what they were doing and came to meet him.

"Mr. Griffen!" Etienne said, shaking his hand and clapping him on the back with his little notebook. "Good to see you!"

"Hi, Etienne," Griffen said. "You called me? Is this important? You got me out of bed, you know."

The werewolf-dragon hybrid immediately flipped to a page in his book. "Time-line," he said. "You still don't have a tuxedo yet, do you?"

"Well, no," Griffen admitted. "I was going to go when I had a chance. Is *that* why you called me?"

"Well, yeah," Etienne said, as if it was self-evident. "It is important, Mr. Griffen."

Griffen felt his neck get hot with fury. It was getting kind of old, having Etienne always know what was happening— or not. But Griffen had talked to other prescient people. The gift was not a friendly one. Shirley, a motherly woman who offered tarot readings in Jackson Square, actually quoted to her clients from the dreams she had had about them the night or the week before, not from the cards. Her record, as far as Griffen's experience with her went, was impressive.

"You're just a servant to the dreams," she had told him. "More than half the time I wish I had no idea of what is going to come. Some people kill themselves. Some drink or use drugs to try and chase the pictures away. The rest of us learn to cope."

So Griffen tried to be patient with Etienne. Still, he had woken Griffen from too short a night's sleep.

"It's just a tux," he said. "I was going to get to it. You probably already knew that."

"Well, I did," Etienne said. "And I know you waitin' too long to get going. As king of our krewe, you gonna get invitations to a bunch of associated krewes, Antaeus, Nautilus, and Aeolus, who share our marchin' day, for a start, but some of the superkrewes are glad to have us up and going again, and they will also send invitations. We return the favor. You could end up goin' to a whole bunch of balls and parties. You gonna need at least three suits."

"Three!" Griffen protested. "Why can't I just have one?"

Etienne shook his head. "They'll be in and out of the dry cleaners all season, so you gotta make sure you don't get stuck without one. Ain't no substitute for black tie. You can't just show up in a sports jacket and say you forgot. And if you miss, it's a big insult, to them and to us. Get enough suits."

Dry-cleaning a suit ran a minimum of twenty dollars. Griffen multiplied that times three tuxedos, which probably cost more to clean, and added the red ink to the mental deficit he was compiling. But there was no arguing with someone who knew the future and had probably seen him renting the suits. He tossed off a mock salute.

"Aye, aye, Captain."

"See, that's good," Etienne said, with his sunny, patient smile. "It'll all work out okay. Here." He gave Griffen a sheet of paper that looked as if it had been copied and recopied many times. "Here's some local tailors who rent tuxes. You probably won' be able to get any in town unless you lucky, but no sense in not tryin'. Metairie is gonna be out, too. They've got dozens of deir own krewes now. Try Baton Rouge, maybe. I tink that's where you gonna luck out."

Griffen resolved to save time and go to the Baton Rouge addresses first. No sense in reinventing the wheel. Langford poked him in the other elbow with his clipboard.

"While you're out looking for tuxes," he said, "I need you to go in for a fitting on your robes for the parade. We had general measurements for you already."

"How?" Griffen demanded. They looked at him patiently. "Never mind, I know."

"And you need to get your ladies together. They have to go in for their fittings, too."

"Sooner's better'n later, Mr. Griffen," Etienne said.

"Hey, Griffen!"

Phil Grover, in charge of charity, looked up from the enormous fountain pen that he was painting, and came over. "I want to thank you for your donation. I didn't expect anything so soon. A lot of money flows through your operation, doesn't it?"

Griffen pulled back just a little, and not from the red paint smeared on Phil's coveralls. He didn't like outsiders asking about the finances of the operation. "Proportionately, I suppose so."

"Well, it's welcome," Phil said. "I can't tell you what it's going to mean to a lot of families here in the city. We have thirty-four families who have been left homeless or partly homeless because of fire in the last eighteen months. Ladybug gives them grants proportional to their situation and income."

Griffen listened until his ears rang. It was unbelievable how much detail each and every one of the lieutenants kept in his head. He interrupted Phil in midspate.

"How'd you get interested in helping Ladybug?"

"Oh, pretty much every krewe has a charity or three that they donate to. Like your business, money comes in large amounts. Contrary to you, we are officially not-for-profit, so when there is surplus cash not allocated against next year's expenses, we donate it. There are always good causes to support."

"There have never been 'next year's expenses' in Fafnir, not since the forties," Griffen said suspiciously. Had he had uncovered the secret Stoner was talking about? Was this a money-laundering operation?

Phil held up his hands and laughed. "You caught me! No, I have been doing the same thing for various krewes here and in Metairie since I was twenty. Not too much younger than you. Now I work for a nonprofit as the vice president, coordinating fund-raising. He named the charity. I started working for the company because I had learned how to fill out the paperwork and shake the can for a krewe, and I keep getting asked to do the same job on krewes because I work in the industry. I suppose you could say that Mardi Gras and my career are entwined. Makes you believe in Fate, doesn't it?"

Griffen was impressed. And puzzled all over again. The krewe seemed to be just what he thought it was. For the life of him, Griffen could not find any sinister meaning in their operation. They were all much, much too busy organizing for Mardi Gras season and doing genuine good works. He didn't understand what Stoner was concerned about.

"Hey, there, Griffen! You listen to this. I know I am right, and this tight-ass is wrong." It was Mitchell, the parade marshal. He came bustling up with a sheaf of papers in his hand. He brandished them at Griffen. "Callum here says I am wasting money, but I am investing for the future of the noble Krewe of Fafnir."

"I am not. I am saying that he is jumping the gun. We have a dozen other places that those funds could go that are more vital."

"What could be more vital than preventing future outlay?" Mitchell asked.

"Preventing a shortfall today! What do you think, Griffen? We would really value your opinion."

"Uh," Griffen said, looking from one to the other. "Isn't this something that Etienne here should solve? I'm only king this year. He's the captain."

Both dragons looked at Etienne and back to Griffen. "But you've got the pure blood, Griffen," Mitchell said, as if it should be self-evident. "You're the senior dragon here. By a long chalk."

Griffen looked at Etienne, worried that he would feel usurped, but Etienne had that serene look on his face that said he had seen what was happening and had learned to accept it or really didn't mind. Griffen still felt guilty, but he asked. "What is it you're trying to work out?"

He listened as closely as he could to Mitchell's explanation of the outright purchase of fifteen small float bodies on a rent-to-own basis, citing the future amortization of assets and depreciation versus rental. Griffen did his best to drag concepts from his Introduction to Business Administration class, but finally held his hands up. "You guys know what kind of money this krewe is bringing in. I don't."

"I can show you, young man," Callum said, thrusting forth his BlackBerry and showing Griffen a complex chart on a screen that was eye-strainingly small. "It isn't nearly enough to cover what Mitchell thinks we need."

Griffen held up his hands. "No, I mean, this is something that the two of you would be better working out on your own. If it takes more discussion than you've given it, then maybe you need to sit down and talk until you've got a real understanding of both positions. I know that if you really ask my opinion . . ."

"Yes," both men said, leaning forward.

". . . All you'll get is a guess, and not an educated one at that."

They looked at one another. Mitchell glowered. "I don't want to hammer all this stuff into this fool's head."

"I'm not sure you could understand what you would need to know," Callum retorted.

Griffen threw up his hands. "Since you asked, my judgment is it's not my problem. Sorry, guys." He turned away. He found that his heart was racing.

"That was a nice, pretty little solution, Mr. Griffen," Etienne said, staying by his side. He smiled. "They each been hopin' you be their own ally, so they haven't bothered to work it out between them. Woulda taken five minutes if they tried."

"That's really why I'm down here today, isn't it?" Griffen asked.

"They had a little lesson to learn, Mr. Griffen, but there's one there for you, too."

"A humility lesson?" Griffen said bitterly. "Thanks a lot."

Etienne looked at him seriously. "In the long run, none of the petty stuff's important. Just gettin' this parade off exactly right is what matters. You keep that in mind." He patted Griffen on the back. "You just what this krewe needs. Just you walk around a little and talk to people. Enjoy youself for a minute."

He went back to a group of dragons in the corner, leaving Griffen by himself in the middle of the vast room.

Griffen took his advice and went on a small tour of the facility. Everyone seemed to have his or her assigned tasks and was executing them confidently. With no experience, he was at a loss. He felt small and young and completely out of place walking past the partially finished floats, the knots of people talking, and the tables pushed against the walls. He had probably better leave.

He weaved his way between the committees and machine tools, smiling at everyone who met his eyes.

A voice rose above the screeching din. "It's *got* to be the flagon with the dragon."

Griffen spun on his heel.

"What?" he asked, not sure if he had heard correctly. "Who said that?"

"I did!" One of the younger men, Jacob, grinned at him from a card table behind the green dragon float. "Hey, Griffen, come on over."

"What are you doing?" he asked.

"We're ordering throws for the parade. You ought to be in on this, young dragon, since you're the king. Bobbie, did you say four thousand?" A tiny woman with pale skin and long black eyelashes nodded. Jacob nodded and noted tiny numbers next to an entry on the inevitable clipboard. Griffen sat down on a stool at the edge of the table. The surface was covered with hundreds of strings of beads. Shiny smooth beads, faceted beads, braided beads, twisted beads in metallic or plain white, some strings with large, ornamental beads, some with multiple strands or a pendant, such as a bottle opener or a flashlight. Griffen let the strings of beads flow through his hands like shining waterfalls. He couldn't stop playing with them. Neither could the others.

"And what about the specials?" asked a fat woman with brilliant green eyes in a tawny face surrounded by ochre hair.

"I have some numbers," said a slender man with hollow cheekbones. "The float captains want a few hanks each, but not too many. They're just too expensive."

"But they are amazing," said the second man. He held up a handful of strands for Griffen's inspection. Spaced between the gleaming metallic beads were five or seven large, shaped beads two inches across. "You'll probably want some for your float, too. We have dragon's-head necklaces, purple with green eyes, green with gold eyes, and gold with purple eyes. A few of the really fancy ones have LEDs inside, and the really, really fancy ones blink." He touched an invisible switch near the clasp of the necklace, and the dragons' eyes flashed on and off.

"I sure do," Griffen said, delighted. "I want some to keep, too."

"What do you say, then? Twenty hanks, forty?" Jacob asked. Griffen shrugged. Jacob eyed the other numbers on his page and made a notation. "Hey, you'll want to see these. We've also got doubloons, and those will have the king's head on one side, the theme on the other. Here's the proof copy." From his shirt pocket, he produced a plastic coin with a hollow-eyed man in profile. With surprise, Griffen recognized the image.

"That's me."

"Yep. We took it from a photo of you Etienne had." From the same pocket, Jacob brought out a photograph. Griffen recognized the room around him as the interior of the Irish bar. It could have been taken anytime within the last few months. "What do you think?" Griffen studied the plastic coin.

"I think . . . I look surprisingly dignified," Griffen said. Bobbie laughed. "You could really feed a guy's ego like that. But what about what I heard?" Griffen asked.

Jacob smiled. " 'The flagon with the dragon' . . ."

". . . 'Has the brew that is true,'" Griffen finished.

"Yes, indeed. You look plenty young to be a Danny Kaye fan, but we already knew you were something different. Isn't that just the perfect quote? We *are* the dragon krewe. We're ordering cups to throw as well as beads and doubloons. The cups'll have an imprint that goes around them, with our dragon on them, and it'll say, 'The brew that is true.' We'll tell people that to drink out of one of these is to give them health and long life." Griffen grinned. "We got you, I can just tell."

"You do," Griffen said. "Give me a bunch of those. However many you think is right for the duration of the parade."

By the time he was finished with the committee, he had put his name down for thousands of necklaces, doubloons, and cups. They would all have to be paid for by February, but Jacob agreed that since Griffen had just joined, he would be allowed to pay over time.

"The treasury can support it," Jacob said in an undertone, though it was unlikely that Callum could hear them over the noise. "Most of the people on the krewe are rich."

Griffen glanced at Etienne, whose pants hems were frayed at the heels. Jacob followed his glance.

"Yeah," he said. "Even the captain. He dresses like a lobsterman, but he inherited natural-gas contracts from his granddad. Didn't have much when he grew up, but he and his mom have a big place out on Lake Ponchartrain, as befits a proper lady dragon. Dragons tend to attract wealth. Even ones with less than a teaspoon of dragon blood."

"He's still a dragon," Griffen said, moved again to defend Etienne. "You guys wouldn't have a krewe to build floats for if not for him."

"Yeah, yeah," Jacob said hastily. "I'm not disregarding all he's done. But I can feel levels of power. I know where he falls in the pecking order, and that's way below everyone else."

"Power's not everything."

"Said the man with the biggest stash in the room," Jacob said. "You don't get it."

"Don't treat me like a kid," Griffen said.

"You *are* a kid. You're the youngest one here except for the children, and you're the most powerful. It's a defense mechanism. You ought to understand that."

That left a question unanswered in Griffen's mind. Mose and Jerome had always told him that dragons sought to conquer one another or sign on with one they perceived as more powerful. These all acted together, as human beings would do. It was unnatural, as he understood it. As the most powerful dragon in the room, he felt as if he needed to watch his back all the time.

"Hello, Griffen," Lucinda said, coming around the open

mouth of the dragon. "Come on down and help construct or paint. It'll be a good example for these other youngsters that people still know how to work hard. Do you know how to apply papier-mâché?"

"I haven't done any since I was in art class in grade school. We made Easter eggs out of balloons."

She smiled. "Then you know enough. Come and get your hands dirty."

Griffen held back. He glanced at the neatly dressed lieutenants talking to one another.

"I can't see *them* getting paste on their pin-striped suits," he said. Lucinda followed his eyes and smiled.

"You can't? Well, then, it'll be a revelation to you when you see them up to their elbows in buckets of flour and water," Lucinda said. "Let's you and I go and recruit some helpers."

Lucinda was more than persuasive. Very shortly, Griffen found himself squatting on the floor plastering tacky strips of newspaper around a chicken-wire armature representing an enormous snapdragon. As Lucinda had promised, the haughty executives abandoned their dignity and buckled down to help, just like the students, clerks, and homemakers all around them. It would have been normal but for the skyrockets of fire and streamers of light going on behind Griffen's eyes. The others couldn't have missed it. He all but blurted out the question.

"What is this feeling of power here? It's not just the people. It's like it's in the air."

Callum wiped the back of his hand across his forehead, leaving a streak of gray glue just under his hairline. "Have you ever made anything, young man? Anything physical?"

"Nothing except love or an inside straight," Griffen admitted. He pasted down a strip of newspaper and wiped it with his sponge."

"You ever heard how lions and tomcats go in and kill kittens that aren't theirs?"

"Yes."

"How do they know?"

"Well, I assume the male's scent is on them . . ." The others grinned at him, so Griffen thought about it harder. The males would not have had any contact with the kits since sperm met egg. "I guess not. I don't know."

Langford cleared his throat. "It's part of a dragon's power. When we make something, we transfer a touch of power to it. More. That's how we can tell it was ours. Usually, the residue is very subtle. Most dragons can't really feel it, and humans can almost never detect it. You're different. Your blood is stronger than ours. You seem to be able to sense very minor amounts of our power. If we had any doubts after your little demonstration, this would convince us you were either a sensitive human, a supernatural, or a very powerful dragon."

Griffen raised an eyebrow. "This was a phenomenon I hadn't come across yet."

"You will," Langford said.

"When we really enjoy making something, it is stronger yet," Callum told him. "When we deliberately imbue something with power, anyone can feel it, but it would knock *you* over. Even puny humans, nonsensitive humans, can feel it a little. It's one of the reasons that dragon-made items of power have been objects of desire by humankind for millennia. They want to possess them, whether or not they can wield them. Many can. Not as effectively as if they were dragons, of course. Whether or not they know what it does, they know there is something special about it. Objects made by dragons have been revered throughout all of human history."

"A lot of the so-called relics of the saints actually belonged to dragons," Mitchell said dryly. "That residual power that bestows blessings, like miracle cures, comes from the dragon power in the object."

Terence grinned at Griffen. "That means, when we make something like a float for Mardi Gras, which we love doing, the floats naturally take on a little of the power that is in our blood."

"Aren't you worried about other sensitives finding their way in here and discovering us? Taking things that have power?"

Lucinda let out a trill of laughter. "Are you kidding? We're dragons, honey darling. If anything, the power signature ought to tell them to stay away. If they don't, then they don't belong in the gene pool. You don't read a lot of fairy stories about the people who enter the dragon's den and get out again."

Griffen cleared his throat. "Well, there's the St. George story. And Perseus. And . . ."

"A few in all of history? It's the ones you *don't* hear, and there are probably millions of them. So, don't worry. Besides, you think that this is the only den with natural magic in it? In New Orleans?"

Griffen grinned. "I guess not. I'm being a dragon snob."

Lucinda twinkled at him. "Aren't we all?"

Working according to Lucinda's exacting standards, Griffen helped finish up the enormous blossoms. Lucinda ordered him to help her wash out the buckets in a janitor's sink in the corner near the restrooms. He had become used to the power in the room. It was benign, even benevolent when put to the purpose as it had been here. Griffen still had no clue as to the subversive element that Stoner said was there. Not even a hint of ill feeling or intent to control was present that he could detect. He suspected, not for the first time, that Stoner was paranoid, or trying to scare him for his own purposes.

When the last of the plastic pails was upside down over a drain in the floor, Griffen wiped his hands on a paper towel.

"I've got to get back," he told Lucinda.

"Well, thank you for your help," she said.

"It was an experience," he admitted. His arms felt soggy and pruny up to the elbows. Paste had congealed under his fingernails, and he could feel a blob of it in one of his socks from when it had dripped off a strip someone else had slapped down and fallen into his shoe. "See you at the next meeting."

"Griffen?" Lucinda asked, as he turned away.

"Yes?"

"Didn't it feel good to make something?"

Griffen stopped and turned back to the partially completed float. It didn't look like much yet, but he could actually sense that piece of the snapdragon he had helped build. He had done that. He would know it forever. Suddenly, the small inconveniences were worth it. Even the squishy sock didn't bother him as much.

"Yes," he said, with a grin. "Thanks."

"My pleasure," Lucinda said.

Seventeen

Griffen was horrified to find that he was right to be concerned about Tee-Bo's reaction to the news of Jimmy McGill.

A singer that Griffen and Fox Lisa both enjoyed had advertised a Solstice Celebration concert at a jazz club just off Bourbon Street near the river. She sat on a stool under a single spotlight, holding her microphone in both hands. Her warm, smoky voice wrapped her poetry with a kind of palpable love. Griffen sat with his chair braced against the wall in the corner of the pale coral room, with his arm around the petite auburn-headed girl, his eyes closed. Music permeated the air like the cigarette smoke. He breathed it in and felt New Orleans's own magic swelling up in him. No wonder so many dragons lived in the area. He had always loved music, but he got a natural, warm buzz from the soaring, twisting, turning flourishes of the jazz trumpet, clarinet, and trombone. It was a solid, mind-changing high, and it was street-legal. He took a sip of whisky. The warmth just added to the sensation of well-being. He grinned down at Fox Lisa. She lowered her eyelashes at him. They both had the same idea about where to go after the music ended.

The singer ended her set to wild applause. Someone handed her a glass of clear, bubbling liquid. She raised it to the audience. The spotlight blinked out, and the buzz of the crowd filled in the silence.

"Hey, Mr. McCandles," said Patches. Griffen looked up.

He was one of Tee-Bo's strong men, a thin, wiry man in a dark green T-shirt stained at the collar. He was missing a canine tooth and an upper bicuspid, both from street fights, but he had won many, many more than he had lost. The other patrons glanced at him nervously. "Can I talk to you for a minute?"

"Sure, Patches," Griffen said.

"Hey, Griffen," Fox Lisa began, concerned.

"Don't worry. Just stay here a moment, will you?"

Fox Lisa glanced toward the bar, where she had left her fanny pack. Griffen knew that inside it was a black-handled revolver. She knew how to use it, and was more than willing to if she thought Griffen was in danger. He shook his head. She sat back in the chair but didn't look happy.

"If you aren't back in five minutes, I'm coming after you."

"No problem," Griffen said.

He followed the enforcer out onto the street. Patches kept walking, around the edge of the building and into a narrow alley. Another of the muscle squad, Tich, was waiting there, his arms crossed. Griffen steeled himself, wondering if he had annoyed the drug dealer without knowing it. But as Griffen reached him, Tich nodded.

"Evening, Mr. McCandles. Tee-bo says hey. He sent somethin' for you."

He tilted his head downward to the side. Griffen realized that the dark lump on the ground was a man. Jimmy McGill slumped against the cracked stucco, his head bowed, chin on chest. His eyes were swollen shut. His left ear was bleeding, as if it had been wrenched partway off his head. Blood trickled from his nose and puffed lips. Griffen drew in a shocked breath. They had worked Jimmy over pretty thoroughly.

"Just wanted you to see the retirement package Tee-Bo gave this guy," Patches said. "He not workin' for Tee-Bo no more, either. He hid out from us for a few days, but we found him. Thought we'd bring him around to you, since he pissed you off, too."

"Tee-bo didn't have to do that," Griffen began. He felt his breath grow hot in his nostrils. He clenched his hands. The skin felt dry and rough. Jimmy *had* lied to all of them, but he didn't deserve that.

Patches shook his head. "Yeah, he did. Jimmy was in for a beating. Tee-Bo considers his relationship with you to be more important than one lyin', low-down snake. This just a little reminder to anyone else who ain't smart enough to comply with the noncompete agreement."

Griffen worked his jaw. He knew he couldn't let himself overreact. This was street justice. He had achieved a mutual respect with Tee-bo and the other drug dealers in town by being honest with them. Jimmy *had* defied the rules, and he had paid for it. He wasn't dead. The gangs were trigger-happy. They could have shot Jimmy and left him in a park somewhere for the police to find. Griffen told himself he should be glad of that, but the violence made him angry. Smoke started coming out of his nostrils.

"Hey, hear you're gonna be in the Fafnir parade, Mr. McCandles," Tich said. "My brother, he have a license to drive a tractor. He's free on the twenty-fourth, if your krewe needs someone. I'll get you his phone number."

Griffen stared at him. How could he talk about something as inconsequential as a driving job when a human being was bleeding at their feet?

Patches nudged him. "Got to go. Have a nice night, Mr. McCandles."

Somehow, Griffen summoned up enough humanity to mutter a "Good night." The enforcers slipped away.

"Come on, Jimmy, we'll get you to the emergency room," he said. He reached for the young man's arm and tried to help him up. Jimmy roused a little and glanced up. His eyes widened until the irises were surrounded by bloodshot whites. He shook his hand free of Griffen's grip.

"No! No! Leave me alone!" he cried. He scrambled backward, pulled himself up against the grimy wall, and fled. Griffen watched him go, confused. Then he caught a glimpse of himself in the remains of a dirty window on the blind wall, and realized he had partially transformed. The bottom of his face had pushed forward, and his teeth, partially sharpened, were showing between his lips. Tee-Bo's men hadn't turned a hair. Did they know he was a dragon, or hadn't they seen, or didn't they care? He knew he had become something of a legend in town. Were they that at home with the supernatural in New Orleans?

Griffen made sure to recombobulate himself and become human again before returning to the club. He caught Fox Lisa's anxious gaze when he entered the crowded room. She relaxed, with a worried smile.

"It's all right," he said. "Nothing to get upset about."

But he wasn't telling the truth. The singer returned, and the second set began. Griffen tried to let the music carry him away, but the evening was spoiled for him. All he could see was the fear on Jimmy's face.

Eighteen

The tailor drew the end of the measuring tape up into Griffen's crotch and dragged the other end down toward his instep. Griffen jumped and tried to flick his hand away.

"Hold still!" the man ordered, steadying Griffen on the cloth-covered pedestal before the triple mirrors. He was a burly, middle-aged African-American with a dark, pockmarked complexion and close-cut gray hair. Griffen would never have guessed seeing him on the street that he was a tailor. He looked more like a gym teacher or a trucker. "This isn't personal. I'm not interested in you, all right? I've got a sexy wife and five kids. Hmm. You got long legs. That's good. I got plenty of trousers in your size."

"He needs three suits," Mai reminded him. "Four might be better." She was curled into a vintage, gray-upholstered chair in the corner of the showroom. The tailor nodded without looking up from his measurements.

Griffen glanced at himself in the mirror. He looked annoyed. Well, he felt annoyed. "I do have a suit."

"That thing? Bought off the rack in a drugstore?"

"A *department* store!" Griffen protested.

"In any case, it is not black tie, and you only have the one. It is unsuitable for this occasion. Stand still, and do not cause more trouble."

Griffen grumbled but obeyed orders. He had been in a formal-wear shop exactly twice in his life, once when his uncle dragged him there to get a suit for his parents' funeral, and early that summer for college graduation. He felt that he had aged hundreds of years since then. He found the racks of black suits oppressive.

"Isn't it weird that in nature, the male has the colorful plumage and the female usually is drab-colored?" he asked. "The cardinal's bright red, and the female is light brown."

"You want a bright red tux?" the tailor asked, raising his eyebrows with interest. "I got those. They're in the warehouse. I thought you wanted proper black tie."

"He does," Mai said.

"Besides, blue is more my color," Griffen said.

"Bright blue, peacock blue, royal blue, or powder blue?" the tailor asked.

"Powder blue would make me look like I was opening for Liberace," Griffen said. "What about royal blue? I'm the king, after all."

"Black," Mai said. "Don't listen to another thing he says."

"Gotcha, ma'am," the tailor said.

Etienne had been right: There were no tuxedos to be found in his size in New Orleans that late in the season. Nor were there any to be had in Metairie.

"You should have reserved them sooner," Mai had protested after five fruitless visits to other rental shops.

"I didn't know sooner," Griffen reminded her.

Baton Rouge was busy with shoppers on the last Saturday before Christmas. Griffen had had to park their rental car a couple of blocks away in a pay lot. He had not had a car of his own since the destruction of his beloved Goblin. Jerome insisted that he didn't really need one in New Orleans, but it had been a personal attack to demolish the vehicle, all the more so since he had been sitting in it at the time. He had always had a car since he could drive one. He loved the freedom of driving, the ability to escape wherever he was and just go somewhere. He loved the rumble of the engine and the feel of the road that vibrated up through the shocks and the springs into the driver's seat. A small part of him

demanded that he satisfy that itch and buy another car as
soon as he could afford one, but that was going to be a long
time in the future. He had withdrawn the remainder of the
membership fee for Fafnir, leaving a balance in his account
that was only four figures. He knew he still needed five to get
through until March. In the meantime, the bronze-colored
sedan reminded him of his curtailed freedom. The occasional
rental would help in the short term.

"That's it!" the tailor said. He rose, grunting, to his feet.
Griffen climbed down from the pedestal and followed him
to the racks. Using a metal pole with a two-fingered hook
on the end, the tailor grabbed hangers from the top rack and
swung them down into Griffen's arms. "Let's just try these
on for size."

Griffen admired himself in the mirror, turning this way
and that. He straightened the satin lapels of the tailored
jacket. "I don't look half-bad."

"You've got a little style," the tailor said. "Let me chalk
up these pants, and you're good to go."

Griffen handed over a deposit of 25 percent against two
months' rental of three tuxes plus all of the small accoutre-
ments that went with them, such as cummerbunds, collar
stays, and studs. The tailor saw them to the door.

"Come back in five days. Everything will be ready by
then."

"Now we will go and buy me a gown," Mai said, taking
his arm firmly as the bell on the door jingled behind them.

Griffen halted. "Wait a minute, this was just supposed to
be a trip to rent suits for me."

Mai pretended to pout, her small lower lip protruding.

"Fair is fair," she said.

Griffen knew when not to continue an argument he had
already lost. "All right," he said. "Where do you want to
look?"

She reeled off an address. "I'll wait until you get the car."

"But it's only three blocks from here," Griffen said. "I'll
end up parking in the same lot again."

This time Mai did pout. "These shoes are not good for long walks," she said.

"Should I carry you?" Griffen asked, playfully, swooping down on her and hoisting her in his arms. "Or are you going to sprout wings and fly?"

"Ooh!" she said, her eyes sparking just as playfully. "That just cost you a higher tier of designer."

Mai knew exactly what size she was and what styles looked good on her. But that didn't curtail the number of things she tried on. The clerks in the boutique carried dozens of dresses to the curtained-in dressing room. Griffen sat in the main room, on a dainty chair with an oval back covered in gold satin, listening to her comments as she tried on one gown after another, dismissing them in turn with terse remarks. Griffen shifted uneasily. He felt the chair might collapse under him at any moment. He didn't mind being fair in terms of spending time shopping for her as they had done for him, but being unable to see what was going on left him bored. All the magazines in the carved wooden racks were periodicals as thick as his wrist, but all about fashion, hairstyles, accessories, and other details about which he just did not care. The owner, a narrow-faced woman taller than Griffen, ignored him as if he were another chair. She sailed past him with a brilliant green gown on a hanger and vanished into the draped enclosure.

"What a lovely figure you have, sweetheart," she exclaimed. "My goodness, look at that! That is just perfect. Turn and let me see the back. Perfect!"

"Well, not quite perfect," Mai's voice said, thoughtfully, for the tenth or twelfth time. Griffen groaned to himself. "The shade is good, but perhaps it should be lower cut?"

"Why don't you let your boyfriend see it and find out what he thinks?"

"Why not?"

The curtain was thrown back. Griffen almost gasped. Mai

came out wearing a bronze-colored satin dress. It revealed a good deal of her modest cleavage, which somehow had been enhanced, nipped in underneath her bosom along her slender waist, then fell in Grecian folds to the floor. When she walked, the skirts parted with a whisper. Her legs from the knees down were revealed at each step. She looked breathtaking.

"What do you think, Griffen?"

Griffen swallowed deeply. "Wow," he said. The ladies of the shop smiled indulgently at him. He goggled at her. She was beautiful, but he had never pictured her looking like a 1940s movie goddess.

Mai walked a few paces and turned to look in the mirror that filled the shop's wall. She tilted her head. "No, I think not. I think the red one was better." She reached around behind her and undid one fastening. The silk dress fell to the floor. The ladies rushed to gather it up.

"I'll get the red one," the owner said. She disappeared into the dressing room. Mai waited, posed like a mannequin in her underwear. Griffen realized she was wearing a strapless push-up bra and a lace thong. Though he found them stunning and intriguing, their import suddenly dawned on him.

"You planned to have me take you dress-shopping?" he asked.

"Of course," she said. "Why else would I have come with you to look for suits?"

"Well, to keep me from renting a blue tux," Griffen said.

She waved a dismissive hand. "I knew you wouldn't end up with that. You are too vain to make yourself a spectacle."

"Maybe I'm not," he protested.

She laughed. "Your poker face is too good, but I know you are nervous. Don't be. You are a dozen times the dragon of any of those people." Griffen glanced at the store staff. The women must have thought the reference was just a personal term between them, but Griffen didn't want the word to spread any further than it had.

The owner came toward Mai with a shimmering bundle

of red held out on her arms like a hank of knitting wool. Mai held her hands over her head, and the owner slid the dress onto them. It slithered into place with a seductive hiss. The owner pulled up a zipper under the right arm that promptly became invisible in the seam. The dress fit Mai almost as tautly as her skin. It hung from one shoulder strap, leaving the other bare. The top was gathered over the bosom, but the long ruby skirt was plain. It could have come out of Veronica Lake's wardrobe.

"What do you think of this one?" Mai asked.

"I like it," Griffen said. He came up behind her and put his hands on her shoulders. The bare side invited him to kiss it, so he did.

"Hmm," she said, smiling at him in the mirror. "I think I like it, too." She reached down for the white tag hanging from the zipper pull, and turned it toward him. "Shouldn't you pay for this, Your Majesty? I am, after all, one of your maids in waiting."

Griffen gulped again. "I . . . can't," he admitted at last. "I'm going to be tight until after March."

Mai looked displeased, but she flicked a hand. "Never mind. I have plenty of money. Daddy still gives me an allowance, as long as I stay out of his hair."

"No," Griffen said. "I'll pay for it." He did some calculation in his head. "It just means I'll have to buy dresses for Val and Fox Lisa, too."

Mai raised an eyebrow. "Val might take your head off if you offer. She is getting very independent about making her own way in the world. Now, I don't mind if gentlemen buy me fine things."

"It's not just that," Griffen said. They both knew that Val was still upset about the bodyguards he had following her. But the guys, who were happy to help Ms. Valerie stay safe, were convinced, first of all, that they would not have to do more than clean up if there was a problem, maybe moving the bodies to a place where they could bleed to death in peace, and second, that he was right about other watchers being interested in her whereabouts. "I'll have to offer, anyhow. And Fox Lisa was excited to be in the court, but right now she's only working part-time." She wouldn't admit it, but it would be tough for her to make rent if she had to buy a dress on top of the other fees.

Mardi Gras was expensive. But Fox Lisa took the yearly festival in her stride. She was thrilled about everything, and insisted it was an honor to pay the three thousand dollars Fafnir demanded for her role as maid. They supplied her costumes, masks, all her throws, and her ball ticket. Griffen was relieved there was ONE expense he was not expected to cover. A dress for her was okay with him.

"Very well," Mai said. "I will pay for my own dress, but you will take me for a very expensive dinner. And you will pay for that."

"Yes, ma'am," he said.

Griffen gestured to the waiter to pour more wine for Mai. He stayed with a single whisky, so he would be sober enough to drive home. If he lost another car, this time it would not be his fault. She lifted the glass to him behind the crystal candlesticks. He toasted her back.

"Thank you for joining me today," he said.

"A pleasure," she said, taking a sip. "How is the business? I have scarcely heard a word from you lately. Normally, you have many stories to tell. I think it is both amusing and ambitious the way you are bringing backroom poker to such high standards."

Griffen made a face at her. "That was one backhanded compliment," he said. "I haven't really wanted to tell anyone about the problems we've been having this week." He told her about the cheating scandal. "This man, an Asian-American guy I haven't seen before, was adamant that two of our regulars had held back a card and screwed up the game on purpose. The victims are very straight. I would trust either of them to hold on to a hundred thousand dollars for me and never think of even borrowing from it for themselves. No way they could have been cheating."

"You think he was responsible?"

"I hate to think so," Griffen admitted. "But there are ways to rig a game for other players. *I* could do it. It's tricky to set up, but it can be done. The whole thing was just a big pain in the ass. Everyone went away mad. Then, in another game, there was a woman—also Asian-American, now that I think about it—Jerome never saw her before, accused the dealer of stacking the deck. The dealer is furious. We had to talk him out of quitting. Another mess. And now I've got this guy who seems perfectly nice, but Jer doesn't like him. I sat in on a late-night game with him yesterday. I just don't feel what Jerome feels. Peter is just too nice. No one is that nice all the time except Mister Rogers. He even loses like a gentleman. Funny, but he's Asian, too."

Mai's internal antennae went up. She didn't like Jerome, who had her number but was not in a position to fight her, but the facts suggested an unseen concurrence of events that she did not like. Griffen picked up on her concerned expression and looked alarmed.

"I'm not picking on these people just because of their background," he insisted. "I'm just telling you about the trouble we've had this week. It's just a coincidence that they were all Asian-Americans."

"No, no." She waved away the suggestion. "I would never think that of you. No. That isn't what I thought at all."

Griffen was not stupid. He made the connection immediately. "You do think there's something in it. Can these three events have anything to do with the Eastern dragons? I thought they were letting me alone for a while."

"I do not know," Mai said honestly. Could there be something more than coincidence? She needed to find out. "I doubt it, Griffen. They did plan to leave you alone." Except for her machinations, of course.

"And on top of that, Harrison is still busting my ass over the murder," Griffen added woefully.

"Murder?"

He leaned close to the candles so the waitress couldn't hear. "One of my dealers was strangled. An Eastern dragon named Jesse Lee. He came over from their operation. He said he wasn't getting the advancements he deserved. He'd been with me for three months. I don't know what happened. Harrison has no leads and no witnesses, but he's sure I'm holding out on him."

Mai was outraged. An Eastern dragon, murdered? That meant someone from one of the families. Who else but they— or the George—would know how to kill a dragon? Her temper flared. The two candles between them responded. Their flames flared high. People turned to look. She controlled herself, and the flames shrank to normal size. She grabbed Griffen's hand. "Tell Harrison you will help him in any way."

"Of course I will," Griffen said. "Did you know Jesse?"

"No," she said. "But I should have."

They finished their dinner over trivial small talk. Mai was quiet and thoughtful as they drove back to the hotel.

"Should I come up?" Griffen asked, as he popped the trunk for the bell captain to retrieve Mai's red silk dress in its plastic bags.

"I think I will go up by myself," she said. She leaned over to kiss him. "Thank you for a lovely day."

"Thank you," he said, looking puzzled. Mai stalked to the elevator and punched the button for her floor. She had a lot of thinking to do.

Nineteen

At 3:43 Sunday morning, the door to the luxury suite slammed open. Jordan Ma leaped to his feet. All night long, he had felt a questing power seeking him, so he did not undress or go to bed. He had sat still in the leather armchair in the darkened sitting room, waiting. Whoever it was grew closer and closer over the course of the hours. At last, he recognized that the seeker had firmed his location. *Target acquired and locked,* he thought. It would be useful to know whether a friend or foe sought him, but it was simpler to wait and find out. He was not without defenses. It was unlikely to be Griffen McCandles, who was far stronger than he, but unschooled, and anyone else in the city was a manageable threat.

A small, slim figure stood silhouetted by the hall lights in the rectangle of the door frame. She stalked in. No dragon of her blood needed lights to locate him, just as he did not require them to see and identify her.

"Well, well, Mai," he said. "Welcome, Princess-who-is-not."

She did not startle. The slamming-open of the door was for effect, not to surprise. She knew he would be alert.

"What are you doing here?" she demanded. In the dark, he saw not the human lineaments of her face but a flickering mask of power that would identify her no matter what shape she wore.

"Since ten o'clock, I have been waiting for you," he said.

"No! I mean, what are you doing in New Orleans?"

"The concerns of the elders are my concerns," Jordan said. "As they should have been yours."

"They are my concerns!" Mai said. The conversation was not going as she intended it to. She tightened her hands into fists. She had crossed paths with Jordan Ma before, several times. He was insufferable and proud, but clever. He had gone to a lot of trouble to make the elders think that he was more valuable than he was. She did not want him interfering in her mission. She must take control of the situation and keep it.

It had taken her hours to scan the city and find him. Of course, he occupied a luxury suite in a fancy hotel. To her annoyance, it was not far from her own hotel. He was aware of her search. She knew that would be likely. She hated that he seemed amused by her.

"What do you want?" he asked, sounding almost bored. "I would like to go to bed, soon. Not with you, of course."

"Are you responsible for the death of an Eastern dragon? One of our own kind?"

"I assume you mean the traitor to our cause," Jordan said. The shadow of his face was drawn into an expression of scorn. "Jesse Lee was warned."

"He was a child! He had promise."

"But not for us. Once he removed himself from the clan, he was on his own, a *ronin*, as the Japanese humans call it. He knew the risks. He chose his fate."

"But why kill him? His desertion was months ago."

"I did not kill him," Jordan said. She could not tell from the shadow of his face if he was lying. He was too good a poker player. "You must ask those who performed the deed. I would see to it that they are well rewarded." He smirked. "You do not care about others. I assume he meant something to Griffen McCandles."

"I do care what became of this child!" Mai exclaimed. Jordan waved away her protest. He treated her as if she did not matter. She resented it. "Why are you here?" she repeated. "What are you doing invading poker games?"

"Do you have any authority to ask?"

"Don't you know who I am?"

"If you must ask me that, then you must know I do not care," Jordan said, with a supercilious smile her claws itched to tear off his jaws.

"Then enlighten me. You will enjoy dangling that little bit of knowledge that you possess."

"The elders are tired of waiting for you to perform the task for which you were sent. You have been making excuses all this time. They are displeased."

"My arrangements are intricate," Mai said. "They want influence over Griffen McCandles. I cannot engineer that in a crude fashion. He is not a fool. He will rebel against blunt force."

Jordan flipped a hand. "The Lee sprout died very easily. It would be as simple to dispose of McCandles if he does not comply."

Mai felt panic rising in her belly. He would not think of trying to kill Griffen? "But the elders want him alive. They have a purpose for him. I am here to steer him to that purpose."

"You are not acting swiftly enough. They think that you have become soft. You prove their thesis, as you are upset over the death of a mere card dealer. You are becoming attached to the subject of your maneuverings. Instead, McCandles has power over you. The elders have warned you before, but you have shown no signs that you heed them. It is time for others to step in. You have become ineffective."

Ineffective? Mai felt her tail grow behind her. Her claws emerged, smooth and sharp as a machete. Mai leaped for Jordan, claws out. She raked her talons across his chest. They ripped open his jacket and shirt, and drew tiny lines of blood.

He took moments longer than she to transform. With longer arms and legs, he had the advantage of reach. He paused as she struck again, then wrapped her in his limbs. She struggled in his grasp. He bent his jaws to the back of her neck. One bite, and she would be eliminated as a nuisance. But she snaked her head back, and breathed.

Fire did not destroy a dragon as it did a lesser mortal, but it hurt. Jordan's muscles contracted. He squeezed. Mai gasped. He was not as powerful as she, but he was strong. He crushed her in his grasp. Her head snaked wildly on its long neck. She bit at him again and again.

"Ow!" he bellowed. He snapped back, and she bit his flickering tongue. Jordan lost his focus. What a dirty fighter the little female was! He dropped forward, still holding her. The floor boomed under their combined weight. Furniture went flying.

"Oof!" Mai grunted. She had landed on her back. She scrabbled at his belly with all four legs until he spread his wings and lifted off her just to get away. He fled to the bedroom, heading for the full-length glass doors that led to the balcony. She gathered herself and sprang.

She crushed his wings to his back. He fell to the floor again. Mai bared her sharp teeth and went for the nape of his neck. Jordan twisted in her grasp. Suddenly, she lost hold of him. She found herself flying through the air. Glass splintered as she crashed into the long mirror on the wall. Mai recovered in the time it took her to fall to the floor. Jordan had the French doors open and stood on the wrought-iron balustrade, ready to spring into space. She shot forward on all fours, and fastened herself around his ankles. He toppled backward and twisted to bite her. Mai slapped his head sideways and hissed at him.

"Is that all you have?" she asked. "Tell me your purpose here! Tell me!"

Jordan's eyes blazed. He snapped at her nose. Mai recoiled in pain. Now she wanted to kill him. She dug her talons into his side.

Jordan bellowed. He clamped his teeth on her shoulder. They rolled on the floor.

The delicate sound of a wind chime tinkled in Mai's ear. Jordan's glowing eyes dampened for a moment. Mai realized it was his cell phone ringing. He used Gilbert and Sullivan's

"Three Little Maids from School" as a ring tone? What a wimp! She knocked his chin upward with the top of her head and bit his throat.

With difficulty, he turned on his belly and tried to crawl toward the bedside table. Mai hung on to him, clawing and biting. He must not reach it. He would not reach it. He was no match for her!

The telephone tittered on through the verse and on into the chorus. Abruptly, the noise stopped. Jordan halted and dropped to his belly. Mai was almost thrown off. He took advantage of her loss of balance to snake a claw up and grab the joint of her wing. He yanked downward. Wings were delicate and prone to breakage. Mai had to follow where hers went. Jordan flipped her over so her throat faced up.

Suddenly, a shadow loomed over both of them, blocking the light from the window.

"Jordan, you didn't answer your phone. . . ."

Jordan looked up.

A woman, a plump, short one with curly hair, stood on the edge of the balcony. Mai rolled back on her flexible spine, kicked Jordan in the face, tumbled across the room, and came up on her feet.

The woman on the balcony was a dragon, too. It took her much longer than Jordan to change shape. Mai went on guard against both of them. So, this must be the woman Griffen had complained about. She was much younger and clumsier than Jordan. She was no challenge to one such as Mai. Mai could finish them both off!

She edged sideways. The newcomer was fresh and full of energy. Mai must disable her first. The young woman bared her claws. Mai brandished hers in response. Jordan sidestepped so he was just out of sight behind the tip of Mai's wing. She spun to face him. As she did, the other woman sprang. Mai was borne to her knees. She clamped her claws on the newcomer's leg and dug in.

"Ow!" the woman howled. She hopped back. Mai was already moving. She ducked between Jordan's legs, then swatted the backs of his knees with her tail. He fell forward. She leaped onto his back and wrapped her arm around his neck. She bore down on his throat, hoping to render him unconscious. He stood up, lifting her bodily. The other woman rushed in to help. Mai turned into a miniature whirlwind, striking and clawing at both of them. They struck out at her in return. She ducked, protecting her eyes from a backward blow by Jordan, only to have her ear and wing chewed by the female. Slowly, gradually, she felt herself being shoved backward. Light flooded over her shoulder until she could see their outline on the floor. They were in front of the window. Jordan bent his head and chomped each of her wrists in turn. The other female grabbed her around the waist, spun, and dropped her out the window.

Mai shrieked as the wind flew upward around her. She spread her injured wings, fluttering desperately. The narrow thread of Royal Street grew wider and wider. At last, she managed to open them and catch the air in their sails a split second before she landed on the street. She hung in the air, catching her breath. Two drunks tottering along the sidewalk gawked at her. They pointed and laughed. Furiously, she exhaled a stream of fire at them and fled upward. They backed up, but they were still laughing.

Funny, am I? Mai fumed, soaring up into the clouds. The frigid upper atmosphere would help to cool off her temper. Ineffective? *I will see about that!*

She flew back to her hotel and landed on the roof, where there were no security cameras. The exercise of a small thread of power caused the heavy fire door to open. She stalked down two flights of stairs to her suite. The door of the room refused to slam. She was frustrated enough to scream, but she did not want hotel security coming to the door in the predawn.

Her own cell phone was in the bottom of her handbag. She dumped the contents of the purse on the bed and pawed through it until she came up with the tiny silver handset. Only then did she restore herself to human appearance.

She swiped at her messy hair in the bedroom mirror while waiting for the other end to answer.

"Honored elder, I am glad to find you in," she said.

"Where else would I be at this hour?" the peevish male voice quavered at the other end. "To what do I owe the honor of a call, Mai?"

"I have just spoken to Jordan Ma," she said.

"Ah. Is he still alive?"

"For now," Mai said. "Honored father, why is he here?"

"Why do *you* think that he is there?"

It was just like the elder one to turn her back with a question.

"He says I am too slow to fulfill your wishes."

"And have you fulfilled them?"

"Well, no! I have told you my plans. You have to remove Jordan Ma and his associates! He will spoil everything! Give me the power to halt him."

"And are you ready to move on your own plans that we have discussed?"

She was torn as to what to say. Elder Father would know if she was lying.

"No," she said, frustrated but unwilling to burst out in protests. Elder Father would find it disrespectful. "I have a few arrangements that need to fall into place before I can move. It will take a few more months, but Griffen McCandles will be in my control after that."

"But we elders wish to move now, over the course of weeks, not months. Can you say that you will be ready soon enough that we must call back the hounds we have put on the trail?"

"I need more time," she said tightly.

"It is too late to allow you to go your own way alone," Elder Father said. "Griffen McCandles will become a threat to our operation sooner than you will be ready. Jordan Ma will at the least hinder him, if not destroy his power base completely. He will do what you have been unable, or unwilling, to do."

"But what is he doing?" Mai demanded. She paced back and forth in her dressing room.

"You do not need to know that. His plans do not cross yours in any way. Do not fear. We will leave you in place. We will need you to continue, particularly if Jordan's scheme does not work. Will you cooperate? Must we question your loyalty? It sounds as if you are experiencing a fit of pique. Or is it something deeper? Do you choose to turn your loyalty to the young dragon instead of your clan?"

Mai was torn. She cared about Griffen the person. She admired his idealism. He always felt that benefit could be found for all. The other part of her, that which served the Eastern dragons, could not condone such an outlook. It knew that, like any commodity, power was limited, and that one must take whatever one could so one was not left without. She could not say for certain that he wouldn't become a threat to her later on. The potential he represented had too many variables for the future. She felt lost and alone. And angry.

"So you condone Jordan's actions?"

"We sanctioned them," Elder Father said. "You still have the support of your family in your aims. Should you accomplish them first, we will cause Jordan Ma and his three colleagues to withdraw."

"Three?" she asked. Griffen had only mentioned three Eastern dragons interfering in his card games. Was there a third dragon waiting to strike?

"I will say nothing more," Elder Father said. "It was good of you to call an old man and brighten the middle of his sleepless night. Perhaps you will telephone again when you have good news. We all hope to hear from you then."

Mai hung up and threw the phone down on the bed. She now had a secret, one she did not wish to keep, but she had no choice. She couldn't tell Griffen what she knew because she didn't really know anything. Jordan had been cagey, laughing at her ignorance. She must find out about their plot. She could not warn Griffen until she did. Any guess she made as to their motive would almost certainly be wrong. He would be guarding against the wrong thing. She also could not take direct action against the Eastern dragons, not when her elders had condoned their actions, but she had to help Griffen.

She would have to steer him to protect himself. That was one of the things she did better than anyone else. She would manipulate from the shadows. And, she vowed, catching a glimpse of her bruises and scratches in the looking glass, she would get even with Jordan Ma. No one threw her out the window and lived to smirk about it. Not for long.

Winston Long and Peter Sing came to Jordan's suite in answer to Rebecca's frantic call. Jordan slumped in his leather armchair in the middle of the wrecked room. His elegant clothes had been torn to rags.

"Will you live, or do you need medical care?" Winston asked.

"They are just surface injuries," Jordan said. It hurt to talk. Mai's headbutt had knocked his jaw out of alignment. The joint was swollen. He held the bag from the ice bucket to it.

"You are covered with bruises," Peter said. "Mai did all of this? Little Mai?"

"Do not denigrate one for her size," Rebecca warned him. "She is a wily opponent. It took both of us to vanquish her."

"Where is she now?" Winston asked.

"Gone. That is all that I care about."

"Didn't the elders warn her not to interfere with us?"

"From her babble, I think they have not told her anything about us," Jordan said, willing the cold to numb the pain. "They will now. She will demand answers. She tried to get them from me. I do not know if she will get them from the elders."

"I hope they tell her to fall down a pit," Peter said.

"She is too dangerous," Winston said. "She must be removed from the scene."

"Mai will never leave," Jordan said. "And the elders want her here."

"She interferes with our mission. I will send her a warning," Winston said, lowering his eyelids dangerously. "If she does not take it, it will kill her."

Twenty

Christmas seemed strange without snow. The French Quarter had gone all out for holiday decorations. Every doorway and lamppost was decked out in red and green tinsel. Statues of Santa, the elves, and the reindeer glowed in store windows and in parks. The dreadlocked contortionist in Jackson Square who folded himself into a small plastic box was wearing a BAH, HUMBUG! T-shirt. Even Salvation Army bell-ringers clanged away in their stocking caps on street corners, but Griffen couldn't feel the holiday spirit when it was still over sixty degrees. He put a dollar in the bucket. The ringer stopped tolling the bell to say thank you. At least that custom was the same all over.

Griffen had gone to the krewe meeting to catch up with the committees, but to Lucinda's disappointment, he didn't stay for dinner. Val, Mai, and Fox Lisa had told him to save the evening. They wanted to hold a small celebration. He had promised to meet them at the Irish bar.

He was a little uneasy having to face all three of them, especially after having just been with the Krewe of Fafnir. None of the three was satisfied with his explanation about the queenship. Griffen had no more news than before. He had asked about who the queen would be. Etienne had laughed and told him if he really wanted to know, he could buy a copy of the *Arthur Hardy Guide*, which ought to be out in a day or two. Griffen knew that would be no answer for the girls. He patted the opaque, white plastic bag in his arm. He might be able to buy a little peace with the contents.

Val looked up as he came in from Burgundy. She waved him over. The bar, which normally had a string of Christmas lights wound around its upper section, had been adorned with more lights, tinsel wreaths, and cardboard cutouts of reindeer. Griffen slid onto an empty stool. The bartender set out a whisky and water on a bright red napkin and pushed it toward him.

"We went for our costume fittings today," Val said. "They look gorgeous!"

"They look like bags," Mai complained.

"No, they don't. And you look adorable in yours. Green's a great color for you," Fox Lisa said.

"But of course," Mai agreed. "Green is a good dragon color."

"What's in the bag?" Fox Lisa wanted to know.

"Aha," Griffen said, mysteriously. He plunged his hand into it and drew out strings of glittering color. They were samples of the throws the krewe had on order. Jacob had let him take a few of the premium throws to give as gifts. The girls dove for the necklaces, yanking the ones they wanted away from one another. The regulars on the family side watched with great amusement and not a little envy as the three women divided the treasure up among them. Mai tried to take the lion's share, gathering them in her small hands.

"Oh, no, you don't," Val said, untangling the hanks of beads. "You've got more than a dozen there. I want one of those." She pulled loose a string of the giant gold dragon heads.

"Look what it does," Griffen said. He flicked the miniature switch in the clasp, and the eyes flickered.

"Ooh, I want that one!" Fox Lisa said, taking the purple dragons away from Mai from the other side.

"Hey, at least leave me my share!" Mai wailed. She put on the remaining necklaces, including the green dragon beads. "There. Beautiful!"

"I thought you said they'd be tacky," Val teased her.

"Well, I have changed my mind," Mai said. "I didn't know how nice they could be."

"They are good," Fox Lisa said, examining the throws with a critical eye. "Fafnir's picked out some fine things."

"Come on, folks, it's too early for Mardi Gras!" Rustic protested. He was another regular.

"They're Christmas gifts," Griffen said. He put a couple of bills down on the bar. "Fred, drinks for everyone on me, and one for yourself. Merry Christmas, everyone."

The bartender gave him a wink. "Thanks, Griffen."

Word of free drinks spread through the room in a heartbeat. Everyone raised his or her glass to Griffen as Fred served them.

"I hope that is not all you have for us," Mai said, with a lift of her eyebrow. "Some plastic necklaces and a drink."

"Of course it isn't." Griffen patted his bag. "They're staying in Santa's knapsack until our party."

The buzz of conversation died away. Griffen looked up as Detective Harrison swaggered into the bar. He made his way over to Griffen. Rustic and the others made room.

"You asked me to come by here, McCandles?"

"Yes, I did," Griffen said. "Merry Christmas, by the way."

"Yeah, the greetings of the season to you, too."

"Is there anything new you can tell us about the murder?" Mai asked him in a low voice.

Harrison gave her a strange look. "No, ma'am. Nothing fresh."

Mai looked disappointed. Griffen was surprised at her concern, but he didn't want to draw attention to it. He grinned at the detective.

"Well, Detective, I've got something for you."

Harrison's face turned purple. "McCandles, I thought you had better sense than to buy me a Christmas gift," he growled. "You want me in trouble, that is a perfect way to do it. And if you bust my pension, you are going to live in hell the rest of your days on this earth."

"I understand," Griffen said. "I swear, that's not why I asked you to stop by."

From a manila folder in his bag, he took a cream-colored envelope. Harrison's name was rendered in ornate script in the center of the rectangle. He handed it over. "This is an invitation to Fafnir's ball. They just arrived. I wanted you to have it as soon as they came. I'm keeping my promise."

Harrison held it in both hands and eyed it as if he were afraid it would explode. He gave Griffen a suspicious look. He opened the flap and slid out the contents.

Underneath a piece of tissue was a piece of heavy, smooth, cream-colored card stock. At the top of the card was a line, upon which "Mr. David Harrison" had been written in beautiful calligraphy. "The Krewe of Fafnir is honored to invite you to its Masquerade Ball, on Saturday, the eighteenth of January, at eight o'clock in the evening. Black tie. *Respondez s'il vous plais.*"

Harrison looked stunned for a moment, then sounded gruffer than usual.

"So you're giving me a present that I have to pay for. Typical of someone like you."

"Dragons?" Griffen asked.

"Gamblers. Don't flatter yourself."

Griffen could tell he was far from offended. In fact, the dour detective was trying not to show how much of a kick he got out of it. "Merry Christmas."

"Yeah, same to you, McCandles. Well," he said, a little hoarsely, "got to hit the streets. G'night." He stalked out. Griffen knew he was touched.

"Where are ours?" Val demanded.

"But you're maids. You don't get invitations," Griffen said.

"Liar!" Val said. She held out her hand and waited. Griffen shook his head, but he passed out the cream-colored envelopes. Val stroked hers with her fingertips. "I have never seen any paper this nice."

"First class," Mai said, critically, feeling the edges. "Cream-laid eighty-pound bond, watermarked. The invitation has been engraved. You can actually feel the raised typefaces on it. They scarcely ever use this for wedding invitations anymore, and it used to be the society standard. That must have cost a—oof!"

Fox Lisa smiled as she withdrew her elbow from Mai's midriff. "Thank you for delivering this, Griffen. I am pleased to accept the invitation."

"Thanks. I'll tell them."

"Me, too," Val said. "I'll be there with bells on."

"So they know the cow has arrived?" Mai asked, and made a face at her friend. Val made one back. "I would be delighted to attend, too. Do you wear your regalia to the ball?"

"No, formal wear."

The bartender came back from passing out Griffen's drinks. "Hey, Val, I almost forgot! You got a package."

"Here?" Val asked. "Who left it?"

"Didn't know her. A lady. From out of town." He squatted behind the bar and rummaged around for a moment. "Here."

He handed her the package. The box, ten by fifteen inches, was wrapped in red, blue, and white Christmas paper with a cartoon winter motif: kids riding on sleds, snowmen in top hats and mufflers, and big snowflakes. Val eyed it suspiciously. "There's no card. But I can guess who left it."

"Melinda," Griffen said. "Do you want me to open it?"

"No," Val said. "If it explodes, I don't want anyone else to get hurt."

Griffen almost said he wanted to protect her but held back. Val was going through enough. If it made her feel in control to open her own packages, he had to let her.

She ripped the paper off. The name on the box was that of a fancy department-store chain. Griffen felt in the air for any trace of dragon power. There was a minute amount, but that could just have been from Melinda's handling it. He was puzzled. So was Val.

She undid the tissue-paper folds inside and lifted from its nest a shimmering mass of blue silk. "A shirt?"

"It's a maternity blouse," Mai said, after studying it for a moment. "Very pretty. It looks as if it would fit you perfectly. Your stomach's just bulging a tiny bit now, but I think it's wide enough to fit until you deliver."

Val felt fury rise in her. Her cheeks felt hot. "How would she know my size?"

"Wild guess?" Fox Lisa suggested.

"No! She has been spying on me! I think that she must have been in my apartment." She thrust the blouse at Fred. "Throw it away."

"Don't be stupid," Mai said, snatching it back from his hands. "This is silk. It will breathe. You are going to want it in the summer."

"But it's from her!" Val wailed.

Mai closed her eyes and concentrated. "No sense of magic in it," she said, with a wry smile for her friend's paranoia. "It's just a blouse."

But Val was right to be concerned. There was a trace on it. She and Griffen exchanged knowing glances. Mai felt the thread of power lead from the seam under the collar, out the door, and around the corner heading south on Toulouse. The spell was meant to trace Val's whereabouts. Mai reached out with a jolt of her own power and destroyed the spell. She felt the power snap like a broken rubber band back to its source. *Hope that stings, Melinda,* she thought nastily. *Merry Christmas, you dried-up old lizard.*

"I don't want anything from her," Val insisted. "She's trying to worm her way into my life."

"She's left you alone so far. Let's not ruin the holiday," Fox Lisa said. "We come together tonight to celebrate the birth of our savior."

"We don't really believe in the religious aspects of it," Griffen mumbled. "Faith just didn't enter into our upbringing."

"Then enjoy the commercial holiday," Fox Lisa said, "and don't ruin it for the rest of us."

A deliveryman in a logo jacket and a Santa cap came into

the bar and caught Fox Lisa's eye. She brightened and waved him over.

"The food's here! Let's go and have our party. Merry Christmas, Fred."

"Same to you folks," the bartender called, waving.

Twenty-one

Griffen sat down in front of the video player in his apartment and went through his collection of disks. He had amassed hundreds over the past few months, but only in December had he concentrated on finding holiday movies that he liked.

"If you put on *It's a Wonderful Life*, I will strike you unconscious with the whisky bottle and set fire to your apartment," Mai said.

"Never," Griffen said, selecting a disk and inserting it into the waiting tray. "This is my favorite Christmas movie." He put in the original Alistair Sim version of *A Christmas Carol*. He waited until the credits rolled, then crawled back to his spot near the couch, where Fox Lisa handed around plastic forks and spoons and stacks of paper napkins.

"What did you buy me?" Mai asked, over mouthfuls of gumbo, corn bread, red beans and rice, and shrimp remoulade. They ate family style on the floor of Griffen's apartment, snagging forkfuls out of whichever container looked good. "Where is my present?"

"What makes you think I got you anything?" Griffen asked, sitting back against the couch.

"Because I deserve it," Mai retorted. "So do Val and Lisa. You need to show your appreciation for us putting up with you all these months."

"I can't argue with that," Griffen said. He reached over the carry-out boxes for the white plastic bag.

"Good things come in small packages," Fox Lisa said,

cheerfully, accepting the palm-sized box wrapped in gold foil. Mai and Val received the same kind of box. Val ripped into hers at once. Mai contemplated hers with pleasure before opening it. Fox Lisa leaned over and kissed Griffen.

Val held up the earrings. Fine, gold-filled wire had been twisted into miniature dragons with tiny blue crystal eyes. "They are gorgeous, Griff," she said. "You have better taste than I thought you did."

"Thanks a lot!" Griffen said. "All the time I spent going over every glass case in the store." He shook his head in mock despair.

Each set was different, but he had gone to a lot of trouble to make sure they suited the recipients. Mai's was a pair of lotus flowers. Fox Lisa squealed with delight over two tiny foxes. Griffen knew better than to have bought identical sets for them. He had not been able to spend as much as he would have liked to, but Jacob had asked him for a deposit on his throws. That eliminated most of his holiday budget. He had to make sure he had enough for rent and utilities, and there was still New Year's Eve to consider.

"I love them," Fox Lisa said, beaming.

Mai immediately took the perfect little square-cut emeralds out of her ears and put the French wires in instead.

"Very tasteful," she said, admiring the swing of the minute blossoms in her earlobes. "I have many outfits that these will complement."

Griffen breathed a sigh of relief. Jewelry was a very personal choice. It had been risky to give it, but it seemed to have paid off.

"We have gifts for you, too," Fox Lisa said, springing up. "Val, do you want to give me your door key?"

"No, I'll help you," she said. The two of them went out and headed for the stairs. Mai stayed where she was.

"You had this all set up in advance," Griffen said.

"Of course. Planning is the key to any good party."

The girls returned with armloads of colorfully wrapped parcels. They giggled as they handed them around to one another. Before long, Griffen had a small heap of presents in front of him. He hesitated.

"Well, what are you waiting for?" Fox Lisa asked. "Open them! We want to see what you think!"

Griffen felt an unfamiliar sense of nostalgia, looking around at the three happy faces. He was related only to Val, and possibly distantly to Mai, if all dragons shared some common ancestor; but this was as close to a family as he had had in years. They cared what he thought. They'd gone to as much trouble as he had, selecting, wrapping, and hiding gifts ahead of time for his pleasure.

"You know, it doesn't matter what's in them," he said. His throat tightened a little.

"I know," Val said. He detected a hint of sentiment in her eyes. "Open them anyhow."

Mai's was a pair of black trousers with the label of an Italian designer in the waistband. The fabric was crisp but not stiff, with just a hint of an elegant gleam. "I had the tailor hem them for me to your measurements," she said.

"They're great," Griffen said.

Fox Lisa waited eagerly as he lifted a tissue-wrapped bundle from a sturdy box. He sensed it was delicate, so he set it in his lap to finish the unwrapping. Swaddled in the tissue was a Carnival mask. He had seen hundreds of them in stores throughout the French Quarter. An oval, blank white face was surmounted by a folded fool's cap of bright green and gold. Around the empty right eyehole was painted a gold star. The molded lips smiled very slightly at the corners, as if the mask knew the punch line of a joke it hadn't delivered yet. It was a work of art.

"It's so light," he said. "I thought it would be made of china."

"It's leather. Masks in Europe are still made that way. A few makers do them here."

"I love it. Thank you."

Fox Lisa beamed. "You're more than welcome. You can wear it to masked balls, if you want."

Val had bought him a history of the earliest motion pictures from the turn of the twentieth century. Griffen glanced through the frames of those crudely made but groundbreaking, hand-cranked films. He had a couple of them in his collection. He felt the urge to curl up with the book and read it immediately. It took an act of will to close it and shove it under the front of the couch, where he couldn't see it.

"That is perfect," Griffen said. "Thanks, Val."

"I knew it was you as soon as I saw it. I was afraid you had bought one for yourself."

He shook his head. "You got in ahead of me. I can't wait to read it. Now, let's see what you have."

Griffen sat back with a glass of whisky as the girls tore into their presents. They thanked one another with hugs and kisses. Fox Lisa reheated the gumbo in Griffen's microwave and brought out more beers and soda for Val. Griffen felt mellow and happy.

"Do you know this is the first Christmas I have had since Val and I were kids that I have really enjoyed? Uncle Malcolm had us flown up to his mansion in upstate New York for the holidays. It was like getting sent to a museum for a week for punishment."

"Who took care of you?" Fox Lisa asked.

"We had a housekeeper. I think she used to work in a prison. I took every chance to rebel."

"So did I," Val said.

Griffen gave her as scornful look. "Yeah, you were great at rebelling. Coming in ten minutes after your curfew was rebelling."

"I was still late," she said, stung. "It made Mrs. Feuer mad."

"Everything made her mad. She was a real . . . dragon." Griffen stopped for a moment and drank whisky. "I never thought of it before, but she must have been. What if we had started manifesting as teenagers? Uncle Malcolm was pretty clever."

"I didn't appreciate his cleverness. I was glad to get away to college."

"You and me both. Uncle Malcolm wouldn't let us go to the same college," Griffen explained to the others. "We wanted to stick together, but he insisted on separating us."

"Control freak," Val agreed. "And he insisted on having us visit him, but he never seemed happy to have us there. It was out of family obligation. He's not a warm person. I think it was torture for all of us."

"I think holidays are a deliberate practice to put people together and make them miserable," Mai said. "Forced happiness only works in Disneyland."

"Hey!" Fox Lisa said, clapping her hands over her ears. "Stop it right now. Let's not get bogged down in happy memories!"

Griffen deliberately turned the conversation to enjoyable subjects.

When *A Christmas Carol* ended, he put on *Miracle on 34th Street*, then *White Christmas*. They played board games. No one could decide on which one, so they cobbled together a combination of Risk, Monopoly, and The Game of Life that Griffen had picked up for a song, still in cellophane, at a used bookstore. They made up rules that Griffen knew he would not remember an hour or two from then but seemed to make sense at the time.

He shook the dice and threw them onto the Monopoly board. He jumped the top hat six spaces, missing the armies bivouacked on Park Place and Boardwalk.

"Wait, you landed on Go," Mai exclaimed, pointing. "You have to move those five armies into Irkutsk!" Griffen winced. That meant that his forces had to face Val's shoe marker and Fox Lisa's red pawn.

"Can I pay a fine instead?" he asked. The girls conferred.

"Spin," Val commanded. "If you get over six, you can retreat." Griffen reached for the Life board.

"Oh, I love this part of Christmas," Fox Lisa said. "My

family always had this kind of togetherness. This and presents. I love getting presents."

"We opened all the presents," Griffen reminded her. He leered. "Too bad there's nothing left to unwrap."

"I've got something you can unwrap," Fox Lisa said, rising to her knees a little unsteadily and putting her fingers on the top button of her blouse. "And I've got a present for you," she told Mai.

Mai tilted her head, interest dawning on her face. "Well, I have one for you, too!"

"Oh, no, I'm out of here," Val said. She was getting tired anyhow, and all the diet soda was pushing hard on her bladder. It was also tough being the only one in the room who was sober. She snatched up her presents and hurried toward the door. "Night, Griffen," she called.

"Merry Christmas, Val," he shouted, as the door opened with a creak.

Just before the door shut, she heard Fox Lisa let out a yelp, followed by a loud giggle. She retreated hastily to her own apartment.

Val had to pull her pillow over her head to shut out the voices and thumping noises as the furniture in her brother's apartment was rearranged by moving bodies.

"Not a creature was stirring, my petite little ass."

Still, it had been the best Christmas she could remember.

Twenty-two

Melinda beckoned gently to her daughter, who stood on the balustrade of the roof of their hotel. *Thank God it's night,* she thought. Only a few drunks down on Bourbon Street had noticed her and were shouting for her to jump. No one paid attention to them in the huge festive crowds on the street.

"Lizzy, bring that man down here. I mean, now! You might drop him. That would be bad."

"He's mine!" Lizzy shrieked. Though she was barely five feet tall and perhaps ninety pounds in weight, she shook the six-foot-two dark-skinned man like a paper doll. Melinda couldn't tell if he was still conscious or not. "I found him. I get to keep him!"

"He is not yours," Melinda said, willing herself to be calm. "He is mine. I am paying for our hotel room. What I pay for belongs to me. I have had to pick up hundreds of thousands of dollars of expenses in the last two months because you had your little accident."

"Not my fault!" Lizzy cried, her eyes filling with tears. The irises looked like disks of fused, multicolored glass. They seemed to whirl when she was upset. They were virtually spinning then. "It was that bitch! That Valerie. She did it! She *hurt* Lizzy! She was mean!"

"I know, my darling," Melinda said soothingly. "But she was not being mean to you. You hit her first, didn't you? Didn't I teach you that was wrong?"

"Ye-e-es . . ."

"So don't you think you should take responsibility for some of the problem?"

"I . . . guess . . . maybe."

"That's not the answer I'm looking for," Melinda said in a light, singsong voice that meant trouble. Lizzy took the hint.

"Yes."

"Good. Now, please give me that man. I want to see if he is all right."

"I don't care if he is all right!"

Melinda put her hands on her round hips. "Lizzy, I am going to count to three, and if you do not give me that hotel porter, you will be very sorry. Do you understand? One . . ."

"All right!" Lizzy screamed. She swung around and heaved the body at her mother. Melinda put up her arms to catch him. Though she was short and on the plump side, she was more than strong enough to hoist a grown human, but the momentum of the weight cannoning into her sent her flying backward. Melinda threw her arms around the porter and braked to a halt on the pebbled tar paper. She felt her Ferragamo stiletto heel snap off under her foot.

Damn!

Then another blow took her from behind, like a gigantic rubber band smacking her in the back. With the man in her arms, Melinda spun around to see what had happened. No one was there. She turned back to Lizzy.

"That's better, Lizzy."

That's better, Lizzy.

"Don't mock me, my darling. It's not nice."

Don't mock me, my darling. It's not nice.

"I'm not," Lizzy said, putting out her lower lip. "You don't let me have any fun. I don't have any friends. Even Valerie, who is gonna make me an auntie, hates me."

"Now, you know that isn't true," Melinda began. *Now, you know that isn't true.* "I've heard you say that many times."

I've heard you say that many times. "Valerie McCandles doesn't really know you." *Valerie McCandles . . .*

The voice continued, but Lizzy's mouth was not moving. Melinda tried speaking again, and immediately heard her own words repeat in her head. In her mind's eye, she saw herself standing on the roof holding a large man and looking up at Lizzy. Melinda knew at once what had happened. The spell she had set on the present she had left for Valerie in that tatty little bar was meant to let Melinda hear and see what went on around the girl. Once she put on the blouse, the spell would have attached to her, so no matter what she wore, or where she went, Melinda would know. The girl was vulnerable. She had no idea what enemies were beginning to gather around a gravid dragon. Melinda wanted to make certain her grandchild was not in danger.

Val must have detected the spell. The energy of it had come hurtling back and smacked into Melinda like a gigantic rubber band. Now she heard and saw an echo of everything *she* did or said, delayed by a few seconds, as if her own words had to travel all the way around the world before reaching her again.

The man in her arms started to stir. His face contorted with pain. Melinda could tell that his arm was broken, and who knew what else? She set him down on the roof. Humans were too fragile.

His eyes opened, then widened to black dots in white circles. "She tried to kill me! She snapped my arm like a twig! Lemme up! I gonna quit!" He tried to sit up.

She knelt beside him and pushed down on his chest with her palm. He fell backward. "You're all right," she said. *You're all right.* "It was an accident." *It was an accident,* the echo in her brain said. "You slipped . . ." *You slipped . . .* ". . . and fell . . ." *and fell . . .* Melinda found herself trying to slow down and let the echo catch up with her, but it didn't work. Curse it! She would have to create a counterspell, but not until she solved the double crisis in front of her. "Never mind!" *Never mind.*

She flattened her palm on the man's forehead. He struggled to get away from her, but he wasn't strong enough. Melinda closed her eyes and concentrated. She reached into his mind.

Forget what Lizzy just did, she thought, and waited. No echo. At least it didn't work in her conscious mind. *You were walking on a slippery floor, and you fell. Your arm is broken. It will heal soon. You like and trust me, but you are shy around my daughter and don't like to be alone with her. You want to sleep now.*

That ought to do it. The porter stopped struggling. He reached over to cradle his bad arm with his good hand. His eyes drifted closed. She sat back on her broken heel.

At that moment, two dragons rushed out through the fire door and gawked at Lizzy.

"Where in hell have you two idiots been?" Melinda asked. "You are supposed to be the finest doctors in the Southeast. How could you let her get out of the suite?" She tried to ignore the echo.

The psychiatrist, Dr. Wivberg, was a genial-looking male with thick chest hair that peeked up through the neck of his polo shirt. "It's impossible," he said. "I gave her enough sedative to make her sleep for a week."

"I told you she was building an immunity to it," said the surgeon and general practitioner, Dr. Kierin. "We should have gone with the cocktail."

"Never mind!" Melinda bellowed. *Never mind.* "Shut up!" *Shut up!* "We need to get her down from there immediately before someone sees us and calls the police. And see to this man. Set his arm." *We need to . . .* Melinda put her fingers in her ears, but she couldn't escape from the sound of her own voice.

Dr. Kierin squatted down beside the hotel porter. "No problem." He took the man's elbow in one hand and his wrist in the other and tugged. The porter woke up with a bellow that echoed off the buildings around them. Shouts down on the street told them that he'd been heard, but no one could see them. Dr. Kierin reached into his breast pocket for the kit both physicians always kept on hand to deal with Lizzy. He knocked the barrel of the dermal infuser with his fingernail, then injected a small dose into the porter's vein. "That'll keep him out for a while. What about memory?"

"Already taken care of." *Already taken care of.* "Dammit!" *Dammit!*

Dr. Kierin regarded her respectfully but curiously. Melinda waved a hand.

"Take care of her. I have another crisis to deal with." *Take care of her . . .* Melinda fled from the roof, but her voice dogged her as she limped down to the top-floor suites. Behind her, she heard the doctors moving in on Lizzy.

"Why, look at you up there, Lizzy," Dr. Wivberg said in a calm, friendly voice. "Do you have a good view of Bourbon Street? Are those men down there shouting at you?"

Melinda stopped on the landing to kick off the useless shoes. She abandoned them where they fell and kept going. She had five more pairs in her closet. How naive of her to have underestimated the McCandles siblings! Melinda did not realize that Valerie had had such advanced training in magical defense. It had only been a few months since she had been made aware of her background. Unless Malcolm McCandles had been lying about what the children knew. She wouldn't put it past him. He ought to have been a politician. He only lied when his mouth was moving.

Melinda let herself into the suite and retreated to her bedroom. If only Valerie were more reasonable, Melinda could have made arrangements with her and been out of the city with Lizzy months before. As it was, she had had to take her daughter out of the private nursing home where she had first been taken to recover. The medical staff there, even though they were also dragons, found her erratic and uncooperative. Once Lizzy was healthy enough to move, Melinda had taken her here, where they occupied two attached luxury suites on the top floor. The doctors were supposed to keep her under watch day and night, but they had become sloppy as Lizzy recovered.

Her daughter was gaining strength daily. With her health, she regained memory of the events of two months before. She wanted to go back and relive them, or live them differently. Melinda never really understood the gift in Lizzy's twisted mind. Melinda had promised Valerie that Lizzy would not cross her path again, but she couldn't send her daughter home. No one there would have been able to control her for five minutes. So she had to use a compulsion on Lizzy to keep her from breaking out and wandering away into the city. Melinda feared constantly that Lizzy would get loose and wreak havoc. Griffen McCandles would have known about it almost immediately. The next time, Lizzy might not be as lucky as to survive an encounter with Griffen or Valerie. Melinda could hardly blame them. As much as she loved her daughter, she had little tolerance for her behavior. Yes, Lizzy was clinically insane, seeing things that had yet to happen or would never happen. It would be a marvelous gift if only it could be exploited in some useful fashion. The talent ran in the family. Melinda had a limited version of it.

Unfortunately, Lizzy's brain was making up for the lack of activity of her body by spreading hallucinations out to a radius of about thirty feet. None of the staff liked to come to Lizzy's suite. After one night, guests in nearby rooms demanded to be moved, bellowing about ghosts, poltergeists, or other supernatural intrusions. As this was New Orleans, the proprietors were torn between having a genuine tourist attraction and mortified that it was cutting into their income. In the end, the wing fell empty except for their rooms. Melinda could not leave until she had settled the situation with the McCandleses, so she put up with the daily visits from the manager and occasional ones from the police.

Melinda sat down on a chair in front of the closet and tried on another pair of shoes, ones fresh out of the box. They never fit exactly right. Ferragamo served a clientele with incredibly narrow feet. Melinda put her thumbs into the ball of the right shoe and pressed outward. The smooth leather spread out about a centimeter. Melinda tried it on and smiled. She turned her ankle from side to side to admire the designer's handiwork. Beautiful. Worth every penny.

She wished she could channel Lizzy's gift. She had a vision of holding a blue-eyed baby in her arms, could feel and smell it. She must make that come true! Valerie and Griffen were hemmed in by protections, both magical and social. Melinda was doing her best to be low-key, but time was fleeting, and so was her influence.

She had had to abandon her own clan to woo Valerie. Running the family from such a distance was beginning to loosen her hold on authority. Her rivals were openly questioning her ability and devotion to the family. She railed at them over the phone, but nothing had the same impact as face-to-face confrontations. If something did not happen very soon, she was going to have to go home and reestablish herself. By that time, who knew what might happen to Valerie and the grandchild?

Not that she was sentimental, at all, she chided herself. She had her reasons for wanting control of that baby. She had failed miserably with her own children. It was Christmas, and she had spent half the night on the roof trying to talk her daughter down. No one had sent her a present or cards. Only her younger son had called to wish her a Merry Christmas.

"Children," she said, sitting down in front of the mirror to prepare a countercurse for her own spell. "They interfere with everything you do."

Children. They interfere with everything you do.

Melinda looked at her own reflection wryly. "You said it, baby. Bah humbug."

Twenty-three

"Hey, thanks for the music player, Grifter," Jerome said, as Griffen slid into a chair next to him in O'Brien's side bar. A couple of legendary blues musicians had scheduled a concert on the "dueling" grand pianos in the lounge. Word had spread among the locals long before the public heard about it, and they had gotten there early to occupy the best seats. "Can't believe it is so small, but it has got some sound on it."

"Glad you like it, Jer," Griffen said, pleased.

The week between Christmas and New Year's was a great time for Griffen's business. Tourists flocked into New Orleans to enjoy the night life and indulge in what it had to offer. The strip clubs did booming business. The bartenders invented holiday cocktails, but they sold just as many Hurricanes, Sazeracs, and Ramos gin fizzes. Every jazz and blues club in the city filled to overflowing with happy people with a week off and money to spend. Griffen and Jerome had had no trouble running two to four games a night at various locations around the city. Harrison, with an unsolved murder on his books and other, more serious infractions against the vice laws turning up in the crowded city, had no time to roust illegal poker.

If the truth were told, Griffen could have used his help. The game on Saturday on the eighth floor of the Omni Hotel had turned ugly. A female professional poker player from Las Vegas insisted that one of the other players had been stealing chips from her stacks. Jerome had gone in to settle the problem, and found himself in a six-way shouting match that culminated in the arrival of hotel security. He had managed to prevent the game being shut down, but the woman cashed in her chips and stormed off, vowing to spread the word to her high-roller friends.

Word seemed to be spreading to the other gambling rings that the McCandles game was vulnerable. Unhappy customers were going to other groups. The hotel concierges, usually the source of their best leads, were steering players away from the spotters. It took personal visits from Griffen and Jerome with assurances that he was on top of the issue, and that it was just the occasional disgruntled player causing trouble, to get them to start recommending his games again. Jerome had put in hours of legwork. Griffen felt he owed him a big favor.

Jerome sat back with a drink, enjoying the show. The two men, both elderly African-Americans, sent musical phrases up and back to one another as challenges. The man on the left, with large, protuberant eyes like Count Basie's, grinned wickedly and played the first lines from "Anything You Can Do, I Can Do Better." His counterpart picked it up, jazzed it up, then added syncopation. The first pianist laughed, repeated what his friend had produced, and drew it out into a trill of music that rolled and ricocheted around the original song. Everyone cheered them on, stuffing money into the jars on the table between the pianos.

"Got three tables tonight," he said. "Everyone's an old-timer. They rather spend New Year's Eve with a handful of cards than their families."

"Four," Griffen said. "Forgot to tell you. I got a call from Peter Sing. He found a few people in his hotel who want a game. We'll play in his room. I called Marcel to deal."

Jerome's eyebrows lowered over his nose. "I told you I don't like that man, Grifter. He's trouble."

"I know! But I'm sitting in. As long as I'm there, what can he do?"

"I dunno, but I don't want to find out! Why do you keep lettin' him in?"

Griffen frowned. At Mai's insistence, they had banned Jordan Ma and the woman from joining any more tables, but he wasn't willing to let Jerome push him around. "I like the guy. He's good company. We get along. I know you don't. I don't see what you think is a problem."

"I told you I didn't like his attitude," Jerome said.

"What's his attitude got to do with it?" Griffen asked. "It's kind of cool that a pro wants to play in our games. It's good for our reputation. We could use a boost about now."

"But not with a dude like him." Jerome looked disappointed. "Grifter, you said you trusted my judgment. Then act like it!"

"You act like you don't trust mine! Who's the—"

The pianist on the left glanced up from his keyboard. "Hey, fellahs, chill. Let's all go with the flow, 'kay?"

Griffen gave him a guilty glance but dropped his voice. "Who's the head dragon around here?"

Jerome raised his eyebrows.

"That mean you know more than the rest of us? You still a baby, Grifter."

"Really? So all the times you come to *me* for advice have been window dressing?"

"I am showing respect to the office, man! The guy occupyin' it obviously don't deserve it!"

A man in a shiny tuxedo jacket and a satin bow tie dipped his head down between them. "Gentlemen," the manager murmured, "sorry to interrupt your argument, but you're ruining the vibes for the other people here. We'd love to have you stay, but only if you have finished your discussion. Otherwise, we'll be happy to see you another time."

Griffen worked his jaw. He felt his cheeks burn. "Thanks," he said. He dug money out of his wallet and set it down on the cocktail table. Jerome shook his head and raised his drink.

"Happy New Year, man."

"Yeah," Griffen said.

He stalked out. Couples and groups raised cheerful go-cups to one another as they passed.

"Happy New Year!"

Griffen responded, though his heart wasn't in it. He felt guilty about Jerome. Griffen depended on him absolutely when it came to the business, but it seemed as if he had a bug about Peter Sing. Sure, he knew Peter was a dragon. He was a demon poker player, and that raised concerns that he had been sent by the Eastern dragons, but he hadn't done anything wrong! At every game he had played at one of Griffen's tables Griffen himself had been present. Was Jerome jealous that he was befriending another strong-blooded dragon? Did this have anything to do with Griffen's Mardi Gras krewe? If Jerome wanted to be involved in that, all he had to do was ask! There was no need for him to sulk.

He found his feet turning automatically toward the Irish bar. The poker game Peter had asked to set up wasn't due to begin until after midnight. He had at least an hour to kill before then.

He passed by a few clubs and bars. Their French doors were wide open to the air, letting the sweet music and loud conversation pour out. Crowds with plastic cups in their hands hung out around the doors, laughing and talking. They were ready to ring in the new year. Griffen felt sorry for himself. There would probably be no one he knew in the Irish pub. Just a few losers who found their way there, who had no one else to celebrate with.

To his amazement, every seat in the house was filled, and the bar was hemmed in three deep with people lost in conversation. The pool tables were both occupied. Practically every regular was there. Half of them were wearing plastic top hats with the numerals of the new year blazoned on them. Blares of toy horns punctuated the usual hum.

"Hey, Griffen!" shouted Maestro, brandishing his pool cue. "Come on and help me rob these poor fools of what's left of their paychecks!"

Griffen was grateful for the invitation, but he waved a hand to decline.

"Griffen!"

He glanced past the bartender to the family side. Val beckoned to him. He went around and squeezed in next to her.

"What are you doing here?" he asked. "I thought you were out with Gris-gris."

"He had to go help one of his aunts," Val said, making a face. "His uncle fell off a ladder and broke his leg. He didn't want me to come and help. Said I might strain myself. What about you? I thought you and Jerome were at the piano concert."

Griffen felt ashamed. "I left," he said. "We had a disagreement over business." He didn't want to rehash it with Val. She wasn't involved in the business, and it stung to relive the accusations they had thrown at one another. She was wise enough not to push it.

"Hey, Fred, a drink for my brother!" Val called. The bartender poured out Griffen's usual Irish and pushed it over the bar. Griffen reached for his wallet, but Val forestalled him. "This one's on me, Griffen. You look like you could use it."

"Thanks, Little Sister," he said. He raised it to her. He felt better. Of all the places he could have been, this was the one closest to a home he had had in a long time. The people there knew his quirks, most of his business, and cared about him. They had accepted him and his sister. It was bittersweet that he had argued with the man he had considered a close friend for many years, only to find out this very year that Jerome was not a human, nor were Griffen and Valerie, that Griffen might be able to make a living at his avocation, that he would meet creatures of legend who lived hidden in plain sight among human beings, and that once in a while people that he had never met tried to kill him. It would have been a lot to take in in a lifetime, let alone a few months.

"Hey, it's one minute to midnight!" Fred shouted.

Everyone turned to look at him. He pointed to the clock. "Let's all count it down! Forty-five! Forty."

Griffen lifted his glass to Val. "So ends the weirdest year of my life."

"So far, Big Brother," Val said, hoisting her Diet Coke to him. She patted her abdomen. "Wait until next year. It's going to be weirder still."

"All together now! Five! Four! Three! Two! One! Happy New Year!"

Griffen drank the toast, but he didn't believe it. How much weirder could it get?

Twenty-four

Matt held Griffen back from entering the function room at the Hyatt Hotel. "You have to wait until you're announced," he said.

Griffen felt nervous. He had met on a casual basis a few of the committee members whose krewes would be sharing their parade date. They had come over to the den to help the builders with crucial parts of float construction. Griffen and the others had been advised then to stay out of the way, or, as Etienne put it, "observe and learn somet'ing." This was the formal meeting of the elite of the four krewes, a ritual ceremony that had not been held in over sixty years, not since Mose had been king. The other three krewes had temporarily disbanded around the time of the war, too, but had reconstituted over previous decades. All of them had been marching since 1979. No one in Fafnir wanted to talk about why it was the last to begin again. He hoped someone at this meeting would answer his questions.

Griffen felt dozens of dragons present beyond the curtain. He was also aware of other powerful personalities. At least one other type of supernatural was present. Griffen couldn't put his finger on it, but he had sensed that kind of power at the conclave. If it was someone he had met, he hoped it wasn't one of the troublemakers.

A lot of the members of Fafnir were present at this reception. They had come to gather around him and shake his hand before going into the main function room to sit down. Apart from its sexist practice of having only men on the committee, men, women, and children of every color and every social class belonged to Fafnir. The one thing they had in common was dragon blood. The heads of committees, the movers and shakers, with the exception of Etienne, had the most, but all of them had a little. The proximity to so many fellow dragons put Griffen's defenses on overload, but he knew kin when he felt it. It was like attending a huge family reunion.

". . . The king of the element of fire, Fafnir! Please welcome Griffen McCandles."

Applause broke out. Matt peeked through the curtain, then clapped Griffen twice on the shoulder. "That's you. Go on!"

Griffen marched out into the room, head high. Hundreds of people turned to look at him, still applauding. As he had been instructed, he kept his face grave and dignified.

The audience was not set up to face one end of the room, as was customary. Instead, it had been broken up into four groups divided by aisles arranged in a cross. Griffen spotted Etienne and most of the lieutenants in the seats along the path by which he entered. The captain gave him a cheerful thumbs-up as he passed.

At the center, Doug was waiting with two men and a woman whom Griffen had never seen before, none of them dragons. He gestured to Griffen to join them. The krewe liaison had a microphone in one hand and gestured with the other like a television evangelist.

"I welcome you all to the Ritual of the Four Elements. According to ancient charter, for the well-being of the city and the environs of this province of New Orleans, groups representing each of the principal elements of nature are called together to grant their blessings upon the coming season. Prosperity, safety, and goodwill toward all!"

Griffen groaned to himself. He had come across mention of pseudoreligious rites associated with Mardi Gras. Etienne had not given him much information about this meeting, other than it was their first with the other three krewes marching on February 24. The woman standing behind Doug grinned and put out a hand.

"Holly Goldberg," she whispered. "Sprite of the Krewe of Aeolus." She had round cheeks and hazel eyes, with laugh lines at the corners. Her hair, which fell well below her waist, was dishwater blond, going naturally gray at the temples. Griffen guessed she was in her forties. She had a solid grip.

"Griffen McCandles."

"This is Costain Wrayburn and Bert Leopold." The other two shook hands with Griffen. Wrayburn was tall, burly, muscular but running to fat, probably in his early fifties. His hair, while still black, clung in a scanty tonsure around a pink scalp. Griffen guessed that he had played football, in school if not professionally. He held himself like an athlete. Bert Leopold had small features but a lantern jaw. His eyes were brilliant green, his tightly curled hair reddish brown and shot with gray. His tawny skin was so weathered Griffen could not guess his age. He could have been anything between thirty and ninety.

"It is a great privilege for me to be here today. This ritual has not been performed in over sixty years. It is only now that Fafnir has been reestablished that all four groups can be brought together again. The need to renew the city's protections is always great, but never more than lately, when this great nation has been under attack by hostile forces, both natural and human."

"Humans *are* natural," Wrayburn growled under his breath. It sounded like an old gripe of his.

". . . Therefore, we begin the process to protect our home. Step forward, the Kings of the Elements!"

Griffen took a pace. He felt like Harry Potter, but this time his name was in the cup on purpose. The audience cheered.

"Now, before we begin," Doug cautioned them, "you must vow to keep the secret of what you are about to behold. Parents, you know if your children are capable of understanding what that means. If not, please take them out now."

No one moved. Doug nodded over the heads of the audience. The people standing by the doors locked them. Griffen felt the hum of voices take on an ominous tone.

"Okay, then, Matt?"

Matt came out from behind the curtain near the east door with a large box like a metal suitcase. It was gilded and ornamented in the style of the Louis kings of France.

"Do you all solemnly swear to keep secret and never tell any living soul the rites you are about to witness? Do you promise to uphold and protect the devices and elements of the Ritual of the Four Elements? Signify now by saying, 'I swear.'"

The audience echoed. "I swear."

"All righty, then." Matt hoisted the box into his arms and presented it to Doug. Doug opened it.

"Oooooh," chorused the crowd.

Griffen reeled backward. He felt as if he had been hit with a two-by-four. The power that had been contained within the case was overwhelming. His eyes filled with tears. So did Holly's. The other two men, though they looked impressed, merely investigated the contents of the box with interest.

Nestled into folds of golden velvet perishing with age were four golden objects. Griffen could not easily define them. In shape and size they were like extralong pancake turners, except the paddle part of each had been wrought into a different fantastic shape. Griffen figured out immediately which belonged to what element. Air was rendered as the outline of many overlapping silver-gilt clouds, dusted with glittering blue crystals. The mountain shape at the top of Earth had dark red and grass green crystals. A glistening bubble dotted with aqua and moss green was Water. And Fire . . . Griffen felt his own eyes glow. The stylized flame of the top almost seemed to flicker because of the red and gold crystals set around the edge and licking upward from the handle in lines like living fire. He reached for it. Holly's hand snapped up and slapped his down. He looked at her in shock. She winked at him. Griffen withdrew it sheepishly.

Doug continued his narration. "These scepters will be yours to wield during the parade, when we charge you to set your element in order. This custom began overseas centuries ago and came over with the European founders of this city. For the protection of all, for the good of all, you must first raise the power of your element in the coming days so there will be sufficient to bind on the destined day, so by the time of penance, known as Ash Wednesday, this city and its environs will know security for another year or," he added, with a grin, "another sixty." The audience chuckled. "We-all don't intend that the next one will be that long after this."

"This is all purely ceremonial, of course," Griffen said.

Wrayburn smiled gravely at him. "No, Griffen. This is for real."

"Earth, our mother, the base under our feet, she who sustains us, and to whom our bodies belong, take your scepter."

Costain Wrayburn grasped the mountain wand and hoisted it over his head. The onlookers cheered. Doug shushed them.

"Hold it to the end, folks. Water, from which life emerged, the pathway and artery of our city, take your scepter. Air, the breath and the wind, guardian of music and flight, take your scepter." As Doug spoke, the next two assumed their devices. "Fire, the divine spark, the power of the sun brought down to us mere mortals, take your scepter." Griffen reached for the last rod in the box and raised it to the cheers of the audience.

As soon as his fingers closed on it, Griffen gasped. Instead of holding the wand, it seemed to take hold of him. A warm force radiated into his flesh, racing down his arm, into his body. It spread out to his head and feet. Finding nowhere else to go from there, it felt like it was shooting around inside him like a pinball banging from paddle to ringer to target, except the pinball was made of lava. Holly reached over and put her hand on his forehead. A cool sensation spread out from her palm.

"Calm," she said. "Control it. Don't let it control you."

Griffen had tried meditation a few times in his life, never seriously, but he knew techniques. He closed his eyes and concentrated on his breathing. The pinball slowed down. It stopped ricocheting around and rolled gently up into a spot just behind his solar plexus. He was aware of it, but it no longer hurt. His head rang as if counting up the points. Griffen opened his eyes. They weren't burning anymore.

Holly took her hand away. "That's better."

Once the energy stopped battering him, Griffen had a chance to examine the scepter. It was far heavier than it looked. It might have been solid gold. The glittering crystals were not glass. They were jewels. The light danced in them, teasing his eyes.

"I've never felt power in an inanimate object before," Griffen said. "It went through me like . . ."

"Shh. We don't speak of it," Holly said. "Come and talk with us later, all right? We'll have a drink."

"Face your element now," Doug instructed them. "Antaeus, you are the north. Aeolus, you are the east. Fafnir, you are the south. Nautilus, you are the west." He arranged them back-to-back, shoulders touching, facing down one of the aisles toward a wall or a door.

Griffen imitated the others when they raised their wands toward the ceiling. He felt a little silly, playacting in front of four whole krewes. They were eating it up, but it was all theater. The scepters were made by people who had some inherent power and really enjoyed what they were doing. What did the audience expect to see? Should he wave it around like a fairy godmother?

"All right, kings, time to call forth your subject. Focus on it. With your scepter, draw your element to you. Call it by name. Now!"

"Fire!" Griffen shouted.

Then, suddenly, it wasn't funny anymore. All the lights

in his quarter of the room strobed toward him, going on and off like neon signs. The huge bulb over his head burst, releasing golden sparks. They fell toward him. Just over his head, they started dancing on the air like fairies. Each grew larger and larger, then exploded like fireworks. Hot air rushed toward him, kissed his face with a touch like a dry, raspy hand. The top of the scepter burst into flame, which roared toward the ceiling. Griffen flinched, but he could not recoil with the others at his back. He waved the wand, hoping to put the fire out. Instead, flickering lights shook loose from the stylized flame and took off into the air on their own. They danced around his head like cartoon Indians around a campfire. He felt something indefinable unlock. All of a sudden, he felt exposed and vulnerable. This was wild power. It would consume him and everyone there if he did not control it. He had never felt anything like it. It intrigued and terrified him at the same time. As Holly had instructed him, he made himself calm down.

You are mine, he thought at it. *I am a dragon. In fact, I am the head dragon around here! You are subject to my command. The element of fire was given to us.* He didn't know whether any of that was true, but it gave him confidence.

The fire didn't believe him. It formed a face with two ears and a mouth. More flames became two hands that stuck themselves thumb first into the ears and waggled. A forked tongue came out of the mouth. Griffen gawked.

WHAT was that? he thought at it imperiously, as a strict father might demand of a sassy teenage son. *I rule you!* His annoyance made the pinball in his belly grow to bowling-ball size. Power raced from it to his arm and to the end of the scepter. Red flames shot out of the gold peaks. They engulfed the wildfire in a cage of glowing net. The mouth of the face opened in a silent bellow of rage. Griffen concentrated, bearing down on the red flames. The cage shrank, until the face was squeezed up against it. It looked at Griffen beseechingly. Its lower lip pouted outward.

Are you going to do what I want now? he thought at it.

The face nodded. Griffen relaxed. The red flames died away, blending with the yellow.

The combined creature retreated, forming streaks of fire that snaked toward the ceiling and down again in spirals and lightning strokes. Griffen enjoyed the show.

He was aware of the other elements in the room. Tendrils of water flowed and rippled through the air on his right, hissing into steam as they struck the heat of Griffen's quadrant. On his left, a whirlwind scooted up and down the aisle. With her scepter, Holly conducted music that presumably only she and the scepter could hear. Griffen could not see what was going on at his back with Earth, but the rumble under his feet suggested Wrayburn had assumed authority over his domain, too. Griffen felt all four of the elements were connected, as he was connected to the other three kings.

"Together we weave the web that keeps our city safe," Doug intoned. "Let it go now. Let it go out and raise the power we need. We'll all meet again on parade day! Send it off. Right now!"

"Go away!" Griffen said, putting all of his will into the command. He didn't expect it to obey, but it did.

Fireballs, lightning, and all, the element of fire gathered itself into a ball like a comet. It circled Griffen once, leaving a black contrail that made him cough, then hurtled toward the curtains that covered the door on the south wall. It vanished with a *bang!* The curtains started smoking. Hoisting a fire extinguisher, Matt stood up and sprayed them. He disappeared in clouds of white. When the steam cleared, Griffen saw a round scorch mark on the yellow fabric. Doug shook his head.

"We are not gonna get the security deposit back this time," he said.

The audience sprang to its feet, clapping wildly. Etienne grinned as he showed Griffen two thumbs-up.

"Great show!" he shouted.

Doug signed for silence. "Together we weave the web

that keeps our city safe. Remember, you can't talk about this with anyone who wasn't here today. But among those of you who were," he said, with a broad grin, "you've got a special story that'll last you a lifetime. See you all later on."

With the power dispersed, Griffen leaned against the shoulders of the others for support. The audience filed out of the room, talking loudly to one another. They were thrilled and impressed. Griffen was, too, but he needed a chance to go somewhere and think about what had just happened.

Wrayburn moved first. "C'mon," he said. "I need a drink even if the rest of you don't."

"I'll beat you to the bar," Griffen challenged him.

"Yeah, you Fire types got no patience," the big man grunted. "The least you can do is buy the first round."

"It'd be my pleasure," Griffen said. "Firewater for everybody."

"Hear, hear!" crowed Holly, putting her hand through his arm.

Twenty-five

Griffen took a solid pull at the whisky and water. He needed it. His nerves were still vibrating from the first spell he had ever been involved in casting. All the fantasy novels he had ever read said there was a price of some kind to pay for raising energy. He'd had no idea how spot-on that statement was. He needed a large meal and six hours of sleep on top of the drink.

The pinball of fire in his midsection warmed at the first swallow to hit his stomach, then went back to sleep, like a cat in the sun.

"You did some fancy footwork in there," Leopold said, setting down his glass. He had drunk half a beer in one long swallow. "Act like you handled fire all your life. Are you an entertainer?"

"No, I . . . I work in the gambling industry," Griffen said. "The truth is, I had no idea what to expect. It was amazing."

"That it was," Wrayburn said. "Hey, since we're bonded for eternity now, call me Cos."

"I'm Bert," said Leopold. "Just think of *Sesame Street*. My wife's name is Ernestine, and don't think we haven't heard all the jokes. Or you can call me Nautilus. It's traditional for the king to go by the name of the krewe. Once the year is up, I'm back to being Bert."

"I'm Griffen. Or Grifter, if you want."

The big man's eyebrows went up. "Like in *The Sting*?"

Griffen shrugged noncommittally. "I played a lot of poker in high school and college. Now I run a business."

"Well, you are a natural with fire," Bert said. "I am third-generation Nautilus. I'm proud as can be that they saw fit to ask me to be king this year. And it don't hurt that I own six car dealerships. The money helps."

"But the ritual," Griffen pressed. He wanted to get back onto the subject. Etienne had avoided telling him anything at all. These were his counterparts. They had to know more than he did. "What do you think happened in there?"

"Some kind of special effects," Cos said, his eyes placid but wary. "I didn't know exactly what to expect. I mean, it's been sixty years and more since that box was opened in public. At least, that's what your man Doug there said."

"We were instructed what to do," Bert said. "The instruction went only so far, you know, where to stand, how to hold the scepter. I know I never seen anything like it before. Never felt anything like it. I expect there was some kind of device in there, some kind of setup in the room, but it seemed more real than that."

"I wasn't told anything except to show up," Griffen said, resentfully. Etienne had blithely given him the time and place but nothing more. He was going to have words with the werewolf hybrid. Small wonder Etienne had disappeared as soon as the ritual broke up. Griffen wanted to confront him. He could have warned him that they were going to be performing some kind of heavy magic in public, before an unprepared and largely nonmagical public. By the time the crowds had cleared, Etienne was gone. With his gift of foreknowledge, he might have had some inkling that Griffen was pissed off.

"Maybe they thought you already knew what was up," Cos suggested. "Are you descended from a member of the original krewe? Lord knows that when we started up Antaeus again, we had to go through all the archives for our history. Amazing how little people write down when they're sure something is going to carry on in living memory. I'm making sure that every single event this year is documented, recorded, and made into a computer file as well so that we don't have to go through it all again next time."

"No. I'm from Michigan. I came to New Orleans last summer. I just graduated from college."

"You did?" Bert asked, surprised. He studied Griffen's face. "You must be some special if they asked you so soon."

"You can see why," Holly said. "He's got a gift for magic. They must have sensed that."

"I reject your supposition that what went on in there is magic," Cos said.

"What else could it be?"

"But what's all of it for?" Griffen interrupted the budding argument. "Why are you involved in this ritual?"

Holly regarded him seriously. "Well, do you believe in the concept of a sacred trust? Can you entertain the concept without going all ironical on us?"

"In theory," Griffen said honestly.

"Well, this is more than theory, isn't it?" Cos said. "It turned out to be the God's honest truth. I was told what I could expect, but I myself did not know what kind of a holy miracle it was until just a few minutes ago, and it has changed me forever. I wish I could tell my whole congregation. It was mind-blowing."

"For me, too," Griffen said, sincerely. "No argument there."

Bert nodded. "What we went through in there is the reenactment of a sacred trust passed down from king to king. It used to be that the king of a country wielded all four elemental scepters to protect his realm, but here we only have our kind of kings, who rule at Mardi Gras."

"The four elements are invoked, with spirit to bind them together, in the name of the Trinity," Cos added. "This is a sacred rite."

"I'm not really a churchgoer," Griffen said. "Would that prevent me from participating?"

"But you're not against goodness, are you?" asked Bert.

"No, just not sure what I believe. I don't impinge on other people, but organized religion is not my thing."

"Are you an atheist?" Cos demanded, his brows down.

Griffen shook his head. "I can't say exactly that I believe in a higher being; but I can't deny that what I thought of as the supernatural is in my everyday life now, since I came to New Orleans."

"I'm not surprised," Holly said, with a grin. "No matter what you believe, things happen in this city that are hard to explain anywhere else. You don't have to be a believer. We all come from different traditions, Griffen. I'm a wiccan myself. I couldn't make it to . . . Well, we'll talk later about that." Griffen understood. He had known a few wiccans in Michigan and wanted to hear more about the local practitioners. "Antaeus is a Baptist. Only Nautilus is a good Catholic."

"I'll pray for you all," Bert said, sincerely. The others groaned. "Sorry, but you are probably all lost to heaven," he said. "I hope for your souls' sakes that you find your way before God calls you home."

"I'll be in the Summerland," Holly said. "He can call me there."

"Are you blaspheming?"

"Can you call it that if it isn't your belief system?" she asked. "Look, Griffen, it doesn't matter what we call ourselves, or how we practice, or what we believe or don't. What matters is that what you did and will do protects New Orleans. It is a special place. Some major ley lines come through here. The energy centers running along the Mississippi alone could power some serious spells . . ." Bert groaned. She rounded on him. "All right, but why does a priest cense the church with incense and chanting?"

"To drive out malign energies. The devil!"

"That is what we do, too! We all call the devil by the name that has meaning to us. Darkness, chaos, evil, greed, anger. Sin is a matter of discussion, but that which hurts other living beings is just plain wrong. Can we agree on that?"

"To place it to do God's work——" Bert said.

"Or Goddess's," Holly put in, earning an annoyed scowl from him.

". . . Is a holy thing."

"I can get behind that," Griffen said. "But don't ask me to put a label on it. It wouldn't be sincere."

"All right," Cos said. "I don't want to get ugly about it."

"I have some other questions, if you don't mind," Griffen asked. "About the ritual specifically. Why, if it's important to bind the energy to protect the city, don't we do it right here and now?"

"We don't have the energy yet," Holly said. "We have to raise it to bind it. Our ritual today will start drawing out the power that is in the city, so, on the day of our parade, we can gather it up and imbue the city with the protection it needs for the next century. Really, it should have been done every decade."

"Like a booster shot?" Griffen asked, grinning. Holly grinned back.

"I don't know what the fuss is," Cos complained. "You know, we all got along okay without doing this for years."

Holly rejected his assertion. "This is a vital focus for the state and the country, even the continent. Most people ignore New Orleans except at Mardi Gras, but what happens here affects people and places for thousands of miles around it. So, we will use the energy that people give while they are here for the Carnival, and from the four elements themselves."

"It all comes from God," Bert insisted.

"I am in no position to dispute that with you," Holly said. "The higher powers are a matter of faith, as you say."

Griffen sensed they were skirting delicate subjects again. "It worried me that all that power has been cut loose without control. It seemed totally wild. Isn't that dangerous?"

"Of course it is," Cos said seriously. "We could be killed

trying to lay the power on parade day. We're all prepared for that. Aren't you?"

Griffen was taken aback. "No! I . . . I didn't really know until now what it meant to be the king."

"Well, in most krewes it's purely ceremonial—or financial. You can understand why this particular ritual hasn't been tried in a long time. When our krewes started marching again, the text was in the archives, but no one wanted to try it until all four of us were back. Now we are. And we are standing up to protect our home."

Bert cleared his throat. "I read in the Book of the Sea—that's our records—that once these scepters are unleashed, they have to be deployed in exactly the right way as soon as possible or problems start to ensue. We can't just play with them. The power has to be kept in balance. Otherwise, there are far-reaching consequences. Yes, that could be death, but if we're careful, it won't be."

Griffen felt his heart sink. He wasn't sure whether he was prepared to die for his newfound city. Etienne hadn't been open with him about the risks. He needed to make Etienne tell him what else he had foreseen. The others watched him curiously. He swallowed his ire.

"If you don't mind my asking, the ritual calls for the kings of krewes to govern the elements. You're female."

"Well, I am glad you noticed that," Holly said, her voice deeply ironical.

"I'm not objecting! But the language doesn't say 'or queens.'"

"Which is funny, when you consider that when Aeolus was founded back then, it could be led by a man or a woman, and our krewe has *always* been part of this ritual. But female kings go back past the common era, Griffen. Haven't you ever heard of Hapshetsut? Or Cleopatra? Technically, I am not a king at all. My title is Sprite of the Krewe of Aeolus. My counterpart, Ethan, is the Cyclone. You see? Nongender-specific titles. The other two, like yours, are more traditional. We actually all started out as one krewe, but it split into four after the first few

years so we could cover more ground and bless more of New
Orleans. We all used to march through the French Quarter;
but when the law was changed, frankly, it was an advantage.
The routes we chose are more specific to the compass direction
our element is ruled by. Have you seen them?" She fished a
magazine out of her large handbag and flipped to the pages at
the back. "There we are, all listed on facing pages."

Griffen examined the routes. "I see! Except for St. Charles
Avenue, we all start and end in different areas. But isn't that
just where your dens are?"

"Why do you think we chose those dens?" Cos asked,
tapping the side of his nose like Santa. Griffen pretended to
smack himself in the forehead.

"We can't march through the Quarter any longer, but
the throws will be blessed—by celebrants of our choice,"
Holly added, as Cos started to protest, "and that will help
to spread the blessing all across the city. Just keep your head
together and concentrate on what you're doing. The diary
kept by the last Sprite to wield the scepter said it was best
to relax and enjoy yourself."

"We can't have fun out there!" Bert said. "It's too serious
a matter!"

But they saw the twinkle in his eyes. Griffen relaxed.
Maybe it wasn't going to be that bad. He was fascinated
by the rituals. He really liked his fellow kings, and he truly
felt as if he had just joined a secret society. Then a thought
struck him. Was this something Harrison needed to know?
What could he tell him? And would it be more than the
man could take, with the murder of a supernatural already
on his hands?

Cos rose and put out a hand to each of them, Holly
first. "Got to go back to work. See you all at the parties,
my friends. After the parades, you are all invited to come
and enjoy some downright serious partying with my krewe.
We'd love to have you."

"Thanks!" Griffen said. "Let's talk about all kicking in to
sponsor an after-party."

"Good man," Cos said, grinning at him.

"I got to go, too," Bert said. "See you all."

"Do you need to run off?" Holly asked Griffen, as the two other men went out the door together. "I'd love to talk to you for a while."

"No problem," Griffen said. "My job doesn't really start for hours yet." He signed to the cocktail waitress for a refill of their glasses.

"My high priestess went to your conclave," Holly said, a little hesitantly. "So I know who you are. I mean, what."

"A dragon," Griffen said. "Some people know. Most don't. But I didn't hide it from the attendees."

"No, they were pretty proud to have you there," Holly said. "It was a big deal. You *feel* different than most people. I have talent, and so do Cos and Bert, though they may not be aware of it. In fact, there are a lot of people in our four krewes who are touched in one way or another, but you don't feel like any of us."

"I am beginning to understand that," Griffen said.

"I could feel the difference between our folks and everyone in your krewe. You're all dragons in Fafnir, aren't you?"

"I can only tell you that I am," Griffen said. "I don't have the right to discuss anyone else."

"But I can feel . . . never mind." She grinned. "You're absolutely right. We have the same tradition in my group. That is so cool. I wonder if you'd like to get together after all this is over and talk about things? Sometime in March?"

"I'd love to," Griffen said. "The conclave was my first exposure to most of you, too."

"Well," Holly said, with a little smile that brought up the dimples in her cheeks, "there's a lot of us out there. You'd be surprised."

"Not anymore, I wouldn't," Griffen said. He held up his glass, and she touched hers to it.

"Cheers, brother king," she said. "We're going to make this a memorable Mardi Gras."

"To the safety of New Orleans," Griffen said.

Twenty-six

The river had had many names since human beings came to live on its banks. It had a consciousness, but it had never given itself a name. Why limit itself with syllables, when its definition was the riverbanks, the earth beneath it, and the sky? When the rains were heavy, it grew. When the air was dry, it shrank, but it moved to its own rhythm.

It had been there millennia, long before the tribes of humans came to stay, long before the first blues musician beat out the long, slow, sad pace of his song inspired by the majestic flow. The Mississippi, as humans called it now, was the life's blood of New Orleans. It was vital to the city. None of its unique history, its music, or its people would be in that place without it.

Usually, the river made little note of the time it spent passing through this place. All water throughout the world was one great pool, like the blood dispersed through the vessels in a living body. But today, it picked up a rhythm of ancient power. It had felt this beat before. It stirred the waters a little, unsettled them. It called for them to wake up and be aware. And act.

The sun's rays beat down upon the river's dancing surface. The heat, coming from both above and deep below, felt the imbalance. Steam rose in tiny curlicues from the surface. The winds, too, felt it, zigzagging against the predicted weather patterns. The muddy bottom of the river rumbled, sending bubbles of gas to the surface. Within one of them, a creature that had been asleep for decades stirred and woke up. It kicked itself free of the diaphanous cocoon and shot away into the flow.

"We'll be dockin' in a moment," the master of ceremonies aboard the *Delta Queen* riverboat announced into the public address system over the mellow strains of the Dixieland jazz band at the stern. "We all certainly hope you enjoyed your lunch cruise with us. Tell all your friends! And come on back! We'd love to see you all again."

The diners seated at the white-covered iron tables didn't notice the hulking figure homing in on the riverboat. It was attracted to the sound of the engine driving the paddlewheel, thrumming like a heartbeat. The creature zipped around under the surface, listening.

Mama? it wondered.

But the boat didn't reply. The river creature, hoping to get an answer, nudged hard. The boat rocked gently. The creature levered itself up and smacked down hard on the surface of the water.

A wave of dirty green water washed up and over the lower deck of the paddleboat. Diners and musicians stood up hastily as the wave swished over their shoes.

"What in hell was that?" demanded an accountant from Illinois.

"River monster," said the trombone player, an elderly black man whose white hair was clipped very short under his straw boater. "Dey turn up once and again."

The tourist shook his head and sat down to empty the water out of his shoes.

"Somebody," he said to his wife, "has had a few too many Sazeracs."

"You saw it, too?" the saxophone player asked his comrade.

"Sure did," the trombone player said, turning the page in his sheet music. "Oh, yeah. Reminds me of dem days before de war."

The boat still didn't answer the creature. It slithered away, listening hard for the right voice.

Twenty-seven

"**Hey**, babe, can a guy get some service around here?"

Val jerked her head up from the book she was reading. The man who had spoken was only two seats away from where she stood behind the bar. She glanced at the clock. It was five thirty. The bar had been empty since she had started her shift an hour before. She hadn't expected to see anyone but a local for a half hour yet. She smiled at him.

"I'm so sorry. What would you like?"

"The house special." He looked her up and down, evidently liking what he saw. He flirted his eyes at her. He had very long eyelashes over dark blue eyes. In fact, he was good-looking enough to be a movie star. The shoulders under the blue pin-striped white shirt were broad and the midriff appealingly slim. "Can I get that to go?"

"Bloody Mary or Hurricane?"

"Hurricane sounds like more fun."

"One Hurricane, coming up," Val said, reaching for a plastic go-cup. She poured four ounces of rum into a shaker, added passion-fruit syrup and a stream of lemon juice, then poured it over ice.

"Is that what you call yourself, lovely lady? Hurricane?"

Val smiled at him and felt for the blackjack under the bar. "Sorry, but I'm not on the menu."

"Too bad," he said. "I'm Dale, by the way."

"Val." She put the drink on a paper napkin in front of him. "Three-fifty, please."

He put a five-dollar bill down and slid it toward her. "Sorry to come on so strong, but wow! I never expected to see anyone like you serving drinks in a, well, dump. You ought to be modeling high fashion."

Val had no illusions about being a member of the ranks of underweight waifs who pouted on magazine pages. "They'd never want me. You look like you probably modeled, yourself," she said.

Dale grimaced. "You guessed my dirty secret. Yeah. I paid my way through college doing catalogs. I'm in town for the convention. I bet you get a lot of people coming in here." He lifted the Hurricane to her and drank. "God, that's sweet."

"They're very popular with tourists."

"Touché," he said. "Normally, my drink is a dirty martini."

"All the martinis are pretty popular these days," Val agreed.

He grinned. "Oops. Didn't mean to be trendy." He was trying hard to make up for being a jerk when he came in.

He *was* cute. Val admired the line of his jaw. His hands were long and fine, with oval nails. "It's quiet in here. Don't you get much business?"

"Not during the day," she said. "This place is a little out of the way for conventioneers and sports fans. We have a lot of local clients starting about now."

"Oh, so you're not getting off for a while." He looked disappointed.

"Not until midnight," she said. She did find him attractive. It might be nice if he came back at the end of her shift. A little attention from a handsome stranger went a long way toward brightening the day.

She's not really showing yet, the thought popped into Val's head. *I bet she'd look sexy in her underwear.*

She frowned. Was she projecting what he might think of her without her clothes? He lifted the glass to her again, drank, then set it far away from him. "That's really god-awful. How about a martini? Would you like to join me?"

"I'll have a Diet Coke, thanks," she said, pouring fresh

drinks for both of them. He paid and added a tip. She liked that he was even generous in offering a gratuity for the drink he had bought her. Of course, it might just be because he was trying to pick her up.

I don't want to have to wait for midnight, the thought came urgently.

Val licked her lips. Her subconscious rarely seemed so loud. Maybe she really did want to be with him that badly. She liked the way he moved, the way he smiled, the warm baritone of his voice.

"So, you thinking of hanging around for a while?" she asked, casually. "I mean, it's a long time."

"If that's what it takes to get a chance to be alone with you, it'll seem like minutes," Dale said, winking at her.

She's going to be impatient if it takes until midnight to get out of here, the thought came.

She? Val didn't think of herself in the third person. Those insistent thoughts weren't hers. She had never had that happen before. Was this a new facet of dragon power that was just starting to manifest itself?

Movement near the door made her look up. Just outside the bar, two people stood on the sidewalk, looking at her intently. They looked like locals. One wore a T-shirt and an old waistcoat over baggy pants and untied athletic shoes. The other had on a flat, shiny leather cap and jeans jacket. Dale glanced over her shoulder.

Who the hell are they?

Val stared at him. Those strange intrusions were *his* thoughts.

"Who the hell are *you*?" she asked.

"Just a visitor," he said, trying to keep an expression of innocence, but it no longer rang true. The two local men came in, still staring at Dale.

She's going to be angry.

Val suddenly figured out who "she" was. She glared at Dale.

"Drink up and get out of here," she said.

"Oh, come on, babe," he said, leaning forward persuasively. He lowered his eyelashes again. It was evidently the move that worked on women the most. "I apologize if I was pushing too hard. We could still have a little date later on," he added. He looked hopeful.

"No fucking way. Tell Melinda that she can shove it up her wide ass, sending a pretty boy to seduce me. Go."

Shit! They didn't tell me she was telepathic!

Val seized the blackjack. "There's a lot of things they didn't tell you about me," she said. "I was captain of my gymnastics team." Setting one hand on the bar, she vaulted over it. Dale jumped backward in surprise. "Now, get out before you're sorry you came in."

"Hey, I don't know anyone named Me—"

His thoughts said otherwise. Val swung a wide arc with the blackjack and slapped him in the temple. He staggered sideways, clutching his head. Val followed up with a kick in the stomach that sent him backward over a chair. He fell on the floor. Val stood over him, brandishing the sack of lead shot.

"You go and tell her to leave me alone! The next person that bothers me won't get a warning. All they will find is pieces of the body! Everywhere! Get out of here!"

She raised the blackjack over her head. Dale scuttled backward on his hands and feet like a crab. When he was safely in between the tables, he got to his feet. Keeping his eyes on her, he edged out the door.

Gotta warn her, was the last thought Val picked up. *Can't tell her about . . .*

No, he wouldn't admit to Melinda that Val had figured he was a fraud or that she had hit him. Twice.

She turned a sour face to the two men near the door. "I suppose my brother sent you?" They nodded. "Weren't you going to help me?"

"Mr. Griffen said that you'd get mad if we helped before you asked," the shorter one said. "Besides, we could tell you could handle him."

"We listened to his thoughts all the way here," said the

taller one, in a fluty alto. "He was countin' on you fallin' for his looks. He couldn't take you nowhere. We heard everythin' he thought he would do."

"Then why didn't you send him somewhere else?"

"It's not the way our talents work, ma'am. We just listen."

"Oh," Val said. "It doesn't work both ways?"

"Thank God, no! It ain't a curse, just a talent!"

"Don't want to have no one hear our thoughts. It's none of anyone's damned business what we think."

"Nope," agreed the taller one.

"Nope," confirmed the shorter one.

Val studied them. "I think I saw you the other night."

"Yes, ma'am, near the diner. Manuel near the door thinks you're gorgeous and wishes you'd go out with him instead of Gris-gris, but he afraid."

"Of me?"

"More of Gris-gris," said the alto. "You should hear what *he* thinks!"

Val blushed. "It's probably better if I don't. But you stop reading my thoughts, or you're next for some of this!" She hefted the cosh.

"Yes, ma'am," the alto said, grinning. "We know you mean it. Y'all have yourself a nice day, now, Ms. Val."

They slipped out the door. Val wondered where they went, then decided as long as they gave her a heads-up on trouble, she didn't need them hanging around.

She walked around the bar and got her cell phone out of her purse. Griffen needed to know about Melinda's latest attempt to trick her.

While the phone rang, she put the blackjack away in its hiding place. When she straightened up, she saw gouges on the inside lip of the bar. Five round holes had been drilled through the wood. She must have transformed, at least a little, when she jumped over it. Her claws had punched them, and she had not even noticed.

"Now, how am I going to explain those to Todd?" she asked.

Twenty-eight

"**All** in favor, den?" Etienne said, looking around at the membership jammed into the increasingly crowded workshop. Dragon's heads, in every stage of completion, loomed over their heads. The captain counted the raised hands. "Ain't no point in countin' dose against."

"Do it anyhow," Callum Fenway said, with an exasperated shake of his head.

Etienne smiled at him placidly. "Whatevah. Dose against? Easy. King Griffen's proposal passes. All jobs open equally to all adult members from here on out. 'Cept mine." He smiled, showing his sharp canines.

Griffen heaved a sigh of pleasure. Several of the members came up to slap him on the back.

"Glad you did that," Louis, one of the department heads said, coming up with a clipboard. Nearly as tall as Griffen, he had an aquiline profile and sharp cheekbones. "My wife's been doing all the work all along anyhow. I'm not as organized as she is. This is my last day on the job. After today, I am just one of her Indians, and she is my chief." The petite woman at his side took the clipboard from his hand.

"Thank you, Griffen," Carmen said.

Griffen smiled. "My pleasure."

The switch to a gender-neutral committee was just the first change he hoped to make. Since the Ritual of the Four Elements, the krewe deferred to him even more than they had after the first meeting at the Fenways'. He figured there was no better time to try to push through his suggestions. Val had been pleased when he had told her what he wanted to do. They discussed joining the krewe on a permanent basis after the season was over, but only if there were no barriers in Val's way.

"Well, we've got loads of work to do," Carmen said. "You forgot to order that small-gauge chicken wire. Excuse us, Griffen." They headed for one of the tables against the wall. Griffen himself went to join Lucinda's papier-mâché squad. They were plastering a figure of an embattled St. George that day, an irony that Griffen enjoyed, having faced off against the ancient hero's modern equivalent twice already.

Once Twelfth Night had passed, New Orleans shifted into Mardi Gras mode and hit the gas. The stores selling throws in Jackson Square and in the stalls at the French Market filled to overflowing with glittering, glowing, flashing stock. Stores put out racks of ready-made costumes and formal wear. Announcements for parties and tableaux that the public could attend were listed in the newspapers and on posters stuck on walls and displayed in windows everywhere in the French Quarter. Everyone pored over the annual guide to decide which parades they were going to watch and discuss the best places from which to watch them. Griffen added a new envelope almost every day to his stack of invitations to masquerade balls and parties. He would have to ask Etienne or one of the other lieutenants which ones he could honorably decline with thanks. The ones he had to accept cut severely into the remaining balance in his bank account. He was finding it hard to keep up on his salary and his poker winnings.

And the crowds started to pour into town. Some visitors would come in waves to enjoy a few days of the run-up or the festival itself; others intended to stay through until Ash Wednesday.

But the party was not and had never been aimed at visitors. It was for New Orleans itself. The tradition of celebrating the period before Lent dated back to 1768. The colors of Mardi Gras were always there in the background, but stores and houses began to dress themselves up with the theme. Harlequins in purple, gold, and green popped up as mannequins clinging to lampposts, toys for children, or wall decorations of all kinds. Griffen noticed the white-faced carnival masks peering blank-eyed at him from window displays and advertisements. People were already wearing masks. He bought groceries from a girl in a fan-shaped yellow-feathered mask, and had coffee served to him by a man in a red-sequined domino and matching derby hat.

The costumers had a steady stream of locals coming and going with at least one and sometimes up to a dozen outfits for the season. Getting into conversations with friends in the Irish pub and elsewhere, Griffen discovered quite a few who had been descended from original krewe members. Nautilus and Aeolus invited him home to see home movies, including new DVD copies of ancient, hand-cranked films that reminded him of early Hollywood newsreels. Though the first parades were primitive compared with what he saw in modern videos, they had mystique and grandeur. If he had not already become part of the upcoming festival, he would have longed for a place in it.

The Krewe of Fafnir wasn't a perfect organization. They had supported Griffen's efforts to change, but mostly because he was at the top of a pecking order that became more evident each time he was with them. Etienne was behind Griffen a hundred percent, not that that seemed to cut much ice with the existing lieutenants. Though they treated him with the respect due the founder, or refounder, and captain of the krewe, on a personal level they were dismissive of someone with so little dragon blood.

He refilled one of the buckets at the utility sink next to the lavatory and came up in the middle of an argument between Mitchell Grade and Etienne.

"Who are you tellin' me what to do? Couldn't light a birthday candle," Mitchell snarled.

"Still tellin' ya what to do," Etienne said.

"The hound dog telling the alligator? That's rich. You got no authority over me, son. Coming from the back of beyond with no more in common with me than a tree. Back off! You don't get it. You couldn't."

"Hey!" Griffen protested. "You act like he works for you. It's the other way around, isn't it?"

"Sorry, Griffen," Mitchell said. "He is just out of his grade here, that's all. I'm making decisions that are fitting to a real dragon, something he can't understand."

Griffen frowned. "This is probably none of my business, but . . ."

"Well, you are right! This discussion *is* none of your business, okay?"

Griffen drew himself up. He felt scales breaking out on his hands and neck. He pushed up to the big man and looked him square in the eye. "Really? And what if I told you I thought none of you were worth *my* time?" The time Griffen had been expecting had come, where they would challenge him. If it turned into a fight, he was spoiling for it. What would Mitchell do first? Go dragon, or try to overpower him with influence?

Instead, Mitchell backed off a pace. "Well, we'd have to take your word for it, Griffen. But you don't, do you? Otherwise, why are you here?"

Griffen aimed a thumb at Etienne. "Because *he* asked me! The one you're insulting! A dragon's *a dragon*!" A roar rose up near them.

"Fire!" a voice near them bellowed in alarm. Griffen turned around. Wild flames were licking up from the float that he and the others had just been working on. They leaped for the ceiling. The fire alarm began to wail.

"Water!" Lucinda's clear voice came over the shouting. "Griffen!"

Griffen looked down. He realized he was still holding a full bucket. He ran to hand the water up to Jacob, who was standing on a ladder beside the sculpture. Mitchell grabbed another bucket and stuck it under the tap. The krewe formed a bucket brigade, pouring pail after pail of water on the blaze. Smoke blanketed the room. The orange tongues of fire flickered, then disappeared.

"Hold it!" bellowed Jacob. "I think that's it!"

Griffen and the others halted. They were covered with water and flakes of soot. His eyes stung from the smoke.

"Damm it all," Callum said. "Did we get it?"

One of the others reached inside the now-blackened, skeletal framework and felt around. "It's out."

"We're gonna have to let the fire marshal in to confirm," Terence said. "He'd better not blab about what we've got going on in here. What the hell started it?"

"I don't know what happened!" Jacob protested. "It was still wet. How could it catch fire like that?"

"No idea," Callum said. "Never mind, it's over."

"What a shame," Lucinda said, bringing hand towels to the firefighters. "That's the part you just finished, Griffen. We'll have to do it all over again."

A hand grabbed Griffen's arm. Griffen turned to blink at Etienne. The captain leaned in and spoke softly.

"Mr. Griffen, you gotta calm youself down. You gonna cause a lot of damage if you don'."

"I was only defending you," Griffen said.

"I can take care of myself, but t'anks, huh?"

"Yeah." Griffen turned to Mitchell, who was wiping smudges off his own face. "I'm sorry, Mitchell. I don't mean to pull rank. But you see what it feels like to be on the receiving end?"

"Yeah, I know. Not like it hasn't happened to me other places in my life," Mitchell said. "Ignorant humans—what do they know? I know I wouldn't like it if you decided to walk away from us, but what could we say? You got to make your own decisions about that. Hoping you won't, of course."

Griffen studied him. "It was pretty arrogant of me to push my views on you, but I really do feel strongly about it.

If you know anything about me by now, I choose the people I hang out with by their merits, not their bloodlines. I'd be an idiot to think I could do better than all of you on this stuff. It's right out of my league. If I'd been in charge, this would be a ten-year project, not two."

"Yeah, but you're learning," Mitchell said, grinning. "I don't mind learning a little, too. You're gonna be a force to be reckoned with one day, son. I just hope you remember the little dragons who helped you along the way."

"Where?" Griffen said, pretending to look around with an innocent expression on his face. "I don't see any little dragons here."

"Man, Etienne, you are good," Mitchell said, slapping both of them on the back. "This boy is a whole lot more than just a hand to wield the scepter."

"That is what I tol' you, Mitchell," Etienne said, no more perturbed than he had been before. "You gots to learn to listen to me better."

Mitchell took in a deep breath. "Yeah, I do."

Griffen breathed a sigh of relief, too.

Twenty-nine

Griffen slid into a booth in Yo Mama's Bar and Grill. He ordered a Peanut Butter Burger, a combination he would never have tried anywhere but the French Quarter. It was not only unexpectedly good, but addictive. Griffen often ordered other things off the menu, but always came back to his favorite. He licked the rich combination of oil and meat juice off his fingers as he made notes in a pocket notebook from a sheaf of paperwork on one side of the table.

He had just come from the last of the four restaurants holding rooms for him. The hospitality directors had all been friendly but harried. They gave him price lists, catering menus, and sample contracts. They were all excellent, top-rated restaurants. It was a hard choice to decide on one of them, but in the end there was one standout, a beautiful white-tablecloth establishment over seventy years old on the edge of the park at the north end of the Quarter. He and Val ate there once in a while and always enjoyed it. It wasn't as fancy as Commander's Palace, for example, but it had an elegance and an easygoing charm. He flipped open his cell phone and dialed.

The hospitality director was glad that he had finally made up his mind. "I'd do anything for Etienne de la Fee," he said, "but people have been hounding me because they know that room is still open. I will be some glad to be able to tell them it's booked. Come in in the next couple of days and we'll sit down and make arrangements. You need the floor plan?"

Griffen sifted through the pile of paperwork, ready to

say no, when he came up with a layout for the grand private dining room. He had not even thought to ask for one when he toured the restaurant. Etienne must have given it to him. That accurate a gift for foresight made him shiver.

"No, I've got one. When can we talk? Say, Thursday?"

"Right. Come after lunchtime. I'll feed you, but let the lunch crowd die down first, okay? We'll be proud to host your king's party. It's an honor, Griffen."

Griffen courteously called the other three restaurants to tell them their rooms were free and they could rent them out, and thanked them for holding them for him. They each asked him to think of them the next time he was planning a party.

"I sure will," Griffen promised. "I love your food." It was the truth. Those were the top restaurants in town. He had come a long way from eating only fast food and microwave frozen dishes, Even though there were days when he still did that, too. But New Orleans had vastly expanded his culinary range.

"Hey, Grifter," Jerome said. He sat down opposite Griffen and accepted a menu from the uniformed waitress. "How's it going?"

"Not bad, Jer," Griffen said. "What can I do for you?"

The two of them never mentioned the New Year's Eve argument aloud, but they had patched up their differences within a day. Jerome reminded Griffen that his choices, however wrongheaded he felt them to be, were final as far as the operation went. With that kind of authority handed to him, Griffen had been very careful to consider what he was doing. He just couldn't see any harm in Peter Sing, and Peter had never caused a single problem.

"Just remindin' you that I won't be around on February 16. Can't answer the phone, can't help out with crises. That okay with you?"

"Sure," Griffen said. "Something wrong?"

"Oh, hell, no," Jerome said, grinning. "That's when my marching society steps off."

Griffen settled back in the booth. "I've heard a little about them. Are they like a parade?"

"They pretty much predate parades," Jerome said. "No floats. A few bands and other units go with us, but everyone is on foot. By the way, Marcel's in my group. A few of the others, too. They'll all need that day off. Might as well shut down the operation for the day."

"We may have to shut down on a few other days during the parade weeks," Griffen said. "You're not the only one to tell me you need the day off. I can't believe how many of the people who work with us are involved in a krewe or a marching society. Or bands. Kitty said she is supposed to play saxophone in five parades. *Five.* I feel out of breath just thinking about it."

"Oh, yeah, boss-man," Jerome said, holding up his cup for the waitress. She poured coffee for him and Griffen. "We really get into it here. History of celebratin' Fat Tuesday goes all the way back to the very beginning of the colony of New Orleans. For me, I started up with the marching society after Mose made me into a functional being all those years ago. I still go out with 'em. You ought to come out and hang with us. It's a lot of fun. Plenty of drinking, bawdy songs. It's a great time. May not get back until after midnight."

"Sounds good to me," Griffen said. "A day off wouldn't do me any harm. I hate to ask this, but how much?"

"Bring your own costume and your own throws and booze, and you're in," Jerome said.

"I love this city," Griffen said, with a laugh. "Hey, I could use your advice. I have to plan this king's party."

"Fancy parties are beyond me," Jerome said. "I'd end up reading Emily Post and Miss Manners to cram for the exam, but I never made one up myself."

"The girls are coming to help me plan. Trouble is, every time I come up with a good idea, it seems to cost a fortune. I've tried calling Mose to see how he handled all the expenses thrown at him, back in the old days, but he's still avoiding me. I hope he's okay."

Jerome waved his coffee cup. "He's fine. I'll tell you what he told me when I didn't know to trust my own judgment. Say no first, then think about it. If you still love an idea later, do it. If you decide against it, someone else had better come up with a damned solid reason why you need to cover it. I'll help in any way I can, you know that, but the final word still has to come from you."

"And that's the big problem," Griffen said. "I have a tough time saying no to myself."

"So show me your plans," Jerome said. "I'll be happy to stick my two cents in."

"Wait until the girls get here. Val has to start work at four, and Lisa gets off at two, so I told them to meet me here."

The three women arrived in a group, giggling together over the contents of a paper bag. Mai sat down beside Griffen before Fox Lisa could get into the long seat. Instead, the redhead slid in beside Jerome.

"Shove over," Val told Mai.

"Pull up a chair," Mai said. Val shook her head. She sat down on the bench seat and pushed in until the smaller woman was jammed between her and Griffen.

"That's better," Val said.

"Thanks for coming," Griffen said.

"We could have done this at the Irish pub later on," Mai said. "In much less discomfort."

"I don't need everyone weighing in with their ideas," Griffen said. "I need some help, but not that much."

"So, what do you have so far?"

"I have a location and a few ideas." Griffen showed them the catering sheets from the restaurant.

"Nice place," Fox Lisa said. "I used to bus tables there a few summers ago while I was in school. Good people. The kitchen's clean as a whistle. Elegant but not stuffy."

"What are you serving?" Val asked.

"That's what I need some help deciding," Griffen said. "Don't go too crazy on me. Take a look at what they want per person for banquets."

"Hokey smoke, Bullwinkle!" Val exclaimed. "I thought they were expensive in the regular dining room!"

"What about sole stuffed with shrimp?" Mai asked. "That sounds delicious."

Griffen winced. It was the most expensive thing on the menu. Trust Mai to go straight for that. "Try to keep the cost reasonable, okay?"

"Forget the expenses, this is your party! When are you ever going to be king again?"

"Always," Griffen said, with a straight face. "That's what I want to be called from now on. Griffen Rex."

"Y'can't be called 'Rex' in this town, pal," Fox Lisa said. "Not unless you actually are. That's taken."

He laughed. "Okay, King Griffen."

"Very well, Your Majesty," Mai said. "What price range are you hoping for?"

Griffen went down the options. The five of them hashed over the set menus and glanced at the à la carte lists. With an eye on Jerome, Griffen said no to everything that sounded too costly until the others justified it as reasonable. In the end, they picked out four entrées: fish, meat, fowl, and vegetarian, plus a soup, salad, and dessert that played to the strengths of the chef.

"That's great," Griffen said, putting the papers in a heap. "Now all I have to work on is the theme."

"Well, what about the parade theme?" Mai asked. "Why don't you use that? It's ready-made for the krewe. Could that work into your dinner?"

Griffen opened his mouth, then closed it again. "You almost got me," he said, as Val laughed uproariously. "I nearly told you."

"But what is it?" Fox Lisa asked. "We've been trying on those costumes, but none of us can guess from the design."

Griffen shook his head. "I'm sworn to secrecy," he said, mysteriously. "Look, I have my own idea for the party." He flipped open his small notebook and showed them a series of crude sketches. "I'm not much of an artist, but here's what

I thought: I want to line the walls of the room with movie posters on easels, only all the titles will have dragon themes." He eyed them speculatively. "Like *Gone With the Wing*."

"Ohhhhh," moaned Fox Lisa. "Not puns!"

"Why not?" Jerome asked, laughing. "How about *Goldbusters*? Who y'gonna call?"

"I thought of *The Wyvern of Oz*," Griffen said.

"*Two Gremlins of Verona*," Val threw out. "Wait, those aren't dragons."

"*Hatching Can Wait*," suggested Jerome.

The others laughed at each new suggestion. Griffen wrote them down as fast as he could. When they finished, he had over twenty that he thought were funny.

"These are going to be great. I'll choose about six or eight of these," he said.

"Who's doing it for you?"

"One of Steamboat's cousins is an artist," Griffen said, naming a fellow barfly in the Irish pub. "He'll draw them up for me and get them printed. Everyone's going to get a miniature poster as a favor, an eight-by-ten print at their place setting."

"That's really clever," Fox Lisa said. "It won't be too expensive, and it's unique. I thought you were going to give everyone a picture of you in your regalia."

Griffen struck a pose. "You think they'd like that better?"

"Oh, well, there's another one for your movie titles," Val said, laughing. "*The Dragon Who Would Be King*. You'll have to have your face on the poster."

"*Goldfinger*," Fox Lisa suggested. "That already sounds like a dragon name."

"No, *Goldwinger*!" Mai said.

Jerome leaned back and shook out a cigarette. "You know you don't have to try this hard, Grifter. They're already impressed to death with you."

"I want to get it right," Griffen said, feeling the need intensely. "Like Mai said, when will I get another chance?"

Jerome grinned at him. "You're on your way to becoming

a pillar of the community. Good job, Grifter." He flicked his lighter. Instead of the inch-high flame, a gout of fire gushed upward. Jerome dropped it on his plate. It didn't go out. The flames seemed to consume what was left of his sandwich and fries as if they were made of tissue paper.

"Put it out," Mai ordered him.

"I didn't do that!" Jerome said.

"Not you. Griffen."

"Me?"

"You started it. I felt it. Put it out. Now! Concentrate."

Griffen stared at the flame, feeling silly. The waitress had hoisted a fire extinguisher from behind the counter and headed toward them. *Go out,* he thought. *Go out now!*

The flames died away into a pool of congealed ketchup. Griffen regarded it with confusion.

Jerome headed off the waitress. "It's okay!" he called. "Sorry about that. I gotta give up smokin'. Maybe this was God's way of reminding me. Sorry!"

"What just happened?" Griffen asked.

Mai smiled. "It looks as if you have a new addition to your secondary powers," she said. "What were you thinking before that happened?"

"I just . . . I just want what I'm doing to work out right," Griffen said.

"You were feeling something deeply. Try it again. Start a fire, right there, but in a small way."

Griffen looked at the charred hamburger. *Burn,* he thought. *Just a little.*

He almost jumped out of his skin when smoke started curling up from the blackened bun.

Out! Go out!

Just as swiftly, the smoke died away.

"Now, that is one useful talent," Jerome said. "You never have to carry a lighter again, Grifter."

"That's amazing," Fox Lisa said. "Cool party trick."

"Do you have it, too?" Griffen asked Val.

Val tried to focus on the remains of Jerome's lunch. She

wrinkled her forehead and her face turned red. "No," she said. "If I'm going to get this one, it'll be later. That's okay. I would be afraid of burning the place down anytime someone lit a cigarette. You ought to be concerned about setting yourself on fire in your sleep, Griffen."

"True," Mai said. "You will have to watch your temper as well."

Griffen looked at her, bemused. It was almost exactly what Etienne had said to him in the den. That meant that he was the one who had made the float catch fire. That suggested to him that it wasn't a natural progression of his powers. It might have something to do with having handled the Scepter of Fire. He'd have to call Holly Goldberg, and ask her if she was having any similar effects from touching her scepter. In the meantime, he needed to be on his guard against excesses of emotion. It *was* good to be the king, but it left him with a new and very dangerous responsibility.

Great, he thought. *Now I'm a walking torch. What next?*

Thirty

"**Shuffle** up and deal," said the dealer, taking her own advice. Her name was Kitty. She fanned the cards out between her slender hands, riffled the two piles together, and combined them with a wrenching sound. The players kept their hands on either side of their stacks of chips.

Rebecca sat at the end of the table, watching the dealer's hands. A second dealer, Wallace, sat in a chair against the wall, keeping an eye on the game. He would step in later, the players were told, to spell the young woman. It was not explained but understood that his job was also to keep an eye out for misbehavior among the players. Rebecca found it annoying. It was far easier to cause mischief when the dealer was tired or looking the other way.

She shifted a fraction in her seat. Because of the previous incident, she had been denied access to any further games in Griffen McCandles's operation. Therefore, Winston instructed her to disguise herself and infiltrate again. If that avatar was thrown out as well, she could shift to another appearance and another. It was, he told her, a chance to explore other states of being. She didn't like wearing a strange face; but if her mentor told her that was what was expected of her, she did it. And what was New Orleans for if not to explore one's sexuality?

To remove all suspicion from the minds of these puny humans that she had played with them before, she had transformed herself into a man. Not just a man, but a tall, thin, fair man with large blue eyes and broad shoulders. Working in a mirror, she based the facial features on a movie star whom she admired, one with a high degree of dragon blood and therefore worthy of her adulation. As a result, she had full lips, a strong chin, high cheekbones, a straight nose and brows. The movie star's eyes and hair were very dark, but she wanted to be a blonde. It was a striking combination. All eyes had turned to her when she entered the room. She had done a good job.

She checked the two cards held facedown. Ace and nine of diamonds. Workable. With professional scrutiny, she examined the way her opponents held themselves. The older man to her left, Mel, who smelled much too strongly of aftershave, was a poor player with many tells. He should not be there. Ira, next to him, was much better, with sharp eyes accustomed to keeping secrets. He was likely to be a corporate lawyer. Beside him, opposite Rebecca, was Nicky, another male almost as handsome as she was. His thick brown hair was just a little too long, and he kept his lips pursed slightly in a sardonic grin. The last player, Penny, was a woman in her forties. She was plain. She kept sneaking glances at Rebecca and the other good-looking player. Her tells were in her fingers. She must have a good hand; she kept checking the cards to see that they were still there. Rebecca would have no trouble with these players. She deliberately lost the first hand.

"So," said the long-haired man across the table, "where are you from?"

"San Jose," she said. She glanced at her hand. A king and a jack.

"Never been there. What is it like?"

"A town," Rebecca said tersely.

"My, aren't you precise!" She glanced up at Nicky's sarcastic tone. His eyes sparkled with mischief.

"I am here to play cards," she said. But she couldn't resist a glance at him. He was very good-looking, and he was clearly interested in her. He winked. Rebecca felt her cheeks redden.

"Ah," he said. "Thought so."

Rebecca concentrated hard on her cards. In a few hands more she would learn enough about her fellow players so she could choose the victim to accuse and ruin the game. She bid. Mel and Ira raised. Penny folded. Another round of bidding left Rebecca and Nicky as the only contenders. The turn revealed another nine. She put in a cautious raise. He matched her.

"So," he said, "what do you like in a man?"

"His liver," Rebecca shot back. "Grilled."

The others laughed. The long-haired man seemed a trifle rebuffed.

"You have got a sharp tongue, haven't you?"

"What do you care, as long as you think you can beat me at this table?" Rebecca said.

"Well, I was thinking of later on," Nicky said. "I hope the rest of you don't mind."

"Oh, I don't," said Penny, though she looked a little disappointed. "You only live once."

"Seriously," Nicky said, leaning over the table toward Rebecca. "I have to tell you, bro, that my gaydar broke out all over the place the moment you walked in."

"What did you say?" Rebecca stammered. The others broke out laughing. She remembered at that moment that she was supposed to be a man. She deepened her voice. "What kind of remark is that?"

Nicky shook his head. "Don't try to tell me you've got a girlfriend back home. You don't do women, do you?"

"No!" Rebecca shouted. "Not that it is any of your business."

"Well, how'd you like to have a boyfriend right here in New Orleans? On a temporary basis, of course. If I go home to Randy with a souvenir like you, he's likely to beat my head in."

"And you think I'm not?"

Nicky looked even more intrigued. "So you like it rough? Hmmm." He lowered his eyelashes at her. "So, do I have to tell you my safe word?"

Rebecca threw in her cards without thinking. Nicky grinned. She realized that he was teasing her, almost certainly in hopes of throwing off her game. Furious, she collected her wits. She would show this ape-descendant how easy it was to trifle with her!

One might almost have heard the fanfare of the "Waltz of the Toreadors" as Kitty dealt them the next hand. Rebecca claimed her two kings and buckled down to serious work.

Within eight hands, she had cleaned out Mel and Penny. Two more rounds took down Ira, who threw her a mock salute.

"I surrender," he said. "Just pleased that I was beaten by a better man."

Man! Rebecca thought, with some satisfaction. At last she was passing!

One more hour, sitting as still as a statue behind her growing stacks of chips so as to give nothing away, she threw bets back and forth with Nicky. At one forty in the morning, both dealers flagging, she turned over the last hand to show the king and ace of spades, to match the king and aces of hearts and clubs on the table. Nicky threw up his arms.

"Wow! Well, would you like to get a drink to celebrate?" he asked.

Rebecca pushed her chips to Wallace. "Cash me out," she snapped.

Her feeling of superior smugness lasted all the way back to Jordan Ma's suite, where he was expounding to the others about the game he had just played. He gestured Rebecca to a chair. She could hardly sit still, so eager was she to tell her story.

"The sad looks on their faces," Jordan said. "That man Jerome did not want to offend the manufacturing millionaire from Ohio, but he did not like yet another accusation of a fraudulent game. We have all our stake back, and the house loses its percentage and, if I am not wrong, at least two of the high-betting players they entertain."

"Cool," Peter said, blowing ring after ring of smoke toward the ceiling. "How about you, Rebecca? Break a few hearts tonight?"

Rebecca smiled. She opened her purse and dumped the piles of cash onto the coffee table. "I did not leave them a single dollar."

Winston Long looked at her blankly. She knew that meant disapproval. "You were supposed to lose."

With a shock, she remembered. Her jaw dropped.

"I am sorry," she said.

Peter hit himself in the forehead with the flat of his hand. "You only had to remember one thing! You are so stupid!"

Rebecca glared at him. "I do not answer to you!"

"But you do answer to me," Winston said, putting a fingertip down on the tabletop. "Why did you not follow instructions?"

Rebecca hated to answer in front of the others. Peter grinned at her. "I lost my temper. But I beat all of them! They did not leave happy!"

Winston and Jordan exchanged glances.

"You are young, child," Winston said. "Are you too young for this mission?"

"No, elder one! I promise!"

"You must calm down. It will serve you well in future. Do you need a mantra or a mnemonic to remember your instructions?"

"No, sir." Rebecca was shamed. She felt her whole body grow hot. She pulled her consciousness in on itself so as not to give Peter the satisfaction of knowing how much she had disgraced herself.

Jordan Ma lit a cigarette with a breath of flame. "It is not all bad that we have taken all the money. That will annoy the players as well. They will go where they have a chance of winning."

"It is not a bad strategy—once in a while," Peter said.

"I agree," Winston said. "Follow orders next time."

Rebecca was stung, but she understood her error. Still,

it had been delightful to see the stricken expressions on the other players' faces. Winning was much better than losing.

"I shall obey, elder one."

"Good. Come with me next time, child," Winston said. "I will show you how it is done."

Thirty-one

Griffen turned over a page, drawn in by the flowing prose. He admired the superb writing, feeling as if he had discovered a marvelous secret. He had heard of Montaigne's essays in college but had never read any of them. At two dollars, the little leatherette volume was a bargain. Griffen tucked it into his elbow along with a Louis L'Amour Western, and went on browsing.

Used bookstores were one of the great treasures among many in the French Quarter, as they were in any other city. Except for Ann Arbor, he had never found such eclectic choices anywhere but New Orleans. The two-story bookstore was Griffen's favorite. It seemed to be the repository for books discarded by superbly literate people with incredibly eclectic tastes. There were always copies of some of Shakespeare's plays, alongside white-spined romance novels by the hundred, cookbooks galore, popular novels, science fiction, travel books, and local history. Hidden among them were antique atlases, medical textbooks, poetry, Restoration drama, and so many wonderful one-off oddities that Griffen could hardly resist visiting every few days to see what had come in. He loved the smell of old bookstores. The combination of dust, a little mold, paper, glue, leather, and the wood polish that the owner used on the glass-fronted cases that held the genuine rarities up near the cash register gave Griffen a feeling of contentment. He never left without making a purchase, even if it cost him only a quarter. The bookstore was one of the great bargains in entertainment in the city. The regulars at his local were big readers, too. He often ran into his drinking buddies in there.

He had an hour or two before a poker game. Jerome had let a few selected high rollers visiting town know that Mr. McCandles himself might sit in. He had a full table booked out in four phone calls. Griffen promised himself that he would be moderate in winning, but he really needed some extra cash.

A dragon walked into the bookstore. Griffen could tell without even looking around by the feeling of power. Thanks to his time hanging out with the krewe, he was learning how to distinguish his kinsmen from the other supernaturals in town. It was a terrific opportunity. Except for Mose, Jerome, Val, Mai, and himself, he had known few others with dragon blood. Now he knew dozens.

Not that it helped him distinguish who was who. He felt tension in the air as lines of force were drawn. He was familiar with the sensation; wards had been used by wiccans and voudons at the conclave to prevent the hotel staff wandering into the middle of an activity that Griffen and the organizers would find hard to explain. So it was not serendipity that brought a fellow dragon in. Nor was this an inconsequential dragon. In fact, the feeling he got was that the new arrival was someone formidable.

Griffen considered leaving through the rear door of the shop. The owner wouldn't have minded. He didn't question why one of his customers didn't want to meet someone coming in. He knew all about jealous girlfriends and overdue rent. Griffen braced himself. If there was going to be a confrontation, it was better to have it in there than out on the street. Fewer people would see it, but more important, fewer could get hurt if it turned into a fight. It could be Stoner. Griffen's consciousness hadn't been raised the last time he met the representative from Homeland Security; now that he could detect dragons from others, Stoner might feel differently to him. He braced himself. But this person was not alone. Griffen could feel five other strong presences, three in the street, and two more that had just entered the bookstore. Stoner would not bring such an entourage. It had to be . . .

"You've been avoiding me," a deep voice suddenly said at his back.

Griffen whirled. And had to drop his eyes.

Instead of the well-built former serviceman with the buzz-cut hair and cold eyes, he faced a short, zaftig woman in a two-piece suit dress, closely controlled, wavy, chestnut brown hair going gray at the temples, and cold eyes.

"Melinda, I presume?" he said, with all the aplomb he could muster.

"Griffen," she said, looking him up and down. "Well, well. You are just as handsome as Lizzy described you. Very boy-next-door."

Griffen could have made a flip comment, but her eyes brooked no nonsense. He knew instinctively that whatever trouble that Lizzy and her siblings had caused him, they would never misbehave in front of their mother. "Formidable" was the perfect adjective to describe her. She could probably command a battalion with that glare.

"To what do I owe the honor?"

Melinda was terse. "Your sister is avoiding me. I have telephoned her several times to arrange a meeting. Every time she hears my voice, she hangs up on me. I have tried other methods to make a connection. She has declined each of those. Therefore, I have sought to speak with you. You, too, have declined to meet me."

"I am busy," Griffen said, just as tersely. "I have a business to run, among other things."

"Neither of you can avoid me forever. I have been here in New Orleans for more than two months, waiting for one of you to take the time out for a simple face-to-face conversation. Valerie clearly would prefer that I deal with you. So, I am dealing. I don't want to harm you. I want to establish friendly connections with your family. We are linked now. And it is important to form a bond of cooperation."

"You might understand that we have no good reason to trust your family," Griffen said. Melinda's eyes flashed as if they were made of crystal. "Your son seduced my sister, and you whisked him out of town so he didn't have to answer for that. Your daughter—you know what she did."

"And your sister took revenge on Lizzy. She is still recovering. I have spent months taking care of her. She is upset that Valerie would attack her like that."

"It wasn't revenge. She was only protecting herself."

"I told you and Valerie I wouldn't disagree with you on that. Lizzy is difficult to control. Nathaniel . . . has his interests. I deplore his approach, but I understand the urge. He behaved dishonorably, but your immediate reaction to him would have been out of proportion."

"I don't think so," Griffen said. "My sister feels that she was raped. Anything I did to him in her defense would have been disproportionately *small* in comparison. To have used glamour on her to rob her of free will is no better than putting rohypnol in her drink."

"That is a very strong accusation."

"You've heard it before," Griffen said, offhandedly. "Your last try to arrange a meeting, as you call it, was another attempt to seduce her."

"And she thrashed my messenger," Melinda said, with a dismissive wave. "Dale doesn't possess the talent for glamour. He would have gone no further than she wanted him to, but it doesn't matter. She sent him away. I thought it better to make my approach directly to you."

"Fine. Tell me what you are here for."

"I want contact. I am tired of waiting. You do not have any right to keep me from my grandchild. I want to see Valerie. I *will* see Valerie."

"I will fight you to the death to protect my sister and her baby," Griffen said. "You know what they say about dragon fighting dragon. I don't give a damn about that. I will use everything in my power to keep you from bothering her."

"Bothering her?" the deep voice rose. The few human customers looked up nervously. No one wanted to get in the middle of an argument between strangers. They had no idea what was really going on.

"You're scaring the straights," Griffen said, with amusement he did not feel.

Melinda visibly put herself under control. "You both are reading more into my intentions than is there. I just want to meet with her. I've been waiting very patiently, caring for my daughter. I don't have all the time in the world. Lizzy will be fully recovered soon."

Griffen felt the hair on the back of his neck stand up. Scales broke out on the backs of his hands. Hastily, he forced both reactions to subside, but she had seen his alarm.

"No, she won't be coming back," Melinda said, with a glint in her pale eyes. She could tell exactly what Griffen was thinking. "I will make certain of it. But my business here is not concluded. I have a right to speak with Valerie. That child will be of my blood as well as your line's. You don't know how important it is to protect it. And the potential it carries is immense. I don't want it to grow up deprived of both sides of its family. The support of one's clan is vital. Dragon families are more vital than any human's. Malcolm McCandles has a lot to answer for, raising you as if you were pedigreed dogs, with a kennel master instead of foster parents. He knew there were other families in the dragon community who would have given you a home after you lost your parents, who would have taught you what you needed to know."

"That's none of your business," Griffen said.

"Both of you like to use that phrase," Melinda said. "But it is my business. Like anyone who wants to assure the future for our species, I am interested in Valerie's well-being and that of her child. I want to give the next generation my full support."

"There shouldn't even be another generation on the way

yet," Griffen said, bitterly. "My sister hasn't even finished college. Thanks to your son. And both might have ended if any of your daughter's attacks had been successful."

Melinda looked pained. "Please. As you say, my children are not good at handling personal relationships or settling down. You can understand that I am seizing the opportunity as I can. This may be my only grandchild."

Griffen felt the poignancy in her words. He almost gave in at that moment, but she was still Melinda. He knew Mai distrusted her, and Mose had been wary of her.

"Maybe we can work something out," Griffen said. "Under normal circumstances I would agree, that both sides should support a baby on the way, but these aren't normal."

"The circumstances are as normal as they get for dragons," Melinda said. "You have no idea."

"I don't want to know. My sister is the only one I care about. But let's declare a truce. I will talk to her. You stop phoning her and having her followed. If she says no, then you leave her alone until and if she wants to make contact with you. Her word is final."

"Nothing is final when you live as long as we do," Melinda said.

Griffen looked grimly pleased.

"The same goes for you," he snarled. He held out his hand and willed the power of the scepter into it. A flame rose from his palm. He clenched his fist, and the fire snuffed out. It hurt, but it was an effective show. Melinda smiled.

"Ah, you are coming into your gifts. Very well, I will abide by a truce. Please assure Valerie I really do only have her best interests in mind."

"I'll tell her. The decision is hers, though."

"Good enough for now," Melinda said. She nodded sharply. The two dragons pretending to shop for books fanned out to flank her. She glanced at Griffen, then headed for the door.

The bell jingled before she reached it. She stopped as the door opened inward. Etienne strode in. He scanned the store. His face lit up as he spotted Griffen.

"Mr. Griffen! Glad to find you here. I gotta ask you somet'ing."

That means money, Griffen thought. "What can I do for you?"

Etienne pointed to the nearest bay of shelves. "Well, let's just take a moment alone over dere where we gots some privacy."

Melinda snorted at him. Etienne noticed her. He removed himself from her path and sketched a deep bow.

"My lady."

Melinda raised her chin and strode out past him. Griffen eyed him curiously. Etienne met him with a bland smile. He took Griffen's arm.

"How do you feel about addin' some extra advertisin' in the newspaper Sunday supplement for the krewe?" he asked. "Half the proceeds go to our charity. Some of the others are kickin' in for a half-page ad. It'd be about a thousand. Mean a lot to have your support."

"Another thousand? This is running into serious money," Griffen said, feeling as if he was being fleeced by an expert.

"You have it, or so I hear," Etienne said. He gave Griffen a knowing glance. Griffen wondered how much of his intel was gossip and how much was clairvoyance.

"Less than I had before," Griffen said. He had a mental picture of bags of cash with wings fluttering out of the window like in an old cartoon. He wanted to say no, but it was hard to appear stingy when everyone else was being generous. Jerome had told him of a voodoo deity that appeared in disguise to ask for charity. It was bad karma to refuse. As tightly as he was stretched, giving to those less fortunate was important. "All right." Etienne slapped him on the back.

"It's all for a good cause. Hey, don't forget. Your final costume fittin' is day after tomorrow. Don't be late, okay? The tailor's fingers are about to fall off, all the people she's gotta fit, even though I told her you're somet'ing special."

"I know, I'm king," Griffen grumbled.

Etienne smiled. "Good, ain't it? See you at the first ball."

Thirty-two

Val held her arms up over her head and stared at the pale green ceiling. She stood in her underwear in the living room of a shotgun house in St. Bernard's Parish, hoping that the thin lace curtain on the window was opaque enough so passersby couldn't see her.

"Hold still, honey baby. I got another pin. I don't want to stick you," Aunt Herbera said. Val felt the plump woman's strong, capable hands gather up another fold of beige muslin and press it against her. "Oh, this is gonna be so pretty!"

"It doesn't look like much," Mai commented. Val lowered her eyes and delivered an annoyed look to her friend, who was curled up in a large, flowered, upholstered armchair under the front window of the small shotgun house. Mai shrugged. "Well, it doesn't. The fabric is dull. You could be wearing a curtain."

Gris-gris's aunt turned with her hands on her ample hips and regarded her with exasperated pity.

"I am drapin', and this is to make the pattern, Miss Mouth. If you never had nothin' fitted to that skinny ass of yours, you had this done on you. Saves fine fabrics from gettin' stretched and ruined. We do all our experimentin' with this." She returned to Val. "What was you thinkin' for neckline, honey? We got to think about expansion of that pretty bosom of yours, what with your little passenger on board, there."

"I've got invitations to parties starting in a week," Val

said. She suddenly worried about the time. "Will you be able to finish it by then?"

Aunt Herbera waved a hand. "You can have it two days from now if you want it."

Val felt shy asking about price, but she had become very aware in the last few months that not getting details up front usually meant she would be socked with expenses she didn't expect. "Will that . . . cost extra?"

"Why, no, girl. That's just when I'll be done. You think I'm gonna hold it up for a while to be dramatic? I've got other things I got to finish, but Gris-gris wanted to make certain I took care of you. Okay, then, maybe a little give, 'cause the season'll run until March 10."

Val was relieved. While there were gowns for every shape, size, and age of women in countless shops in New Orleans, she had not found a single decent evening dress for a six-foot-plus pregnant woman that she could afford. She had called Gris-gris to ask for the name of his relative who made clothes. Aunt Herbera was happy to oblige. And she wouldn't cost an arm and a leg, either.

"How many relatives does Gris-gris have?" Val asked. "Just out of curiosity. He seems to have uncles and aunts and cousins for every occasion."

"There's plenty of us," Aunt Herbera said, as she worked. "And there's some who ain't relatives but they is now. You know what that's like."

"I really do," Val said. "Our friends are just about the only family that Griffen and I have. Our parents are dead. Our only blood relative is our uncle."

"Why, you poor thing! You want some of ours, you just ask. We tired of feedin' them."

Val laughed.

"All right, you take a look at that." Aunt Herbera turned her so she was facing the long mirror attached to the wall next to the white-painted fireplace. "That too low-cut? You can stand to wear it because you're so young and fresh."

Mai was right about the muslin being dull in color and

texture, but it had transformed in the dressmaker's hands into a work of sculpture. The fabric was pleated over each breast into a strapless bodice. The small folds met in the middle in a woven V that showed the cleft between them. The rest of the muslin fell smoothly down around her body to the rectangular bolt lying at Val's feet from which it had been unrolled. Even in that color, the shape was perfect for her, youthful and, she was almost embarrassed to realize it, devastatingly sexy.

"That's unbelievable," Val breathed. "You did this just by draping?"

"All the time," Aunt Herbera said. She regarded her work critically in the mirror. "It does look good." She reached up to tweak the left side upward under Val's arm.

Val's eyes widened. Something was moving in the fireplace. She didn't worry that something was burning. Even during that winter, it was rarely cold enough to light a real fire. Most people relied on furnaces, most of which had been retrofitted to the old wooden houses. Val could hear the low hiss of baseboard heat. But the ornamental screen attached to a white wooden frame to match the fireplace surround was moving. Perhaps her cat was playing in there? Val was just about to mention it, when the screen went flying violently outward.

It hit Aunt Herbera in the back of the leg. She spun around.

"What was that?" she demanded. A shape rolled out of the chimney and sprang to its feet. It looked around and snarled. It was the size of a teenager, like a wiry human in build, but its hands and feet were too big for it. What looked like gelled-up spiked hair on its head was a mess of big gray-brown scales the size of leaves. Its pointed teeth were made for tearing flesh. Its tongue, Val was horrified to see, was forked. It flicked at her, tasting the air. Bizarrely, to Val's eyes, it wore a brown T-shirt and gray sweatpants, "A clinker! God save us, get out of my house!"

The creature laughed at her. It jumped high and kicked

off against the fireplace as if it were the side of a swimming pool. Over their heads it flew, claws out, straight for Mai.

The small Asian woman saw it coming. She was braced in the big armchair long before it got there. She lifted herself on the arms and kicked upward, smacking the clinker in the jaw. It tumbled backward and landed on the floor. In a split second it was up again, ready for another attempt. Mai jumped to her feet and stood hunched over with her hands flat on the air, martial-arts style. Val felt something strong hit her, something invisible. It made the clinker stumble backward.

"Who are you?" Mai demanded. "Who sent you?"

"You know who," it cackled, in a hoarse, gravelly voice like that of a four-pack-a-day smoker. "This is a warnin'! You better back off and stop interferin'!"

Mai's eyes widened, then narrowed again. "I don't take warnings from lowlifes like you!"

"Then how's this instead?" It raised its long hands and spread its fingers out. Flame gushed from the fingertips in thin streams. Mai leaped out of its path and landed near the front door. The curtains started to crackle. Val ran to beat them out with the folds of muslin.

Aunt Herbera snatched up the ornamental fireplace poker and started belaboring the creature over the head from behind. "You get out of my house, you spawn of Satan!"

"Ow! Ow!" the creature bellowed. It ran around the room with the old woman in pursuit. She chased it into a corner and rained blows down on it. "Knock it off, you old sack of bones! That don't even raise a bump!"

"It don't, do it?" Aunt Herbera asked. She raised the rod to hit him again.

The thing straightened up, grinned evilly at her, and grabbed the poker out of her hands. "No." It tied the brass rod in a knot. Aunt Herbera gasped. The creature flung the piece of metal away and pushed her to one side. "Good thing you ain't on my schedule!"

Mai was still on guard. As she got closer, she turned in a circle and let go a roundhouse kick. The clinker fell back,

its jaw knocked sideways. It rolled on the floor and came up
on its hands and knees. Mai hit it again with another dose of
force field. Though the invisible hand pushed Val backward
five steps, it had no more effect on the clinker. The creature
scooted toward Mai as swiftly as a lizard and wrapped itself
around her legs. Mai screamed. She flailed at its head with
her fists. The clinker seemed to flow up her body until she
was wrapped up in its limbs. Smoke rose from her clothing
and hair. Val gawked, horrified. She and Aunt Herbera
rushed to try to and peel the clinker away from Mai. Its skin
was burning hot. They snatched their hands away, gasping
in pain. Aunt Herbera retreated.

Mai fell to her knees. The clinker clung to her, cackling
in her ear.

"You stay out of business that don't concern you. You get
one warning, and that's all! After that, I don't stop!"

"Tell Jordan Ma that he can stuff his warnings up his
ass and dance!" Mai gritted out. Her teeth were clenched
together. She clawed and kicked, but her movements were
jerky with pain. Val took a deep breath, and dug her hands
between the clinker and Mai's body. She pried outward.

"Leggo, girl!" the clinker roared. "I got no problem with
you. I'll spare your life and the old lady if you let me have
this female."

"No way, asshole," Val snarled. She doubled the effort,
grunting as she pushed outward.

Val felt the creature's muscles loosen slightly. It might
be fast, but she was stronger. She put all her strength into
pulling it away from her friend. The creature's right-arm
grip popped loose. It scrabbled at Mai's shoulders, trying to
keep hold. Val put her foot into the clinker's neck, pushing
it down and away. Its hot skin burned her, but she was
determined to eject it no matter what it took. The other
arm came loose. Before it could regain its grasp, Val grabbed
the clinker by the neck and heaved. Mai collapsed on the
oval rag rug, gasping. Val dragged the clinker out over the
living-room floor. It wasn't very heavy, but her hands felt as

if the skin were going to boil off her bones. She dropped it and blew on her palms.

The clinker turned over to scuttle back to Mai, but Val stomped down on the back of its neck with one foot. It flipped over and made to grab at her with all four limbs. Val smiled viciously.

"I was hoping you'd do that," she said. She brought her foot down hard on its crotch.

"Oooh!" It contracted in on itself, clutching at the injured spot. It rolled side to side, moaning with pain. Val felt herself growing bigger, but she didn't care. She kept on kicking and stamping on whatever part was closest. "Girl, leave me alone! Uncle! Uncle! You killin' me!" Val looked down to see if it was badly hurt. In the brief pause, it flipped over again and tried to head for Mai.

By then, Mai had risen to her knees. She had her claws out, but she looked bad. She was in no shape to defend herself. Val grabbed the clinker by the nape and hauled it upward. It couldn't have weighed more than thirty pounds. Val shook it and slapped its face back and forth. It swung its legs up and battened onto her forearm. It scratched at her, but it could not get a toehold on dragon skin. Then it began to glow red. The heat increased. Val felt blisters rising on her skin. She punched at the clinker's back, where the kidneys would be on a human, willing it to let go. The pain was temporary, she kept telling herself. Only temporary!

The creature's hot grip seemed to grow weaker and weaker with every blow. At last, it let go and dropped to the floor. Val was on it in a heartbeat, kicking its head and belly until it lay in a pool of its own blood, which flowed from its mouth and nose. The blood flickered blue and purple like a gas fire. She stood back, gasping.

"That was amazin', young lady!" Aunt Herbera said. "You are as strong as iron."

"Sometimes she doesn't know her own strength," Mai said weakly. Val and the old woman ran to help her up. Her lovely designer clothes hung in scorched tatters on her body. Her usually pale skin was red where the clinker had touched her.

"Well, I am impressed to death. Gris-gris ought to be proud to be on your arm, Ms. Valerie."

Val knelt beside Mai. "Are you all right?"

"I am getting better," Mai said, swallowing hard. "It felt like it was trying to burn the life out of me. If you hadn't stopped it . . ."

Val smiled at her. "Well, I did, so don't think about that. Come on, sit down." They helped her into the armchair and found a quilt to tuck in around her. Mai watched Val bustle around, completely unself-conscious about displaying that magnificent body of hers in a scanty pink bra and panties. Apart from her burns, which went almost bone deep despite what she had told Val, Mai suffered from an uncomfortable and unfamiliar feeling. She had to search deep in her memory for a similar sensation, one that she had felt seldom in her long life.

Oh, yes. Gratitude. Mai nodded.

She had given friendship to Valerie McCandles and received friendship in return. Mai was humbled that the girl who did not know her that well and did not understand the danger into which she was putting herself and her unborn baby had thrown herself at a creature she had never seen before to save her friend's life. It was not that Val had so much faith in her dragonish abilities; she had merely seen her friend in trouble and acted.

Would she have done the same? Mai doubted it. She was ashamed.

How many roles had Mai nurtured carefully over the years? Dozens, or more. Siren, leader, thief, muse, lover, daughter? Yet her favorite was the simplest of them all: friend. In her long life, she had never really had one before. It was a genuine revelation to her. It made Mai rethink her strategy, or part of it. Whatever Mai would do in the future, Val would never suffer from it.

"Thank you," she said.

"No problem," Val replied. She looked down, and realized she was in her underwear. "Oh, my God!" She reached for the fallen swaths of cloth and wrapped them around her.

They heard a moan coming from the clinker. It was stirring on the floor where Val had left it. Aunt Herbera stood over it and glared down.

"In my younger days, I would have hung you out with the washing! Crawl back into the sinkhole from which you climbed!"

"Are you kiddin'?" the creature asked, showing its bloody teeth in a grin. "That ain't even poetic!"

"You want poetry?" Val demanded, coming to loom over it.

"No, I want you to drop the towel. You got some body on you, babe." It leered at her.

Val kicked it in the neck. "I want you to swear an oath to me. I want you to promise to serve me."

The clinker let out a pained laugh. "Oaths? We don't swear no oaths! That's fairy-tale stuff."

Val hauled him to his feet by his unspeakably dirty T-shirt. "You don't? Well, how about this oath? If you don't swear to leave me and my friends and family alone and do what I say *when* I tell you to do it, I swear that I will tear you here and now into little quivering bits and burn them until you will wish you were swimming in a Lucky Dog cart to ease the pain. You owe me."

"For what?" the clinker asked.

"For not killing you right away and asking questions later."

The creature looked alarmed. "What do you want, Ms. Beautiful, three wishes?"

Val grimaced. "No. I'll figure that out later. In the meanwhile, you had better not hurt my friend, or this lady, or me, or anyone in our families, now or ever. Or I'll find you again. I've got friends in high places. And low places. And a bunch of other places. I'll find you, and I will finish the job. You know what I am."

"Yeah. All right, all right! Agreed," said the clinker. "Gimme your cell-phone number."

"*What?*"

"Well, how the hell you expec' me to find you in all of New Orleans when you want me?" he demanded.

"You have a *cell phone?*"

"Get wit' the twen'y-first century, lady!" He reached into his pants pocket and pulled out a battered flip-phone. Val reeled off her number. The clinker punched a button, and Val's purse erupted with her ring tone. "Now you got mine." It grinned at her. "You don't wanna give me one more look at that bodacious body of yours, huh?"

"No! Now, get out of here!"

"Dang, what a bitch!"

Val made a move toward him and stamped the floor. He fled for the fireplace and zipped up into the chimney. He left a contrail of sparks that winked out.

"That was absolutely amazing," Mai exclaimed, turning to offer Val a smile of admiration.

"Hurts," Val said, folding up like an accordion on the floor. She clutched her hands. Mai noticed for the first time that both arms were covered with blisters up to the elbow.

"It'll heal," Mai said. Now was the time for her to help. She rose from her nest and folded the quilt into a pillow to put under Val's head. Aunt Herbera left the room and returned with a glass mayonnaise jar filled with green salve.

"You both need my special burn cream," she said. "This come from an old family recipe my great-grandma learned from her great-grandma. You can't buy this in stores." She started slathering it onto both girls.

In spite of the eye-watering smell of menthol, the salve smelled good. After just a few moments, the redness went away. Within fifteen minutes, most of the blisters had flattened out. Mai looked down at herself in dismay.

"Will you look at my blouse? It's ruined!"

"I told you it was a waste to buy designer," Val said, fingering the pieces of cloth.

254 ROBERT ASPRIN AND JODY LYNN NYE

Mai smiled. "Darling moose-butt, it is never a waste of time to buy designer. It is a waste if you wrestle demons in it, though. I will kill that creature. What did you say it was?"

"A clinker," Aunt Herbera said. "Dragon-kin, but real distant. I thought it was a legend that mothers tell their children to keep 'em from goin' out at night and raisin' hell. That was as pretty as anything, the way the two of you faced it down! And you, Miss Val, stompin' it like a cockroach. You wouldn't mind if I tell that story? I participate in folktale circles. That is as good as anythin' else that ever won first prize."

At first, Val was horrified to realize that she had just fought a fire-wielding creature in front of a stranger, and one of Gris-gris's relatives at that. But the older woman's eyes were full of admiration, not fear. She believed in supernaturals. She lived with legends, and she was not at all surprised that Val and Mai had handled themselves like one of her peers.

"No problem," Val said, relieved. "As long as you make sure I don't look fat in my dress."

Aunt Herbera touched her arm. "Honey, they will all be wondering what you got under there by the time I finish with you. You'll look like a woodland nymph. Not that I ever met any. But I bet you have."

"No," Val said. "You'll have to ask my brother. Wood nymphs are more his speed."

"Do we have to ask you not to tell your nephew about this?" Mai asked.

Aunt Herbera shook her head. "Wouldn't matter if I did. He already thinks this girl here can walk on water. The fact that she can wrestle fire-demons will just make him worship her more. But if you don't want me to, I won't. You go on, now. I'll call you when your dress is ready. It'll just give me something pleasurable to think about while I'm sewing. Let me give you something to wear home, honey."

They heard her cackling with delight as they left.

"And so a legend begins," Mai cracked. A borrowed

blouse of Aunt Herbera's that would have wound around her twice hung from her slim shoulders.

"So," Val said, "you want to tell me who sent you that guy as a warning?"

Mai hesitated. "Not yet. Forgive me, but I don't want to involve you in my troubles. Not yet. I must thank the two of you for saving my life. And healing my wounds."

"That salve of hers is great," Val said, thoughtfully. "I wonder if it will work on diaper rash."

Thirty-three

Griffen ran off the elevator in the Royal Sonesta Hotel. He had had to leave a stimulating discussion over drinks with Holly and Bert, about magic being sacred or profane, but the phone call sounded urgent. The rising annoyance in Wallace's voice told him he had better get there quickly, or there was going to be violence.

Not as many games had been running lately as there might be during this season. The people who normally played one or two nights a week were involved in Mardi Gras activities: going to parties, tableaux, building floats, and all the other activities that Griffen himself was doing on the side. That meant that not as much money was coming in as he and Jerome had hoped. They were feeling the pinch. Griffen had had to cover part of the last payroll out of his savings. Word had also continued spreading about the crooked games—or at least the losers' perception that they were crooked. Once a rumor started, it was hard to stop it. Griffen hoped this was not going to be another disaster.

He heard the shouting from the open door of the suite and winced. He hoped the windows looking out over the pool were shut. A hotel security guard raised his head when he saw Griffen. There must have been some complaints. Griffen made a gesture to assure the man he had seen him, and the guard leaned back against the wall. He had a bribe coming later on for not shutting down the room.

"Hello, folks," Griffen said, coming in with his hands

raised. "I'm Griffen McCandles. What's all the fuss?" The combatants stopped yelling and turned to glare at him. A short, round-bellied man with a few strands of hair plastered on his scalp jabbed an angry finger at an equally short, round man on the other side of the table.

"Griffen! This sonovabitch accused me of slipping cards under the table! He says I'm cheating! You have known me for how long?"

"There has to be some kind of misunderstanding," Griffen said. He felt pressure like a drill driving right into the third eye on his forehead that Holly insisted he had. "Mr. Stearn is an old friend of ours. What is it that you think you saw happen?"

"Think?" the other man said. He was a Chinese-American about the same age as Stearn, but with a good deal more hair. "Just because I am old doesn't mean I'm blind, or that since I retired I have enough money to lose to criminals."

"Criminals! Why, you sonovabitch!" Stearn launched himself toward the table, fist first.

Griffen leaped in and pulled him back. "All right, can we just talk about what went on?"

"No! I am going to call the police!" the other man said. "He is a friend of yours, is he? Perhaps the problem is collusion! You get a share of whatever it is that he takes away from the rest of us?"

Griffen felt his temper flare. He damped it down with difficulty, as the cigarettes that had been snuffed out in the ashtrays on the table edge started to smolder again. "Sir, I am sorry I have given the wrong impression. My operation only provides you with the time and place to play a friendly game of poker. The other players are, as far as I am able to determine, honest, upstanding citizens like you. My business runs on its reputation. I do not plant shills. I don't support cheating. If I have proof that there has been some dishonest play, then I will do my best to settle the matter. Now, what proof do you have?"

"How about an eyewitness?" the old man asked. "Aha,

you think I am the only one who saw what went on?" He turned to the others. "Tell him. What did you see?"

Up until then, Griffen hadn't paid any attention to the rest of the players in the room. Only one other beside Mr. Stearn was a regular. Mr. Diener shook his head. The other two were a tall black man in a polo shirt and long shorts, a former professional basketball player on the Boston Celtics who Griffen recognized from television, and a small woman with red hair who reminded him of Fox Lisa. She wore a cotton dress and a lightweight cardigan with the top button fastened.

"He looked furtive. Yes, that's the word," the woman said. "Furtive. He could have done something." Stearn glared at her.

"I saw the guy slip a card down onto his lap," the ballplayer said, after a glance at the old Asian. "Next hand, he had two kings. Can't tell me that's an accident."

"It was the deal!" Stearn bellowed. "That's all! I have said it a hundred times now. I got pocket kings. I never slipped a card anywhere!"

"It's fraud," the old man said. "I am calling the police."

"I would rather you didn't do that," Griffen said. "Can't we settle this here and now in a civilized way?"

"He can give me my money back," the old man said.

"I won that!"

"And damages, for pain and suffering."

"This isn't a court of law," Griffen said. "We don't award damages."

"Then I am calling the police! They'll get it for me!"

Griffen could see the look on Harrison's face if he had to roust one of Griffen's games out of the Royal Sonesta. He also foresaw having to bail Stearn out of jail in the middle of the night. But to agree to blackmail was to open the door to further demands. He shook his head. "I can't do that, sir. I'll make good your losses plus a hundred dollars, but that is all I will do."

"You pussy!" Stearn said, glaring at Griffen. "Maybe I should demand damages, too, for having my character impugned!"

"I didn't say you did anything wrong, Mr. Stearn," Griffen said.

"It would be nice if you at least defended me!"

"I wasn't here," Griffen said. He turned to the dealers. "Wallace, Ezra, what about you?"

"Didn't see nothing that they say happened," Wallace said. "It was all goin' real nice until then."

But the situation had reached a stalemate. Griffen reached for his wallet. It was flatter than ever. He managed to scrape up the amount that Wallace said the Asian gentleman had lost, plus the promised C-note. The Asian pocketed the money. Stearn swapped in his chips and departed without saying a word.

Griffen left, after offering praise to the dealers for handling the difficult situation. They felt bad for him. He could see it in their eyes though they didn't insult him by saying so. He was devastated. Whatever had happened there had ruined a nice game. Yet another rumor was going to hit the mills, and he could not do a damned thing about it. His head ached. The frustration sent unquenched fire rushing through his blood.

I am getting addicted to that scepter, he thought. He headed for a side-street bar for a drink. He didn't want to have to talk about what had happened with anyone he knew.

The rest of the players reached the ground floor and scattered. The short Asian man headed into the Mystic Bar for a celebratory cocktail. A few minutes later, the tall basketball player joined him. In the shadow of the corner booth, the tall form shrank into a compact, slender one, looking rather incongruous in a polo shirt and long shorts that almost reached her ankles.

"That was magnificent, elder one," Rebecca said, breathlessly. "I bow to your expertise."

"Thank you, child," Winston said, patting her on the arm. "Now you have seen, I expect you to go out and do."

"I will!"

"Good. Go and get us some drinks."

Thirty-four

Val clutched Griffen's arm as they waited in line amid dozens of couples in black tie and floor-length gowns. Griffen was proud to observe that he and his sister fit in perfectly. Her new dress was a column of blue silk that skimmed over the small baby bump at her waist. The strapless top showed off her slim, athletic shoulders. He noticed more than one man looking her over with interest.

"I feel like we're in a movie," she whispered. It did look like a classic movie set, with men in tuxedos and ladies in evening dresses posing against heavy swagged curtains tied with tassels and tall, Art Deco flower vases overflowing with blossoms. Somewhere an orchestra, heavy on the strings, was playing Cole Porter. Any moment now, someone was going to burst into song.

"Maybe *Shall We Dance*, or *Top Hat*," Griffen suggested. "Something that starred Fred Astaire and Ginger Rogers."

"Everything is so elegant!"

"And this is just the first one," Griffen said. He had thought that because Rex and Zulu were two of the most important, they would have the first formal balls, but another superkrewe had beaten them to the punch. As Etienne had predicted, Griffen and the other members of the court and committee heads were sent invitations. He had a whole stack of them on the table where he paid his bills. Of course, the response had to be accompanied by a check or money order; but on peering into the ballroom ahead of them, he saw that they were getting their money's worth. Busby Berkeley would have been proud of the detail the organizers had gone into. Silver, crystal, and china gleamed on perfectly white tablecloths. The centerpieces on the tables were towering, fairylike sculptures of green, gold, and purple. They were impressive, but not bulky enough to prevent the diners from seeing one another.

"I won't know what to say to people."

"Don't worry. They're all thinking the same thing."

Val shot him an accusatory look. "I thought you were going to ask Mai to this ball."

Griffen shrugged. "I thought you'd enjoy it. She wanted me to bring her, but I told her family took priority. You are my sister, so you get to go first. She has her own invitation. She said she might come if she found an escort."

Val leaned close to him. "Do I look like a watermelon in this dress?"

"No! You can't even tell. It hides, uh—"

"You feel that uncomfortable mentioning my baby?" she asked, wryly. "When you can discuss sex and dead bodies out loud with people?"

"It seems like pregnancy should be private," Griffen said. He did feel uncomfortable. "I mean, the baby's inside you, and what's happening there is no one's business."

Val shook her head.

"Don't be so squeamish! Babies are natural. But . . . do I look big?"

Griffen was at a loss for words. If he told her the truth, that people could see the small bulge when the soft fabric flattened against her stomach, she would get upset even though she had just insisted it was natural. If he lied, she would be upset, too. He was rescued by a suave voice at his shoulder.

"You look lovely, Ms. McCandles. And *both* of you look very healthy."

"Thanks, sir," Val said. She smiled shyly at the older man in black tie and bright red silk cummerbund. The lady on his arm, who matched him in age and elegance, wore old-gold damask brocade. She smiled at the McCandles siblings. The man bowed to Val.

"You don't know me. I met your brother at the conclave in October."

"Right," Griffen said, searching for a name. "I don't recall . . ."

"Milton Pelletier. This is my wife, Emily. We are very proud that you are gracing our krewe with your presence. Enjoy the evening. Nice to see you, Griffen. Miss Valerie, I hope you will honor me with a dance." He bowed to her. Val giggled at the old-fashioned gallantry.

"Thanks, Milton and, uh, Emily," Griffen said. "See you inside."

"Did you meet him at the conclave?" Val whispered.

"I don't remember his name."

The older couple turned and passed through the doors.

"Who are you talking to?" the hostess in the pale blue lace jacket asked him, as he reached her and handed over the invitation cards.

Griffen gestured toward the direction the couple had gone. "Uh, that man in the red cummerbund. And that lady in gold. Mr. and Mrs. Pelletier? They said they were on the krewe."

"Really?" the hostess said, puzzled. She thought for a moment. "We haven't had anyone named Pelletier in the krewe since 1937. They were the king and queen then."

"Maybe I heard the name wrong," Griffen said. He accepted a seating card from her.

Val's eyebrows were high on her forehead as Griffen escorted her into the ballroom. She was holding back with difficulty and exploded as soon as they were out of earshot of the others.

"Why couldn't she see them?" she demanded. "Were they ghosts? The ghosts of a king and queen?"

"I guess so," Griffen said. "There were ghosts at the conclave, Rose and some others. I didn't have time to get to know everyone there. I had to handle a lot of problems then."

Val whistled.

"I guess you never stop being into Mardi Gras," she said. "Do you think they've been coming to the ball since 1937, or just since they died?"

"If you see him again later, you can ask him," Griffen said. "Just don't dance with him,"

Val looked offended. "Why not?

He grinned. "Because if no one else can see him, then you will look as if you're crazy."

Val made a face at him.

"Mr. Griffen!" Etienne homed in on them just inside the doorway. An older lady in coral-colored satin held on to his arm. "Mama, you know Griffen McCandles. And dis is his pretty-as-a-picture sister, Valerie."

"Pleased to meet you," she said. "I'm Antoinette. Come and sit next to me, Valerie. I want to gossip 'bout some of the outfits that the other ladies here are wearin'. I cannot *believe* that they left the house 'thout lookin' at the mirror!"

Val smiled at Griffen. "I think I am going to enjoy this party," she said.

A jazz trio struck up soft music as the guests found the tables with their numbers on them.

The table they were assigned was already occupied by Terence Killen, Mitchell Grade, and their wives. Griffen introduced them to Val. Secretly, he was relieved to have a few people he knew present. They could answer questions for him.

"'Scuse me for working business into pleasure, Griffen," Terence said. "Got a call from the restaurant about your party. They're happy to hold the room on your say-so, but their suppliers need a deposit for the food. Do you think you can just drop by there and put one down? They only need about 25 percent."

"Sure," Griffen said, feeling pained. That amount would strip his bank account down to a few hundred. He hated to have that small an emergency pad on hand.

Val leaned over. "Do you need a loan, Big Brother?" she murmured.

"I shouldn't," Griffen said, swallowing hard. He needed to get in on another game. Or twelve.

Terence jumped slightly, as if his wife had elbowed him hard in the ribs. "Well, that's it. Not another word about that. Pretty nice decorations they put up here. Nice and traditional, with the jesters. I wonder if that has anything to do with their theme."

"I always guess, and I am never right," Mitchell said. "My wife, here, she is always right. What do you think, honey?"

Mrs. Grade glanced around the room. "I think it's kind of generic. If I had to say for certain, I think they are going to make us wait for the tableau. But they did hire the very best musicians. Listen to them. I want to get up and dance."

"Later, honey, later. Wait until they've made the speeches."

Griffen saw no flaw in the grandeur of the room. The adornments that Mrs. Grade called "generic" were still hand-painted and beautifully made. He was impressed once again with the level of detail that had to be put into every Mardi Gras event. Real royalty would have to push to equal the beauty of this setting. Pages in damask satin and eye masks helped guests into their seats and brought around drinks. "I know that we're a smaller krewe. Is our ball going to be as grand as this one?"

"Ours will be better," Etienne assured him. "Dis is just a warm-up. Don't you fear; we'll be shown up by nobody."

Thirty-five

Griffen sat back, stone-faced, as a trio of players tried to guess whether he was bluffing about the quality of his hand. The game could end now. Griffen held a straight flush, two to six of clubs. It could be superseded by a higher-ranking suit or a better straight flush. He hoped his luck was going to hold out. He had plenty of chips in front of him to intimidate other players.

"I think yer bluffing, Griffen," said the millionaire from New York. He pushed his stack forward. He took a carrot stick off the plate at his right and crunched it. Through shards of vegetable, he mumbled, "Five thousand."

"Fold," said the tough-faced woman from Kansas who ran a confectionary empire.

Griffen didn't change expression. Too bad. He wasn't going to be able to make a clean sweep of everyone's pot.

He felt so much more at home in this setting that he wanted to beam at the others, but they would have thought he was crazy or up to something. The latter was true, certainly, but not the former. He was just relieved to be out of the tuxedo and back into familiar clothing. His dreams had been haunted by imagined social missteps, with choruses of howling banshees laughing each time he did or said something wrong. Not that the ball itself had really gone that way. He was just suffering from the reaction to having had to spend all night guessing what to do next.

"I call you," said Peter Sing. Griffen didn't meet his eyes.

"Five thousand," the dealer recited, counting the chips in a single glance. Griffen pushed in his own stack to match it. He couldn't afford to lose. He had put an IOU in the bank for his stake, seen by no one but the surprised dealer. He really had to win, to pay back the house, plus help take care of his expenses. He was pretty sure he could beat the others. Their tells said they were holding nothing. All except Peter. Griffen could not penetrate the other dragon's façade. He was good. If it had been anytime but Mardi Gras, Griffen would have enjoyed playing him on a regular basis. He studied Peter again for a moment, then turned over his cards. Peter grimaced and pushed his away without revealing them.

"Ohhhh!" the others moaned. Griffen raked in the pot. He glanced at the clock. After 2:00 a.m. A couple of the players were beginning to flag. Griffen had too much adrenaline in his system to be sleepy. He was prepared to play until dawn.

"So, what's it like being king of Mardi Gras?" Peter asked. "I don't know if you heard, folks, but we have royalty among us. Griffen is king of the Krewe of Fafnir."

The others applauded him.

"Congrats, Griffen!" said the millionaire. "I've always wanted to be king on one of them floats, but everyone tells me I don't qualify. What's it like?"

Griffen grinned sheepishly. "Expensive. I never dreamed when I said yes that it was going to cost me something every time I turned around."

"But isn't it a great honor?" the confectionary queen asked.

Griffen pulled his wits together. Running down the very institution for which New Orleans was known above all else was bad business, as well as uncharitable. "It really is. I was knocked sideways when they asked me. I mean, I haven't been here very long, and I'm pretty young. The history behind the festival goes back hundreds of years, but the one here in New Orleans is unique. There are so many other men that they could have given the post to, but I'm really glad for the opportunity. It's been an amazing time so far. I've been invited to a lot of parties. Formal parties. I was just at one last evening. It was the most elegant event I have ever attended. We have our own masquerade ball coming up. And you ought to see the float that I am going to ride on in our parade. In fact, all the floats are unbelievable. It's going to be a great day."

"Wish I could see it," the millionaire said. "Got to get back after this weekend. Maybe I'll get back in time for the parades."

The woman from Kansas put in five chips. "Why is it called Fafnir? That sounds silly."

"Well, most of the krewes are named after someone in mythology," Griffen said. "Fafnir was a dragon in Norse myth."

"You like dragons?" asked the New York millionaire.

"Yes, I do," Griffen said.

"Me, too," added Peter, with a conspiratorial grin at Griffen. "So you don't mind coming back to the real world in between?"

"It's a relief, to be honest," Griffen admitted.

The ball had been a challenge to his pride as well as his powers of observation. The krewe elite made him feel all too keenly the disadvantages of his middle-class upbringing. They talked about their swimming pools and jet-setting around the world. The women were all wearing diamond-encrusted jewelry that his senses told him was real. Val's eyes gleamed with envy though she had nowhere to wear anything like that in her ordinary life. Only there and in similar occasions would it ever be appropriate, and this season was probably the only time in their lives when they would be rubbing elbows with the social hierarchy.

After the tableaux, which revealed the krewe's upcoming parade theme in a series of little sketches by ladies in gorgeous gowns and elaborate headdresses, he had met the king, queen, and court of the host krewe. Introduced by Etienne as the king of Fafnir, Griffen was shown much honor as a brother monarch. They tried to include him as an equal in their conversation, which made him feel all the lower down the social chain. He hated it. Americans had no titles, so they felt compelled to invent their own nobility: politicians, movie stars, and now once-a-year monarchs. He did his best to enjoy himself but felt guilty for enjoying it. That voice at the back of his mind was the equivalent of the slave standing on the back of Caesar's chariot during one of his triumphs in Rome. It held the figurative laurel wreath up over his head, all the while whispering, "Remember thou art mortal." On Ash Wednesday, he would be back to being Griffen McCandles.

Why did he feel put down by these equally ordinary people, when he played poker with richer, more eminent, more famous people and never felt out of place? Presentation did so much. Presentation and personality. The industrialists and celebrities who found their way to his tables didn't expect to be treated more deferentially than the shoe salesman or cocktail waitress who played cards with them, and the kings of Mardi Gras did. Admittedly, like his games, the price of admission was to have money, lots of money. But Mardi Gras royalty required acclaim by someone else who decided you were worthy to hold that exalted office, for however short a time. And that let one into the club.

Perhaps he had not learned yet to aim higher. He had never really anticipated having to socialize with the upper class. It was telling that this particular upper class did not have as powerful a bloodline as he did; but they had been raised with money, privilege, and, most important, the knowledge of what and who they were. Griffen felt at a disadvantage. He didn't know how to respond to some of the little nasty comments. Sometimes he felt that he wasn't even speaking the same language. Without meaning to, they treated him like an idiot cousin. He didn't like it, but it wasn't his party. He was just the king. It was a temporary post, and a hazardous one. He had not asked enough questions at the beginning, not that he'd known which ones to ask.

At least they never denigrated Val or made her feel an outcast. That would have made Griffen go for the throat. Instead, Antoinette de la Fee protected Val like a mother hen. Antoinette was gracious and welcoming, as were the other women at the ball. They praised her looks and her dress, included her in their conversations, and listened to what she said. They gave her advice, made little comments about other people, and pointed out what was going on around them from their point of view. At first it sounded as if they were patronizing her, but as Griffen listened more carefully, he saw that they were treating her as if she was a daughter who had not learned the social conventions yet. Val was eating it up. She was rapt. She had never had a circle of maternal older relatives.

They had been so isolated in Ann Arbor. For the first time, Griffen felt a pang of deep loss. Not for himself, but for Val. He had managed to get along in the world. He had his social network, like the players around the table, his drinking buddies and friends. Mose had insisted, then proved, that Griffen didn't need a mentor. He had made his mistakes, recovered from them, grown, and prospered. Val had had to help herself grow up. Mrs. Feuer had been pretty clinical about such things as menstruation and birth control. She had not been any emotional or practical support to a maturing girl who needed to know how the world worked.

There, in the middle of a fancy-dress ball, Val was getting lessons in becoming a woman of society. He could forgive the rougher treatment he was getting from the men of the krewe, if only to make sure that Val kept getting from their wives and mothers what she had never had after she had lost her own mother. He hadn't really considered keeping up relationships with them after Mardi Gras was over, until that moment. Val had given him a look of happiness. He had never seen anything like that on her face since they were small children.

Peter threw in his hand. Seven and two, the worst possible combination anyone could hold. Griffen glanced at the millionaire. The way he chewed on the left half of his lower lip said he had nothing in his hand. Griffen could beat him with his pair of nines. "Call," he said.

"Fold," said the millionaire. Griffen didn't make any triumphant sounds as he hauled in the pot. There had to be several thousand dollars there. If he could keep from losing most of it, he would feel a lot more secure.

"Shuffle and deal," said the dealer. "What game, folks?"

The confection queen glanced at her small, diamond-rimmed watch. "I've got a meeting in the morning, guys. Cash me out, honey."

"Yes, ma'am," the dealer said. He flashed a smile, gleaming white except for a missing front tooth. She collected her winnings, dropped a hundred in front of him, and departed.

"I better go, too," said the millionaire. "Great game, Griffen. Nice to meet you, Peter. Let's play again, huh?"

"A pleasure," Peter said, shaking hands with him. "Anytime. Griffen will tell me when there is an open table."

"Good thing I can afford it," the millionaire said. "Night, guys."

Griffen hesitated as Peter sat down again. He started to push another ante into the pot. If anyone could take the night's profits away from him, it was Peter.

"No, I do not wish to play anymore," he said. "I wanted to talk to you alone."

"I'm takin' my break," Ezra said, hastily getting to his feet. He moved across the room to the wet bar and had the caterer pour him a drink. Griffen welcomed his discretion.

"What's on your mind?" he asked Peter.

The other man looked uncomfortable. "Well, I do not know how to bring this up. I have always found you to be a friendly host, and I admire the way you run your operation. When I retire from the professional field, I wouldn't mind having something like this. In a city where it is legal, of course. I would not enjoy running the gauntlet as you do."

"I wouldn't recommend that part," Griffen said, "but I came into a going concern."

"I know. But that is not what I wanted to say. I will be blunt. I find you honest and straightforward. Your business is fair to the customers. Five percent of the tables for the house is not out of line. The house share is much more expensive elsewhere, and in much less pleasant circumstances. But I get into conversations . . ." He hesitated. "I am hearing from other sources that players think that your games are being rigged. Not all of them, but enough that people are nervous to trust their money to you."

Griffen felt as if his heart had been cut out. "Do you know the name of anyone who said that? I'd like to talk to them, straighten this out."

Peter shook his head. "I have a great card memory, but I'm not so good on names. One guy said he was going back to Atlanta and not coming back until things get better. If they ever do."

Griffen flipped through his mental Rolodex and came up with three regulars that it might have been.

"I just thought you ought to know," Peter said. "People who see me on television think they know me, so they tell me things. As a friend, I thought I'd better tip you off."

Griffen sank into a chair. His world felt as if it was collapsing on top of him. The one thing that he had built up this operation with was his integrity. He had been straightforward with everyone he dealt with. He counted on that pool of money from games to pay his expenses, rent, bar tab, food. He never took anything that might indebt him to someone else. He paid his way. Why was it so important to someone to take away the small operation he was running? The atmosphere was becoming so soured that the majority of players who were not cheated felt as if it could happen to them. Griffen was at a loss.

"Thanks," he said. "Yeah, I'd rather know. I will have to figure out a way to deal with this. I appreciate that you aren't one of the ones who is jumping off the ship."

"Oh, I can spot a cheater," Peter said. "I'm not afraid of being taken. I'd tell you if I saw one. He wouldn't stand a chance against the two of us."

"You're a friend," Griffen said. "I've . . . I've got to go."

He paid the two dealers and left the suite, feeling miserable.

He didn't notice Peter grinning ferociously as he gathered his winnings and put them in his wallet. Jordan and the others would be pleased. There were many more ways to undermine an operation than merely depriving it of its clientele.

Thirty-six

Griffen spun Mai around the room to the soft strains of a waltz. The orchestra, nine musicians of ancient years but excellent caliber, nodded and smiled to him as he whisked her past them. It was Thursday. He had two parties that week, both can't-miss invitations. Fox Lisa had campaigned to come to this dance, but so had Mai. In compensation, he promised Fox Lisa the biggest ball of all, the masquerade ball held that Saturday by a superkrewe who wanted as many kings and queens as possible. She had not been pleased to be third choice, and had made it known to everyone in the bar. Griffen had a lot of people's sympathy.

Mai had a few bones to pick with him, as well.

"Why was I not made queen?" she demanded.

"Look, I still don't know more than I told you," Griffen said, utterly tired of the topic. "All I know is what the krewe tells me. Callum Fenway said it was Etienne's choice, and they could vote up or down, that is all. So they voted up."

"On M. Wurmley," Mai said. "I saw the entry in that magazine. You haven't met her yet?"

"No," Griffen said. "I bet she's someone's rich aunt."

"Mmm," said Mai, sounding preoccupied.

"You look beautiful," Griffen said. She was clad in brilliant green. The fabric fell from tiny straps on her shoulders in a smooth flow to her feet, accentuating her figure in the simplest way. He had expected her to wear the red dress she had bought while out with him, but she had informed him she was saving it for the Fafnir ball. Naturally, she had a closetful of eveningwear.

Mai tilted her head. "Very well, I shall drop the subject. It's done now."

"Right. Let's talk about something else."

"Is there any more information about Jesse Lee?"

Griffen almost choked. "Something positive?"

"I do care what happened, you know."

"I know." Griffen sighed. "But Harrison hasn't told me a thing. He's coming up empty. I put out word among my watchers and some people I met at the conclave. No one seems to have seen anything, or they are too scared to come forward."

"I see." Mai tapped her fingers pensively on Griffen's shoulder.

Her own investigation, asking questions among her spies in the Quarter, had come up with no other information on the murder. Jesse Lee would likely never be avenged. That irritated and frustrated her. She wanted badly to connect Jordan Ma to the killing. If she could do that, she could prevail upon the elders to remove him. Perhaps permanently.

"Wait, there's someone I want to talk to," Griffen said. Mai glanced in the direction he was looking. A tall man with a potbelly stood beside a woman in a yellow dress, about a size sixteen, she estimated. They wore eye masks.

They swung to a halt next to the couple just as the music ended.

"Hello, Eric," he said.

"Griffen McCandles?" the masked man said, startled. "I didn't expect to see you here."

"No?" Griffen asked.

"Because you're so busy," the lady in the matching mask on his arm put in hastily.

"Yes, right," Eric said. "That's what I meant."

"I'm king of the Krewe of Fafnir," he said.

"Yes, I saw. Congratulations. We're in the court here."

"Congratulations to you. This is Mai."

"As in Mai Goodness? Pleased to meet you, lovely lady,"
Eric said. "My wife, Gloria."

"That's a beautiful dress," Gloria said.

The tiny woman preened. "Caroline Herrera," she said,
turning slightly to show off a better angle.

"Well, it looks wonderful on you," the woman said. "Not
everyone can carry off a silhouette like that."

"I am fortunate. Your dress becomes you, too. Is that
Armani?"

"Yes! What a good eye you have, dear."

"So, doing the rounds, are you?" Eric sounded nervous.
Griffen put on a polite and disarming smile. Eric was a
Louisiana businessman with ties to a number of politicos.
Griffen had done his best to strike up a friendly acquaintance
with him, making sure games were open when he wanted
them, bringing in his favorite liquors and snacks. It would
be useful to have an in with the local government. Influence
of that kind opened doors. Griffen was beginning to think
about his future, beyond running a few poker games.

"Like yourself," Griffen said. "Say, Eric, it's been a while
since we've seen you at a game."

"Oh, you know," Eric said. "Pretty busy right now. The
season's getting started, and we have a big pile of invitations,
but I've got to keep up with business matters, too. Probably
the same as you."

"That's true," Griffen began.

The orchestra near the wall struck up a soft jazz tune.

"Let's go and sit down, Gloria," Eric said hastily. "Nice
seeing you, Griffen."

Alarmed, Griffen saw his useful connection getting away.

"Eric, I'd just like to talk with you for a moment."

Eric held up his hands. "Maybe later, Griffen. Really. Not
now."

Mai put a hand on Eric's arm. "Won't you ask me to
dance?" she asked sweetly.

Eric looked at his wife, who nodded. The expression in
her eyes was not jealous. Mai was glad. It would make this

effort somewhat easier. As they moved away, Griffen bowed to Gloria.

They moved off together to the strains of a glorious old standard. Mai allowed Eric to plant a large, heavy hand in the small of her back and press her against his chest. It was his way of guiding her around the floor. It did not leave her a good deal of room to move her legs, but she was nimble enough to keep his feet off of hers.

"Griffen speaks well of you, sir," Mai said, bending gracefully as he twirled her out to arm's length and back into his arms.

"Good guy, Griffen," Eric said absently. He gave her a quick smile. She could read agitation in his expression.

"But something is troubling you."

"It's not his fault, I guess, but I have a reputation to look after in this state. I hear things."

"About Griffen?"

"The games. Been a lot of controversy lately. I ended up talking to a guy in a bar who had been at one of the games and had his whole stake wiped out by someone who turned out to be cheating. Asian like you."

"I probably do not know him," Mai said, coolly.

"No! Not saying you do. But if I'm not wrong, one of these days the cops are gonna raid a game, and I'd get my picture in the paper. All I want to do is play some poker. If I want hassles, I can stay home and talk to my wife."

Mai gave him a playful smile. "I see. I know that Griffen would certainly like you to come back. He respects you so much, Eric. You are a man of power."

Nothing loosens up a man's inhibitions like flattery. "If he can clear up the problems, I'd be back there like a shot. Never had such good hospitality. He picks the best players. And I win a lot." He smiled, some of the nervousness abated. Mai smiled back. They finished the dance, and Mai curtsied prettily to him. She came to squeeze Gloria's hand.

"Thank you for letting me dance with him. He is very good."

"He's not bad at that," Gloria said. "Your Griffen is a good dancer, too. Nice to meet you, dear."

The elder couple squeezed their way through the crowd and disappeared. Mai took Griffen's arm and pulled him off the dance floor. She told Griffen what she had coaxed out of Eric.

"The word is out," Griffen said, angrily. "We ought to have had eight games this week. We're down to five. The rumors are killing us. We'll be wiped out in a few weeks if this keeps up."

"Come and sit down," Mai said hastily, glancing around. Almost everyone else had taken their places.

"I don't think I can sit down," Griffen said. "The Eastern dragons are destroying not only my life, but that of all my employees. Do you know how many people rely on me for their livelihood?"

"Poker face!" Mai hissed. "Play the part. This is no time to let your anger get the better of you."

Griffen looked around and realized that numerous eyes were upon him, including Eric's. If there was ever a time that he had to conceal all his tells, this was it. He smiled and put out his elbow to Mai.

"May I escort you to our table?" he asked.

"It would be my pleasure," Mai said. She alone could feel the fury in him, but as they passed each of the tables, the candles in the centerpiece flared up. Mai was grateful that the guests at their table were all strangers.

"I will get them," Griffen whispered to her, attacking his salad as if it were one of the Eastern dragons. "I just hope I can do it before they wipe me out."

"You have allies," Mai said. "I will do everything to help you."

Griffen smiled, the first genuine smile he had put on in an hour. "I know. I'm counting on you."

Mai went back to her salad. Something told her that she ought to be ashamed of herself, but she was simply not accustomed to it.

Thirty-seven

Griffen blanched at the figures on the balance sheet. "I didn't know it was that bad."

"Believe it, brother," Jerome said, tapping the page with the edge of a coaster. They were alone at a corner table in the Irish bar. The other patrons sensed a personal and painful discussion and left them alone. Griffen glimpsed eyes slewed toward him from the pool tables and other places. They looked sympathetic. "We are down this entire month. I have got only one game scheduled, at the Omni, of all places."

"What happened to the high rollers who were going to meet at the Royal Sonesta tomorrow evening?"

"Canceled. No points for guessing why. The rumor mills have been working overtime and double time. The concierge won't even talk to me."

"Can we fill the suite? Less high-level players?" Griffen took a sip of the one whisky and water he had allowed himself. In order to make sure he could pay his rent, he had cut back on everything that he possibly could. He knew he could run a tab, but Fred would expect to see it cleared at the end of each week, and he did not know if he'd have the extra income to pay it. As much as he hated cooking for himself, it looked like the only way to eke out his food budget for the week. Peanut butter tasted better on hamburgers than on plain bread with jelly.

"Not unless you find out why they're not coming," Jerome said. "Their expectations are low at the moment. This is a bad precedent, since our expenses are not going down, even if the intake is."

"Can we handle payroll?"

Jerome pointed to an entry in red at the bottom left of the sheet. "Only if we don't pay ourselves, man. I'm okay, but how are you doing?"

"Flat broke," Griffen admitted.

"I'm your friend, but there is no way I can't point out the irony of a member of the local royalty more down-and-out than the peasants."

"If I remember my history, plenty of monarchs had empty treasuries. The difference is that they could rob the peasants to raise money."

"Well, the peasants aren't coming. I'm gonna have a face-to-face with a few of our formerly most helpful connections and see if I can't convince 'em to send us some prospects. I suggest you do the same."

Griffen agreed. "Let's split up the list. We'll see if we can at least fill that suite day after tomorrow. If not, we'll have to lay people off."

"They'd feel that was unlucky, losing their jobs during Mardi Gras season," Jerome said. "Not to mention the practical side of needing the funds same as you for the festivities. We've been through tough times before."

"Not with someone trying to put us out of business on purpose," Griffen said. "I just wish we could figure out when they were going to strike and how many of them there are."

"Mai told you not to trust three of them, but it seems like there's more than that, and they aren't all Eastern."

"That's the problem," Griffen said. "We're not spotting them, and it's killing us."

"We'll get by," Jerome said. "We went through worse before you got here."

Griffen made a face. "That's not so much consolation," he said. "But let's start the charm offensive, and see if we can pull it together that way. I'll talk to the spotters. I'll offer them a percentage of the table if they can deliver players."

Jerome shook his head. "I dunno, Grifter. That will have them bringing uncles out of the bayou or prison just to fill seats."

"There'll be rules," Griffen said. "I'm not completely desperate. Not yet."

His cell phone warbled, reminding him there was another bill that he had to pay, and soon. He raised a finger. "Sorry, Jer, just a minute. Hello?"

"Griffen! Peter Sing."

"Hey, Peter," Griffen said. Jerome's brows drew down over his forehead. He made a throat-slitting gesture. Griffen waved it away. "What can I do for you?"

"Well, I got a call from your assistant. He said that the game on Sunday is canceled."

"Yeah, sorry, Peter. The other players who were going to be in on it dropped out."

Peter clucked his tongue. "Well, that is a shame. I am in the mood to play." There was a brief silence. "Would you like to come up to my suite and play a few hands, just for fun?"

Griffen winced at the thought. "I'm pretty busy with Mardi Gras assignments right now."

"Don't say no." Peter interrupted him. "I'm bored out of my mind. I could go down to the casino, but there's no one of your caliber there. Come on up. I will order some food from downstairs, exactly as you would if you were hosting. Just a little friendly one-on-one. Say you will come. In an hour or so? We can play for chips instead of cash. We can talk technique. It will be unofficial."

Griffen was torn. Jerome was shooting him poisonous looks, but a friendly game with such a skilled player as Peter would cheer him up.

"Okay. Thanks. I would enjoy it. See you"—he checked his watch—"in two hours?"

"That would be great," Peter said. "I can pick your brain about betting on Omaha games. It is a weak spot in my repertoire."

Griffen knew Peter was just saying that to help cheer him up, but he appreciated it. "See you then." He hung up.

"Grifter, I do not trust that man."

"I know," Griffen said. "But he hasn't done anything. Not once at any game has he caused a problem. In fact, he's bent over backward to be nice to the other players. It has added cachet to our games to have him there. You can't deny that."

"I know. I just have a feeling that he just hasn't erupted yet, like ragweed. And to offer to play you a game for no money? He knows more than you tell him."

"He's pretty damned observant," Griffen said. "I think he knows I've got my back to the wall, but he's not adding to my debt."

"It's just too convenient," Jerome said. "He might be acting like a nice guy, but he's an Asian and he's a pretty strong dragon and all my vibes go off when I'm around him. I think he's got to be involved with the Easterns even if Mai has never seen him before. But you're the big dragon. You get to make your own decisions, for better or for worse. I'll be there to pick you up again if he knocks you down, but just remember that I get to say, 'I told you so.'"

"If he does, I'll have earned it," Griffen said. He got up and put a dollar on the table. "I'll make some stops before I go see him. Let me know how it works out for you."

Jerome pushed his chair back and stood up. "One thing's for sure," Jerome said, brandishing the balance sheet, "it'd have to sink a whole lot to be worse than it is."

Thirty-eight

"**What** do you mean, you lost?"

"I mean, I lost," Peter said. He did not like being under scrutiny, but sitting in the brocaded armchair with the other three circling around him like interrogators, all he lacked was the bright light in his eyes. Rebecca would gladly have turned one on him if she had thought about it. Luckily, she lacked imagination. "Griffen McCandles took all the money I put up as my stake on the table. Three thousand dollars against the three hundred he had in his wallet, and he won it all in five hands. I applaud him."

"You're too soft," Jordan Ma said. "You let him take your money."

"I am not soft, and I did not let him take it. He really is that good. You have not played against him at a table. I have, many times now. When he begins to concentrate, it is as if his opponents' minds are open books. It is most disconcerting. And he cannot read minds in the traditional meaning. I have tested the theory. It is just uncanny card sense. He did not want to play for money—he is close to broke right now—but I persuaded him, to the detriment of my own wallet. I could have won it all back, but only by cheating, and I would rather shatter a pure jade vase than stoop to such a level."

Jordan let his annoyance show, a rare event. "He is our quarry. You have befriended him."

Peter shrugged. "I do not deny it. I like him. We have

become friends. He is open, unlike the rest of you. It is refreshing to speak with someone who means what he says. Poker is my life, unlike the rest of you. I have learned a few tricks watching him that you probably wouldn't understand."

"But Mai must have told him what you are!"

"Did she? She plays her own game. If he does know, then he is a better player than I would have dreamed and has had better training in controlling his emotions. I sense no power spikes such as Rebecca here is constantly sending off." The female sputtered until Winston Long held up a hand. She subsided, glaring. "If he knows me to be the enemy, then he is playing a dangerous game. I like it."

Jordan Ma was furious. "You are becoming bewitched by him. This will not do. We should remove you from this operation."

Peter snorted in derision. "The elders won't like it if you send me home. I will tell them what I know."

Rebecca stuck her face close to his. "Not if you cannot draw breath to tell them."

He didn't move even though her breath smelled aggressively of spearmint. He smiled, knowing he held a hand higher than hers. "Really? Are you really suggesting murder because I have colored outside the lines a little?" He ignored her. She was not the chief of the operation, after all. "I am not a fool, Jordan. I tell him nothing about what we are doing. I am no less useful to the assignment than I was when we arrived. But I am paying attention to what I am doing."

Winston Long grunted, "It is the Stockholm syndrome. You are befriending the enemy, hoping that you can work out some solution that will see us all survive the encounter."

Peter groaned elaborately.

"Old man, you watch too many movies. He confides in me. I don't confide in him."

"Then what information do you derive from these conversations?"

"The operation is close to collapse," Peter said, feeling

reluctant to let the words escape his lips. Jordan's eyes gleamed. "I believe that except for what he left with, he has no assets remaining to him."

"But you have helped to fund him for another day!"

"Air is leaking out of the hole we have made. It does not matter how fast. It's still leaking, and soon it will be empty."

"But it could have been tomorrow! Now it could be next week, or the week after!"

"You know we could be going about this all wrong," Peter said, offering a thought that had been on his mind for days. "He could be an ally instead of an enemy."

Jordan made a slashing gesture with the edge of his hand. "No. He *is* the enemy if he can turn our own forces against us."

"I can help to arrange for an accident," Winston said. "It is much swifter than waiting for the bitter end, if you are so impatient." He turned to Peter. "And you had better not tip him off, or you will incur the same accident."

Rebecca came to sit on Peter's knee. "Just like the other one. It will be fun to watch another one die."

Peter raised his hands. "I am not keen to commit suicide. I just think you are misusing a potential asset. I would be inclined to allow Mai to continue on her tack. It would be better to have someone like Griffen McCandles in our operation than to destroy him. It would be like burning a work of art."

"Whether or not, it is our job," Jordan said. "The elders make the decision. We do not. You are doing well so far. Stick to the program. No more improvisation. If we bankrupt him and prevent him from running his operation, we can move in to take it over immediately. Do not prolong the endgame."

Rebecca looked smug that he was getting dressed down. Peter didn't care. "You are making a mistake," he said. "Am I the only one who can see it?"

"It doesn't matter what we see," Jordan said. "Our perception is not what matters, in the long run. The elders make the decision, and we carry out their wishes. Feel free to call them, Peter. I will tell them I said you may."

"I will call them!" Peter said.

Jordan shook his head. "It will change nothing. But if they tell you to follow my orders, I expect you to do so or suffer whatever consequences I wish. Do you understand?"

The other three sets of eyes bored into Peter. For the first time he actually felt fear, but his poker-playing self refused to show it. "I understand," he said. "And I will obey."

Thirty-nine

Val put her hands over her ears, but the horrible noise persisted. She backed away, but there was only so far she could go in the storeroom of the bar.

"Valerie, I only have your best interests in mind," Melinda said.

"I am not listening to you anymore," Val cried.

She had only glanced down for a moment to read a few lines from her latest book. The bar had been completely empty at three thirty. The last customer had drained the final drops from his beer, slapped a tip on the counter, and departed with a grin at her. Then, suddenly, the place was crawling with people. Men in suits, who looked as if they were packing, covered the doors, front and back. One closed the shutters over the windows and turned the sign from OPEN to CLOSED. Val had reached for the phone to call for help, but another besuited man had taken it from her and ripped the cord out of the wall—and up inside it for five feet. Plaster dust was still sifting down.

In the center of it all was a small, slightly overweight woman with reddish brown hair and a no-nonsense demeanor. She wore a two-piece suit of pebble-textured, mahogany fabric that shouted "money" at the top of its lungs. Her Stuart Weitzman shoes had five-inch heels, but they only brought the top of her head to just under Val's chin.

"Hello, Valerie," she said. "I'm Melinda."

Val's attempts to escape had only caused cascades of glasses and bottles to shatter on the floor everywhere in the bar. The coffered ceiling had scars in it, one from a head impacting the painted panels, and two from flying feet. Three chairs she had tried to use as bludgeons had been reduced to firewood, along with the table one of the men had landed on. It had been no use. She was desperately outnumbered. They had backed her slowly but inexorably behind the bar and into the storeroom, Melinda marching on her like Napoleon Bonaparte, whose face was on a brandy bottle not a foot from her shoulder. Then she had started talking.

Val screamed and fought, but there was no way out. Melinda had her where she wanted her at last.

". . . And you have to stop sleeping with every handsome man that goes past you! Why don't you have any self-respect? You're a beautiful girl. You're twenty-one years old. You should care more about yourself."

"I have self-respect," Val shouted back. "I've got a boy-friend!"

"A street thug? He's beneath you, Valerie," Melinda said. "A mongrel human. Nothing special."

That really inflamed her temper. Valerie straightened her shoulders, growing a foot taller in the cramped room. "Nothing special? Gris-gris IS special! He's a gentleman. He treats me like gold. He wooed me, unlike your 'special' son. If Nathaniel was really so wonderful, he wouldn't have had to use his talent on me, would he?"

"It's a dragon's way to take what she wants," Melinda pointed out. "You've done that, haven't you?"

A trifle guiltily, Val thought about the way that she and Gris-gris made love, with Val firmly in control. Melinda nodded.

"Yes, I know. It's none of my business. Then, on to what IS my business. You. You and this precious child you are carrying."

She glanced over her shoulder at the armed men in suits. Val went even more on guard. Melinda turned back. She smiled like a shark. But instead of moving closer, the men edged back. They were still between her and the door.

"What do you want?" Val asked.

"To give you a world of opportunity," Melinda said. "Come with me. Right now. I have a limousine waiting."

"No! You'll take me away. This is *my* life."

Melinda smirked. "Mai told you I'd kidnap you, didn't she? I can just guess what that little oriental bitch has been telling you. Make your *own* judgment! Are you a dragon?"

"Yes! That's what everyone keeps telling me!"

"Don't do that! Decide based on what you know, not what other people tell you. Here are the facts: I have been within reach for almost three months. Have I laid a single finger on you?"

Val paused before answering. "No."

"Am I coercing you to get in a car with me?"

"Well, no, but . . ."

"Just no! Then how am I impinging on your life?"

"You're here! You keep calling me. Nagging me! I want time to make my own decisions. Back off. Leave me alone. I'll get along fine without you."

Melinda shook her head. "You need advice. I spoke to your brother. He is concerned that you are taking this step too soon on your own. I have a proposal for you. Let me take your child and raise it. You can get on with your life. You will have full access, but you can finish growing up."

"I am grown-up!"

Melinda clicked her tongue. "My mistake. I shouldn't put it that way. Let me say it differently: I want you to have the opportunity to fulfill your potential. Being a very young, marginally employed, single mother will make it harder for you to achieve it. Do you want to finish college? Do you want to have a career? I can help."

"Your help? I would rather have a goiter and two broken legs!"

"You can have all three," Melinda said calmly. "They're

not mutually exclusive. Let me raise the baby until you feel ready to take care of it. I'm a mother. I love babies. I have been through all the stages: colic, sleepless nights, teething, head colds, diarrhea. I can handle it. I'm not the monster you think I am."

Val reminded herself that not all monsters looked like monsters. Some of them looked very pretty, like those crazy changelings that had been all over the conclave dance. And some of them looked like the president of a powerful corporation. But only one thing was keeping Melinda here, terrorizing her. She steeled herself.

"You had better get out of town while you still can," Val said, dropping her voice to a cold whisper. "I don't have to bring your grandchild into the world. You've got three kids. Let one of the others have a family. This one doesn't have to be your pawn."

Melinda's eyes narrowed. She understood what Val was implying. "You wouldn't dare."

Val knew she would not, but Melinda didn't. She put her chin up defiantly. It was hard to push the words out, but she managed.

"Some of my friends have had terminations. It was horrible for them, but they couldn't handle having a child too soon. Maybe it's the same for me. I . . . I know where to go."

Melinda's face turned purple. "You can't!"

Val looked down her nose at the shorter woman. "I can. Anything rather than having you hounding me and hovering over me for the rest of my *life*!"

"You'd really do it?"

"Yes! Anything to get you to go away!"

Melinda threw open her arms. "Come here, darling! You really *are* a dragon!"

"What?" Val found herself enfolded and pounded on the back.

Melinda held her at arm's length and beamed at her.

"Only a dragon could make a statement like that to tip the balance of power. It's immature and misguided, and I know that you would rather tear your own intestines out and drape them around your neck than harm a single scale on that baby, and you were reluctant even to think about it; but I really admire you, Valerie. I was beginning to wonder if being raised as a human had made you too soft. Boy, was I wrong! You are the real thing, sweetheart."

Val pushed away and retreated out of reach. "I still don't want you bothering me."

Melinda waved a hand. "You'll get over it. You will need my help. I can be a resource for you. You can ask me anything. I don't mind. I do not embarrass easily."

"Yeah, I figured that out," Val said. "Otherwise, you might have civilized your own kids."

Melinda put an arm around her and patted her on the back. "I tried. You have to believe me. But after a while, they go their own way. And Lizzy—never mind. I don't want to rehash the past. She will not bother you. I can keep her busy somewhere else. All I want is to be in my grandchild's life as it grows up. Malcolm doesn't understand the softer feelings. He sees them as weakness. I know that you need the entire range to be effective. I can be brutal, but real loyalty comes when you love someone."

"I know that," Val said.

"I will limit my contact with you, if that's what bothers you so much," Melinda said, "but you have to allow me some. You are a strong woman. I do believe you now when you say you can handle what's coming. What I ask is if you feel something is going to be too much for you, that you swallow your pride and ask for help. It's harder than going it alone, I know. But you have talents of your own that even your prodigy of a brother will never have an inkling of."

Val was confused. "What kind of talents? I can grow big and I'm superstrong. What else?"

Melinda regarded her pityingly. "You don't even know what you have got there under the hood, do you? No, of course not. That Mose didn't want you to know that your potential is greater than your brother's."

"What?" Val was suspicious.

"I am not lying. They haven't told you about female dragons, have they? They fear us, darling. They *fear* us. We can run circles around them. There isn't a male dragon that can equal us, and they didn't want you to know that. I will help you reach the pinnacle. You can learn to control all your talents. Ask Griffen. He knows more than he has ever said. They call us female dragons wild. But we can control that savagery and make it work for us. You shouldn't be wasting your time pouring drinks in a side-street bar and rolling the occasional man who catches your eye. You could be running a major corporation or a small country."

Val pouted. "I like my life the way it is."

"Shut up!" Melinda roared. It was the first time she had turned on her own power. Until then, Val had thought of her as what she looked like, a middle-aged East Coast matron who might have just come from a mah-jongg game. Now she looked like a dragon, a fierce, bloodthirsty beast. "You can't be serious! Living in a dump of an apartment, with thirdhand furniture and thrift-shop clothes? At least you should learn your capabilities before you throw them away. Take responsibility for yourself! Live, don't just exist. If I give you no other gift, as the mother of my grandchild, I will give you that. You don't have to like me, but you should respect me. I am what you could become."

Val had regained her aplomb. "And who says I want to be that pathetic?"

Melinda's eyes narrowed, but she seemed pleased. "You are so young," she said. She patted Val on the cheek. Val flinched backward. "I want you to think it over. I'll be in town. Good-bye, dear. I'll call you."

She seemed to vanish among the ancient wooden shelves. Val rushed out of the storeroom, expecting to see chaos in the bar, but it was clean. The stoic-faced men in suits had cleared up the room while she and Melinda had been in the back. Not a shard of glass or a drop of liquor was on the floor. They had reopened the shutters. Even the broken chairs had been repaired. All that was left was to turn the CLOSED sign back to OPEN.

That woman! That woman was going to haunt her the rest of her life! Val looked longingly at the whisky behind the counter.

No.

As much as she hated to admit it, she found sense in some of what Melinda said. She did need to take a harder look at where she would be a year from then, or five, or ten. Griffen was working for the future; why shouldn't she?

And what was that information about female dragons that she claimed he was concealing from her?

Forty

Griffen fingered his tie. He was getting used to formal attire. In fact, he looked good in it, something that he had resisted knowing. It was just so much trouble! How women went through all of the fussing and froufrouing to get ready for a date, he didn't know. He knew his gender was not innocent of having expectations about women that were difficult to meet naturally. Long, dark eyelashes, for example. Rosy cheeks and lips. A smooth, curved figure. Men, as Val had remarked with some asperity, could show up in anything and, as long as it was clean and in good repair, would be accepted at any event up to white tie. He had seldom had to rise to the occasion. He had failed to appreciate how much the women he had dated did to look nice for him.

He sat in the middle of the rear seat of the taxi, between Fox Lisa and Mai. Both of them looked spectacular. Mai, in the red silk dress and lipstick to match, dripping with expensive jewelry, sat serenely on his right. Tourists staggering down Royal with plastic cups in their hands stared through the window at her. She waved to them with her fingers together as Griffen had seen the Queen of England do. The gesture didn't seem at all out of place. On his left, Fox Lisa, in electric blue, had become a queen herself. She held her head high. Her red hair had been swept up into a chignon with a peacock-feather eye nestled against it. Griffen realized he hadn't noticed how long and slender her neck was. He felt like leaning over to kiss it. Her many tattoos peeked out from the brief, tight black dress like jewelry. He had never noticed that the twining snakes on her wrists resembled 1920s enameled Cleopatra bracelets.

The streets were more crowded than he had ever seen them. He understood why many of his friends who had lived in the French Quarter longer than he had hid out during the two weeks before Mardi Gras, and why "tourist" was a dirty word though the persons were a necessary evil. It was like one long, very intense spring break, in a much smaller area than Miami Beach. They came to drink and carouse. They came to listen to the music. They came to bare their breasts for strings of beads. They came to scream at the parades and join in dancing on the street once the last band had passed by. Yet there was an entire stratum of the carnival that they never touched, and many of them never knew existed. Griffen looked back on what he had learned in the last couple of months, and marveled. The citywide party that seemed so obvious was multilayered, intricate, took months, if not years of planning, and accommodated hundreds of thousands of celebrants of every kind. He watched the staggering men with pity, knowing that he could well have been one of them as recently as the year before.

They pulled up into the taxi queue in front of the hotel. "Now, remember," Doreen said, putting her elbow on the seatback, "use the glass doors to the ballroom only. The police won't let you in again if you use the main hotel doors. There was a big fuss a few years ago. One of the superkrewe kings got locked out of his own ball because he got arrested for starting a fight with the cops. Don't make me come and get you from the lockup."

"Thanks," Griffen said, handing her the fare plus a large tip. He had taken the winnings from his unexpected game with Peter Sing and paid off his employees, and had been eking out his own expenses with the residue. At least he had enough for taxi fare home, as well.

Fox Lisa slid out on her own and waited on the curb.

Griffen alighted and went around to help Mai out of the other door. With both ladies on his arms, he sauntered inside to join the crowd already assembling in the anteroom.

Molly Harting, the wife of the ball committee chairman, waited at a table by the door of the ballroom. She examined their invitations and checked off their names on a list. An ornate display featuring a gold dragon wearing a domino mask and dripping with beads loomed over little tent cards that stood in rows on the table. Each had a picture of the same gold dragon curled around the calligraphed name of a guest.

"That's your table number," Molly said, handing Griffen his card. Mai and Fox Lisa found their own. "Of course, all of you are at the head table. Enjoy."

"Thanks," Griffen said, gallantly. "May I reserve a dance with you?"

She giggled with pleasure. "Your dance card is likely to fill up before I can write my name, Your Majesty. Thanks anyhow. See you inside. Oh!" She reached behind the figure of the dragon and brought out three masks. "Put these on, and don't take them off until your name is called."

"Griffen!" Val called.

Griffen turned to look for her in the crowd. The women in evening gowns and coiffed hair were all strangers. One of them broke away from the crowd and came over to Griffen. The most attractive was a statuesque blonde in blue silk and a white lace shawl over her bare shoulders whose hair had been sculpted into Grecian coils. She had amazingly long eyelashes and very pretty blue eyes. Griffen was speculating on who she might be, when she came over and hit him in the arm with her fist.

"You look great, Big Brother!" she exclaimed.

"Val?" Griffen gulped. He had been checking out his own sister! He hoped no one else had noticed. "Wow, you look absolutely amazing."

Val primped her hair with a careful palm. "What do you

think of the updo?" she asked. "And they did my makeup at the salon."

"It makes you totally unrecognizable," Mai said. "I mean that in a good way." Val wrinkled her nose at Mai, who made a face back.

"I love your wrap," Fox Lisa said, fingering the edge of the shawl.

"Isn't it lovely? It's from Gris-gris," Val said, pulling her date forward.

"My aunt sent it," Gris-gris said. "Val and Ms. Mai impressed her plenty."

Val and Mai exchanged glances and grins.

Griffen had to do another double take. The slender man, who had never worn anything fancier than a polo shirt around Griffen, had on a Brooks Brothers tuxedo that framed wider shoulders and a narrower waist than Griffen ever would have suspected him of having. The white shirt gleamed in the muted lighting of the anteroom, and his silk bow tie was more perfectly knotted than Griffen's. Griffen would not have known him at all except that he was escorting Val.

"Looking good," Griffen told him. Gris-gris ducked his head shyly.

"It's the lady on my arm that makes it all work," he said. "I never done nothin' like this before. I worked a bunch of krewe parties in days past, but I never came to one."

"Neither have we," Griffen assured him. "Come on, let's go find our table."

All but Gris-gris donned masks, and they entered the room.

"I love my dress," Val told Gris-gris, holding on to his arm. "That was one of the most fun experiences I've ever had."

"Aunt Herbera said she'd be happy to fit you out again anytime."

"Local talent is all very well, but the real cutting-edge

fashion comes from New York couture," Mai began. Griffen nudged her hard. Mai started to give him a dirty look, then ducked her head in shame. "But she does impeccable work, I must admit. There is not a stitch out of place, and this is the second time Val has worn it. It is a classic that will last many years." Gris-gris looked pleased.

"My aunt, she been making dresses for kings and queens of Mardi Gras for forty years," he said. "This the first time I've seen 'em bein' worn. She will be thrilled."

The huge ballroom was even more dimly lit than the anteroom, but enough to see the decorations. Around the perimeter and flanking the amazingly long head table were white pillars with gold dragons perched on top. The dragons' tails wound down the columns, almost to the spotlights that shone upward, projecting the winged shadows on the ceiling. Softly rippling banners hung on the walls. One of them, fringed in heavy swags of old gold tassels, looked old enough to Griffen to have been made before World War II. The others were newer but just as beautiful. Round tables filled most of the room around a large dance floor.

An archway made of trelliswork crawling with dragon figures stood at one edge of the dance floor. A photographer stopped them as they reached it and snapped several exposures.

"Trying to go incognito?" a stocky man asked them when the photographer let them go. "It won't work."

Griffen smiled at Detective Harrison. He touched the mask on his face. "I don't know what the mask is for," he said.

"Plausible deniability," Harrison said. "Consorting with known criminals."

"But here you are," Griffen said. "You look good."

"Thanks. Cost me enough to get here, between the ticket and tuxedo rental. Mine wasn't fancy enough for this blowout."

"You have your own tuxedo?" Griffen asked, unable not to sound astonished.

Harrison frowned at him. "You think you can live in New

Orleans and never get invited to a Mardi Gras party? Thanks a heap."

"I don't mean to be offensive," Griffen said. "You could fill a library with all the things I don't know about Mardi Gras."

Harrison waved a hand. "Never mind, Griffen. Anyone can tell *yours* is a rental. But the rest of you cleaned up pretty good."

"Didn't know we could do it, huh?" Gris-gris asked, grinning. Harrison did the same double take that Griffen had.

"Gris-gris? Well, I will be damned. But this is the season for costumes. For everyone, I guess."

Gris-gris was enjoying himself too much to be offended. "That's right, Officer. I hide my inner prince most days. But today I had to reveal myself to take this lovely princess on my arm." He patted Val's hand.

"Enjoy yourself, Detective," Griffen said. "They're signing to us to sit down."

He escorted both of his ladies to the long table at the end of the room. Several people in domino masks were already seated there. All the men rose as the ladies approached. Griffen recognized most of them in spite of the nominal covering, and introduced them to his party.

"These are the dukes and maids," Etienne explained, giving everyone's name. "Lieutenants and committee heads are out dere." He gestured toward the sea of round tables.

"A pleasure," Griffen said, bowing over the women's hands and shaking hands with the men.

The dukes followed suit, in "pecking order," as Mitchell might have put it. The ladies all curtsied to him and shook hands with the others. He had heard some of the names. They were prominent in business or society or both in town. He felt proud to be titular head of a group like that.

"What are the masks for?" Mai inquired.

"We reveal the members of the court later on in special introductions," Etienne said. "After you are so obligin' as to assist us in the tableaux. I know y'all are all ready to go on dat."

"We've been practicing," Val assured him.

"For what?" Griffen asked, feeling like a rug had been pulled out from under his feet. "You're presenting a tableau?"

Val winked at him from behind her mask. "You don't know everything that's going on, Big Brother." She let one of the masked dukes lead her away

Etienne's seat was at the center of the table. Griffen was at his right hand, and an empty chair was on his left. The rest of the court spread out boy-girl-boy-girl on either side. Griffen took a moment after sitting down to look at everything.

Etienne had kept his promise: Fafnir could hold its masquerade ball up beside any of the krewes, super or not, with pride. The decorations featured the same masked dragon that had been on the Fafnir invitations. He—or she— had been made into wall hangings like medieval tapestries that hung suspended all around the walls, etched into the champagne flutes at each place, and printed on the name cards. A white card with the sequence of events printed on it was propped against the pristine white napkin folded on his plate. Two bands would play that evening, one jazz and one orchestra. The jazz band was playing at the moment off on the side of the room.

"Canapés, sir?" asked a waiter in black tie. He extended a silver tray to Griffen. Griffen accepted a small plate and napkin. The waiter used a small silver tongs to fill it with a pastry shell an inch across filled with pink crabmeat and topped with a dollop of remoulade, a single perfect shrimp on a black-and-white crust made of sesame seeds, and a globe of salmon paste with a flag made of cucumber sticking out of it on puff pastry. He kept doling out tiny sculptures in food until Griffen held up a hand to stop him. The lady to his right, Regina Bellaut, owner of three trendy exercise studios, exclaimed over her morsels.

"That is just the most delicious thing!"

"It's the best food I've had at any of these parties," Griffen said. He had become quite a foodie since moving to New

Orleans and was pleased to be able to identify the delicacies
to his seatmate.

"Well, I am mightily impressed," Regina said. "It's so
nice to have Fafnir up and around again after all these years.
My great-granddaddy was a duke of Fafnir."

"Really?" Griffen asked. He realized that she was a dragon
and wondered if she knew it. "Did he know a man named
Mose?"

"Yes, of course he did! A fine gentleman. He and Great-
granddad used to chat about once a week. Probably still do
though I don't know. Great-granddad is in Arizona for the
climate."

Griffen noticed that beside his water glass was a china
figure of a dragon with the date and the name of the krewe
on a banner snaking down its chest. The dragon was wound
around a treasure chest made of real wood banded with
metal.

"What is this?" he asked.

"It's the favor," Regina said. "I think it's a little jewelry
box, a ring box, for little valuables or paper clips. This is
so much nicer than most of the table favors at other balls.
Very pretty, Captain," she said, raising her voice so Etienne
could hear.

He offered her a seated bow. "We do it all," Etienne said.
"It's got a witchin' on it so you never lose half of a pair of
earrin's or have you necklace clasp break. It's good luck."

"Well, thank you, Captain," Regina said. "I will treasure it."

"Me, too," Griffen said.

"Quality's what we aim to offer," Etienne said.

The meal followed suit. Griffen enjoyed a shrimp etoufée
that rivaled any he had had at the best restaurants in the city.
All the courses were, he thought with a self-deprecating
grin, fit for a king.

After dessert was served, Griffen sat back with a full
stomach and a sense of well-being. People came up to take
pictures of him, alone or with the spouse of the camera-
wielder. He felt like a minor celebrity. This was a lot more

fun than the conclave had been. There he had been a curiosity, one of a kind. Here, he was among fellow dragons. His mask limited his vision to what he could see ahead of him, but that was a minor annoyance.

Etienne stood up and banged on the side of his water glass with a fork. His lean, sharp face was lit with eager energy. Griffen could see how that enthusiasm had inspired a new generation.

"Attention, folks! I want to welcome y'all to the revival of the Krewe of Fafnir and our Masquerade Ball! In a moment, we'll see a tableau of this year's theme, which I'll tell ya, just to whet your appetites, is Dragons Rule!"

The diners burst into wild applause. Etienne held up a hand. "All right. But first, I wanna introduce you to the court of Fafnir. These are your royalty, ladies and gentlemen. I want you to give dem all your respect. Let's start with our pages!"

Three small boys of about ten or eleven years of age stood up at tables throughout the room. They were wearing satin dinner jackets and gold silk bow ties. Their hair was firmly slicked down, as if their mothers had gone to work on them with a comb just before they were introduced. Etienne reeled off their names, to tremendous applause. As each boy's name was called, he took off his mask.

"Dat's great! We're proud of 'em. Next, give a big hand to our gorgeous ladies of de court, the Maids of Fafnir!"

One by one, the women at the head table rose and removed their masks.

". . . And, finally, Miss Valerie McCandles!"

Val stood up, looking shy, and got the biggest round of applause. Griffen pounded his hands together and whistled loudly. She blushed and sat down in a hurry.

"Our honored dukes!"

The nine men whom Griffen had just met stood up and bowed, revealing their faces. Griffen realized he had seen a few of them before. They were leaders of the community, one a noted journalist on the *Times-Picayune*, and another the owner of a jazz club off Bourbon Street.

"Next, her fiery majesty, who is second only in our krewe to the king, I am forthrightly honored to introduce you to Mrs. Melinda Wurmley!"

Griffen clapped madly as a strongly built woman in fire gold satin stood up from the chair on the other side of Etienne and lifted her mask. His hands froze in midair. She turned to accept the accolades from the crowd and glared at Griffen.

M. Wurmley was *that* Melinda.

Griffen realized that he had not known Nathaniel and Lizzy's last name. He had seen the name "M. Wurmley" in Hardy's guide and not thought anything about it except that it sounded like a dragonish last name. Never in a million years would he have associated it with the dread Melinda.

Val rose and rushed out of the room. Mai followed her. Gris-gris shot a look of concern toward Griffen, who gestured to him to go. Gris-gris rocketed away, weaving among the tables and servers like an oiled snake. Griffen barely heard his own name. Etienne shoved his right foot into Griffen's leg to get his attention. Still reeling with shock, he rose to his feet.

"Our king and honoree at our parade on the twenty-fourth of February, the dragon who rule the Dragons Rule, dis is Griffen McCandles!"

Griffen lifted his mask and did his best to smile at the crowd. His head was spinning as he sat down. How in hell did she come to be Mardi Gras queen? He leaned toward her.

"What are you doing here?" he hissed.

Melinda looked indignant. "I was asked by him!" She tossed her head toward Etienne's back. "What are you complaining about? I told you I would abide by a truce with you, at the very least until the baby is born. Don't you trust my word?"

"Well, yes . . ."

"Then shut up and act like a king, even if you have to pretend! This is not the time to have this discussion."

Griffen felt rage throttling him. "No! The time was months ago, when I could have refused to be here!"

"Don't be ridiculous," Melinda growled. "We both need to be here. I am not a threat to you or your sister!"

"*She* doesn't see it that way."

"She's not hurt—she's only surprised. Both of you need to *grow up*!"

"Me, grow up?"

Etienne, seemingly oblivious to the verbal sniping going on behind him, went on to introduce the dozens of lieutenants, heads, and members of the various committees. After the last round of applause, he held up his hand for silence.

"So, now we come to the fun part y'all been waitin' for. I turn y'all over to Mrs. Lucinda Fenway, who will present our parade tableaux. Then you can tell people you saw it here first. Ms. Lucinda!"

Lucinda, gorgeous in rich, Prussian blue satin sewn with rhinestones, stood up and gestured to the members of the court, who followed her out of the room.

"Now, I'll just turn you over to our master of ceremonies, Mr. Matthew Winger." Etienne stood aside as the slender man came forward to take the microphone.

"Evening, everybody!" he called.

Griffen took advantage of the bustle to excuse himself from the table.

Forty-one

In the anteroom, the other ladies of the court and other women, each designated by the float captains to represent a float's theme, laughed as they helped one another to don flowing, open-fronted satin cloaks over their dresses and put on hats the size of those worn by Las Vegas showgirls. Most of those had a dragon in some position, some heroic, others comical, but all recognizable by Griffen as representing one of the giant floats in the den.

Beyond the place-card table, Val stood against the wall with Gris-gris on one side of her and Mai on the other. Her careful makeup was streaked on her cheeks from crying.

"Why is she here?" Val demanded. "I was ready to put up with seeing her once in a while when I had to."

"I don't know," Griffen said, upset for her sake. "She said Etienne approached her months ago, even before he talked to me. She said he saw her in a vision, standing on a parade float."

"Everything he does is for that damned parade!" Val snarled. He realized that she was over being shocked and was just angry. She looked around for something. Gris-gris whisked a handkerchief out of his impeccable suit pocket and handed it to her. She dabbed at her eyes. Mai took it from her and cleaned the mascara off her face. "I can't go back in there."

"You'll have to," Mai said. "You can't let her win."

The first of the maids got her headdress in order. It depicted a dragon lounging in an airline seat with a drink in its hand, watching a small television set on a bracket. Her escort, one of the dukes, took her arm and led her into the ballroom. The jazz band struck up a fanfare, which resolved into a peppy, cheerful melody. Griffen heard Matt's voice boom off the ceiling.

"Ladies and gentlemen, Flying First Class!"

Roars of appreciative laughter greeted the maid.

Fox Lisa, dwarfed by the massive sculpture on her head of a short, stout red dragon holding a gigantic quill feather, hurried up to take Val's hands.

"What's the problem?" Fox Lisa demanded. "You shot out of there like you were on fire!"

"The mother of the man who knocked her up is here," Mai said.

Fox Lisa looked around, an impressive feat considering her headgear. "Where? I will kill her!"

Griffen held her back. "You can't do that. She is the queen of the parade."

The little redhead's face was set in grim lines. "It doesn't matter. She's going to wear a mask anyway. Now she will *have* to."

"My, my, she's fierce. I can see why you keep her around," Melinda said.

Fox Lisa spun on a dime and went for Melinda with her nails out. Melinda merely shoved backward on the towering hat. Fox Lisa staggered back. Griffen caught her. She pushed away from him, ready for another sally. Luckily, Lucinda arrived on the scene with a handful of hairpins and ribbons.

"Ms. Lisa, are you ready?" she asked, smiling at all of them. "Come on, dear, it's almost time for your entrance!"

She gestured to a tall, very slim dark man, the journalist Griffen had met. He bent to offer her his elbow. Fox Lisa gave a dubious look to Melinda, but allowed herself to be escorted away.

"You better not miss me," she called over her shoulder.

"I want to see," Val said, her voice thin but firm. She cut Melinda dead and sailed past her. Melinda raised her eyebrows but didn't protest. Gris-gris kept his arm around her. Mai and Griffen stayed close.

Matt held the microphone close to his mouth.

"Ladies and gentlemen, you all know that history is written by the winners in any confrontation. That'd be why we have to make sure we got scribes who are worthy of the feats of dragons, and who better to tell the story than one of our own? So, here is Arthur, Pen-Dragon!"

The contrast of a very tall man and a very short woman struck the eye amusingly enough, but the stout red dragon had been made with such a knowing, sly expression on his face that Griffen found it hard not to smile. Fox Lisa carried herself like a queen. She sailed gracefully along in her kimono-like cloak, dipping her shoulders but keeping her head straight. She got to the area below the podium.

"They say that the pen is mightier than the sword," Fox Lisa said, making it sound incredibly suggestive. "But I'll try either one on for size."

The audience roared with laughter. A few men at the front tables rose and whistled with their fingers in their mouths. Fox Lisa beamed. Mai adjusted the huge golden snapdragon headpiece and marched in in her turn.

The jaws of the flower moved, chomping closed with an audible sound effect that had the audience rolling on the floor.

"Yes, sir, you gotta watch where you put your fingers," Matt was saying. Mai pretended to snap her own teeth at him. He waggled his hand as if she had nipped him. She delivered her lines to applause and shouts.

Val watched, but she kept muttering to herself.

"Val, you have to calm down," Griffen whispered. "There's too much glassware here."

She gave him a pained look. "I'm trying," she whispered back. "I'm telling myself she's nothing to me. But why didn't we know?"

"I don't know, but I will find out," he promised.

Lucinda came over and tied a huge and ridiculous-looking

hat on Val's head that looked like a turtle with a slab of granite on its back.

"Honey, you have got to go," Lucinda whispered to her. "It's all right. You look wonderful. Ben, sweetheart?"

One of the dukes, a big, broad-shouldered man silvering elegantly at the temples, glided to Val's side and put out an elbow to her. She slipped her hand onto his arm and allowed herself to be drawn out into the room. The applause that greeted her was as loud as thunder.

"The Nine Sons of the Dragon!" boomed Matt's voice over the public-address system. "The ancient Chinese knew that dragons were the wisest of all the legendary beasts. Looks like old Pappy Dragon got around, because a whole lot of these nine sons don't look a lot like the traditional one. But the wisest of all the children was the tortoise. He brought him some reading matter with him." That got another big laugh.

"Is she all right?" Melinda asked, coming up to his side.

Griffen let himself tower over her.

"You did this. You ruined this event for Val."

Melinda shook her head. "No. If anyone did, it was the captain of this krewe. I was tremendously impressed by his prescience. He told me things that no one else could possibly know. A genuine talent like that is precious. I went along with his request because it seemed like a good way to look after you and your sister."

"We don't need your help!"

"Yes, you do," Melinda said, patiently. "Don't be so stubborn! At this moment, I am the best friend you have in this world."

Louder applause than ever resounded through the ballroom. Matt, at the podium, bowed over his microphone and handed it back to Etienne.

Lucinda came to lay gentle hands on their shoulders. "That's it," she said. "The tableaux are over."

Griffen made a face. "I . . . hardly got to see them."

She smiled. "I know. Don't worry. Y'all had other things

on your mind. It was videotaped. You can get a copy from
Etienne in about a week. You two need to get in there now."
She shooed them toward the ballroom as the orchestra sat
down and struck up the beginning of a waltz.

"Come on," Melinda said.

"I am not going anywhere with you," Griffen said.

She lowered her voice. "You idiot, this is the first dance.
You are the king, and you have to have the first dance with
me, your queen."

She took his arm. Griffen felt a shock. Besides himself
and Val, he had not sensed any dragon that powerful before.
She seemed to have an electrical current running through
her skin. He wondered if people felt that in him, too.

Melinda towed him toward the dance floor. She smiled
graciously at everyone they passed. Griffen plastered a smile
on his face that hurt to retain. Melinda stopped in the middle
and stared at him.

"It's a waltz," Melinda said. She put up her hands. "Hold
on to me, idiot!"

Griffen obediently reached out and put his left hand on
her waist and took her left hand with his right.

"One, two, three, ONE, two, three . . ."

Normally he was nimble on his feet, made more so by the
fencing classes he took with Maestro, but his tension made
him clumsy. Melinda was scornful.

"Straighten yourself up," she commanded him. "Slower!
You're skipping the beat. One two three, ONE two three.
Get into it. That's better. You hardly look like the dragon
of the prophecy when you're tripping all over yourself.
And me."

"Do you believe in that legend?" Griffen asked.

"Whether I do is not as important as how many others
do. Perhaps I believe that this child of my son and your
sister is the one." Her light eyes glinted. "We won't know,
perhaps not for years."

They glided together around the floor. The musicians
changed key upward a third, and Etienne stepped onto the

floor with Regina on his arm. He stopped before them and bowed.

"May I cut in?" he said.

"Of course," Griffen said, grateful to be rid of Melinda. He took Regina in his arms and danced away with her. His feet immediately regained their coordination.

As they swept away, he heard Melinda say, "I've never had an invitation based upon a dream before."

"Well, look at you, pretty lady. You look like a dream."

"So that is Mrs. Wurmley," Regina said. "You know her?"

"She's a, uh, distant relative," Griffen said.

It took an effort, but he kept his expression pleasant and his conversation noncommittal. Stifling his impatience, he finished the dance, bowed to the lady, and handed her off to another male dancer who approached. Ignoring a woman who gave him a hopeful glance, he marched over to confront Etienne, who had just turned Melinda over to Callum Fenway.

The krewe captain took another lady and spun her around the dance floor like a dust mop. Griffen had to resort to a brisk stride to catch up with him. The lady in Etienne's arms looked disappointed when Griffen tapped him on the shoulder but didn't cut in.

"I need to talk with you."

"You coul' wait until the end of the dance, but I know you won't." Etienne sighed. He bowed to the woman and escorted her to an empty chair. "Pardon me, but dis is krewe business."

"I understand," the woman said, with a smile.

Griffen grabbed his arm and pulled him to the wall near the bus trays.

"You knew all along!" he snarled. "Why didn't you tell me? My sister was incredibly upset. Of all places to trap the two of them together!"

Etienne looked at him with disbelief. "Trap? Dis ain't no trap. She won't hurt her here. Fact, she won't hurt her at all. She be a great queen, Mr. Griffen. She got de blood, just like you and Miss Valerie. Not as strong, but stronger than de other ladies in town. She the best person to ask. I knew she would be here, so I asked her, and she said yes."

"She didn't say anything to me or Val," Griffen said.

"She knew how you felt," Etienne said. "Everybody do. I asked her to keep it to herself. She agreed."

"I can't tell you how pissed off I am," Griffen said.

"I know," Etienne said. "But what would you have done different if you knew?"

Griffen huffed and puffed with fury, but at last common sense overtook him. "There's nothing I could have done. Except walk away."

"And are you gonna do dat?" Etienne's pale brown eyes studied him. Griffen wanted to grab him by the throat, wanted to jam him through the wall and storm out. But the parade was coming. He wanted to be part of that magic. And he had bonded with his fellow ritual-makers. He couldn't let them down.

"No," Griffen gritted out at last.

"'Zactly. So, savin' you months of frettin' is bad how?" Etienne patted him on the shoulder. Griffen flinched back. The werewolf smiled. "Enjoy yourself. This is the chance of a lifetime. Enjoy bein' king, Mr. Griffen. It's all just temporary. And I say, what harm do it do to honor another powerful dragon with the queenship? It's all good for the krewe, and for N'awlins. I know you care about dat." He signed to a waiter, who homed in on them with a tray. He presented Griffen with a whisky. Griffen glared but he snatched the drink and downed it.

"You even knew to get that set up, too?"

For a moment, the werewolf-dragon hybrid's eyes looked weary and tired. "Mr. Griffen, I seen everyt'ing that matter. Everyt'ing gonna work out. Go ahead and hate me today, but you'll see."

At that moment, Griffen did hate him. He hated everything about the krewe, the party, the parade, the fussy decorations, the formal wear, the people—especially the people. With a whoosh, the tray next to him blazed up. Griffen let the orange flames dance for a moment, then extinguished it by clenching his fist.

"Watch it, McCandles!" Harrison's voice interrupted him from his funk. He glanced up. The bulky figure of the detective in his black-and-white suit made him look like a thirties G-man instead of the street cop he was. He danced by Griffen with long, slow steps. Harrison looked happier than he had ever seen him, but with an expression of sad longing. Griffen would not have hurried the dance, either. The dark lady in his arms had a divine figure, to which clung a swirling dress of purple, gold, and green in narrow stripes that made it look like a pinwheel. She lowered the lorgnette mask in her hand to smile at Griffen.

It was Rose.

"I received your invitation," she said. "Thank you. I am glad to have this chance to be with David at such a distinguished gathering."

"Yeah," Harrison said, holding her firmly to his chest with his outspread hand in the middle of her back. "Thanks, Griffen."

"You're welcome, anytime," Griffen said, sincerely. His own throat felt thick. He watched them move away, feeling like a matchmaker. He would never have thought of them as a couple, but they were. Griffen desperately wanted to know the history of that relationship, but he doubted he would ever get it from either of them. All he did know for certain was that Harrison had been devastated when she died. It was none of his business, but he would have liked to know just the same.

Since Griffen never knew when he would see the voodoo priestess's ghost, he had left the cream-colored envelope addressed to her on the park bench on the Moonwalk where they sometimes talked. She had obviously found it. He was glad. It was the least he could do for Harrison.

He managed to enjoy the rest of the ball after all.

Forty-two

Griffen frowned at the map and its multiple overlays that Cos Wrayburn had prepared and spread out on Holly's kitchen table. He followed the four colored lines along St. Charles, around Lee Circle, to Canal Street, where three of the lines diverged.

"Only Aeolus keeps going," Holly pointed out. She poured coffee for all of them from a copper-colored pot. Her kitchen suited her, furnished in sunny colors and sturdy furniture and appliances. "That's east, Air's cardinal direction. We're going in along Rampart as far as St. Ann."

"I know we turn right on Canal and go south to Tchoupitoulas," Griffen said. "Mitch has been drilling us. We step off forty-five minutes apart, from five fifteen on."

"So," Cos said, pointing a thick forefinger at the map, "all the routes intersect at the corner of Canal and Rampart."

"So we release the energy then?" Bert asked.

"No. That's when we *bind* it," Cos said. "Haven't you been paying attention?"

"You think I do a lot of this on the used-car lot?" Bert asked. "Build living sculptures of water out of my hoses?"

"Get you a lot of customers," Griffen joked.

"I can use them to wash the vehicles on my lot, maybe." The king of Nautilus laughed.

Griffen didn't laugh. He had the Scepter of Fire in his hands. Holly had shielded the little white-painted house and overgrown garden with wards as soon as the three others had come inside, and let them take the heavy gold wands out of the metal-bound chest. Griffen felt the warmth grow in his solar plexus like the return of a happy memory.

"It'd be good if we all knew our capabilities on parade day," Holly reminded them. This was their third practice session. Every time Griffen touched the long-handled object, he found it hard to let it go. The sensation that went through his body was like the twanging of harp strings or guitar strings. The vibration went on and on.

"Has anyone had any, uh, element-related incidents outside?" Griffen asked. "Maybe it's my imagination, but fires seem to start around me more easily than usual."

Cos let out a gusty breath. "I thought it was just me," he said. "I left some footprints in concrete the other day."

"So?" Bert asked.

"It was dried hard. And the plants around my house are just busting out like crazy. They don't know it's February."

Bert looked at them all sideways. "You all don't believe what you're sayin', do you? I'm a man of faith! The things been happening around me are coincidences—just coincidences."

Holly nodded. "It could look like that. What are you talking about?"

Bert seemed to find it embarrassing to put his thoughts into words. "Well, I get wet when it rains, same as everyone, but the moment I step inside, I'm dry as a bone. And I never get thirsty anymore. Never. Doc says there's nothing wrong with me."

"It's the scepter," Cos said. "I, too, am a man of faith, but I see nothing more than the Hand of God working through us."

"It's uncanny, though," Bert agreed. "Only, I do agree that it's benevolent, whatever its source."

"I know I'll find it hard to pass on the scepter to next year's king," Griffen said. "It really makes me feel connected to all of nature, not just things associated with fire."

"Learn to let go," Holly said. "Practice thinking about it. I know it's hard. I feel it myself."

"Never felt nothing like that," said Wrayburn. "It's a test. God wants me to do my job and walk away. I can do that."

"You are every inch Antaeus," Holly praised him. She looked at Griffen in concern. "It's Griffen I'm worried about. We three have been preparing for ages. You didn't even have any reading material."

"I'll handle it!" Griffen said, disliking being singled out. "And if you say I'm too young . . . !"

The wineglasses on the table began to hum, then dance on the surface. Holly grabbed for the stemware and held it steady.

"What's going on?" Cos asked. "Is there something that the scepters caused? Is it you?" he asked Griffen.

"No!" Griffen protested.

"No," Holly said. "I doubt that's him. He's not radiating that kind of destructive energy. You'd be able to feel it yourselves, sitting that close to him. Let me concentrate. Something is attacking the wards." She squeezed her eyes shut. "It's coming from outside, not inside."

Griffen felt pressure on his chest, like invisible walls closing in on him. He swiped at the air, but there was nothing solid to push aside. Cos fingered the collar of his polo shirt.

"I'm choking. What's happening?"

"Are we under attack?" Bert asked. "From who? And what?"

"No idea," Holly said. Even she looked shaken. "It's some kind of external force. It's trying to get in. It doesn't feel elemental, it feels malign."

"How in God's name would you know that?" Bert asked.

"I do know," Holly said. "Just like you would know the word of God when you heard it. This isn't the time for an argument, Bert."

"Let me out there," Griffen said, even though fear planted a cold hand on the back of his neck. "I'll take care of it."

Holly knew what he was talking about. "No! We must

not break the wards. They are giving us more protection than you can. We'll ride this out."

"What if they don't hold?" Griffen asked.

"We can hope they do."

"What can we do?" Cos added.

"Pray," said Bert. "Pray hard."

"I agree," Holly said. "Guys, I'm going to do something a little premature and use some of the energy we're raising to protect us.

"You can't do that!" Cos said. "It's too soon."

"The energy will still be there," Holly said. "But we might not. Don't you feel that?"

"'Course I do," Cos said. He put a hand on his chest. "Feels like . . . asthma attack."

Holly took his hand and squeezed it. "Lend me your power. Concentrate on putting the force of your element into my hand."

"This doesn't seem right," Bert said, even though his face was gray. "Need to save power . . . for the parade."

"Don't you want to live to ride those floats?" Cos asked, his head beginning to droop.

"God will protect us if He finds us righteous," Bert said.

"Sometimes we have to help ourselves to get His help," Holly said. "Don't be a self-righteous fool. Remember that story about those footprints in the sand?"

Bert gave her a crinkle-eyed grin. "I always thought the man in the story was the . . . biggest idiot ever born. All right. I just wish . . . I could breathe."

"You will, soon," Holly promised. Her voice was the strongest of the four of them. Griffen marveled at that, but Air was in her power. "Lend me your power. Let's do it now."

"All right," Cos said. "Do what you know."

Griffen was full of admiration for the other two men. Humans were more resilient than he would ever have guessed. These men, who didn't officially believe in magic, were putting their lives in trust to a wiccan, whose practices were condemned by their own churches. They were handling the whole supernatural thing a lot better than he did when he found out he was a dragon. Unlike Harrison, who had been in love with a voodoo queen, these were adherents to more formal sects. He admired them, but he was concerned for his own involvement.

"Holly, I don't know if I should," Griffen gasped out. "I'm afraid of setting everything on fire."

She turned intense eyes to him.

"It'll be all right," she said. She laid the Scepter of Air on the table with its top at the center. Griffen, feeling as if he were in a dream about drowning, dropped his with a thud and pushed it with clumsy fingers until it touched hers. Bert's head was sagging. He needed both hands to put his scepter in place. Cos made a mighty heave and put his point forward with the others. Then he dropped back in his chair with his eyes closed.

Holly tossed back her long blond hair, tilted her face to the sky, and let out an eerie wail. It resolved into words. "We ask thy aid. Let that which others send to us return to them threefold! Lend us thy will. We ask this for the good of all, according to the free will of all. Let all that comes to us return to the giver threefold! Let it happen now!" She let her hands fall on the junction of the four scepters. Griffen felt something rise from it like a hot burst of steam. He squeezed his eyes shut. The howling of a hot wind swirled around them. Grit tore at his skin; rain lashed it. Griffen's heart pounded. He felt it tearing him and the others apart.

Suddenly, it stopped. He panted for breath.

He opened his eyes. Nothing was there but four people sitting around a table in a small kitchen with gingham curtains. No water or sand dripped from the walls. The cheerful copper-colored clock above the stove clacked.

"That was scary as hell," Cos said. "But that pressure's gone."

Bert regarded her severely. "I don't agree with what you just did."

Holly was outraged. "What? I sent the power back to where it came from."

"But the threefold stuff, that's punitive. You're hitting back more than we were attacked!"

"If you listened, you heard me say that all good things shall also be returned threefold. And I am not the one doing the meting out of justice. That is the universe's job. I am just asking. Just what you do when you pray. And it seems to have worked, thanks to all of you."

Cos cleared his throat. "Hard to argue with that," he rumbled. "Got to ask my preacher."

"But why did that happen?" Griffen asked.

"I don't know," Holly said. "We might never know. It could be a function of our power-raising, or from someone who doesn't want us to do it."

Griffen immediately thought of Stoner, but how could he know about the scepters? They hadn't been out of their box in six decades.

"We'd all better get going," Cos said. "Just in case it starts again."

Holly held her hands over each one of them. Griffen felt as if she had just sprayed a suit of armor on him.

"You'll be protected for a while," she said. "But be careful." She smiled at Griffen. "See you all at your king's party."

"Yeah, Griff," Bert said, shaking his hand. "Lookin' forward to it."

Griffen kept all his senses sharp as he went home.

Forty-three

Griffen, black bow tie crisp as a potato chip, shook hands with each person who entered the dining room. Val stood beside him, smiling and gracious in her blue dress with her long golden hair flowing over her shoulders. By tradition, the queen of the krewe would have been next, but Val threatened to boycott the whole party if Melinda was closer than three feet.

"It's silly," Melinda had declared, but she went along with it. She was fifth in line after Etienne and his mother, Antoinette. She wore pale green scaled jacquard with a little jacket over her shoulders. Even Griffen had to admit she looked queenly. He stopped thinking about her and concentrated on his party.

The restaurant had come through for Griffen in every way. Waiters and waitresses in immaculate white aprons poured red or white wine or delivered drinks on tiny round trays. Hors d'oeuvres that smelled and looked marvelous were circulated on large silver platters with white napkins. The guests nodded or shouted compliments to Griffen.

The movie posters were an enormous hit. Griffen had five of them arranged on easels for the guests to see as they came in. Everyone laughed at *The Dragon Who Came to Dinner*, with an illustration that looked like Griffen with his leg in a cast. Most of the guests were dragons, so they appreciated the jokes more than the humans, but there were plenty of movie buffs from both species.

Griffen gave a thumbs-up to the leader of the band he had hired. The Crescent City Brass Band had been highly recommended to him by a singer he knew in the French Quarter. Their audition CD had sold him, and he watched his guests bobbing their heads and tapping their feet to the heady beat. Later, there would be dancing. Fox Lisa would have the first dance, to be followed by Val, then Mai. The ladies had worked out the order themselves. He was happy to abide by their agreement. All the decisions for the evening had been made. He had his speech on note cards in his pocket. The menu cards were on the table.

When the last of the guests had shaken his hand, the reception line broke up. Griffen allowed himself to mingle, wandering into the crowd to exchange a few words with people he knew. Holly and her partner Ethan waved at him from a group near a pillar. He couldn't guess what they were discussing by their hand gestures, but it had something to do with either belly dancing or sex. Terence Killen slapped him on the back without breaking off his conversation. A couple of ladies who had been promoted to lieutenant because of his efforts came up to give him a kiss on the cheek.

"Looks mighty fine, Your Majesty," Etienne said, catching up with him. "Pretty close to an ideal."

"I hope so," Griffen said, smiling whenever someone caught his eye. He plucked a bacon-wrapped scallop off a passing tray. He planned to enjoy the dinner all he could. He had been living on carry-out food, a thousand miles away from this in quality. Until the games picked up, his access to gourmet food was limited to krewe events for which he had already paid.

"This is just brilliant, Griffen!" Callum Fenway said, holding up the souvenir poster from his plate. Griffen bowed over Lucinda's hand and shook her husband's. "Lucinda here wants to swap hers with Madeline Grade's, if you don't mind."

"Not at all," Griffen said. "Glad you like them."

"I think these are just so clever," Lucinda said.

"Whatever you would like," Griffen said, pleased. "Enjoy

he evening." He and Etienne made their way to the table at
he center of the room, where Antoinette was holding forth.
Griffen's ladies and Gris-gris were already seated, as was
Melinda. Val was angry to have her at the same table, but
Griffen had pointed out, it would have attracted attention if
he were not seated in a place of honor. With a look that told
him he would pay for it later, Val subsided. She made sure
Gris-gris and Mai were on either side of her.

He signed to the bandleader, who played a fanfare on his
rumpet. Griffen took his cards from his pocket.

"My friends, I want to thank you all for coming tonight.
The king's party is an opportunity for me to express gratitude
o you for the honor of naming me as king of the Krewe of
Fafnir for this year. I am a newcomer to New Orleans, but I
have never felt so at home anywhere as I do here in this city.
To give me a chance to participate in this most famous event
is far beyond my wildest dreams. To see New Orleans prepare
for Mardi Gras seems as if it's getting dressed up, but what's
really happening is that the city's revealing to the rest of the
world what it really looks like all the time, only on the inside.
The good times roll. We take things easy, big-time. But we
work hard at having fun, too, but all the fun leads up to a time
when you take your faith seriously. A krewe is set up to hold a
parade or a party, but most of them, Fafnir included, do some
serious work for charitable institutions. I respect that.

"I want to offer a special welcome to all my fellow kings
and queens and potentates and whatever names you've given
o the honorees who ride at the front of our parades." Cos
waved a languid hand from the table nearest him. Everyone
laughed, including Griffen. "We're one of the first things the
paradegoer sees, but we're only a minor part of the whole.
Behind each of us, literally, are hundreds, if not thousands of
people who make Mardi Gras happen. I had no idea how far
in advance everything has to be planned or how much detail
has to be seen to—and I'm grateful I didn't have to."

The audience chuckled again.

Griffen smiled at them, feeling expansive and relaxed for

the first time in ages. The warm glow of the candles cast
golden light on the ladies in their finery and the gentleme
in their tuxedos. He'd seen many of them in sweatpants an
T-shirts slinging paint and papier-mâché. It was his night t
shine, but theirs, too.

"There are too many of you to name individually. I wis
I could. First, I want to thank Etienne de la Fee for ge
ting me into this in the first place. Second, I want to curs
Etienne de la Fee for getting me into this in the first place.
Everyone laughed, especially Etienne, who slapped the tab
and guffawed. "Credit also goes to the Fenways, the Grade
the Killens, my sister Val . . ."

As he named each, the audience applauded. Griffen ju
barely heard the noise of a cell phone blaring its irritatin
beep. Someone hadn't bothered to turn his off when he cam
into the dining room.

With a shock, he realized it was his. The clapping die
away, and everyone laughed again when they heard th
insistent peeping.

"You better get that, Mr. Griffen," Etienne shouted.

Griffen knew he had to go with the flow.

"Excuse me," he said. He took the phone out of his brea
pocket. The screen said that it was Detective Harriso
calling. "Hello, Harrison. I . . ."

The detective's voice bellowed in his ear. "Don't you Ha
rison me! I'm at one of your goddamned games. It's turne
ugly, and I want you here, now!"

Griffen grinned uneasily at the tables of guests. "Detec
tive, I'm in the middle of something. It's going to have t
wait a few hours."

"I don't care what you're in the middle of!" A loud crash
followed by shouting, erupted out of the receiver. "Get you
ass down here, McCandles! If you aren't down here in te
minutes I'm sending a patrol car. Damm it, you stop tha
Hold on to her, Sherer! Move it, McCandles. This is you
business and your problem." The connection snapped off.

Griffen found himself staring at the handset in dea

silence. He looked up. "Uh, folks, there's an emergency. I . . . have to leave for a little while."

"Anyone hurt?" Callum Fenway asked, his forehead wrinkled with concern. "Anything the rest of us can do, Griffen? We'd do anything you need."

Murmurs of agreement swept through the room. Griffen was grateful and ashamed.

"I don't think so. It's, uh, business. I should be back pretty soon, after I straighten everything out. I want everyone to stay and have a good time." He looked around desperately. The faces at his table looked up at him. He needed a substitute host to carry on with the dinner.

"I'll take over if you wish," Mai said.

"Or me," Val said, though she didn't really look ready to step in.

Val wasn't an organizer, and she could be shy in public. Mai could be charming, but mostly in one-on-one situations. She wasn't good at putting others at ease. Fox Lisa had that gift, but the snobbish crowd had sensed her low dragon blood and wouldn't treat her with the respect she deserved. He turned to Etienne.

"Not me, Mr. Griffen," the captain said, raising his hands. "Not my place."

In desperation, he turned to Melinda. The senior female regarded him suspiciously. "I have an emergency. You are the queen of this krewe. I need you to act as hostess while I am away."

Val gawked at him. "Griffen, you are not serious. *Her?*"

"You don't actually trust her," Mai demanded.

"I can't stay," Griffen said, seriously. "She's got the rank and the blood, and the experience if something . . . goes wrong. It's appropriate. Will you do it?"

"I certainly will," Melinda said, not looking as smug as he thought she would. "I have to say I am surprised but gratified that you can pick the best person for the job whatever your misgivings. I accept. I'll take care of your guests. Go ahead. Everything will be fine."

Griffen met her eyes. "Protect my sister."

"I don't need her help!" Val shrieked. Melinda pressed her lips together grimly. She knew the risks; she was one of them. But they had a truce, and he didn't have a lot of time. She nodded.

"You know I will. Get going."

Griffen noticed Etienne's eyes glitter behind her.

"Why didn't you warn me about this?" he demanded.

Etienne shook his head. "Got nothin' to do with *my* business, Mr. Griffen. I don't see everyt'ing about everyone. Just what the Fates tell me I need to know. But it'll be okay. Go on."

Melinda stood up and tapped a water glass for attention. "Ladies and gentlemen, Griffen has to excuse himself for a while. In the meantime, please let me call on Mr. Callum Fenway to say a few words. Callum?" She gestured gracefully toward the lieutenant, who stood up, fingering his collar.

Griffen called for Doreen on his way out of the building. Whether he liked it or not, he was leaving his party in good hands. He hoped it wouldn't take too long to resolve whatever Harrison was in the middle of.

He felt glaring eyes bore into his back. He would have to make peace later on, but that had to wait.

Forty-four

In the weak light of morning, Griffen limped into his apartment and locked the door behind him, glad to be home. He had no idea where his tuxedo jacket was. His pristine white shirt and silk tie were stained and crumpled.

When he'd arrived at the Embassy Suites, he heard shouting and banging coming from the double doors at the end of the corridor. Inside, chairs lay on the floor around an upended table. A bottle of gin lay on its side leaking into the carpet. Chips were strewn everywhere. A lone twenty-dollar bill was plastered to the wall. The room was full of people, all yelling and gesturing at one another.

Wallace, his poker dealer, was up against the wall between two vice cops, bellowing at the officer taking his statement. Three players, two of whom he recognized as high rollers and one who was a stranger, were being interviewed by a black female cop. Kitty, his alternate, sat weeping into a tissue as Harrison took her statement. When he saw Griffen, the detective came up out of his chair and homed in on him.

From that moment, Griffen would have had to have instant replay video to straighten out everything that he heard, saw, and had happen to him. It seemed that one of the players, a factory-farm owner from Oklahoma, had arrived a little tipsy. He drank gin and tonic steadily through the game. After an admittedly bad beat, for which one of Griffen's regulars apologized, the man had erupted and accused both the player and the dealer, who at the time was

Kitty, of colluding to cheat him. Wallace had immediately called Jerome, who arrived to mediate. The man couldn't be mollified or bought off, and had started throwing punches, then furniture. The player got a chair in the face and lost a tooth. The hotel management arrived, followed quickly by the police. As soon as the responding officers saw what was going on, they had summoned Harrison from a night off to handle a case involving his "friend, Griffen McCandles." Griffen understood why he was upset.

Harrison refused to let him talk to the complaining player. The man had been taken to district headquarters, to give a statement and press charges if he so chose. So had Jerome. Griffen couldn't raise him on his cell phone. The next thing he knew, he was up against the wall being handcuffed.

"I can't ignore it," Harrison growled. "Running an illegal poker game in my town! Softening me up with your phony overtures, you are so slick you can slide under a closed door. You're responsible. You'll be named in the indictment."

Griffen rode to the station jammed against the rear door of a patrol car with Wallace and the poker player whose tooth had been knocked out. The latter was taken out for a while to get medical attention, but Griffen and Wallace had been shoved into the drunk tank, the only holding cell with any room. Mardi Gras was a busy time for law enforcement. Griffen got the rundown from Wallace and the other players on what had happened during the game up to the chair-throwing incident. It fit into the pattern. The customer from Oklahoma, whom no one else had met before, accused them of cheating, and said he wanted all his money back plus damages and pain and suffering. He got more and more aggressive, until he had started swinging furniture. It helped clarify the situation in Griffen's mind, but he needed to talk to Jerome.

He tried Jerome's number dozens of times, but got shunted to voice mail each time. Either his second-in-command had gotten badly hurt in the fight, which seemed unlikely, or the cops were interviewing him and wouldn't let him call out for Griffen or a lawyer. He wondered when his turn was coming.

In the meanwhile, he made several more calls, to Val, Fox Lisa, and Mai. Unfortunately, anyone else he could think of who might have the wherewithal to loan him bail was at the party he had left, and had his or her phone turned off. They had been smart enough to shut them down during the party. He wished he had been.

No. Harrison knew where he was holding the king's party. He would just have had the maître d' summon him to the phone. This was going to happen no matter what.

His phone rang. He grabbed for it. "Mai?"

"No, Grifter, it's Marcel. Man, I wanna apologize. I heard what happened! The guy seemed cool. I didn't know he was crazy."

Sitting against a wall between a drunk who had vomited all over his own clothes and a furious man who had been picked up for refusing to pay a hooker, Griffen did his best not to sound angry at the spotter. After all, Marcel really was trying, and his instincts about people were usually good.

"It wasn't your fault," he tried to assure him. But Marcel felt guilty. Griffen tried not to be resentful, as the hours went by. He had no money left to pay his own bail, let alone that of the players and dealers. The stink in the cell was unbelievable. Even if they had offered them food, Griffen wasn't sure he could have kept it down. The only good news was that he overheard one cop say that Harrison may have solved Jesse Lee's murder.

He called everyone he knew to ask for help. All of the messages went to voice mail. By an hour before dawn, he started getting calls back, but they weren't the kind he was hoping for. "I don't know if I ever want to speak to you again!" Val snarled. "Oh, she queened it over us all right! That bossy bitch! And she kept putting her arm over my shoulder. You can just sit and rot for a while. What is the *matter* with you?"

She had hung up. Fox Lisa was next. Her usual cool had been burned away.

"They made fun of my tattoos! They treated me like a toy.

I had to slap one of them, and he laughed at me! What kind of people are these? They were perfectly nice at the ball, but you turn your back, and they act like they are all that and a bag of chips! I didn't walk out because there is no way I would cede the ground to them, but you are in big trouble, Griffen. Bail? I am not going to waste my time. I am going home to take a long bath."

Mai was short and to the point. "You trust her, and you won't trust me. Your priorities are screwed up, Griffen."

But about dawn the jailer came to the cell door and leaned in.

"Griffen McCandles!"

He figured it was Jerome, or perhaps Val had relented. Instead, waiting for him on the other side of the solid steel door was Melinda. Griffen stopped before he crossed the threshold. The jailer nudged him from behind until he moved.

"You're free," Melinda said. "You can pay me back sometime when you're solvent again. Your little redhead told me about your financial situation. It happens. Businesses have their up-and-down years."

Griffen's cheeks burned. "Did the party go all right?"

"Oh, yes," Melinda had said, with a broad smile. "It was a wonderful party. You can see the photographs. Too bad you weren't there. All the gossip was about you. By the way, thank you for the honor of your trust. I'm sorry your family and mine got off on the wrong foot. Several wrong feet. But, thank you. I won't forget it."

Griffen hated being indebted to Melinda, but he had had no alternative. His voice was more gruff than he intended, but it had been a long night. "You bailed me out, so we're even. I will pay you back as soon as I can."

"Come on," she had said, gesturing toward the door but careful not to touch him. "I've got a car waiting."

There was nowhere else to go but home. Griffen sat on the couch in his satin-striped trousers and formal shirt, his silk tie untied. He had no reason to go out again. He had missed his own party. He had the headache to end all headaches. No one was speaking to him. He decided he was going to stay in his apartment forever.

His cell phone rang.

"Griffen? It's Kitty."

"Hey, Kitty, I didn't see you last night. I'm sorry I couldn't bail you out."

"It's okay. My mama came down and got me out. Can I talk to you? I'm right outside your building."

Griffen buzzed her in. Kitty came in. She looked so different in street clothes. When she didn't have to wear the tuxedo shirt and black pants, she favored bright colors. Her scarlet blouse was almost blinding to Griffen's hypersensitive eyes.

"Can I talk to you, Griffen? I don't know whether I'm crazy."

"Sure," he said. "Please, sit down. Do you want a drink?"

"No, thanks." She hesitated for a moment. "Griffen, you know that Jordan Ma who made such a problem at that game back in December?"

"I sure do," he said. "I wouldn't have let you deal for him, but he hasn't asked to play again. I haven't seen him since."

"Well, it's not him, but it feels almost like it has been. He had this tell, he liked to run his first finger around in a little circle on his cards. He'd hold them down like this and move his finger?" Kitty demonstrated, putting her hand on the arm of the couch. Griffen watched her. "He did it when he had a good hand. But there've been three different people since then who do the same thing, especially right before they kicked up a fuss. It sure hasn't been the same guy. I mean, I won't ever forget what he looks like! But that guy from Oklahoma last night who caused all the trouble—he did it, too. And there was a woman, too, who got stinking drunk and talked all kinds of shit until everyone else left. She did it. Maybe they belong to the same club or something?"

Or maybe, Griffen thought, *they were the same man—or*

dragon—shifting shape to be four different people. He had to trap one of them.

"Kitty, I don't think you're crazy. I think there is some kind of club or society that is trying to shut us down. When you see that again, no matter what, call me. I want to talk to . . . one of them. Can you do that?"

She set her small jaw resolutely and squeezed Griffen's hand.

"I sure will, Griffen. No one is gonna screw up *our operation* like that. It means a lot to us, how you take care of us. I never had such a good job in my life. I will be damned if I will let some out-of-town assholes break us down."

Griffen smiled. "I don't appreciate my employees enough," he said. "Keep your eyes open, and tell the other dealers to watch out, too."

"I promise," Kitty said. "Thanks, Griffen."

Griffen let her out. They would help him catch Jordan Ma and his squad of Eastern dragons—if he ever had another game to run.

He called Jerome again. At last the phone rang. "They kept me sequestered, Grifter. Took the battery out of my phone. Kept losing the paperwork. Had to stand before the judge . . . Grifter, it was another dragon. I don't know how many there are."

"It seems there are fewer than we may think." He told Jerome what Kitty had described to him. Jerome clicked his tongue.

"So we're dealing with shape-shifters. Experienced ones."

"Yeah. And this was the worst yet. Just when things were picking up, thanks to the town being full for Mardi Gras. We were both too busy to be there. If one of us had been able to drop in, we'd have known we had a dragon on our hands."

"Yeah, and you know why that is?"

Griffen knew it before he said it. "No, Jer!"

Jerome was inexorable, and Griffen knew he deserved it. "Yes, Grifter. Your pal Peter. He knew you were gonna be completely occupied this evening, and I bet you told him I would be hanging out with my marching buddies then, too."

Griffen's heart sank, but he couldn't deny it. "Sounds like you were right all along."

"There is no satisfaction in 'I told you so,' man. You're the big dragon, and this is your operation. He probably didn't cause any other trouble until now."

"Well, they have succeeded in taking us down. Harrison said I couldn't run any more games, or he will bust me. I can't take a chance on going to jail. The parade's just a few days away."

"Uh-uh," Jerome said. "What you need, my friend, is plausible deniability. You don't know a damned thing. In fact, you are not going to hear from me about anything. It will be just like the old days. You know I told you to keep closer to the business? Well, now I want you to back off and not be involved. You have too much to do as Mardi Gras king. Mind that business. We'll get this done. No cop is going to shut us down. You go and have a good time."

Griffen smiled for the first time in hours.

Forty-five

Now Griffen really began to feel like Nathan Detroit. In case the NOPD had managed to put a tap on his phone, he fielded all calls asking to join a game with an apology. He kept Peter Sing at arm's length.

"I'm sorry. There isn't anything going for the foreseeable future, Peter. All of my people are tied up with . . . Mardi Gras obligations. I hope we can resume normal operations soon."

"That is a pity," Peter said. "I have really enjoyed our games." The voice on the other end of the line sounded genuinely disappointed. Griffen felt a pang. He really liked the other man, but now that he was convinced of his perfidy, he had to protect himself. "I will come and see you march."

Harrison kept the heat on him. Vice rousted his known runners in the hotels, but they couldn't be around all the time. Griffen went about his business, hoping Jerome could keep ahead of them. He hoped once Mardi Gras was over, they could build up the operation again, but who knew how long it would be before they could stop the Eastern dragons, if they could stop them?

Around one in the morning Thursday night at the Irish bar, Griffen's phone rang. He pulled away from his discussion with Bone over the quality of movie remakes.

"Griffen, it's Kitty. One of them is here, one of the guys from the club. This isn't the one who draws circles, but one of the gang who blinks. I think this guy is gay. He's acting just like the other gay guy who brought down a game. He makes comments. He scares me."

Griffen's heart started pounding.

"Just keep it going exactly as you would with any other group, Kitty," Griffen said. Another exemplary employee. He was going to have to institute some kind of reward system. If he ever got things back to normal, that was. He excused himself and called Jerome on the way over. If Harrison busted him now, it was all over, so this was his best and only chance to take one of them down.

"Sorry I'm late," he said, dragging another chair up to the table.

"Grifter!" cheered Jacomo Bernucci, a businessman from Baltimore.

"Jock, good to see you," Griffen said, shaking his hand. Good. One player he absolutely didn't have to worry about being the mole. The others, though not as familiar as Jock Bernucci, had been in town at least once before during Griffen's tenure as "head dragon." Lacey was the wife of a politician in Grand Cayman. Her family owned part of the power company, the telephone company, and almost all of the main Internet service provider in the islands. Oliver Stanton was blue blood from the East Coast, but in Hollywood he was a well-known character actor with a profile like Burt Lancaster's. Only the fourth was a stranger. He seemed ordinary: tall, blond hair turning white, hairline creeping upward, strong chin and straight brows; from all appearances a niceish guy in his fifties. Kitty shook her head at Griffen's interrogatory glance. So he had not started making a fuss yet but had made some comments. The other players didn't seem as relaxed as they usually were. The newcomer was the cause of the tension.

Once Griffen arrived, he subsided, but they both recognized another dragon. Griffen pretended not to notice. The other dragon relaxed a little. There were a lot of people with a little dragon blood around. Perhaps Griffen did not understand the significance.

He put all the money he had in his wallet in front o
Kitty, $320, most of it borrowed from Val in the bar. Kitty
counted out the chips.

"Are you planning to clean the rest of us out, Griffen?"
Oliver asked, with a practiced wry expression.

"It's a good exercise for me," Griffen said. "If I can't play
for at least an hour on this much money, then I had better
find another job."

They laughed. He was short-stacked compared with
the others, but it didn't take him long to double up and
double again. He kept a deliberate eye on the blond man.
He thought Kitty was probably wrong about his being gay.
When one took shape-changing into account, the effeminate
movements were probably just that. The mystery guest was
a woman.

He, or she, tended to tuck his cards underneath his right
wrist, leaving the right hand free to play with the stacks o
chips. He leaned on the left wrist. The dragon did blink a
lot when he, or she, had a good hand. Griffen started reading
the signs and began to chip away at those stacks.

"Are you picking on me, Griffen?" the dragon asked.

"Me?" Griffen said, blandly. "Just playing a little poker."

It would take a lot of guts to go ahead and spike the
game, but Griffen assumed that the Eastern dragons knew
how much risk he and the others were taking to have se
it up. He had to be prepared to cause trouble and call the
police. Griffen merely had to beat him to it. It needed to be
a hand that the other dragon was prepared to lose.

It didn't take long. Griffen palmed a card from the
deck and kept it hidden until the other dragon glared a
Jock Bernucci, who had just won a hand with king-jack o
spades.

"You are cheating," he said. Griffen felt his heart speed
up. Here it came.

"What?"

The other turned over his cards. "I, too, have the jack o
spades. So you had an extra one in there? Hoping that none

of us would notice an extra card in the deck? What kind of game is this? I thought it was honest!"

"I am honest!" Jock exclaimed. "Griffen!"

"Don't worry, Jock," Griffen said. "He's the one who is cheating. Look at this." He reached across the table and wrenched the other dragon's wrist up, scattering chips, and slipped the other card out. "He's got one he was saving for a rainy day, too. Look at that, another jack of spades." He hoped the illusion would hold. It didn't have to be good for long.

Jock gawked at him. He sprang to his feet. "Stand up, jerkface. Stand up and let me take you to pieces." The other dragon jumped back, alarmed, tipping over his chair.

Griffen rose and put his hands between the two of them.

"What just happened, Griffen?" Kitty asked.

"He cheated," Griffen said. "He had some spare cards in his sleeve. Nice of him to accuse Jock when it was him."

"I . . . I never noticed," Kitty said. "I'm ashamed."

Griffen kept his eyes on the other dragon, who looked as if he wanted to dive for the door. Griffen had to be ready to prevent an escape. "Don't be. He's one of the best there is. I've heard of him from . . . back East."

"Atlantic City?" Lacey asked.

"Uh, yeah. Atlantic City. Atlantic City Steve they call him. Very tough player, but dishonest as hell."

"Atlantic City Steve? That's a really dumb nickname."

"You think Minnesota Fats is complimentary?"

"Well, no, but it was descriptive."

Griffen kept his eyes leveled on the tall blond man. The other dragon glared at him. "I'm sorry, folks, but I think it'd be better if we call it a night. I need to handle this. Steve and I have to have a little talk. Thanks for coming. Kitty, count them out, please."

The other players departed. Kitty lingered for a moment, but Griffen chased her off. "You did great," he assured her.

When the door closed behind her, he looked at the other dragon. "Take it easy. We're going to be here for a while.

Why not drop the disguise. I'm curious to see the face of my enemy."

The tall blond male seemed to collapse in on himself. Griffen had watched shape-shifters of other species, but except for Val had never watched another dragon change. The body shrank at the shoulders and grew slightly at the chest. He was right: It was a woman, a short one with frizzy brown hair, dark, almond-shaped eyes, and a blunt nose. She stood rigid on the other side of the table.

"You can't keep me here," she said.

"I sure can. Now, call the others."

"What if I won't?"

Griffen knew his poker face was the best around. He just looked at her.

She faced him down but grew more and more uncomfortable as the silence prolonged. Griffen sat down in a chair blocking escape through either the window or the door. He blew a smoke ring, slowly, insouciantly.

Finally, she took out her cell phone.

Forty-six

Griffen kept his eyes fixed on the woman until a knock came at the door. "It's open!" he called.

Three men sidled cautiously into the room. Jordan Ma, whom Mai had warned him about, the old man called Pack, who had challenged Mr. Stearn a few weeks back, and Peter Sing. Griffen was disappointed but not surprised.

"I knew you were one of them."

Peter looked regretful. "I'm sorry. I came to like you. But business is business."

"The same goes for me," Griffen said.

"Rebecca, are you all right?" Jordan Ma asked the woman, who began to back away when they came in. She opened large, resentful eyes to him.

"No! He has kept me here for ages! You try holding it after six wine spritzers!" She turned and fled for the bathroom.

Griffen gestured to the other chairs. "Sit down. We still have a lot of refreshments. Can I pour you a drink? I'm Griffen McCandles, but you already know that. Won't you introduce me to your friends?"

When Jordan didn't speak, Peter said, "This is Winston Long, and that was Rebecca Tan."

"How do you do?" Griffen asked.

"Not bad for an old man," Winston said, amiably. "Call me Pack." Rebecca returned and plumped down in a chair but didn't say a word.

"Why are we here?" Jordan Ma asked, but he sat down and

signed to the others to do the same. Griffen made himself a whisky and water and took the seat opposite Jordan.

"You came here to take down my operation. Naturally, I don't want you to."

"I do not mean in New Orleans. Why are we here in this room at this time of night?"

Griffen lounged back in his chair and studied the other dragon. "You have been trying to take me down for months. Why?"

"You have something we want."

"Good. And you have something I want."

"And what is that?"

"Your absence," Griffen said, toying with a stack of chips on the table. "I am finding it difficult to run my operation with you people causing trouble. I don't want you in this city. I challenge all of you to a single game of poker, any game, any rules, winner take all. You can put up whatever you have against what I have."

"And what is that?"

"What did you come for?" Griffen countered.

"Your fiefdom here," Jordan Ma said.

"Then that's it," Griffen said. "I will play you for everything you have against what I have. If I win, then you butt out and don't come back. Never. If you win, then I will pack up and move back to . . . well, maybe not Ann Arbor, but somewhere."

"Somewhere not in the Eastern dragons' command," Winston Long said.

"Fine," Griffen said. "You give me a list, and I'll avoid them. If I lose. Which I doubt. What I do after that is none of your business. This is what you are here for, now. Play or don't. I'll take you down one by one. I know who each of you is now."

"What about your sister?" Jordan Ma asked.

"She's independent," Griffen said, casually. "I'm the one you're worried about. So play me. My share is worth exactly what all four of yours are together. Everything you have against everything I have."

"Who the hell are you, Sky Masterson?"

Griffen smiled. "Up until now I would have thought of myself more as Nathan Detroit, but if you want to play me for what I have, then I guess I've graduated to Sky. That is my proposition. If you don't think it's worth your while, then why have you spent months here in disguise trying to undermine my business? This is your chance to take the whole thing in one game, winner take all. If you know anything about me, you know my word is good. I will walk away. You will win. If you can."

It was a dare. Griffen could feel the excitement in the air.

Peter grinned at him. "I love it," he said. "This is the final table to end all tournaments. There has never been a larger prize."

"Who will deal?" Winston asked. "I don't trust your humans or any of your feeble dragon hybrids."

"Mai," Griffen said.

The four Eastern dragons looked startled. Rebecca tapped the table.

"Why her? She is one of us."

"Because I don't trust her," Griffen said. "But maybe you do."

"No," Peter said. "None of us trust her."

"That's perfect," Jordan said. "I agree." The others nodded.

Griffen hit her speed-dial number on his cell phone. Mai answered, sounding irritable.

"Griffen? It's after three. Why are you calling so late?"

Griffen explained what was going on. "I need you to deal poker for a private party," he said. "A few old friends. Jordan Ma and some of his associates."

"Jordan! Where are you?" she demanded.

"In your hotel, on the fifteenth floor." He gave her the number of the suite.

"I will be there in five minutes."

It took six. She hurried in through the door and stopped short when she saw the others. She let out a hiss like a snake. Jordan Ma smiled. The others merely looked perturbed. Griffen could tell they had some kind of history. Someday, he might be able to persuade it out of Mai.

"We will use our own chips." Jordan said.

Griffen frowned. "What's wrong with mine?"

"Ours is our stake." He nodded to Peter, who took a heavy leather bag from under his coat and poured the contents out in the center of the table. Hundreds of metal disks clinked, cascaded, tinkled to the felted top. Their color was pure, brilliant yellow.

Griffen's eyes popped at the sight. "Are these . . . solid gold?"

"It is commonplace among the Eastern families to hold hard assets," Mai said, waving a dismissive hand. "Very showy, but it is just money."

"Each of our chips is worth eight hundred dollars," Jordan said. "We have approximately a thousand of them. Is that what you think you are worth?"

Griffen resumed his casual pose. "No, but you will never have enough gold to cover that. I'll play for what petty amount you have."

"I will need coffee," Mai said.

Griffen waited while she brewed a pot, then accepted a cup. He needed a clear head. He had to prepare himself for the game of the century—of his life.

Griffen helped Mai set up the table. A basket of new decks of cards stood nearly full. She stripped the first one and shuffled it deftly. She flipped half the deck with the edge of one card and flipped it back again.

Griffen watched her, trying to let the rhythm take his mind off the flips his stomach was doing. He was scared. His entire livelihood was on the line. He didn't want to leave New Orleans and the life he had built there, but no other offer could prompt agreement from these very powerful and inexorable personalities. He was scared, but also angry. The latter was by far the more important emotion if he didn't let it overwhelm him. *Channel that,* he told himself. *Be cool. Think of every trick you have ever known. Know that what you are doing is important.* He stretched out his arms, intertwined his fingers, and cracked his knuckles.

"Ladies and gentlemen," he said. "Let's play poker."

"The challenge is yours, so the choice of weapons is ours," Peter said. "I declare that we play Texas hold 'em."

Griffen shrugged nonchalantly. Peter knew that he disliked the game and was taking every advantage. He would have done the same thing in Peter's place. "It won't make any difference," he said.

Mai put out the button, and dealt the first round of cards.

The first several hands were trials, as Jordan, Pack, and Rebecca felt Griffen out. Griffen, doing the same, saw that his dealers had been right: All of the tells that they had spotted belonged to one or another of the three against whom he had not played himself. Peter's he knew, just as the cocky dragon knew his. That information canceled itself out between the two of them but did not redound to the others' advantage since Peter did not have time to convey it to his cohorts. Griffen coolly judged by the discards how daring each player was, how much risk he or she could take, and how good each was at calculating the odds. They were all very good; he found it a compliment that the Eastern dragons had thought enough of him to send real pros.

His phone rang several times during the game: Jerome, Val, Fox Lisa, members of the krewe, all wanting to know where he was. Jerome wanted to come down immediately, but Griffen assured him there was no need. The matter would be settled then and there; nothing Jerome did or could do would change the outcome.

He missed last-minute krewe meetings, fittings, even meals. The sun rose over nearly silent streets that swiftly filled with shouting, raucous crowds of tourists. It was

Mardi Gras out there, but inside, poker was the only thing on Griffen's mind.

He only stopped to eat when his hands started to get shaky. After finishing the one whisky and water, he skipped liquor, drinking coffee or diet soda exclusively. The Eastern dragons did the same thing.

About four hours in they were all desperate for the bathroom. Griffen glanced at his fellow players through a gradually increasing lens of yellow, but he wouldn't go first. Rebecca finally broke, headed for the toilet.

"You must have the weakest bladder in the world!" Jordan Ma snapped at her, the first sign of temper from him. Griffen was glad. It meant the cool-headed dragon was breaking.

Rebecca shot him a hateful look. "I drink when I play. I have been playing. It is good to stay hydrated!"

The others, glad of the excuse to take a break, followed in her wake. Mai threw the old decks into the wastebasket after every few hands, setting them on fire with one gentle breath so no cards could be retrieved. She was like a coin-operated fortune-teller. Only her hands and eyes moved. She didn't speak to anyone, not even Griffen. She was probably angry with him for roping her in and would probably take it out on him later when they were alone, but he was glad for her silence. He focused on every turn of the card, every chip that clinked into the pot. Griffen was playing for real.

To the others, this was not life and death. Except possibly for Peter, poker had never been their sole support. Only Griffen knew the desperation of needing to make money by his wits and skill. They could not have that edge. He did. This was more than life and death. He had barely begun to acknowledge his heritage, to learn what it meant to be a dragon, to take on his own power and learn about it. He was not going to get driven out of town by a bunch of *tourists*. His muscles ached, and the chair padding felt thinner and thinner as the raucous afternoon became loud and musical night, but his mind stayed sharp. It had to.

Gradually, the stacks between his wrists grew larger and

larger, as the piles belonging to the others shrank. Winston Long went all in on a hand that Griffen knew from his twitching eyelid was a bluff. He confidently matched the call as well as a side bet from Peter, and stripped the table bare of brilliant gold coins when his hand proved the stronger. Pack removed himself from the table, with a philosophical half smile. The remaining players showed signs of desperation. Griffen found himself grinning ferally at them. This was real card-playing. He felt more alive at that moment than he had in months. Being an executive, a responsible human, a lover, a friend were satisfying, but not like this, not like a game of chance where every move was significant. Every hand could bankrupt him and send him into exile.

Rebecca got more nervous as her stash of gold ran down. Griffen took advantage of it by making large raises against her in each hand that she seemed to have mediocre cards, according to the rapidity of her blinks. Peter let out an amused snort when he saw what Griffen was doing but didn't intrude or try to rescue his fellow dragon. In fact, he seemed almost pleased when Griffen finally wiped her out. Rebecca pulled away from the table with a grim face and went to join Winston. Griffen heard her whispering angrily. Winston tried to calm her. She got up and started pacing.

"Stop that at once," Jordan Ma ordered, without looking up from his cards. "Winston?"

"Sit down, child," the old dragon said.

Rebecca regarded him with dismay. "But he has taken all my gold!"

Winston raised weary eyes. "You lost, young one. He won. That is how it works. You knew it was at hazard. Now it is gone."

"I want it back! He can't keep it!"

"Stop it!" Jordan ordered. Rebecca glowered at him. Griffen watched his hand carefully. Jordan circled his forefinger on the back of his hand once. So the cards were good, but not that good. Griffen pressed his lips together.

He had ace-three unsuited, but Jordan wouldn't know that. He pushed out eight stacks of the heavy yellow coins.

"I am putting you all in."

Jordan looked up at him in surprise. Rebecca's distraction had made him lose track of the betting. He looked down as Mai turned over the river card. It was an ace. One pair. Jordan hesitated.

"Call or fold," Griffen said.

Jordan glanced at his hand. "Call." He stacked his remaining eight piles of chips and gold in the center, his advancing armies meeting Griffen's.

Griffen turned over his hand. Jordan bent his head a fraction of an inch. "Very neatly done, Mr. McCandles. Very neat. You caught me off guard, and I fell for it." He threw in his cards without revealing them. Mai gathered them up. Griffen wished she had shown him what he had beaten, but it wasn't really that important.

That meant the last dragon standing was Peter.

Griffen looked at him. He still saw the friendly young man with the gelled-up hair who had become a friend to him over the last couple of months. He realized that on the one hand, Peter had betrayed his confidence to the others. On the other, they had played some good cards, each relishing a really worthwhile opponent. Griffen gulped coffee to prepare himself for a multihour session. It would take a long time to finish Peter off. Griffen was getting tired, but he could do it.

Then he changed his mind.

"It's not worth it, Peter. Let's get it all over with. One hand, winner take all."

Peter was surprised, but the idea appealed to him. He nodded slowly.

"Why not?"

"You're not serious," Mai said.

"I am," Griffen said. He had relied upon skill, cunning, courage, and patience, but to win in a single hand required luck. If he didn't have that, none of the others would make a difference in the long run. If he was meant to stay in New Orleans, let the Big Easy prove it to him. "Let's play."

"Okay, then." Peter sat back with his fingers interlaced behind his head.

Both of them sounded casual, but they were deadly serious. Mai opened the last new deck and shuffled it crisply. She doled out two cards to each of them and set the deck down.

Griffen didn't even look at his cards.

"All in," he said. "I'll match what you are holding."

"Griffen, no!" Mai exclaimed. "Don't do it like that!"

"You are joking," Peter said.

"Not at all," Griffen said. "Absolutely nothing I do now would change what I've been dealt. It's one hand. You have exactly the same chance of winning or losing that I do. It's a major stake. What do you say?"

The other dragon smiled broadly, showing sharp white teeth. He put his hand down without looking at it. "I agree. Just lay out the other five cards, Mai. No sense in prolonging the agony."

Griffen held his breath. This was a turning point in his life. Mai flicked out the flop, the turn, and the river facedown, then showed them one by one.

Three threes and two twos. Griffen laughed out loud.

"Let's see 'em," Peter said.

"You first."

Peter grinned. He flipped over the first card. A king. Then the second.

Another king.

"Full house," he said.

Griffen's heart pounded, but he was trusting to the little voice in his head. He turned over the first card.

An ace.

His mouth was dry as he went for the other card. Another ace would cement his victory. There were three more in the deck. He fervently expected, no, hoped, to see one. How badly did the Big Easy want to keep him there? He wanted desperately to stay. He had changed his whole life to be there. Let chance show him that he had made the right decision. He turned the card.

A three.

Four of a kind. The only card other than an ace that would make that hand work was right there under his fingers.

He stared at it in disbelief, then let out a whoop that echoed through the fifteenth floor. Then he sat down in his chair and leaned back, resting his left ankle on his right knee.

"Gentlemen and lady, get out of my town. I'll know you in the future. I am vetting every player in every game from here on out. I will know if there's a dragon there, in whatever disguise you wear. You can do what you want, but not at any of my tables. Sorry, Peter, this means you, too."

"Okay, Griffen. Congratulations."

"We will keep to the agreement," Jordan Ma said though his face twisted as if his mind were carrying on an internal argument. "I will report to the elders that we have failed. You are smart as well as a fine poker player. I am sorry that this was not for pleasure."

"I found it pleasurable," Griffen said.

"Me, too," Peter said. He put out a hand. "No hard feelings, I hope?"

"I wish I could say that," Griffen said. He looked at the hand but decided to shake it anyhow. "Maybe someday."

"Let us go," Rebecca demanded. "I want to go home. Aaggh! You will have to use your credit card to pay for a taxi, Jordan!"

"I told you she was too young for this mission," Jordan Ma told Winston Long, as the elevator doors closed on them.

Griffen stood up and stretched. His muscles felt like lead. He looked at the clock—8:00 p.m. He had been playing for thirty hours straight.

"Thank you," he said to Mai. "I owe you."

"You don't," Mai said. "You did it all yourself. It was difficult to be in the same room with them. They have caused me a lot of trouble in the past. They are very tricky. I am surprised that they played the game honestly. I watched for ruses, but they did not use any. It is a compliment to you."

"I'm glad you didn't tell me that until afterward," Griffen said. "I might have screwed up."

"I doubt that very much. But it was very satisfying to see you beat them so thoroughly."

Griffen went into the bathroom and splashed his face. His eyes were red, and his chin was covered in stubble. He came out wiping his face with a towel.

"Good riddance to Jordan Ma. He can catch a plane to anywhere but here."

Mai looked smug. "Oh, well, he may make it to the airport, but he is not leaving New Orleans for a while."

"What? Why not?"

"I gave him a going-away present. A priceless relic of the Ming Dynasty."

Griffen looked at her suspiciously. "What kind of 'priceless relic'?"

"Oh, a dagger. It has a jade hilt in the shape of a dragon, eight-inch blade. Ruby eyes. Utterly beautiful and completely priceless." She grinned up at him sideways. "I called someone I know who went to Jordan's room and hid it in the lining of his suitcase. Oh, and there is a rope matching that which strangled Jesse Lee in the lining of Rebecca's luggage. They will probably sit in the Transportation Safety Administration office cursing my name." Mai smiled, a chillingly bloodthirsty expression. "I am enjoying the thought. They are responsible, after all."

Griffen returned the smile, uncharacteristically enjoying the sangfroid. "So am I. Do I want to know how you knew that?"

"No. It is better if you don't."

Griffen reached into the heap of coins on the table and offered Mai a handful.

"Are you trying to insult me? I don't do tips."

"But you do gold." He had seen her eyes glowing the

same color as the game went on. "It's a gift for not killing any of them until I could clean them out."

Mai smiled. She took the coins in her small hands. "Yes. Thank you. I can see why they use them. I would find them impossible to resist." She held one up to her ear. "No, too heavy to use as earrings. Perhaps I will have one set in diamonds for a necklace. As a symbol of your success."

"Won't you get in trouble now, helping me against them?"

"If you had lost, it would have been me helping them," she pointed out. "You make your own luck. Even the elders must respect that."

Griffen nodded. "Will they try again?"

"Of course."

"Do you know what the next attempt will be?"

Mai was silent for a moment, considering her own plans and orders. With Jordan gone, her plan was back on the table.

"No. I don't know what will come next," she said.

That was honest but not helpful. Griffen knew then that he did care for her, but as he had told Jordan, he didn't trust her. He smiled. Her eyes twinkled at him.

"Congratulations."

"On what?"

She gestured at the gleaming heap of coins. "You have your first hoard. It is an important day in the life of a young dragon. You did an impressive job. You earned this. It is time to enjoy it."

"Not yet." Griffen listened for a moment, then leaned out the door. "You can come in now, Jer!"

Jerome seemed to detach from the frame of a doorway down the hall as if he were part of the molding. "You knew I was here?"

"Since about five hours ago," Griffen said. "Looking after your investment?"

"Well, I can't let the big boss go without protection," Jerome said. "What would Mose do if I lost him his replace-

nent after lookin' for so long? My, my, isn't that pretty!" He
dmired the sprawling heap of gold coins.

Griffen was conscious again of how much he owed Jerome
nd Mose and so many other people in New Orleans. He
ook another handful of the gold disks and let them clink
ownward onto the tabletop. He gathered them up again
nd offered them to Jerome.

"Now, what's that for, Grifter?" Jerome asked, his dark
yes blazing.

"You've put up with a lot this last few months. I didn't
ive you the credence you deserved. I was pretty stubborn. I
now I thought I was right, but I was wrong. I admit it. You
arned this. Call it a bonus."

Jerome shook his head. "You get to think you're right
nce in a while, brother dragon. You didn't have the feelings
 did, and truth to tell, there wasn't any other evidence to say
hat Peter was involved with the troublemakers. So, call it
ven." He looked down at the handful of coins, and carefully
elected one. "Tell you what, I'll take this as a souvenir, but
o more. Gold gets to you, changes you. I don't need it."

"What will you do with the rest?" Mai asked.

"I don't know. Pay off my debts."

"But that will take only a fraction of this fortune."

"Call Mose," Jerome said. "This call he might take. He's
ot about five hundred places that he puts things he wants to
eep for later. Don't tell me which one of them you choose.
Don't even trust me. This is too big a treasure to rely on
ommon sense. But it is yours. You may need it one day. I
uggest you plant it and forget about it."

"But what about my debts?"

Jerome pointed at the gleaming pile. "Sell a few of these
nd pay your debts. Won't take but a few. I can tell you who'll
;ive you the best price and won't ask too many questions.
Then just cache the rest. I promise you won't need it for
ow. Good job on handling the situation. Mose would be
proud. I am, too."

"Thanks, Jer. That means a lot to me."

Griffen took his advice. He also set aside one gold coin each for Fox Lisa and Val. Maybe he'd present them as special doubloons from the dragon king.

It was good to be the king.

Forty-seven

"'Scuse me, dude," said the big blond youth in the Florida State T-shirt. He hoisted what was left of his Hurricane and continued on his stagger up Royal Street.

Drunk as a skunk at noon on a Sunday. Griffen moaned and blotted liquor from his favorite blue shirt. He had avoided Bourbon completely over the last few weeks, but lately even the side streets were jammed with tourists, all of whom were increasingly more drunk and uninhibited. Almost everywhere in the French Quarter, girls on the wrought-iron balconies were flashing the crowds. Everyone seemed to be wearing hanks of glittering throws and donning masks, crowns, or hats in the three colors of Mardi Gras. Griffen was looking forward to Fafnir's parade. After that, he planned to hide out in his apartment until the stroke of midnight on Wednesday morning, when the street sweepers came out and washed the whole festival away. The entire city had gone crazy. There could be, he mused, too much of a good thing.

Griffen did not see a single face he knew in the mass, but he had the odd feeling that someone was watching him. He scanned the faces but never caught anyone looking at him. Still, he had learned long ago to trust his instincts. He ducked into the next alley and made a few turns, in case someone was following him. He came out on Decatur, a block north of the Café du Monde, but the feeling didn't go away.

His cell phone rang.

"Glad to see you're close by," Stoner's voice said. "Wh[y] don't you join me for coffee?"

"No, thanks," Griffen said. "I've got things to do."

He moved just before the hand caught his elbow. He spu[n] around halfway, and found himself facing a tall, muscula[r] man with a long, rectangular face in khakis and a polo shir[t.] Stoner's voice squawked tinnily out of the small receiver.

"Just go with Pearson, McCandles. We need to talk."

Pearson had to be an agent, but he was also a drago[n.] Griffen knew the man didn't have anything near the pu[re] blood that he did, but Pearson was better trained and almos[t] certainly armed to the teeth. He had deep blue eyes tha[t] fastened onto Griffen's like glue. Griffen considered mak[-] ing a run for it, but Stoner knew everything about him[,] including where he lived and where he liked to hang out. [It] would be better to get the confrontation over with.

"All right," he told the phone. "But he does not lay [a] hand on me."

"Fine," Stoner said. Pearson seemed to listen for a mo[-] ment, then nodded. "Come on in. I'm ordering you coffe[e] and beignets."

Griffen went into the café. Jason Stoner sat at the bac[k] at a table near the long-leafed plants outside the rails tha[t] surrounded the restaurant. As Griffen went inside, Pearso[n] peeled off and waited, looking as if he was deciding wheth[er] to go in for a snack.

A very slim black waitress stood by with a cup on a tra[y.] She didn't set it down until Griffen reached the table.

"Thought you'd prefer to see it delivered," Stoner said.

"What can I do for you, Stoner?"

"I told you not to get involved with anything tha[t] interfered with Homeland Security."

"And I told you I wouldn't," Griffen said. "I haven't."

"And not to participate in any magical spells that woul[d] endanger the country that you claim you love."

"Of course I'm not!" Griffen's face got hot.

"I find that hard to believe when there is some seriou[s]

hoodoo going on that is counter to the interests of the United
States of America, and I find you right in the middle of it."

Griffen held his temper. "I don't want to cross you, Stoner,
but you keep accusing me of being involved with things I'm
not, or doing things that I not only am not doing but have
no idea as to what you are talking about."

Stoner regarded him without expression. "Then you will
have no objection if I stop the people who are endangering
this country."

"Not at all," Griffen assured him. "I think it'd be a good
thing."

"In that case, I want those scepters," Stoner told him.

"You want what?"

Stoner's impassive face twitched just a millimeter. "Don't
pretend you don't know what I'm talking about, McCandles.
You have seen them and touched them."

"Yeah, but they're just relics. They're meant to protect
the city of New Orleans. They're elemental."

"Do you even know what that means?"

"Not really, but I know people who do. They say that
they're part of an ancient charm that keeps the city from
disaster." He didn't know how much more he was able to
say, considering the vow of secrecy he had taken, but he
guessed that Stoner knew as much or more about it than he
did already.

"That protection, as you call it, interferes with the
spells that we have running to surveil the United States of
America. When it is operational, it blocks all scrying or
distance-viewing powers. In other words, it blocks this city
from view."

"What about ordinary cameras? Microphones? I'm sure
you have all that stuff in place."

Stoner didn't even blink. Griffen wasn't sure he ever
did. He had eyelids, but perhaps they didn't close—like a
snake's. "Our equipment deployment is classified. But there
are things that ordinary technology cannot monitor. The
spells must not be laid down."

"*Now* I don't know what you are talking about."

"You're a bad liar, McCandles. You do. I want you t help me."

"I told you I don't work for you."

"National security is at stake here. We cannot adequatel protect this country if one part goes under a magical black out. I warned you not to become involved in a subversiv activity."

"This is New Orleans. Half of what goes on in this city i subversive," Griffen pointed out.

Stoner, notably, had no sense of humor. Griffen shoul have known better than to try. "Not that endangers thre hundred million people and their way of life. You hav access to those scepters. Bring them to me."

"I can't do that. And I don't have access, except . . ."

"Except when?"

"Except once," Griffen said, lying again and hoping his poke face was good enough to fool the Homeland Security agen "They let me touch them. I thought it was just a game."

It didn't. "I'm not a fool, McCandles. No one with an sensitivity would miss the punch those things pack. We hav been looking for them for years. They are well shielded mos of the time. There have been a few times they were detectec We have tried to obtain them at those times. They were . . protected." Griffen knew what he meant. He realized tha it had to be Stoner who was responsible for the attack o Holly's house, the one that he had just barely survived. H was horrified by the thought that Stoner would kill fou innocent people to get what he wanted but not surprisec "The next time you have access to them, I expect you to pas them on to me."

When hell freezes over, he thought. "When I get hold c all four scepters, I'll talk to you. But I have no idea if that even possible."

"That's the cooperation I expect," Stoner said. "I don' want to have to take action when there are so many innocen citizens around who might get hurt. Don't force my hand.

expect to hear from you, or I am going to come and get them myself before they can do any harm."

The Homeland Security agent rose and placed a perfectly crisp new ten on the table. He left. Pearson and another man in nondescript clothes joined him. They went south on Decatur.

Griffen was relieved when Stoner left. He hated to have the man as an enemy, but his demand put them on opposite sides of the situation. To be a noncombatant in Stoner's battles was all Griffen could hope for. But he had no choice. Griffen could not give up the scepters before they had done their job. New Orleans deserved to be protected. No matter how powerful or all-seeing Homeland Security was, it couldn't guard the city all the time from all events. They had to look out for themselves.

In the meantime, they had to protect themselves from Stoner and his agents. Griffen had no choice. He had to warn the other krewes. They would have to prepare.

"We'll be ready for you," Griffen vowed. He left the coffee untouched and ordered a fresh cup and a plate of beignets. He opened his cell phone and hit a speed-dial number.

Forty-eight

Lucinda Fenway bustled around her unexpected guests with all the aplomb of a practiced hostess. She saw to it that everyone had a chair and a drink in the large conservatory. "Edith will have some nibbles set up soon. You all relax now." She started to leave.

"Don't go," Griffen asked. "You're part of the krewe, too. You need to know what's happening."

"Well, all right, Griffen," she said, sinking into a handy chair. "You sound so serious."

"I have to be." He stood with his back to the fireplace, looking out over most of the same faces that had been at his party: all the lieutenants of Fafnir who could make it, the other three parade kings and their captains, Val, and to Val's annoyance, Melinda. Jerome and Gris-gris sat on folding chairs near the back. "Thanks for coming. I know it's the day before our parades, but we have a problem that will affect all of us."

Without using names, he told them about Stoner, and described him and the two agents he had seen. "He intends to get the scepters between the time they come out of that shielded case and before we bind the energy that has been building up. To me, that means he is going to try to take them before we get to St. Charles and Canal Street."

"He can't do that!" Callum said. "He can't stop the ritual! We've waited sixty-four years to get this done!"

"He sure is going to try," Griffen said. "He's tough, and

e isn't working alone. You have to be prepared. Fafnir is
nder control. I'm worried about you other three krewes."

Cos Wrayburn leaned back in his chair. "I highly doubt
hat with all the police out there and the crowds, someone
s gonna try and jump us during the parade. We're in plain
ight!"

"Look, call me paranoid if you want," Griffen said, "but
ou don't know what you're dealing with. You've honored
ne by taking me into your . . ."

". . . Fellowship?" Holly suggested.

Griffen smiled at her. "Yes, fellowship. That's a good
vord for it. I wouldn't mislead you, but you don't have to
rust me. You all know Etienne?"

"For years," Bert said, grinning at the Fafnir captain, who
hrew him a mock salute. "He's a little crazy, but everything
ie has ever said is going to happen happens. I can't explain
t, but I accept it."

"Well, Mr. Griffen is right," Etienne said. "Dere's gonna
>e an attempt on all of you. Strong men, out-of-towners who
lon't respect the tradition or Mardi Gras, either. We gotta
>rotect de scepters."

"So what are you suggesting, Griffen?" Cos asked. "Are
ny of us in danger?"

"Not physically, unless you resist giving it up. I suggest
hat I put a rider aboard your float who can help protect your
cepter at least until the power is harnessed, and at best until
he parade is over and it gets put away again for next time."

"Oh, no," the captain of Antaeus protested. "The king
loat is special for our king. He rides alone."

Cos sat up. "I don't want anyone else on that float with
ne. I don't need help. If I am to do God's work, God will
>rotect me."

"But what if this is one of those cases in which you're
upposed to help yourself?" Griffen asked. "Look, what
bout a squire? Someone who will hand you doubloons
nd necklaces when you want them? Snap your fingers for
. refill?"

"I kind of like that," Bert said, grinning. "Okay, you ca
put one aboard my barge. Especially if he can pour drinks.

"All right," Cos said, reluctantly. "But nobody who'
gonna act out of turn. I don't want someone who's gonn
draw attention away from me. I've been waiting years fo
this chance, Griffen."

"I have a couple of good people," Griffen assured him. H
signed to the two men in the back, who stood up. "Both o
them work for me. I will vouch for them absolutely. Gris
gris will ride with you, Bert. He's tough and fast. He follow
orders. Cos gets Jerome. He can help you spot the peopl
you have to be on the lookout for."

Cos looked Jerome up and down. "You've got goo
shoulders. You'll look good in a toga."

"Oh, no," Jerome said, holding his hands in the air. "N
toga. But I will wear full mask and costume. I won't loo
like anything special. I will blend right in."

"That'll do," Cos said. "We're in, Griffen. What abou
Holly?"

Griffen hesitated. Melinda had offered him some of he
men, but he didn't want to use anyone he personally coul
not trust. "I'm still checking around for someone who is fas
smart, and tough that I know can handle this situation."

"No problem," Val said. Griffen looked at her curiously
She whipped out her cell phone and dialed a number. "Yeah
It's me. Ms. Beautiful. Get here. I want to call in my favor.
She smiled at Griffen. "This shouldn't take long."

They waited. Suddenly, squawking came from the hallway
Edith arrived just in front of a short, thin, scruffy-lookin
male who pushed his way into the conservatory. "He just cam
out of the fireplace!" she shrieked.

"It's okay, Edith," Callum said. "He's with us."

"Okay, babe, I'm here. What do you want?"

"He'll do it," Val said.

"I'll do what?" the man asked.

"Just say yes," Val told him.

"Yes," he said, obediently, though his face was set in a mulish expression. "What am I agreein' to do?"

"I'll tell you on the way uptown," Holly said, rising to take his arm. "Come on with us. Griffen, don't worry. We'll be ready for anything. And thanks."

"One more thing," Griffen said. "We need to keep in communication. I brought walkie-talkies. They have earphones so we don't have to hold them up all the time. They're all on the same frequency. It's an open one, but I can't help that." Jerome passed out the plastic blister packages. He and Gris-gris escorted the others out of the house.

"What about us, Griffen?" Callum asked. "You got a strong man to ride your float with you and take care of that scepter? Protecting this city from fire's the most important thing of all."

Griffen stared at him. "I don't have to have anyone else with me. All of you are going to be riding right in front of me."

"Well, what do you expect us to do if this guy turns up?" Terence asked. "He sounds pretty dangerous."

"You're dragons!" Griffen exclaimed.

"Well, but we're not really fighters," Mitchell said.

"It's part of what we are!" He looked around at their puzzled faces. No wonder they had never attacked him or challenged him. They had forgotten what they were. "Look, the guy who is attacking us is another dragon. He's pretty powerful, and he has agents with him, but there are twenty of us against three of him. We can do this! You all claim that your blood makes you more important than anyone else."

"Well, yes," Callum admitted. "So what?"

"Well, what do you think having dragon blood means? What it used to mean? You transform for party tricks? And you were pretty rude to my friend Fox Lisa at the party, and all because you have dragon blood running in your veins. Is that all your heritage means to you? Picking on someone else? Well, I have more, and I am saying you have forgotten what it is to be a dragon."

The group looked at one another.

"You shame us, Griffen," Callum said, reproachfully.

"I hope so," Griffen said. These people had lived all their lives in comfort and privilege. They had gone soft. There had been no such thing as someone like Stoner the last time Fafnir marched. In those days, anything someone did to protect their home was understood. It was more important than letting the government eavesdrop on you. The presumption of innocence meant something. "You don't know what it's like to be under threat. This is it! We are being threatened. I need you to keep these men from taking over something that is important to our whole city. As dragons, you have the power to prevent that. If you want this ritual performed, that is. As your king," Griffen added, though he couldn't believe the words were really coming out of his mouth, "I need your help."

The lieutenants gawked at him as if he were suggesting they dance naked in public.

Melinda flung herself up out of her seat. "What is wrong with you? Never in my life have I seen so many self-righteous complacent people! What will it take to get you to rise and do something difficult? You have worked tirelessly for the parade and the parties, but not for the ceremony at the heart of your involvement? I don't believe it! Back home, we would eat you cowards for lunch!"

Lucinda's eyes flashed. "We have a different way of doing things here, Mrs. Wurmley."

Melinda turned to regard her. "Well, Mrs. Fenway, how is that working out for you? Look at you! Never mind, Griffen. We don't need them. All it will take to repel this foolish intruder is you, me, and Valerie."

"Hey!" Val protested. Melinda put her hand on Val's shoulder, ignoring her efforts to shrug it off.

"Together we will be far more of a force than all of you put together. This girl here has ten times your potential. She hasn't known of her heritage for more than a few months, and she's more prepared than you are to face a threat."

Griffen watched Val's face change from open hatred to

open astonishment. Melinda did honestly seem to appreciate his sister. Val was just starting to realize it.

Mitchell cleared his throat. "We haven't forgotten who we are, Griffen. It's just that y'all are opening up cans of whoop-ass that we sealed up decades back."

"When this is over, you can go back again to the way you were before. This won't change your relationship with your allies. You have a common enemy. What about it? Will you help me?"

"I will," Etienne said. "You'll save the ritual, Mr. Griffen. You'll see to it that dis city and everyone in it is protected from fire."

"I'll do my best," Griffen said. "Look, if I am wrong about these men, then you can blame me later on. If I'm right, then you have to admit that. In any case, I insist. You respect pure blood. I'm invoking it."

"Well, you don't have to put it that way," Callum said. "Of course, if there's going to be a problem, we'll help." The others chorused their agreement.

Griffen almost collapsed with relief. "All right, then let's discuss strategy."

"**That** was weird," Val said, as they waited for Doreen to pick them up on the curb in front of the Fenway house. Melinda had already departed in her chauffeured car.

"Are you all right?" he asked her.

"Yeah. I . . . have a lot to think about."

Griffen nodded. "If you want to talk, let me know. Excuse me, I have one more call to make."

He took his phone out of his pocket and dialed. "Harrison? It's Griffen. Stoner is in town. He didn't call you? He said it was a matter of national security."

Forty-nine

The deafening blare of horn music filled the street outside of Fafnir's den. A giant knight in silver armor over fifteen feet high was the first thing that met Griffen's eye. Only when he got closer, he saw the puppeteer underneath the mannequin's legs, as if he were giving it a piggyback ride. It raised a huge hand and saluted him. A huge green dragon, riding on the backs of two puppeteers, came over to menace the knight. Griffen left them to their game. In the street, hundreds of musicians in a rainbow of uniforms vied with one another to be heard as they tuned up. The smaller floats sat between the super floats. Each had a float captain who shouted at the riders around him to finish setting up and get on board. In turn, Mitchell, the parade captain, shouted at all the float captains through a megaphone. Hooks on each float were loaded with swaying hanks of necklaces. The weather prediction was for sunny but cool, in the upper fifties. Griffen was glad of his gold silk livery and the hearty lunch he had eaten. Both would keep him warm on the front of his float on a cool February evening. He went up the line looking for it.

He had not slept well the night before. Excitement and worry gave him strange dreams. He felt as if he were still in them, passing among crowds of krewe members in full costume, dogs dressed as dragons, and the giant heads on the brilliantly colored and neon-lit floats all looking at him with insane grins.

"Griffen!" Val shouted. She stood up on the maids' float

and waved. Fox Lisa and Mai were with her. Their silk gowns and headdresses made them look like ladies from Castle Anthrax. "Good luck!"

To his astonishment, he noticed that Melinda was with them. They were all wearing earpieces. "What's going on?" he asked.

"I am mustering your secondary force, Your Majesty," she said. She pointed to her own float, which was next in line. "I will be able to hear you, but they won't. You were going to waste a valuable resource: these girls. We have made our own preparations."

"Good idea," Griffen said. Val was openly less hostile to her than before. He leaned close to Val, and murmured in a low voice, "Are you all right?"

"I . . . still don't trust her, but she treats me like I matter."

He smiled and patted her arm. He was glad the truce was holding. "You do. Good luck. I know you all know how to take care of yourselves." Fox Lisa patted a fanny pack slung over her shoulder. Griffen blanched. "You're not riding armed, are you?"

"No!" she exclaimed. "But I've got pepper spray. You never know."

Mai smiled at him. "Those knee breeches show off your calves, Griffen. You should wear them more often."

Griffen shook his head. "Next time I'm king, maybe. I'd almost rather wear a tux!"

A handsome white horse trotted up to them. Etienne was on its back in green-scaled mail and a helmet. "C'mon, Mr. Griffen. Get on board! We step off in less than half an hour!"

Griffen followed him to the front of the line, where the rest of the lieutenants milled around on twenty matching white horses. He mounted his float, which looked like the head of a dragon with its mouth open. Hidden inside the lower-front fangs were boxes of throws. He checked them all: the shining metal doubloons, glittering necklaces, and stacks of The Flagon with the Dragon. He grinned and settled himself on his golden throne. Nothing to do now but wait and enjoy.

Antaeus had stepped off an hour and a half before. Griffen had been monitoring their progress through his earpiece. So far, Jerome had reported no suspicious activity or other dragons. Harrison had been in touch, furious about Stoner. It took a lot to convince him that Griffen had not known about Stoner's designs on the scepters all along.

Griffen touched the walkie-talkie attached to his costume inside the back of his belt.

"Antaeus, this is Fafnir. How are you doing?"

"**Just** passed Lee Circle," Jerome said, toggling his radio. He had a padded stool at the front of the king's float, handy to pass more throws from the concealed cartons to the King of Antaeus. He wore an all-enveloping robe of purple silk with a gold headcloth tied around his forehead with a green cord. The band behind them was playing an energetic rendition of "You're Nobody 'Til Somebody Loves You." "Nice night. Plenty of kids. Make sure you throw a bunch of stuff toward that hotel on the south side of St. Charles. There's a forest of ladders!"

"Everything's fine, Griffen," Cos Wrayburn put in. He stood tall in his leopard-skin toga, brown tights, and boots, a crown of tall crystals on his head, waving to the crowds with the mountain-topped golden scepter. He stood on a half dome painted to resemble the northern hemisphere. "Jerome and I are having a good time."

"Yeah, it's different *riding* in a parade," Jerome commented.

"Never belonged to a marching society myself," Cos commented. "Sounds like good people."

"They are," Jerome said. He liked the big man. They had had a lot of time to get to know one another since the parade mustered on the side street. "We have a get-together on Lundi Gras, next Monday. You ought to come along."

"I will! You come to our party, too. It'll be a blast."

Jerome felt rather than saw a dragon coming toward them. He turned around just in time to see a man with a long face in a pale blue polo shirt jump up on the float. It had to be a dragon; no one else moved like that. Even in twilight, he could see that well enough.

"Get off my ride!" Cos demanded.

"I am from the United States government. I am here to confiscate that scepter." He showed Cos an identification card with a badge. Cos studied it and started to hand the golden wand to him. Jerome stood up between them just in time. Cos protested.

"Jerome, he's the law."

"No. Grifter, we've got one."

Cos added, "Griffen, you didn't tell me we were dealing with US agents!"

"Cos, calm down!" Griffen's voice came from the earpiece. "Does he have a warrant?" Jerome repeated the demand to the agent.

"No, he doesn't."

"He's not acting on official orders," Griffen said.

The long-faced man was adamant. "I represent Stoner. Do you know who he is?"

"No," Cos said, his big face turning red. "And if he has a warrant, he can come and see me after the goddamned parade. Now, get off my float!"

Faster than one would have thought the big man could move, Cos grabbed the other's wrist and tossed him toward the side of the float. The agent recovered almost in midair and landed on the step just before hitting the street. The crowd cheered, thinking it was an act. He sprang up and made a grab for the scepter. This time, Jerome was ready for him. He rushed the man with his shoulder down and flipped him. The man rolled up and tried to make a counterattack, but Jerome knew more martial arts than just street fighting. The two of them traded punches, kicks, and blocks to the delight of the onlookers. Jerome panted into his mike.

"Grifter, call the cops!"

The agent halted, alarmed. Suddenly, big men in uniform began to converge on the float. Jerome took advantage of his opponent's momentary stiffness to cannon into him. They leaped off into St. Charles Avenue just as they reached Canal Street. Jerome grappled with him, but he broke every hold. The man had training! The officers flanking the parade route moved in and grabbed him. The man fought free of their grip and tried to catch up with the king float, but Cos already had the scepter held high.

"I bind the element of Earth!" Cos bellowed. "Let the power be settled and protect this city, in the name of God!"

Jerome was knocked sideways as a shock wave hit him. It felt as if he were standing in the surf and got hit by a major roller. It felt heavy but natural, a little dangerous but good. Invoking his Maker gave Cos the strength of the pure. That was nothing to be sneezed at. Jerome respected a man with genuine faith.

The surge of power disoriented the police, too. They staggered. The agent took the opportunity to shake free of their hold. He fled into the crowd. Jerome thought about chasing him, but there was no point. He hadn't gotten what he came for. He clicked his mike.

"Griffen, we're good! One down, three to go!"

He caught up with the float. Cos leaned down and hauled him up.

"Wow," Cos said. "Did you feel the earth move back there?"

"Yeah," Jerome said. "That was pretty good. Normally, I have to have a lady with me for that, but this was cool, too."

"That was some pretty fighting," Cos said. "Come and

have a beer with me when this is over. Meanwhile, hand me some doubloons! We got kids shouting at us."

"So you're really a clinker!" Holly said, admiring the cockscomb scales on the small male's head. Wearing her diaphanous chiton, she sat strapped into her pale blue throne surrounded by fluffy white tulle sculpted into clouds and lit by twinkling LEDs. Her float was fashioned into the image of an enormous cumulus cloud with a screwed-up face that looked like it was blowing her throne down St. Charles. All the floats that followed hers were based on the theme of Stormy Weather. The jazz band marching behind them played the classic blues song as they went. Chinese kite flyers made their neon-lit toys dance on against the night sky, to the laughter of the children watching. She waved her scepter at the crowd with one hand, blessing them, and tossed necklaces with the other from pots of throws on either side of the throne. She had cups, doubloons, fans, and a special box for later on.

"You keep sayin' that, lady," the clinker said, crouched in the mass of fabric. "My name's Charlie."

"Charlie the clinker?"

"Don't call me that!"

Holly cocked her head sympathetically. He swore like an X-rated movie, he was cocky as hell, but he fascinated her. She was delighted to meet another genuine human—something else hybrid. He had demonstrated his fire-starting powers for her, to her open admiration. Since then, he had responded to her in a pigtail-inkwell kind of way. This had been her favorite day ever since she joined the craft. "Is that a sore spot?"

He made a sour face. "Every damned day!"

"I'd really like it if you would come and talk to my coven," she said.

"Lady, I don't do no lecture tours. Unless you pay," he added, hopefully.

"Wait a moment," Holly said. She listened to her earpiece. Charlie heard it, too. "Heads-up. Antaeus just got attacked. Jerome says we're next. Look out after we pass Lee Circle."

Charlie braced himself. "They be sorry they try us."

She kept in touch by radio with Ethan, five floats behind her, and her captain, Nish, riding with her lieutenants at the front on Harley-Davidson motorcycles.

"Anything?" she asked, over and over.

"Nope. We'll see 'em if they come in from anywhere," Nish replied, over the roar of her engine. Holly acknowledged it as she bent down for another handful of doubloons. They couldn't sneak up on her unless . . .

They came from behind. A large man with no expression on his square face was suddenly there. He grabbed her wrist and pried at her fingers, trying to take the scepter.

"No, sir!" Charlie bellowed. He jumped onto the man's back and held on. The agent let out a bellow. Smoke started to rise from his clothes. He let go of her and batted at the clinker, but Charlie's grip was too good. The man fell off the float. Nish signed to the other riders, who gunned their bikes to surround him and held on to him until the police could run in and arrest him. Holly breathed a sigh of relief.

But he wasn't alone.

A taller man with a long face appeared on the other side. He snatched the scepter right out of Holly's fingers. He dove off the float and did a barrel roll on the pavement. Charlie ran after him. The man drew a gun. The people in the crowd screamed.

Charlie dodged from side to side, then sprang. The man tossed him off before he could get a good hold. The clinker landed in the crowd. The people he landed on yelled as his hot skin burned them.

"No!" Holly shouted. "Let him have it! Please! Come back!"

The clinker looked at her. The man dashed away, shoving over ladders full of screaming children as he went. Irate parents hurried to straighten them up. He vanished, under cover of darkness. Charlie's shoulders collapsed. He trudged

back to the float. Holly pulled him up, ignoring the heat
from his hand.

"I blew it!" Charlie wailed. "Ms. Beautiful is gonna tear
me a new one!"

"No, we haven't failed," Holly said calmly. "Have you
ever heard of the Law of Contagion?"

Charlie looked at her sideways. "Yeah, if you cough without covering your mouth, you can make other people sick."

Holly smiled. "No, not that one. If you touch something
to something else, they are bonded forever and have the
same properties." She opened the last sealed cardboard box.
It was full of scepters just like the one that had been stolen.
She started throwing them to the crowd. "That was plastic,
just like these. I enchanted all of these last night with the
original, which is in a safe place, by the way." She raised one
of the substitutes as they reached the intersection at Canal
Street. She felt the down-to-earth strength of Antaeus, and
concentrated on tying in that of Aeolus. "Air!" she cried,
and recited the words of the ritual. She activated her radio.
"Griffen, we're clear!"

"Y'all know you look like Aquaman," Gris-gris told Bert
again, as they turned onto St. Charles from Jackson Street.
The king of Nautilus had a scaled, marine blue hip-length
tunic and black tights with black boots laced up the front,
and a crown made of spiral shells. Gris-gris didn't feel much
better about his own costume, which looked like it came
out of the *Gladiator* movie. At least it had leather pants, not
a skirt.

"Yeah, I know. I told the seamstress that when she
showed me the fabric, but she said it's sea blue, and what
do I expect?" Bert gave him a wink. "So I just settled for
thinking there's something for the comic-book fans, too."
His throne looked like a big shell. Gris-gris sat beside him
on a clump of fake red coral filled with neon-edged clown
fish. Giant seahorses attached to the front of the float looked

as if they were pulling it. Stick-manipulated giant puppet
that looked like sea monsters danced around them as th
nearest band played "Under the Sea."

The Nautilus krewe had welcomed Gris-gris as a
asset. He felt disadvantaged, thrown into a social group h
normally slunk around, resenting, but his Val had brough
him into a new world. He'd live up to the situation for he
So far, if he was honest, it had been fun. If he was afraid he'
be made fun of, most of the people he hung around wit
were driving tractors that day. *He* was riding on the king'
float. So how do you like that?

"Hope someone takes my picture for Val," he said.

Bert grinned at him. "That's some girl you have there."

Gris-gris felt a moment's tenderness for Val, somethin
he wouldn't admit out loud even under torture. "Yeah
Never found anyone I cared about like that."

"How much? Would you die for her?"

"In a minute, but then I couldn't be with her, so that's
waste." He grinned back.

They were having a fine time. Gris-gris made sure Ber
had whatever he needed for kinging. He kept him supplie
with necklaces, bottle openers, inflatable beach balls, an
other trinkets to throw to the yelling watchers. Gris-gri
stowed a few of each to take home later for his nephews an
cousins. There was plenty of beer on board. Nautilus wa
never dry, Bert commented drolly.

A dancing octopus draped its tentacles over the foot o
the seashell. Gris-gris leaned back out of its way.

When it passed, a big man dressed as a merman wa
standing on the float. Gris-gris knew all the dancers wh
were supposed to be at the head of the parade. This was
stranger. Immediately, he leaped up and pushed the man i
the chest.

The man staggered back and swung a fist. Gris-gri
ducked. As fast as a greased snake, the man turned an
reached for Bert's scepter. Bert walloped the man with i
that had to hurt. Gris-gris leaped on his back. He reache

into the pocket of his costume for the rope he had brought with him. Griffen had warned him not to use a knife. If he couldn't drive him off, the best thing to do was tie him until the cops could get him. The man bucked like an unbalanced washing machine. Gris-gris held on. He couldn't get the rope around his arms. Instead, he went for the knife hanging in a sheath under his arm. This guy was not going to ruin the parade for Val's brother!

He plunged the knife into the man's back. The blade went through the costume, but skidded off the skin. The man bellowed, but he was unhurt. That was impossible! He must be wearing a bulletproof vest! Gris-gris was surprised, but he went after the man with everything he had. A couple of punches to the kidneys ought to bring him down. Like lightning, the tall man turned around. His hand seemed to change before Gris-gris's eyes from fingers to talons. He brandished them at Gris-gris. He must have believed that just seeing a hand turn into a claw would scare him, but Gris-gris grinned.

"That all you got, man?"

The man plunged one talon into Gris-gris's stomach. Gris-gris gasped, but hung on. He shoved his head upward into the other's chin, then forward into the windpipe. The man staggered, but he recovered fast. The talon came across and gashed Gris-gris through the cheek. He knocked Gris-gris's hands upward, breaking his hold. He grabbed him by the shoulder and hip, lifted him high, and brought him down on the seahorse at the front of the float. Gris-gris moaned. His back hurt him and he couldn't feel his legs. He lay on top of the cardboard boxes, staring at the sky.

"Gris-gris!" Bert shouted. "Tritons, come and help here! Hey, damm it, let that alone!"

The captain and lieutenants raced to help, but the big man snapped Bert's arm sharply up and down on the arm of his throne. Bert heard a crack and knew it was the bone. His hand opened nervelessly. He grabbed for the intruder, but he couldn't reach him. The merman snatched up the scepter and jumped straight for the head of the lead horse which sent it bucking and whinnying. He vanished unde the thrashing hooves. The lieutenants grabbed for him, bu he evaded them and leaped over a barrier.

"How bad are you hurt?" the captain asked.

"Arm," Bert gritted. The pains shooting through his arm were almost as bad as the humiliation he felt. "Griffen, I los it. And we have a casualty."

"Who?" Griffen's voice demanded.

"My defender. He's valiant as an old-time hero. He's wor thy of better. Dammit, I hate to be the weakest link!"

"Not your fault. What about Gris-gris?"

Bert's float stopped as stretcher-bearers rushed in from the side. They settled Gris-gris onto a backboard and fastened a collar around his neck. A paramedic in a white tunic came up to see to Bert's arm. One of the lieutenant threw his horse's reins to another and stayed on board to toss necklaces to the crowd. "Medical staff taking him of now. I'm still blocks from Canal Street, Griffen. I didn' have a chance to weave his scepter's power in with the others. I am so sorry."

Gris-gris signed to Bert. His high-cheekboned face had a gray pallor. Bert's heart went out to him as he leaned over the stretcher. "Don't tell Val. Spoil . . ."

"I won't. You hear that, Griffen?"

"I did. You did all you could, Bert. We're dealing with pros." Griffen felt a pang of worry, for Gris-gris, but also fo Val. "Melinda?"

"She won't hear it from me," Melinda's voice insisted "Just hang on to yours."

Fifty

Fafnir was already two hours into its march. Except for worrying about Stoner and the missing scepter, Griffen had been enjoying himself immensely. He had gone through three boxes of throws already, including the special LED dragons. He waved his scepter at everyone. Kids jumped up and down on the curb, yelling for necklaces and doubloons. He threw them in generous handfuls. The cups were a big hit. Everyone who caught one laughed at the slogan and nudged their neighbors.

Griffen couldn't believe how the corps-style bands could keep playing for hours on end. He would have been exhausted. Etienne said some bands earned as much as two thousand dollars a parade. They were worth more. The flag twirlers were still as perky and energetic as they had been when they set out, even though it was late in the evening.

The band behind his dragon's-head float played "If Ever I Ceased to Love" over and over in between other popular favorites. The monotonous slow waltz was like a reminder that Stoner was out there somewhere. He could just about feel the other's presence, like a sinister shadow looming. The disaster aboard the Nautilus king float made him think again how vulnerable he was. Bert was riding now with his arm in a quickset cast. Griffen was concerned about him and Gris-gris, but Etienne and Melinda reminded him again and again that his duties lay in what he was doing at that moment.

He knew how to be a parade king. He had seen enough

parades in the week before. He nodded and smiled and threw goodies to the eager crowds. He brandished his scepter feeling the sensation of heat in the air. He was surprised how much more power there seemed to be than the first day they had wielded the scepters. It was wrong that Stoner had prevented Bert from settling Water's force before he stole the wand from him. Griffen was determined that wouldn't happen to him. Having to be on guard, he almost couldn't enjoy what would be the greatest honor he had ever had, or might ever have.

"Throw me something, mister!" a little voice cried out from the sidelines. Others joined in. Oh, yes! That was something he was supposed to do.

He reached for the hooks containing more neat hanks of beads, thousands of them, in every color, and pitched them toward the watchers on the side. The crowd surged forward like goldfish feeding in a pond, snatching at the glittering snakes that flew through the air. Griffen felt the magic spread out. *Remember,* Etienne had told him, *you have plenty. Be generous, Your Majesty.*

He made sure to aim for the children sitting on the top of ladders. The kids caught the offerings with both hands against their chest, their faces full of glee. He plunged a fist into the bucket of doubloons at his side. Like a real king, he spread the largesse to his public. Roars of approval all but drowned out the music behind him.

"Any sign, Griffen?" asked Melinda's voice in his ear.

"Not yet," Griffen said. He peered ahead into the lamplit street. They were only half a block from Canal. If Stoner wanted to prevent a second scepter from doing its job, he didn't have long. But Griffen was well protected. He was surrounded on all sides by fellow dragons, in front of him occasionally dropping back beside him, behind him . . .

Behind him.

He had forgotten Stoner's gift of stillness. Suddenly, he felt a cold metal ring touch his neck. He didn't have to look down to know it was a gun.

"Hand me the scepter, McCandles."

"You've been back there the whole time, haven't you?" Griffen said. He stared out at the approaching intersection, keeping a smile pinned to his face. The pinball of fire danced in his belly, itching for a fight. Griffen told it to quiet down.

"The question is immaterial. Give me the scepter."

"I can't," Griffen said. "If you know what it is, you know why I need to use it."

"It will create difficulties for my department," Stoner said. "That threatens all of national security."

"But it leaves this city vulnerable."

"You can't make yourself responsible for that."

"It's my home," Griffen said. They were a hundred yards from the intersection. He could feel the waves of power that were left by Holly and Cos. He needed to join to it immediately. He lifted his hand.

Stoner shot out his hand and grabbed for the scepter. Griffen held on to it with both hands. He realized with a moment's wry humor that the agent was dressed as St. George. He had been hiding behind the curtain concealing Griffen's backup supply of throws. Griffen fell onto his back, trying to break the other man's grip. Stoner brought his other hand around in a chop that made Griffen's wrists tingle, but he turned his shoulder into Stoner's chest. There wasn't time to waste. He had to finish the ritual early, even if it made it less effective.

"Fire, I call . . ." he began, trying to lift himself to a standing position. Stoner kneed him in the back. Griffen fell to his knees. They grappled with the scepter between them. Griffen felt it turn in his grip. The fire in his belly sang. A wave of heat blasted from the scepter toward the side of the street.

Children screamed as fire burst out of the windows of the hotel at their back. Emergency crews on the sidelines mustered to move them away from the blaze.

"You see what kind of danger you are putting your home into? This device must be locked away!" Stoner said.

Griffen couldn't leave the paradegoers in danger, but he couldn't pull away from Stoner. The agent plunged two fingers into the muscles of his upper arm. His hand went numb. He switched the scepter to his left hand.

"Melinda!" he choked out.

"We see it," she said in his ear. "Leave it to us. Valerie and I have this under control."

"Mr. Griffen, we're comin'!" Etienne's voice announced.

"Let go now, and I will see to it no charges are filed against you and your colleagues," Stoner offered.

Griffen was so mad that he could hardly see straight. Ruining the parade, putting thousands of people in danger, when there were other times Stoner could have demanded the scepters. Like at Holly's house. He was furious when he recalled the force that almost crushed them. The pinball jumped up and down, demanding satisfaction. Griffen was inclined to deliver it. He looked straight up into Stoner's face and brandished the golden rod.

Fire burst from the dragon's mouth and washed the two of them in a crackling blaze. The watchers let out a shout of surprise.

"What are you doing?" Stoner demanded.

"Get off my float now, or it goes up," Griffen said. He was aware of the flames. They licked at his costume and hair. He didn't feel his skin burning, but he'd deal with that later. "You can't stop me now."

The float continued to roll down St. Charles as they battled for possession of the scepter. Stoner held up a hand to protect his eyes. He stabbed for Griffen's Adam's apple with the other hand. The crowd cheered them, thinking it was all part of the act, St. George battling the dragon. Well, this time the dragon would win.

"This is an obscenity!" Stoner gritted. His sleeve caught fire. He batted it out. "You are in violation of a hundred different laws!"

"I want to see the official paperwork," Griffen said, fighting to get the words out in the parching heat.

"Don't be obtuse. You know this is off the books. The government needs the results, but not everything has official sanction."

"Then get lost," Griffen croaked. "Protecting this city from natural disasters is also in the government's best interests."

Griffen looked up through the smoke. His eyes watered. He blinked them clear. They were still a hundred feet from the intersection. It was a little premature, but it was his best chance. He staggered to his feet. Stoner swept a leg forward and kicked them out from under him. Griffen turned up the heat. The pinball danced with joy. Tongues of fire blazed up from the floor, hiding Stoner from view. Stoner bellowed in pain. Griffen huddled down with the scepter clutched to him, feeling the cape smoldering on his back. He tried to remember the words of the binding ritual.

Suddenly, clouds of white hit him from five different points. Griffen gasped as the fire extinguishers played up and down his body. He just saw Etienne grinning at him over a black plastic cone. He was hauled off the float by dozens of hands. He coughed. More hands pounded him on the back. When his eyes cleared, he found himself on the street in a ring of New Orleans police officers. Stoner, too, was surrounded, but he looked less happy about it. Harrison shoved his face into Griffen's field of view.

"Get back up there, McCandles!" Harrison ordered him. "You've got a parade to finish!"

"You can't let him go, Detective!" Stoner said.

"You tellin' me what to do in my own city again?" Harrison exclaimed, rounding on the government agent. "Get up there!"

Griffen didn't hesitate. He stood up and pointed his scepter to the burning building. A fire truck was parked out front, but its little streams of water would be a feeble aid for a centuries-old wooden structure. Tongues of red began to lick out from under the eaves. The roof would catch any moment.

"Fire, go out!" he bellowed.

The fire went out. It seemed to suck away suddenly into another dimension, so swiftly did it vanish. In delighted amazement, Griffen put out the fire on the float just as quickly. He hoped this new talent lasted beyond his involvement with the scepter. It was really useful. The watchers cheered wildly. They were loving the Fafnir parade and all its unexpected special effects.

Griffen could have cheered, too, as they hauled Stoner away. He could hear Harrison haranguing him all the way to the police van.

He settled into his throne. Ten yards more to go. He felt the lines of Antaeus and Aeolus intersecting over his head. It wasn't the triple knot he was hoping for, but maybe next year. Now was the time for him to call the energy raised by the first ritual and bind it with the others. The city would be protected from wildfires and explosions, better than Homeland Security could. The government could not be everywhere, but this could.

"Fire!" Griffen called. He put his entire will into the command. "Come home to me!"

From all over the city, wild flames flew toward him, out of windows, chimneys, and out of thin air. Dragonfire, fox fire, sparks from gas flames, embers like the ends of burning cigarettes, all sailed toward him. He called to it, not willing to take no for an answer.

The fire gathered around him like translucent curtains of red and orange. He was already burned from the fire on the float, but though hot, this formed a nimbus around him. The crowd was delighted. They roared their pleasure at what they thought were realistic special effects. A photographer with a huge camera jumped out to take a picture. He threw Griffen a triumphant thumbs-up. Griffen vowed to hunt the man down later and get a copy. But nothing was more important at that moment than doing the job he had been assigned. He held the scepter high like a beacon.

"I am king of Fafnir, lord of fire. You'll do what I say."

The sensation of heat closed in on him, protesting, as if to say, "Aw, *Dad*!"

And Griffen responded. "I mean it! Calm down! I bind you and order you to lay a shield over the city. And the environs." Whatever that meant, but it was in the ritual. Holly had said it, and so had Matt. In his mind's eye, he saw a sort of old-fashioned, hand-drawn map, all that fire calming down to a warm glow. The pinball inside him faded away to a pinpoint.

Griffen suddenly felt the weight of the solid gold scepter in his hand. He lowered it. He was exhausted. The job was done.

A little voice interrupted the haze in his brain.

"Throw me something, mister!"

A little black girl sitting on the top of a ladder waved to him, a large man bracing her back. Griffen smiled. He reached into the front of the float, which had been miraculously spared from the conflagration, and pulled out the remaining boxes of throws. He flung a flashing green LED dragon's-head necklace to her. It landed right in her little hands. She shrieked with joy. Griffen kept on flinging.

The day had been so strange, what with spells and power and mystic binding, it didn't seem to have been real. There was something missing, Griffen knew. The whole experience wouldn't be complete until . . .

The bands behind him struck up a loud brass fanfare.

Yes, there it was: "Second Line." People on the sidelines began to tap their feet in time with the music.

Griffen was suddenly and thoroughly content with his lot. This was his city. He was king of Mardi Gras, and the world was wonderful. He waved and gestured with his scepter, loving the day and the event, being in the here and now. He understood Zen for the first time.

He rode the rest of the route in his scorched costume, on his burnt-out chicken-wire shell of a float, throwing doubloons and cups to the eager faces and hands of the crowd. He had nothing left that he had to worry about. Not until the parade ended, anyhow.

Fifty-one

"I was amazed those horses didn't panic at the fire!" Melinda shouted over the jazz band's cheerful music as they climbed off the floats when they reached their terminus point on Tchoupitoulas. Buses were waiting to take the riders to the after-party.

"Dey my hosses, Mrs. Melinda," Etienne said. "Raised 'em all myself. Dey not afraid of no dragon, nor dragonfire. Dey owned by dragon."

"I can't believe how fast that hotel fire went out," Mai said.

"It was the scepter," Griffen said. He was glad that Matt had marched in so soon and locked it up again in the case. He was beginning to miss the pinball, which vanished as soon as the scepter was gone. "I'm glad no one was hurt in it."

"No, and Melinda got everyone organized to soothe the kids," Val said. The marchers from Ladybug, Ladybug were right between our float and hers. She organized them and us maids to soothe the kids, and sent out a volunteer with a whole bucket of doubloons, compliments of the queen. Distracted them right out of the fear." She sent a shy smile to the older woman. "We're going shopping for the baby."

"Maybe later," Griffen said. He took out his cell phone. "I'm getting us a taxi. We need to go to the hospital first."

"Are you that badly hurt?" Fox Lisa asked, pulling aside the torn fabric to look at his skin. "You look okay."

"It's not me," Griffen said.

Val seemed to read his mind. "Gris-gris? He is hurt? Damn you, Griffen, why didn't you tell me!"

"He didn't want us to," Griffen said.

"And you listened to him? I'll go by myself!"

"I will take you," Mai offered.

"No, dear," Melinda said, taking her arm and pushing in between Val and the others. "*I'll* go with you. The rest of you go to the party. You deserve to have some downtime. Go on."

"Call me when you find out how he is," Griffen said. Val nodded. She was still upset with him. He didn't blame her.

Griffen saw them into the taxi. Everyone else was slapping one another on the back and swapping stories. The rest of the beer and throws were loaded onto the bus with them.

The party, thrown by Antaeus, with donations from the other three krewes, was being held in a huge auditorium. A lot of paradegoers who had bought tickets were there to share the fun and dance to the music. Three videographers had a huge flat-screen TV showing raw footage of the parades that they had just shot, complete with audio. It was so loud that Griffen had to put one finger in his ear to get a report from the hospital.

"Val says that Gris-gris will be okay," he reported to his friends and fellow kings. They were all laden with necklaces and other trinkets from one another's boxes. "He's going to keep the scar on his face. 'It's currency in the Quarter,' he said. Now she's going shopping."

Bert laughed. His temporary cast was covered with signatures from all four krewes. "I owe Gris-gris a lot for fighting that hard," he said. "He did more than I could to try and stop that man. He was like a supervillain!"

"At least we got the city protected against three elements," Cos said. "We'll try again next year."

"It won't be my problem then," Griffen said, cheerfully toasting his fellow kings.

"But you did it when it matter most," Etienne said. "Dat's why it had to be you, Mr. Griffen."

"You did a great job," Holly said. "Let me know if you ever want a third girlfriend."

Griffen found his throat had dried out. "Uh."

She laughed at him. "Just joking. You're sadly outnumbered as it is." She gave him a kiss on the cheek. "I'm looking forward to continuing our fellowship."

"That was a damned dangerous thing, that ritual," Co said.

Etienne nodded. "Coul' been worse. Rest of you was okay, but half the time in my dream, Mr. Griffen didn' get up again after the fire."

Griffen looked at him aghast. "You mean I could have died?"

The hybrid waggled a hand. "It was possible. But it didn happen. No, sir."

Griffen sat back in his chair, speechless.

"Well, that explains a lot."

"What?"

He gestured with his drink toward the lieutenants. "Why no one in this group attacked me. I've been warned so many times that dragons either fight their way up the food chain or sign on to someone who has more power than they do."

"You was the sacrificial king. It wouldn't have worked without you. You did good, Mr. Griffen. All of N'awlins would appreciate it if they knew."

Griffen gave him a sour look. "Thanks a bunch."

Etienne smiled. "Well, okay, but would you have said yes if I tol' you everyt'ing I seen?"

"No!"

"Then you see why I didn't. Had to be done, and y'all did great." He grinned. "Didn't you have a good time?"

"Yes, I did," Griffen admitted. He felt a warm feeling over the whole experience. Literally. But a pebble of resentment had taken the place of the pinball of fire in his belly. "I have been used by people for their own purposes since before I got here. I'm tired of being the symbol for the union of dragons. I hated being thrown into situations for which I

was not ready. It's no consolation to realize I could rise to the
occasion. I have just been too nice to say no, I'm not ready,
I'm busy, I'm tired, I'm not interested."

"But all the opportunities might pass you by," Jerome
said.

"Let them," Griffen said. "I need to learn who and what I
am. I *know* that I am not really everybody's patsy. I just have
to stop acting like it."

Fox Lisa patted his arm. "You've been true to yourself, in
the pacts you have made, the promises you have kept."

"Yes, that is me. But what do I want to do, once I learn
who I am?"

She smiled up at him. "It will be interesting to find out."

"Oh, you will, Mr. Griffen," Etienne said. "I seen dat, too."

"When?"

Etienne shook his head. "Ain't good for ya to know dat,"
he said. "I'll tell you one day if you gotta know somet'ing."

Mai smiled at them, but her thoughts were troubled.
Griffen was learning to think for himself. She would have to
throw him off-balance again, or she would never be able to
put him under her control.

Harrison came into the room. He made his way toward
them.

"Have a drink, Detective!" Cos bellowed, hoisting one
of Fafnir's plastic cups. "The flagon with the dragon has the
brew that is true."

"Maybe later, Cos," Harrison said. He turned to Griffen.
"Thought you might like to know I just had an instructive
talk with our friend. He tried to tell me I didn't know who
I was up against. He didn't have a warrant or probable cause
for confiscation, or anything he can take to a grand jury. But
I do, having him and his minions jump on floats during a
Mardi Gras parade. I think the country's just sore enough
about the Patriot Act to love a story about Homeland
Security sneaking in and usurping the authority of the legal
police force of the sovereign city of New Orleans during a
unique heritage festival like Mardi Gras. I told him to get

out of my city and don't come back." Harrison gave him
mean smile. "He said he won't. Homeland Security won'
bother to set foot in this city ever again."

"Good," Griffen said. "Good riddance." He toasted th
police detective. "Come on back and have that drink whe
you're off duty."

"I will," Harrison said. He looked pleased to have solve
his murder and tossed the intrusive agent out of town. "
earned it. That and many more."

The party went on for hours. Griffen danced with dozen
of ladies. The event was catered by one of the best houses i
the city. He stuffed himself on crawfish etoufée and banana
Foster, washed down by the best Irish whisky. One excellen
band succeeded another. It was a great party, capping a
incredibly eventful day.

"And it's not even Fat Tuesday yet," Fox Lisa said.

"As far as I'm concerned, I'm just an observer from nov
on," Griffen told her.

He felt a soft kiss on his cheek. He turned. Rose stoo
there beside him.

"Thank you," she said. "I know it was hard. You did well
The city is almost completely protected."

"Thanks," he said.

"I owe you a favor," she said. "Ask me if you need me.
She smiled at Griffen and slipped away into the crowd.

"Was that who I think it was?" Fox Lisa asked, wide-eyed
Griffen nodded. "Wow. This might be the best day ever."

Griffen's cell phone rang. He almost didn't hear it ove
the rendition of Fats Domino's "Walking to New Orleans.

He reached for it. "Hello?"

"Griffen?"

He stiffened a little. A voice he had not exactly though
to hear for a while, or really wanted to.

"Hello, Uncle Malcolm," he said. "Happy Mardi Gras."

"Yes, thank you," his uncle said, dismissively. "Griffen
we really need to talk. Where is your sister?"

"She went shopping," Griffen said. "With Melinda."

ROBERT (LYNN) ASPRIN, born in 1946, is best known for the Myth Adventures and Phule series. He also edited the groundbreaking Thieves' World anthologies with Lynn Abbey. He died at his home in New Orleans in May 2008.

JODY LYNN NYE lists her main career activity as "spoiling cats." She lives northwest of Chicago with two of the above and her husband, author and packager Bill Fawcett. She has published more than forty books, including six contemporary fantasies, four SF novels, four novels in collaboration with Anne McCaffrey, such as *Crisis on Doona* and *Treaty at Doona*; edited a humorous anthology about mothers, *Don't Forget Your Spacesuit, Dear*; and written over a hundred short stories. Her latest books are *A Forthcoming Wizard* (TOR Books) and *Myth-Fortunes* (Wildside Press), her seventh collaboration with Robert Asprin in the Myth-Adventures series.

THE ULTIMATE IN FANTASY FICTION!

From magical tales of distant worlds to stories of those with abilities beyond the ordinary, Ace and Roc have everything you need to stretch your imagination to its limits.

Marion Zimmer Bradley/Diana L. Paxson

Guy Gavriel Kay

Dennis L. McKiernan

Patricia A. McKillip

Robin McKinley

Sharon Shinn

Steven R. Boyett

Barb and J. C. Hendee

THE ULTIMATE
WRITERS OF
SCIENCE FICTION

John Barnes	Jack McDevitt
William C. Dietz	Alastair Reynolds
Simon R. Green	Allen Steele
Joe Haldeman	S. M. Stirling
Robert Heinlein	Charles Stross
Frank Herbert	Harry Turtledove
E. E. Knight	John Varley

penguin.com/scififantasy